Life Interrupted

By

Bobbie Anthony

Copyright © 2021 Bobbie Anthony

ISBN: 9798715600028

This is a work of fiction. Names and characters are the product of the author's imagination and any resemblance to actual persons, living or dead, is entirely coincidental.

www.publishnation.co.uk

Chapter One

The Nightmare (Vicky)

I closed my eyes in an idle attempt to dull my senses and block out the reality of the vortex I've been sucked into. To shift my mind to a better place. Anywhere, just not here. Surprisingly, I'd cradled myself to sleep, a real deep sleep.

Startled by an unfamiliar tone, there was the hum of a young girl sobbing.

Usually, the first thing to lodge in my head when I wake is where am I. Though not always, the cold and uncomfortableness of this place rapidly catapults me back down to earth.

This is me, stashed away from prying eyes, locked in a basement. Purgatory for want of a better description. Disappeared.

My world, my life turned on its head, thrown into utter turmoil. My waking hours given over to nightmares, flung into a dream which has no end in sight, my new norm misery, squalor and degradation.

This horrendous nightmare is not mine alone, there are others, we're all trapped. Young women similar to me who were plucked up one by one. We were strangers a few weeks back, never so much as clapped eyes on each other. Now it's a whole different story. We're a family of sorts who cling to each other as if in a sinking lifeboat, desperately trying to keep each other afloat.

As in most families we extract strength and comfort from each other in a vain attempt to prevent one another from breaking. We are sucked into that deep dark place, the rabbit hole where experience affords us the knowledge there is no return.

Remaining strong for each other is paramount.

Survival the name of this game.

1

In this cold dark place it's a wonder we're able to sleep, but we do. Emotional exhaustion encumbers every fibre, every cell, then you're away. Tonight it'd gone my way and I'd drifted off.

It's escapism, it relocates the mind to other places like a favoured holiday destination. My mind meanders round a cute village in Yorkshire, England, where I grew up.

We often talk of our dreams and lives. Our lives before this, our real lives as we refer to them.

My roaming mind took a back seat as I momentarily absorbed the unrecognisable tone, the cries and whimpering dominating the dismal scene.

My ears weren't deceiving me, the youthful, muffled tone was definitely that of a child. She'd picked a spot furthest from the door in a corner. Good call, I remember I did that, not that it helped. She'll have no choice but to do as the rest of us do and fall into line.

As yet the poor girl is unlikely to have grasped the enormity of her predicament, notably how and why she's here. There is only one reason she'll be permitted to leave through that dungeon door she'd entered earlier. How she'll be turned out as a commodity. Become a vessel, a nonentity, a slave for the paying perverts.

I must have been comatose having not stirred at the latch sliding across, hearing the new person being dumped in our cold, nasty abode. A new captive, a new sex slave.

There had to have been a commotion, there always is, noise, yelling, pleading... Then you up the ante, offer bribes, followed by promises. Cries of sheer terror as the magnitude of your plight begins to take hold. It suddenly dawns on you that no amount of begging, yelling, offering money or anything else is going to make them open that huge wooden door.

My fuzzy half-awake brain is going all out to assimilate the recent development and is taken aback that these scum have actually kidnapped a child.

Contemptible, loathsome individuals that they are, they had the brass balls to keep us here against our will. But kids?

Surreptitiously torn from our ordinary everyday lives to do their bidding, I guess anything is within the realms of these poor excuses for human beings. There's probably more money in it the younger the girl.

Curiosity and compassion had me reach out to our newest cellmate.

I whispered gingerly to the little voice who didn't as yet have a face or name.

"Hello, what's your name?"

The crying persisted, growing progressively louder. Again, I muttered, "What's your name?" unsure she could hear me over her own sobs.

"Keep it down will you?" bounced out of the mouth of my fellow captive and friend, Claire. "Quit your snivelling, take it down a notch. Do you know what'll go down if they hear us? You soon will do if you keep that up." Her delivery was prickly and harsh.

"My names Susie," she responded in a barely audible whisper.

"What's going on? Where am I? Where are we?"

"We don't know where this place is exactly, I'd say someplace way out in the middle of the desert, twenty, thirty miles out of Vegas. Maybe more," I offered.

"Why have I been brought here? I want my mum, I need to go home," the exasperated cries hailed from the young girl.

"For christ's sake, how old are you?" Claire chided, upping her irritation a few degrees.

"I'm fourteen," Susie offered meekly.

"Old enough then." Claire's tone was so sharp she could have cut herself.

"Old enough for what? What are you talking about?" cried Susie.

"Please, Claire, button it. What's the point in terrifying her?" I said, in an attempt to calm the mood.

"It won't be me doing the terrifying though, will it? Assaulting her and forcing her to participate in all manner of perverted acts and stripping her of her dignity," grunted Claire rhetorically, shaving off not one iota of the sharpness in her tone.

3

"Wind your neck in, Claire. What's up with you?" I shot back equally as sharp, the last part a tad stupid as I knew exactly what was up with her.

The obvious, plus why they'd allowed her a pass tonight. Pulling up the vision of her face at the motel before we were steered into the waiting van, the van purposefully adapted to ferry us back and forth and to ship us back here in the early hours after they'd done with us.

Brutally beaten senseless by punters, refusing to comply meant that some of them would beat the crap out of her, the lowlife pummelling her with his fists resulting in horrific injuries. Moreover, the worst I'd had the displeasure to witness since I'd been embroiled in this sordid mess.

Slits as eyes, face bruised, puffed, bloodied and sore, bruises forming over other parts of her body. For whatever reason, the sadistic brute had really gone to town on her.

"Bad for business," the throwaway remark flew out of the mouth of one of the caring souls on the payroll.

"Leave her here a of couple nights until her face don't look so bad."

Oh, the compassion of the man, these words a hair's breadth from exploding from my lips.

I kept my trap shut. What choice did I have? Here in this hell survival is what it's all about. In the beginning there was no halting my smart Yorkshire mouth. I paid dearly for daring to impart my thoughts, my opinions, my boldness.

The old me would have let rip and fired both barrels.

The only words Claire managed to whisper out of her bloodied swollen lips were, "You want to see the other guy."

We'd concluded there and then our Claire had a death wish.

For once they'd made a concession with the blindfolds. The one named Pete gestured to us to help her. Like we needed to be prompted, I'd thought rhetorically.

One thing to come out of it, those few minutes we weren't blindfolded afforded us a clear view of where we were, instantly recognising the bright lights of Fremont Street a couple of blocks up.

It was a stroke of luck I'd not been shipped out tonight. Catching the tail end of one of the jailer's phone conversations,

4

I heard there were less rooms available in the motel. They would either split us up or leave a couple of us here. Convenient for them but Claire was unworkable. For reasons only they knew they'd picked me to stay with her. There was no questioning from my end.

At least being here I'm able to offer a little solace to the whimpering kid cowering in the corner. A desperate scared kid who if nothing else could use a hug and a splodge of empathy.

Unlike my fellow captive who's patience had withered, I couldn't stand to hear Susie's cries. In terms conjuring up words which might make a difference my thought process had drawn a blank. Platitudes and untruths rallied round my brain, but I hadn't the heart to come forth with such crap.

I am reflecting back to what was whirring round my head when I first had the misfortune to wake in this cold, nasty place. I remember I cried, as I bet Claire did, and still does at times. We all do.

My eyes adjusting to the darkness, I warily shuffle my body to the mattress in the corner. It's vital I quieten her or at least give it my best shot. Tell her it would be alright and not to worry. But of course I knew that would be pointless. And a lie.

"Hush, Susie," I ensued, placing a blanket round her shoulders and pulling her close.

"Unfortunately, Claire's right, it doesn't pay to aggravate them. They barely need an excuse to come down here as it is. We have to pretend we're following their stupid rules."

The nonsensical rules put in place to show us who's boss, wield their power. Keep us in line. Plus, we're never able to determine how many of them are upstairs at any given time, or the mood and state of mind they'd be in. Volatile and unpredictable were the words that came to mind.

It was evident they drank, the sickly smell of booze on their rancid breath inches from us as they untie our wrists and yank off the blindfolds. Slaves in a chain gang, ushered back down here where we huddle together and pray.

They never ease up with the torturous routines however sozzled. Blindfolded with zip tied wrists as we are bundled into the van each night. Frantic and scared because we know what's coming. Different motels, different faces. Same faces, same motels.

We are constantly threatened, exposing their guns in case we doubted the veracity of their threats. We had to eradicate thoughts of escape, we'd seen and known girls who had vanished into thin air.

A few, and I strongly suspect Claire joining the ranks, are on the verge of breaking. Throwing in the towel. I'd noticed a distinct change in her over these last couple of weeks.

I guess I'm a glass half full sort of girl. My ideology, there is always hope, otherwise what do we have to cling to? I'm possibly deluding myself, it's only a matter of time and I'm right there with her, a ticking time bomb is what we all are.

My ponderances side-stepped to my friend Fiona and how she was here one minute then gone the next, snatched from us by a great hulking monster of a man who was hovering above us whilst we lay huddled together on the mattress on the floor. The rhythm of his twisted voice repeated the phrase "eeny meeny, miny moe" over and over, he wasn't going back up those stairs without one of us. Governed by his own twisted desires, it could have been any one of us, and not for the first time he chose her.

Tiny Fiona scooped up as in a sack of trash, a piece of meat. Flaying through the air, her long flowing auburn hair used as a tool against her.

The hurt and depravity awaiting her required no explanation.

Inwardly tortured, not one of us slept. We waited. We waited with bated breath so that we could hold and comfort her.

That moment never came.

My beautiful, big hearted friend gone forever.

Thuds, bumps, the banging of furniture and blood curdling sounds spoke volumes. We took it she fought and dared to refuse. Only a few feet away above our heads, but we couldn't save her. Helpless, we listened and prayed, straining our ears with the hope of hearing her voice, the ruckus given over to deafening silence.

Is this how it all ends? What's in store for all of us?

During these endless six weeks I listened and absorbed the horror stories.

I caught snippets from some of the others of what they'd been put through – sadistic torture, bites, cigarette burns and worse, much worse. One guy had a penchant for sex whilst rendering the girl unconscious, strangling her until she blacked out, bringing her round then repeating. He'd requested her specifically and paid more for the privilege, unashamedly imparting he'd gladly cough up for extra time.

Now that really sticks in my gut. I am not sure what is worse, to hear his monstrous deeds, or her take on the whole thing.

On the return journey in the van she is barely able to form words; dazed, woozy, striations around her neck, regurgitating his actions, divulging she'd hoped his hands would squeeze longer and tighter. Letting it slip, maybe next time would be it, lights out, game over.

Navigating through this daily trauma, emotionally and physically pulls up every ounce of strength and resilience we own, and then some. Forced to adapt to these inhumane conditions beyond the pale is not something I'd wish on my worst enemy.

All this is running through my head as I nestled close to Susie hugging her gently, kindness and warmth all I'm able to extend in this awful place. Her weeping took on a steady rhythm.

"What's your name?" she questioned in a mousy tone.

"I'm Victoria, but call me Vicky," I whispered. "That pugnacious specimen over there is Claire in case you missed it earlier. What's your story? How'd you end up here? You seem young to be online dating. Where did you encounter Jake or whatever name he's going by these days?" I warily questioned in a hushed voice.

"No way would I do that. Absolutely not. I'm not that stupid. Who's Jake anyway? I don't think I know anybody called Jake." Her snivelling reply came with unyielding purpose.

Well, that's me told, I thought.

Doing my best not to take offence at the disparaging comment, I continued to probe, knowing full well how I, Claire and a few of the other girls had ended up in this hell hole. Though there was no arguing with her logic.

She began painting a picture of how she'd been snatched off the street, literally in broad daylight.

I listened intently as the teenager tentatively reeled off a fairly detailed account of how she'd come to be here.

In a soft broken tone between painful sobs she outlined how her abduction occurred. She took a moment then bravely pressed on, offering up specific details of what was clearly a terrifying ordeal.

"I just can't believe it, my mum and dad will be frantic with worry…"

Barely stopping to catch her breath Susie's voice trailed off.

"You're very brave, Susie, just keep being brave, they'll be looking for you I am sure of it," I offered, giving her a little squeeze. "You need to focus on staying healthy and alive until you can either escape or be rescued. Like I said, people will be looking for you."

I immediately regretted using the word "alive", a momentary lapse of judgement on my part, tiredness making me forget I was speaking to a new victim, a child.

Once more the floodgates opened, silent irrepressible sobs. I pulled the blanket around her and hugged her tightly, a hollow attempt at consoling the terrified youngster.

"For God's sake shut up! You're not helping by being nice to her. This is reality now, little missy. It doesn't matter how you ended up here, the fact is you're here. Deal with it and stop your snivelling. We're all in the same boat so suck it up," Claire hissed.

"Precisely," I said in a hushed, sombre voice.

"We need to stick together, help each other. She's only a kid, give her a break, Claire. Compassion, ever heard of it?" I whispered sarcastically.

"I'll show compassion when those demonic morons upstairs show me some, namely letting me go and stop pimping me out to line their bleeding pockets," snarled Claire a little too loud for comfort.

Susie completely lost it at this point.

The penny had dropped, and it finally dawned on her why she was here. More to the point what lay ahead, the reality of her predicament hitting her on the head like a wrecking ball.

At that she became even more inconsolable, crying for her mum, dad and sister.

It dawned on me she's probably their youngest captive, although how would I know? There could have been younger girls taken before I landed here. Maybe, just maybe, they're setting a new trend getting rid of us "oldies". My mind was rambling.

I was remembering how I'd spent my last birthday. Doing unimaginable things, dirty, disgusting things, there was nothing half full about my glass that day, that I do remember.

Random thoughts come seeping through and dart into your head out of nowhere. Having very little to occupy us the mind tends to migrate to the past, the past which seems a world away, a life lived by someone who looked just like us, a parallel universe.

Unlike Susie it could be argued that I am at least partly responsible for where I find myself.

I'm guilty, guilty of being a dork. Gullible. Prompted by friends, I joined an online dating website.

Like the rest of the population I knew the risks, had heard the stories, the hidden dangers meeting strangers, weirdos. I could've dealt with weirdos. A master manipulator is a whole different ball game and certainly not what I bargained for.

Enter the charmer known to me as Jake.

My online suitor. My maybe boyfriend.

One stupid mistake. Albeit a momentous mistake.

As far as stupidity goes this has to be up there.

I couldn't deny I found it a welcomed distraction considering where my life was at. In the throes of grieving from the loss of my dad, I began to look forward to our little interactions. Mr slightly flirty possessed the ability to make me smile.

The guy's persona was that of a sweet, kind, caring individual, and clearly intelligent.

He stood out and showed interest in the mundane aspects of my life, differing to the usual flannel and bullshit. Flattery came easy and often, not in a creepy way, he was too classy for that. Then it came, the offer. The offer which if I chose to accept held the power to change my life forever and change me as a person.

The words that I had secretly been yearning for out of sheer curiosity more than anything were staring back at me from my phone.

Are you free Friday evening? If so, do you want to meet up?

Little did I know accepting would lead me to this. The tall, dark, handsome stranger had me in his sights, and unbeknown to me and the rest of the female population he owned a hidden dark side. A hidden evil dark side.

There was no denying I was flattered. I questioned, "What does he see in me, an ordinary office administrator who'd moved from the UK to the bright lights of Vegas?" He simply oozed charm and charisma. Could I really have got this lucky?

I chose the restaurant at his request. A nice touch on his part. The fact he suggested I choose the location gave me an air of confidence. It pointed to him being on the level, not some crazy guy.

It just goes to show, I'd thought many a day while locked up here. Here, waiting for the next instalment of this horror show where I share a starring role.

Articulate and interesting, he was engrossed in every word that came out of my mouth. What more could a girl ask for?

A gentleman to a fault, courteously getting to his feet as we were leaving, gallantly pulling out the chair and reaching for the door. Chivalry alive and well on this Friday night.

Until it wasn't.

He apologised profusely at having to call it a night, stating how he'd really love an opportunity to make it up to me, suggesting perhaps a club next time, dinner first of course.

Why in the world would I be suspicious?

Flashy beamer aside, it would have been rude not to accept the offer of a lift home.

Why oh why had I been so compliant and accepting? It didn't take me long to conclude I had made a rookie mistake, an incredibly foolish mistake.

I'd fallen for his patter good and proper. God only knows what went through my champagne soaked brain. All the claptrap spilled out of my mouth over that dinner. A second drink ensures every morsel of common sense I've managed to cling to evaporates in a puff of smoke.

The more I drink the more I rattle. The more I rattle the more personal information tumbles out, a bit like attempting to put the toothpaste back in the tube I guess. I should've kept my mouth firmly shut. Zipped.

My gregarious date is showering me with compliments, notably paying attention to every detail with regard to my everyday interactions. The people I'm closest to and my work colleagues. On reflection, I'd made myself a target like shooting a fish in a barrel.

He reeled every one of us in using the same method. If you have a tried and tested formula then why deviate? Even the way he leaned in a little with the ruse of making sure the seat belt was secure.

Reminiscent of a venomous snake, he swooped, swiftly securing its prey, me and my friends fitting the role of the unsuspecting prey.

Recalling the moment our eyes met, the toerag was leaning in for the kill. Smiling sweetly, his warm breath wafted over my cheek, his fingers gently untangling a strand of my long blonde hair snagged under the seat belt.

A painful jolt ran through me, a bolt of electricity. Done for, out cold. I learnt later a taser gun was his weapon of choice.

Now here I languish, paying the hefty price for my foolishness.

Chapter Two

And Then it Began

The car journey to which I have absolutely no memory came to an end, and with it another end. Life as I knew it. Unprecedented terror began to unfold as horrific pain punctuated my drowsiness, the synapses darting back and forth in my head attempting to assimilate the predicament I had somehow fallen into.

One minute I'm on cloud nine, happy and safe. The next minute hell on earth. I'm utterly terrified and I hurt all over. My vision is impaired though my other senses are amplified. I can hear, smell and feel, and am aware I have been taken to an unfamiliar location and am being brutely assaulted in the most humiliating way.

Why and by who?

Pitifully, I plead, beg and lie announcing I'm pregnant. Whatever outlandish thing creeps into my head shoots straight out of my mouth. All to no avail. My pleas fall on deaf ears. They, and I know there are two of them, continue with the brutal assault.

The vulgar, disgusting, derogatory remarks directed at me flow unreservedly. Sore and with a throbbing headache from hell, my mind is going in a hundred different directions. I can't comprehend how this could be happening to me. Who are these two monsters?

Sneers, grunts and obscenities pour out of their nasty foul mouths as they worked themselves up into a frenzy, egging each other on.

Though the tone is alien to me, and through a fogging haze one voice is familiar. I connected the dots.

Jake. It had to be Jake. And a second person. A second rapist.

12

It's slotting into place, the car, the seat belt. That knowing smile.

The superficial charm and soft appealing tone is replaced by vulgar profanity, ratcheting up the vileness in his voice with each assault. Words from his fiendish friend are limited to the odd word.

It's imperative I fight. Not physically, that would futile and a non-starter. I'm not a huge person, besides, being trussed up by my arms on some kind of beam puts the kibosh on any thoughts on that score. Coupled with wide sticky tape over my eyes, I'd no hope of escaping nor lessoning the hurt.

The one thing I quickly garnered from their foul mouth battering is that they revelled in my anguish. My pitiful ramblings, crying and begging for mercy, gave them pleasure.

It's a game and I'm the star of the show. Tonight's entertainment.

My only recourse is to close off my mind or attempt to. Control my emotions. Emotions, self-pity and anger. A neuron fired up and blew a thought into my head. If only I had the strength to distance my mind from my body; dislodge my thoughts.

I had to give it a stab. What had I to lose?

If I'm to remain sane it's incumbent I take my mind to a better place, someplace nice in my head. Anywhere, just to freeze my thoughts and to quit whimpering and screaming.

To close off my mind and hope for it to stop. And to pray silently.

The better place is impossible to find. I resorted to the Lord's prayer then "All things bright and beautiful". Other psalms broke through as well as prayers and hymns from my school days.

Inevitably the outcome I'd visualised came to fruition. No more prayers and then I passed out. In and out of consciousnesses. Semi-consciousness brought with it a repeat of my terrible singing. Mute singing. I'd enough nous to know not to rile my tormentors.

Unable to see what was coming next, I squirmed inwardly at their touch. I'd no grasp of time and was completely unaware of the length of time the assault persisted or how long I was unconscious for. I was lost in the midst of a nightmare. Lost to a couple of sadists. I couldn't comprehend why anyone would do this.

Jake sadistically violating me was abhorrent in itself, but inviting a buddy to join him in his perverted quest was beyond sick and a whole new level of depravity. Or could it be the other guy was the instigator? Jake hooks 'em, the other does his worst.

I'd prayed they'd let me go when they were done having their fun. I questioned if I would ever know who this other rapist is. It crossed my mind, although maybe it was wishful thinking on my part, that I haven't seen this other individual so surely it's a good sign. If they weren't going to free me I wouldn't have been blindfolded throughout the attack. Then Jake popped into my head shattering that theory.

Eventually it ended.

My hopes faded with the realisation that my nightmare hadn't even got off the ground.

My head was thumping frantically as I attempted to get a grip with this, my new situation. I was now in the throes of a second wave of unbearable horror, another dire predicament I had to get my head round.

Different room, different surroundings, different smell even. And people. People like me, young women.

A new kind of torment.

I'm in a similar position to Susie and Claire and about ten other girls locked in this hell hole with me. This chamber of horrors.

Above Susie's crying I caught a sound. A recognisable thud. The lock and bolts sliding across the door overlooking the basement steps. That loud creak as the huge wooden dungeon door opens slowly.

For a brief second the light and brightness are appreciated. Accompanying the light a slight breeze drifts in, diluting the stale smell of our abode.

Accompanying the light and breeze is something, somebody, unwelcomed and unwanted.

The light paved the way in outlining a big brute of a man. A face we unfortunately knew all too well.

Our jailer, the gatekeeper. The devil, well, one of them. This thug, the animal who snatched my friend Fiona. And others. One of Jake's many sidekicks standing there, the look of wrath on his obnoxious face like some sort of fiend from a sixties horror movie.

The light from above enabled me a glimpse of the young angelic-looking Susie. The young girl had the appearance of someone far younger than her fourteen years.

A cursory thought, perhaps she'd been snatched because of her youthful appearance. Then maybe not. Most likely age didn't factor into it. Her pretty features probably had more to do with it, I surmised, catching sight of the vivid green eyes enhanced by lovely long lashes. Tiny with waist length blond hair, the girl is striking in appearance, indeed quite stunning.

"What did I tell you?" snarled an older green-eyed blonde, Claire.

As if she hadn't been scared before the pretty youngster was beside herself, bawling her eyes out with terror etched across her sweet innocent face.

Exploding between sobs she says, "Why am I here? What do you want? Why can't I go home? Please, please let me go home. I won't tell anyone, honest. I really won't," she begged.

Obnoxious face sniggered. He was having a field day deriving pleasure from Susie's cries and pleas.

"Now what makes you think we'd want to do that, pretty little schoolgirl? I'm taking a big risk all round adding you to our little harem. Our band of merry hookers." A dirty snigger accompanied the guiling response.

I knew the last comment would rile Claire. No matter the state of her, she just had to bite.

"Who are you calling a hooker?" came her angry retort.

"I'm sure you have been called a hell of a lot worse," countered the great ugly one.

"But I'm a virgin," offered the scared little voice.

I said nothing though couldn't help but think she should have kept that under wraps.

15

Shaking his head with a grotesque smile, "Oh my, we've really hit the jackpot this time. Wait until boss man Jake gets hold of this. Pretty, blonde, cute and innocent, all in one tiny little package. This little snippet has just netted us double, no, forget double, make that a treble payday. Cheers, Susie, for that one." Nastiness was oozing out of every pore.

"How do you know my name?" she blurted.

Ignoring her question, instead exploding with nasty observations and innuendos, he said, "Oh boy, they forgot to pass this little nugget on. Me, I've never had a virgin myself."

He was licking his lips and dishing up vile taunts left and right.

"Oh yeah, I could teach you a thing or two. All of 'yer for that matter. A real man is what 'yer need."

Bulging frog eyes were searing into Susie, the taunting in no way easing, exacting too much pleasure from her reactions by the look of his contorted face. It was like he'd found a new hobby, something, or someone to alleviate his boredom.

"Don't suppose any of your cute little mates fancy joining us? Make it worth their while we will. Always room for one more. Mind you, we can always go help ourselves, see how you pan out. I hear your mates are all lookers. Having a little 'ole party on my own upstairs if any of you fancy joining me? I'm a tad bored and lonely tonight drinking on my lonesome," he sniggered.

The protruding frog-like eyes were darting back and forth as if just like that he'd tempt us and we would jump to it and take him up on his offer. As he spoke, his big hairy hand was waving what I could only assume to be Susie's phone. A sparkly pink girly phone. I didn't have him down as a pink phone man.

"Oh, by the way, love, don't you look a doll in those holiday snaps?"

His eyes squinting like he needed reading glasses, he resumed perusing the photos coming forth with lewd comments directed at different girls.

There was no holding back with his filth on how the girls carried off their beachwear and other outfits, audaciously referring to them by name and providing running commentaries

16

on their figures. Diabolical, disgusting statements were teeming out of those vulgar fat lips.

"Aren't they just the prettiest little bunch?" his ranting continuing like verbal diarrhoea.

"Your sister's got it all, ain't she? Wow! What a pair. Older? Younger? Got that Britney Spears thing going on I see."

He was clearly getting his daily fix of fun, bullying and frightening the young girl. Top dog as he considered himself, in no way expected a peep out of her. Moreover, nor did we.

Barely hanging on before he'd put in an appearance, now all of a sudden as if someone had wound her up, it had pressed a button. With fire in her eyes and an eruption of raw anger she went at him all guns blazing. Full throttle, screaming and yelling. There was no holding back, bringing the guys who'd snatched her into the mix just for good measure.

He'd awakened the angry teenage Susie.

Hollering more than a few choice words, and intent on letting the bastard know what a disgusting, dirty excuse for a human being he is, she stated he'd burn in hell. She yelled that he'd never get near her sister Jess or her friends, he'll be locked up way before ever clapping eyes on them.

Tears of anger trickled down her face. The girl sure had a pair of lungs on her.

Maybe this was her real character surfacing. Silently crying, nevertheless exploding with rage, she sure had plenty to say.

After she'd finished her tirade I saw her through fresh eyes.

Suddenly, panic swirled in my stomach. I was scared for her, for us. It didn't do to goad them, any of them up, especially this clown.

Fiona's disappearance was forever engrained in my mind and heart, and as much as I agreed with every sentiment I felt it vital I simmer her down.

I'd been there exacting my frustration and anger, the consequence of my outburst still fresh in my mind. I didn't want that for Susie.

Part of me was surprised Claire hadn't joined in and added her two cents worth. Instead, she'd hidden her face with a blanket in an attempt to dissolve into the mattress, disappear,

17

out of sight out of mind. Let the focus of his attention stay on the newbie and me.

Both of us were acutely aware of his agenda and where he's heading with his filth. The question being with who. All this dirty talk working himself up, we didn't need drawing a map. It went without saying Claire was still in the running, and the fact she'd been beaten to a pulp the previous day wouldn't deter him.

The monstrous brute never ceased to disappoint. It was always going to be a case of who would be the unlucky recipient, the next on his hit list. He had to get his rocks off somehow and tonight we were it. Well, at least one of us would be. Since we were down to three the odds weren't looking particularly good.

This guy who could give Shrek a run for his money started towards me and Susie.

Her cowering demeanour returned. Huddled behind me on the mattress she shook uncontrollably, again crying and whimpering with fear.

I attempted to calm her. We were both frightened. Me because I knew what stirred in his tiny, perverted mind, Susie for obvious reasons now reality had well and truly kicked in.

Arms clinging tightly to my waist, her tears soaked the back of my top. She'd abruptly ceased with the hollering and obscenities and once more her tone exemplified fear.

Could I persuade him to leave? Could I appeal to some lobe in his bonce responsible for empathy and pity? Surely some cell in his body held a speck of decency.

I felt it imperative I go all out for all our sakes.

Sensing it to be useless, my voice began with the only thing that managed to make it to my mouth. Bypassing my brain altogether, I heard the words but wondered who put them there.

"Look, I'm sure you're not an unreasonable man. You have sisters? Nieces? A mother?" I pleaded. Pleading turned to begging. "You can see she's petrified," I implored.

"What gave you that idea?" he spluttered, face contorted, his eyes like huge marbles. "Unreasonable is 'ma middle name."

18

"Amongst other things," I heard Claire mutter cynically but quietly from beneath her covers.

For a minuscule of a second I wondered if Claire had sealed her own fate. He turned slightly as if to start towards her.

You could always rely on Claire to be garrulous. Regardless of the situation she couldn't keep it buttoned, no matter the consequences. I suppose I couldn't blame her. We all had our moments and yesterday's beating undoubtedly dragged her further down than I had ever seen her.

Before I knew what'd hit me the monster pounced in my direction, lunged at me, and made a grab for my hair. The hideous specimen began pulling me by my ponytail along the coarse hard basement floor, swearing and ranting for good measure.

Susie's screaming escalated as she witnessed the barbarian doing his thing.

Directing his threat at the frightened young girl he said, "You can shut the fuck up or you'll be next."

I knew further pleading was futile, a waste of my much-needed breath. I braced myself knowing this wasn't good, also knowing if he thinks I'm going to lay down and take it he'd better buckle up. I ain't making it easy for him, I'm not going down without a fight and that's a given.

Chapter Three

My Eureka Moment

As he dragged me my bones hit the cold hard steps one at a time, scuffing every inch of my aching thin body, the egotistical piece of shit pulling my hair allowing me no possibility of gaining my footing.

Domination and terror drive this sadist brute, pure pleasure etched across his face demonstrating to the two left behind what a big man he is. Sadistic charm overflowing, the ruse was that his pathetic rules were being ignored.

Eventually arriving at the top of the steps his huge hand relinquished his grip. Dropped like a stone, albeit a small stone, I couldn't determine which part of me hurt most. My head throbbed and felt as though clumps of hair had been tugged out. I'm picturing a lump forming at the point his knuckles connected to my skull. The rest of my body was grazed and sore, the brutality levelled at me totally unnecessary.

The compulsion to swear and curse consumed me. I'd have liked to offer up my rendition of what Susie had chucked at him, but on reflection I knew better.

It probably only took thirty seconds for me to end up exactly where he wanted me, dumped as a piece of garbage on the hard stone floor. Blood was beginning to seep through what few clothes I'd managed to hang on to, and bruises were forming on my thin hips and the top of my legs. Battered, bruised and in pain, this before the bastard begun with what we both know was rattling around in his tiny pea brain.

My weeks in captivity had come to this, pathetically crumpled on that floor. I was next in line, waiting, anticipating the fight of my life the realisation this could be the end of the road.

The degradation served up daily was chipping away at me. My endurance was withering and disappearing a little each day.

It's all too much. I'm slowly becoming physically and mentally broken. The front I exhibit is just that, a front.

Maintaining my position I purposely clocked every clumsy move he made. He reached for the key which by the look of it he'd left in the dungeon door. He turned then quickly deposited it back in his pants pocket.

After locking the door his huge stretched arm reached to the bolt at the top and then bent to slide the lower one across.

I could barely hear Susie, though not for a minute did I think she'd settled down. Witnessing all this would have added an extra layer to her fear.

I guess Claire was still being Claire but trusted she'd comfort Susie until I got back. I know only too well there's a decent compassionate person hiding underneath that smart mouth. I also knew she'd plummeted way down, and I had yet to see a sign of her pulling herself out of that dark hole we've all circled from time to time.

As I sat there on the floor akin to a wounded animal I scrutinised my surroundings. I thought I could hear voices.

He'd purported to be drinking alone but I'm damned if I'd take anything out of that mouth as gospel. I was expecting to clap eyes on one of the other bods at any second. It didn't look like any of the others were around so lucky for me just this one, though this ghoul was the worst of them all.

Again, I could hear voices, chatting and laughing. No sooner had the tones hit my ears when my brain assimilated what and where they emanated from. They weren't real, it was a television switched on in the adjoining room.

Guessing that room a lounge, this room, where we'd obviously stepped through countless times to reach the basement, was ostensibly a kitchen. Their version of a kitchen, a messy hovel more like.

A large refrigerator stood next to a cluttered countertop adjacent to a sink, the sink barely noticeable due to the amount of rubbish strewn in and around. Stacked on the surface area were empty food cans, plates and other crap piled up to the brim.

I was tempted to make a suggestion regarding housekeeping but had a swift rethink knowing what and who I'm dealing

21

with. There was nothing good heading my way so there was no point in making a bad situation worse.

I'd been in this place for six horrendous weeks with absolutely no notion of the layout. Of course, we'd speculated, now here I am sitting on the floor catching a bird's-eye view.

My vantage point allowed me a view of more or less the entirety of the house. It had a TV and various pieces of furniture but looked plain and basic.

It was imperative I get my bearings and suss the place in the event it necessary to scramble away from the brute and hide. Or run but I doubt that was going to happen. After all, where would I run to? I'm trapped.

I could see three windows all blacked out by black trash bags held in place with that familiar stuff, silver duct tape.

A mountain of women's clothes caught my attention nestled on top an expensive-looking backpack. Susie's I guess.

Breaking my ponderances, the huge grotesque brute took steps toward me.

Motionless, I hadn't budged. I remained where he'd deposited me a foot or so from the basement door. I scanned the floor in the event there might be something to hit him with. No dice, there was nothing.

His gait was that of a man on a mission. Him the big man, the jailer, me, the disposable commodity. I have but one purpose, to indulge his needs and whims.

I guess it depends how compliant I am whether I end up back downstairs or where Fiona ended up.

Reaching for my arm he roughly pulled me to my feet, forcefully shoving me on one of the chairs positioned around a huge table. Appreciative of the size of it, to my way of thinking it acted as a barrier, mercifully setting me down directly opposite him.

Instinctively I yelped as a sharp pain ran through my arm and shoulder. An expletive jumped out of my mouth, he either didn't hear it or chose to ignore.

It was me and him at this rubbish laden table with two empty chairs either side. Hopefully they'll stay that way, empty. Having no desire to look at him I glanced round. In addition to the huge table there was a fridge, sink and countertop, and as with the table they were strewn with trash, the majority of the rubbish being beer cans and empty junk food containers. Amongst the trash on the table stood a nearly full bottle of vodka. Obnoxious face was having a party for one by the look of it.

Suddenly, he trotted off into the other room to switch off the TV. Due to the compactness of this dump he's back within seconds sitting in the same spot. He's sitting and staring as if wanting to say something. Or am I supposed to speak? I tried not to look at him but it was difficult.

A sidewards glance at the pile of clothing and other things, I couldn't help but wonder how many girls had ended up here. Could it really be girls have been killed and buried?

I found myself in this labyrinthine of hell feeling weak, hungry and petrified. How much longer could I go on? How much more of this could I take? Am I doomed? Here's me doing my best or at least what I'm able to do to protect young Susie, but who's here to protect me?

My soul is shrivelling and eroding rapidly from the inside out. I'd had all I could take and knew for the sake of my sanity I had to somehow get the hell away from this place and these evil individuals.

My sanity demanded I buck up and sharpen my senses. Moreover, extract from my tired brain an escape plan before it's too late and do what I do best, utilise my intuitive thinking and imagination. I had to stop waiting for the rescue party which up to now hasn't materialised and is a mere pipe dream. It's imperative I get my thinking cap on, be proactive and get out of here.

I had to do something. The realisation hit me that there is only one person who will be my saviour – me. It's like when you have a eureka moment, Susie being taken, that jerk picking me, I had this surge of something telling me this is it, now is the time to take back control of my life.

I had chosen to get into that car with Jake, now I'm choosing to get out of this place. This is my time. I had always been capricious. At this juncture it was now or never, do or die. Or die trying. I'd reached the point of utter despair. It has to be now, today, the one night I'm not taken out. For the moment only, there was only one monster to contend with.

I concluded it was fate I'd been selected by Mr Congeniality tonight. No question, I'm frail, aching from head to toe and weak from lack of nutrition. Nevertheless, I'd retained a steely determination and know 1 have fight left in me. Fight, strength of character and a hell of a lot of bottle.

My gut instinct told me this had to be it. Resolute in my mission, one way or the other to emerge from this nightmare, my Yorkshire grit and sheer tenacity surged through every inch of my body.

I wasn't going back to that fetid smelling dungeon, of that I was sure.

Chapter Four

Let the Game Begin

Without a second glance at the two-legged monster splayed opposite me, I rose to my feet. Unsteady, a little wobbly, but undeterred, I readied myself. Using my peripheral vision I stole a glance fortuitously clocking his reaction, and as difficult as I found it I turned and offered a small smile. I went on to slowly, almost seductively, brush the dust and dirt from my clothes, behaving as if his exploits evoked nothing in me. I'm over it. For all intents and purposes, his words and actions hadn't impacted me, didn't even ruffle my feathers.

The look of bewilderment added nothing to his fine features. Shocked and not knowing quite how to react, he regarded me quizzically, almost bemused.

The creepy expression hadn't eluded him. His eyes widened and mouth stretched forming a smile, half of one at any rate. I could see it in his eyes, hope and wonderment. Could this really be his day? His lucky day? The one and only day in his miserable life he has actually found himself a willing partner?

I took from the befuddled look on his mush things didn't usually, if ever, go down like this. By my earlier protestations and pleading, not to mention me screeching with pain as he did his caveman impersonation, no way should I be compliant. Or willing. Why would I? Why would anybody?

My mind set I was focused. I had no intention of acceding to this monster of a man. The priority at this juncture was to come up with a stalling tactic. I had to think outside the box and it was imperative that somehow I find a way to buy some time.

The blood pumping quickly through my veins swirled round my brain. I could almost feel my heart thumping in my chest.

My brain hammered at me, doing its upmost to pull up an idea. A plan thus enabling me to make my escape knowing full well that most of the time there is more than one guy here.

Therefore, any minute there's a distinct possibility things could become twice as difficult and twice as dangerous.

The objective was to escape from this revolting place with the least amount of pain and degradation as possible. I really had no idea how this would play out. As yet I had no plan to speak of, but undeterred I was gonna give it my best shot. Unrelenting in my quest I dawdled making a meal of dusting myself off. As if job done, I tentatively started very slowly towards him. Not too close, only a little closer. I was careful not to allow myself to be in a position which would enable him to make a grab for me.

Although in my mind I was ready for it, I was anticipating what his next move could be. Just dare, I said to myself, as I eyed that large bottle of spirit thinking how much damage I could do to his head.

His eyes bore into me, he clearly had no intention of allowing me out of his sight for a second.

Predictably, he's bound to be cagey, struggling to get a handle on the situation or believe his luck. I tugged at the band holding my ponytail in place and shook my long blonde hair.

The motion hurt my head which was pulsating from the brutality dished out by mine host, the pain giving me incentive and adding to my determination.

A wave of nausea nestled inside me as I crept forward in my stocking feet, having not had the opportunity to put shoes or anything else on. Admittedly they would've gone flying at the point he began with his usual brutal shenanigans.

I decided to take the initiative and begin the dialogue.

"Were you just teasing earlier when you mentioned a party?" My tone was flagrant disguising my utter contempt. Going all out and feigning sexiness, my best acting skills were rising up out of nowhere. "How about pouring a girl a drink?"

Without a word he pulled his hulking torso up off his chair. I guess he daren't turn his back on me so he didn't, he sort of craftily edged his way to his "bar". He proceeded to get a clear plastic cup and pour a copious amount of what appeared to be cheap vodka.

Not a word left those puffy fat lips. It was probably all in my imagination, but at this stage of the game I felt a minuscule ounce of control prompting me to wing it and make conversation.

Offering a half smile, I started with the buttering up.

"Wow, that's generous, you're very kind."

"Ice?"

That's when to my utter surprise he did turn his back on me, if only for a second or two as he opened the freezer part of the refrigerator to retrieve an ice tray. But still, mistake number one.

As he watched me I watched him while making a mental note of his every move. I can't believe he is buying this little charade. The flicking of the hair and my wanting to party with him, the halfwit was not picking up on how disingenuous I was.

I came to a swift conclusion. This guy must be really, really drunk or stupid. Or both. Or perhaps lonely as he'd touched upon earlier. Probably sees a future for us!

That vodka must be good stuff if he thinks he is on a promise.

He iced both drinks then beckoned me to sit back on one of the chairs by the cluttered table. I couldn't help but wonder if these were all his empty beer cans or if he'd had company, one of the other "jailers". No wonder he's buying into my sham if he's downed all this then he's halfway pissed.

The one thing more than anything I yearned for at this point was food. All I wanted, needed at that precise moment, was something to quell the hunger pains and gurgling noises in my empty stomach.

Ridiculously it entered my head to ask him for something to eat. A sandwich maybe? God, that would have been heavenly.

Although I doubted I'd be hungry enough to eat anything he had a hand in making, at the same time I hadn't eaten for nearly twelve hours. There was no getting away from it, I was absolutely ravenous.

I also knew if I drink alcohol on my empty stomach I'll be out of it in no time, moreover sick. I couldn't risk that, no way do I intend to allow myself to become vulnerable, more vulnerable than I am right now sitting here waiting for him to pounce.

27

I need to keep my wits about me, remain focused, staying one step ahead is the name of this game. I'm probably delusional but I could sort of feel I had control over the situation. A welcomed and strange feeling, I hadn't had such feelings in a very long time.

He swigged his drink and proceeded to pour himself another. I put my hand over my plastic cup thus preventing him refreshing mine. To my surprise he didn't push it. More for him I suppose but I wouldn't have had the confidence to argue at this point.

I couldn't gauge or be sure who is playing who here. Is he buying this? Maybe he's waiting to see my next move.

The cadence of his voice had changed slightly. He took on a softer tone.

I carried on pretending to sip my drink, twirling the ice round with my finger, placing my finger in my mouth as if to lick it, my attempt in dragging this little performance out.

My eyes periodically glanced his way throwing him a closed smile now and again. I was keeping up the deception that I'm willingly partaking in his one-man party. I was waiting for the opportunity to empty that drink without his beady eyes spotting me. Hopefully, my drinking buddy was half cut therefore oblivious to my sneaky move.

Part of me was secretly praying the fat lump would drink so much he'd pass out right there on that chair in that grotty kitchen. It would have to be a minor miracle for that one to go down. What are the odds of me being that lucky? Still, I kept hoping and of course secretly praying. Please, God, let him fall off the chair drunk and crack his head on that concrete floor. Alternatively, stay down long enough for me to whack him with that bottle.

No way would I have anticipated him to be thinking it on the cards that me and him could become best buddies. Surprisingly, the drink was bringing out his chatty side. He's rabbiting away in full flow and I'm fantasising and playing scenarios in my head what I'd like to do with that bottle and where I'd like to shove it.

I made overtones intimating I'm paying attention, listening, nodding and smiling in all the right places. The great lump was making like this is a normal everyday situation and we are two people simply having a beverage or two. Three, four, five or six in his case. Oh yeah, sitting here like two acquaintances, old friends, him and me.

I have a notion that'll be something else lacking in his world – friends!

There was no letting up. He gave the small talk his best shot going on about how I'm one of Jake's special girls.

He'd heard this and that from Jake and the other guy, the person who he's referring to a mystery to me. It was someone who had clout and their opinion mattered by the sound of it.

"You've got a natural look, pretty all the same."

"Thanks," I reply, my sarcasm struggling to stay hidden. Am I supposed to be flattered? Is this meant as a compliment?

Also citing this girl, that girl, none of whom I'd ever met or heard of which I found mind-boggling and thought provoking. I had to stop myself pressing him for details for fear of undoing the rapport I figured we'd started to build. It was probably wishful thinking on my part and his for reasons which I didn't want to think about.

I was all too aware that in order to survive I had to play the game. His game. To a point that is.

Play for time. Allow him to talk. Continue knocking back the booze, that'll do for now. Hopefully his backside will stay put, planted on that chair the other side of that table. I'm thankful for now at least that he's keeping his grubby hands to himself.

I didn't know how to converse with such an individual. Full of trepidation I realise that if my plan has any hope then I must make a determined effort to reciprocate. Especially since he's putting on a show, presenting himself as friendly and part of my fan club.

Although in what world he lived, what planet he occupied, I should be flattered by his, Jake or the other dude's compliments was quite unfathomable and totally beyond comprehension.

Listening to all the bullshit I'd noticed his demeanour had shifted. Now behaving like this is just a typical night for him, and lucky me I'm his date. I'm almost blinded to the fact I'm being held against my will and have been kidnapped.

The only thing which jumped out at me to talk about was family. I put my best foot forward and went for it. "Do you have a family? Kids? Siblings? Mum, dad, dog, cat, pet rat?"

As precarious as my situation had become sitting here with a potential killer and rapist I'm giving my best, or at the very least acting cordial.

Obviously, I got that wrong. Boy did I get it wrong. You'd have thought my question had been on the lines of, "Are you out on parole? Been kidnapping and raping women long have you?"

He was back to his usual tone with a vengeance. Up one minute down the next. A psychopath.

"What? What 'yer saying? What business is it of yours, heh? Why do you of all people need to know that? Bit of a nosey slut aren't we?"

There he goes, he just couldn't keep it up. The facade of normality evaporated as quick as a flash back to what I'm used to, foul mouth, nasty and vicious.

If ever damage limitation is called for this is it, I said in my head.

"I didn't mean anything, I'm simply interested that's all. It occurred to me you must miss spending time with them while you're stuck out here with us."

My tone was a little reticent as to my mind I'd already blown it. Being sweet and friendly to this ogre is no easy feat. All I could think of whilst he rattled on was dare I risk lunging for that vodka bottle? Is it possible I could grab for it without him grabbing my arm?

"What do you mean 'out here'? You don't know where the fuck you are or where here is," he declared sharply.

At this juncture it's clear I'm falling way short in my efforts. Straining to connect on some level, any level, is evidently going down the pan quicker than an express train. The hope that maybe he would start to see us differently as human beings with feelings and families waiting at home was way off.

He continued knocking back the booze like there was no tomorrow. Stupidity on his end he hadn't noticed mine wasn't dissipating. Perhaps he had but really didn't give a damn.

With small talk clearly not working his mind turned to other things. Me. His true intentions were creeping back to the surface.

The usual perverted voice was re-emerging, a dirty snigger tagged on for emphasis. "How's about a little lap dance?"

I was not entirely sure what to do next, thinking maybe he'd caught on that I'm playing for time here.

My plan thus far consisted of getting him blind drunk and hoping he'd pass out was way off the mark. His tolerance for the liquor was truly something to behold. This guy could drink the Hoover Dam dry. Worryingly it appeared to be having the opposite effect.

"Yeah, why not?" I responded, feigning the sexy voice once again.

"You got any music?" I asked in a more normal voice having forgotten to use the sexy tone.

Keen as mustard, I guess imagining what he thought was going to play out, he sloppily got off his chair almost taking a tumble into the bargain. Steadying himself using the table, he came close to ending up on the concrete floor.

Shucks, nearly, was my immediate reaction, though naturally keeping it zipped.

Me, I was pretty close to something too. Flipping the junk filled table in the hope some part of it would hit him, then on doing so diving for that bottle then making a break for the outer door.

Instead, he grabbed the bottle and staggered into the other room.

"Now what?" I muttered to myself.

Maybe all's not lost, I thought, the stupid idiot could barely stand.

As he occupied himself, no doubt rooting through his extensive music collection in the adjacent room, my eyes darted haphazardly from one area to another. Predominantly the outer door. I was contemplating how many steps it would take for me to reach it. Again, for a split second I almost made a dash for it. Could I make it? Would it be locked? Why would it not be locked?

31

Obviously, they live like slobs but appear to be tuned in when it came to security, following their little routines to the letter.

The music started up. I couldn't see where it stemmed from, I just heard the thumping sounds. First came the blast from the past, well not exactly my past, a seventies song I recognised echoed from the other room. Clearly someone was enjoying the moment and having a good old sing song.

"She's crazy like a fool, just like daddy cool, daddy, daddy cool..."

It was repeating over and over as he "daddy cooled it" round the room, prancing back and forth the noise emanating from his gob akin to a wounded walrus.

I'm guessing he does this in the hope of impressing the opposite sex. I'm also guessing it doesn't have the desired effect.

"Get your sexy butt in here," demanded the wounded walrus.

As slowly as humanly possible I obeyed, devouring the room with my eyes as I entered. I was doing my upmost in making a mental note of his little domain, what and where everything is positioned. I tentatively made my way into the lion's den.

As with the room we'd just left the place was scruffy and pretty sparse of furniture. A long frayed burnt orange couch dominated this room. My first thought eyeing the couch was I'll bet he flakes out on this when the other guys are not around and when he's drunk himself into oblivion.

Against the far wall, directly behind the long couch, stood a sort of sideboard, wall unit or maybe a bookshelf. I couldn't make it out. What I did determine was it contained various items dotted here and there on a couple of the shelves, one of which appeared to be a bronze trophy of some kind fixed firmly on a thick wooden stand.

A television set on a little flimsy table stood opposite the orange couch.

Daddy cool was really getting down to it, strutting his stuff in the middle of the room, no doubt expecting me to join in now we were back to being best buddies.

Praying with everything I had I hoped he'd knacker himself out and collapse onto that couch. Or launch himself and break a bone. That'd work also.

Had he forgotten about the lap dance? I could hope but I seriously doubted it, although I was now seeing a different side to him. This wasn't the usual growling, twisted features man I'd encountered on and off during my captivity. Weirdly, in his own bizarre way, the guy is "letting loose".

I couldn't stop the crazy thoughts running rampant through my head. If I stealthily manoeuvred my way toward the outer door would he cotton on? The dancing walrus appeared to be lost in his own little world.

Could I make a run for it, make for the door? Just run and keep on running? Would he be in a fit state to give chase? The questions were bombarding my head all at once while daddy cool was still going for it in the background.

I have always been accused of being overoptimistic, but surely it wasn't going to be this easy. Of course not, I'm being naïve.

As I stood in the doorway of the TV room he tugged at my arm pulling me towards him, my drink almost flying through the air. That's one way to get rid of it, I thought.

"You haven't forgot why I put the music on have you, little English girl?"

No, but I was hoping you had, very nearly leapt out of my mouth.

Catching the smirk on that ugly face as he undressed me with those peculiar bulging eyes made me feel sick.

My stalling was about to come to an abrupt end as he surprisingly let go of my arm. He flopped down smack bang in the middle of the big orange sofa, incessantly staring right through me and jiggling his fat hips giving Boney M a run for their money.

Legs sprawled, not for a moment did he let go of the drink held firmly in his right hand, the other hand on his crotch. That image alone I'll forever struggle to expunge from my brain if I live to be a hundred.

Clarity hit me and out of the blue an idea flew my way. It was probably the most stupid plan on earth, but a plan nonetheless.

This would take guts, strength and energy. One out of three ain't bad. My feelings towards him gave me the guts.

Determined not bottle it, I knew it to be a gamble and a one off. I wouldn't be permitted a second chance.

If I don't pull this off I'm dead. No two ways about it.

Chapter Five

The Great Escape

Digging deep within myself to summon up the energy to do what he wanted me to do, namely dance like a performing monkey, took some effort. In the guise of doing a lap dance I attempted to slowly sway to the music. Sore and in pain I did the best I could.

Leisurely, seductively, I began to unbutton my blouse real slow, turning my back on him periodically as if to titillate and tease. Provocatively peeking over my shoulder, my intention was to subtly string it out.

There was always the possibility he'd get bored and nod off. One can hope, I thought, and prayed inwardly.

This couldn't be further from clumsy old me. I couldn't do provocative if my life depended on it. The thing is my life did depend on it and I was still crap. Oh, this is me giving it my best shot alright, although I needn't have fretted. He was in his element. Talk about lapping it up.

At the point I turned his way I caught a glimpse of him licking his lips, eyes transfixed on my full breasts clearly thinking he's onto a winner here. I'm guessing this would be a perfect end to a perfect evening for the pissed-up gatekeeper, getting shit faced and forcing himself onto a petrified unwilling girl.

I strongly suspected he couldn't get a girl if he were the last guy on earth.

Of course, this was not an issue in his world. He could take his pick. There was always going to be at least one kidnapped victim at his disposal under lock and key in a room below his feet. Of course, he had to rough her up a bit just for good measure. Show her who's boss, beat her into submission or ply her with cheap booze.

Glancing over at him I could see those beady eyes boring into me. Undressing me. It was clear all manner of perverted scenarios were playing out in that fat head, the excitement building up in his putrid face as he kept his hand on his crotch. I could have retched at the sight of him still hanging onto his glass as if it were precious, plainly not giving up his booze for anyone.

"How's about taking all your clothes off?" he muttered creepily, his eyes almost bulging out of their sockets.

"All good things come to those who wait," I breathed, as tantalising as my mouth would allow.

I was not quite pulling it off. Recalling a scene from *Silence of the Lambs*, my tone was akin to Hannibal Lector addressing Clarisse rather than that of a seductress.

My winging barely cutting it, the situation was plainly becoming dire. I had to make my move fast before I lost my bottle or he cottoned on. It had to be now or never or I would be at his mercy and that vision made me ill.

Without warning I pounced on him. Literally. I ended up in a straddle pose with legs either side of him.

His eyes lit up like he'd been plugged into the mains. "Oh yeah, who's in charge now, fat boy." He loved the fact I had taken the initiative. Boy, did he love it.

He thought Christmas had come early by the look of that cheesy grin splashed all over those disgusting features.

Oh, please be as stupid as you look, I prayed.

"Give me your drink", I demanded in a tone reminiscent to a teacher asking for whatever you've been caught red-handed with passing around the class behind her back.

He complied willingly. Now for it, the moment of truth.

Is the plonker buying all the crap coming out of my mouth? Little 'ole me minutes earlier, plucked from the prison below, conspicuously doing a U-turn, unashamedly making a play for him?

Keep on dreaming, buster, it ain't happening!

My brazen command exploded out before I knew it, before I bottled it, part of me not daring to say those few dynamite words let alone action the next bit. I hesitated for a second and grimaced inwardly. In my most seductive yet commanding tone I heard the words come out as if spoken by a stranger.

"Close your eyes."

This whole thing was unbelievable. Enchanted by the whole little routine he complied and was putty in my hands. The delusional monster was under a spell. My spell. Jeez, where do they find these morons?

In a split second before he cottoned on he'd been duped I'd reached over his left side, stretching my already raised arm over his left shoulder.

With all the power I possessed I grabbed the heavy bronze trophy. Undeterred by the weight of it I firmly gripped it with both hands as I dropped his drink on the couch and brought it down with as much force as my small body would permit.

Rather than the top of his head, it had made contact with the right side of his head slightly toward the front of the skull above the brute's ear.

Good, that'll do. At least I didn't miss.

I'd done it. Result. A gash appeared. A deep gash. I'd drawn blood. Adrenaline still pumping, my stomach was doing somersaults and a little voice inside me said, "Don't stop. One whack's not enough, keep going." Somehow another rush of adrenaline and hate devoured me, and with every ounce of strength I could pull up I clobbered him again. I was fully engulfed in rage and this man was getting the brunt of every creep who had laid hands on me since my abduction.

The second blow rained down with more intensity. Another inch and I'd have lobbed his ear off. Feral and out of control I was getting the hang of it, scarily enjoying the power and violence erupting from within me.

My yoga moves resurfaced. With trophy in one hand and as quick as a flash I jumped back almost frog like. I dropped my weapon, my backwards jump did me proud apart from almost falling on my backside. Like greased lightening I regained my balance, got to my feet and moved well out of his reach, knowing full well any second now it could be me bleeding all over the place adding to the dried blood splatter on the ceiling above and on the scruffy sofa.

Immediately he kind of slithered to the floor, rolled and ended up on all fours in front of the couch, the scruffy orange couch which now contained splatters of his blood.

Mission accomplished he appeared dazed and speechless. My plan had always been to head for the outside door. The humongous worry and concern was would it be locked? If this turns out to be the case I'm in one hell of a mess.

I didn't have a plan B, I barely had a plan A.

I turned for a brief second. He hadn't shifted from where he'd first landed and was in the same position on all fours with blood dripping from the wound. Wounded walrus noises were emanating from his mouth.

It was a good sign from my perspective, but would he jump to it on seeing me bolt for the door?

Catching sight of him on the floor looking all pathetic made me want to go back and clobber him again. Obviously, I'd subdued him, concussed maybe? More than that I couldn't say, I simply daren't risk it. I knew seconds counted and most likely made the difference between him coming at me and making me pay. This would more than likely be my one and only shot at escaping.

Knowing only too well my life depended on it, I ran like hell for the door.

I looked over my shoulder briefly half expecting him to be on his feet giving chase.

Catching a glimpse there was no movement. He was on his hands and knees muttering expletives, fingers bloodied as his fat chunky hand attempted to stem the blood from the gash. He was obviously not quite grasping what had hit him.

As I zoomed towards the door I grabbed a handful of clothing from the heap, desperate for something to cover my body, common sense telling me it will be even colder outside if I made it that far. Outside, where I will be on my own. If luck stays with me, on my own and free.

As the word "free" entered my head I lunged for the door handle, my gateway to freedom. Tremendous relief engulfed every tiny cell in my body. Utter shock and disbelief. The door was unlocked!

The cold air lodged in my airway as I ran for my life. I ran like never before leaving a trail of clothing as I speedily made my escape.

Moving forwards into the cold dark night, my only plan was to keep on running. Again, adrenaline gushed through every inch of my body.

I'm lost. I hadn't a clue where I was or where to go from here. The only certainty was that I am a free person once again, but for how long remained to be seen.

I could not believe I'd made it this far, albeit in terms of physicality at this point within spitting distance of that wretched place I'd created an opportunity and followed through.

The cold night air was piercing my lungs as I breathed hard and fast. My moment of high fiving passed quickly as I came to terms with the here and now. My anxiety threatened to overwhelm me and I felt sick with nerves.

Governed by instinct and the desire to be free I pressed on. "Don't look back," I said over and over in my head.

Little stones and pebbles were digging into my feet but nothing affected me. A small price to pay, a very small price. I hadn't the foggiest idea which way would take me to sanctuary, someplace where I could get help not just for me but for the rest of my friends, my new family.

Maybe there is a possibility of rescuing Susie before any real harm comes her way, but after being snatched off the street in broad daylight and witnessing that brute's antics it had already impacted and terrified her.

If this is to work I'd better focus and strive to stay one step ahead. It was important I take note of my surroundings and concentrate on my goal. My plan had miraculously worked so far, though I was fully aware I have a way to go before I'm free and clear. Keeping my wits about me I kept moving forward and knew that whatever happened I must not become overconfident.

My thoughts turned to my environment. Maybe there is a house nearby where I could summon help?

Having ventured a fair way down the dirt road I decided to check out the clothes I'd been clutching to my chest.

Tentatively I veered off the road to find somewhere suitable, stumbling across a sizable brush area surrounded by small trees. Fortunately for me a full moon occupied the clear sky. This afforded me enough light to rummage through the bits of clothing I'd managed to hold onto. Lady Luck was shining on me once more.

To my astonishment I'd done good. Well, at least good in having the gumption to grab the stuff and good in terms of I could get warm. I'd got a big jumper, a pair of dark-coloured leggings and a grey hoody. The hoody could have done with being black but beggars can't be choosers. It'll do the job.

I was all togged up and ready to do another round with the elements, my mind forever racing back and forth. Big questions loomed and I had big decisions to make. It's not enough I'm out of there, I knew I could be dragged back at any minute.

Should I run hell for leather down the dirt road until I see lights, civilisation or hide here where I am? It could possibly result in me succumbing to hyperthermia knowing my luck.

I was grateful for the warmth my new garb provided but I couldn't help think who they belonged to. I needed to eradicate these thoughts and replace the fear and negativity with the belief I will survive and, dare I hope, go home.

Staying alive without allowing those evil people to catch me should be all I'm thinking about, and my friends of course, my aim being to secure their release.

The crux of my new predicament is I continue to be in mortal danger, and the possibility I could be recaptured at any moment stays with me. Scuttling along, sore feet an all, my thoughts are pierced with scenarios of being punished.

Out of nowhere comes a flicker of a good thought. From now on my life could be my own. Just maybe I've made the first step in taking my life back.

On and off since I'd legged it, the hotel van crashed into my thoughts. Ordinarily we didn't return until the early hours, sometimes as the sun came up. My senses were telling me I need to be long gone from here should it or other vehicles appear.

The guys who held us were very unpredictable. We frequently caught the sound of vehicles at random times, therefore we knew they came back and forth all the time.

I couldn't stop my imagination running riot. I'm envisaging myself being caught in the headlights by one of them, and that would be curtains for me.

Contemplating the return of the girls in the van made me think of food. Normal routine dictates they would have brought back a little something to eat. I've lost out on that little treat, l thought to myself.

The hunger I felt earlier had long since dissipated, the nerves wandered from my head to my stomach erupting in nausea. I felt dizzy and light- headed. I suspect hunger will hit me later. For now nervous energy is the only thing enabling me to put one foot in front of the other.

I'm putting money on walrus features not being in a happy place. He would have been right there behind me, big hairy hand dragging me back. At least I haven't damaged his good looks, I smirked to myself.

He'll have to give Jake his version of why he has a great bleeding gash on his head. It will probably be more pertinent to them as to why there is one less prisoner in the grotty basement and how did I manage to leg it out of there half naked. Yeah, he'll have that one to explain. More likely he'll think I'll freeze to death overnight in the desert.

I could be wrong but I don't think he caught sight of me grabbing the clothes. The thought crossed my mind more than once. The freezing cold out here could bring about my demise.

Chapter Six

A Sudden Realisation

My eyes strained to take in the vista before me, turning left then right, the moonlight doing what it could in terms of throwing up a little light. Miles of desert terrain was surrounding me. I knew one thing for sure, I did not go through hell on earth to die in the desert like a wild animal.

Although eager to remove myself as far away from that house as possible, I knew I ought to make a mental note of where we'd been held. The names of roads, landmarks, street signs if and when I happen upon any.

I got back to thinking about Claire and young Susie and the other girls. Guilt consumed me as I knew it would. If only I could have released the two of them relentlessly hammered at me.

Claire, more times than I could count, had acted like a complete jerk being mouthy and downright nasty at times. A product of the circumstances she's been forced into. It wasn't lost on me she'd been abducted a couple months before me which was why I cut her some slack when she came out with all the negative crap.

Having briefly met Susie I had her down as a real nice kid, feisty, level-headed and sweet.

To think those bastards have got their hands on her conjures up rage and anger in me on a whole new level.

Of course, I knew I shouldn't be thinking about this. The task in hand is where my head should be at, namely getting clean away and making contact with the cops. And if I'm really lucky magic myself something to eat and drink into the bargain.

Back to dreaming again. Maybe, just maybe, there's a 7-eleven at the end of the road. Or a CVS? Then it came to me, I've no dosh. Tempted and hungry I'd have to snaffle a sandwich. At that the cops would show up and bang, mission accomplished!

Plodding on my thoughts continually harped back to life with the girls, the life I'd unfortunately been steered into.

Food, burgers and fries more often than not. The occasional pizza. We sat in the back of the van, hair wringing wet, wolfing down what came to be our one and only meal of the day.

Unbeknown to our drivers a few of the perverts brought us bits to eat. Perhaps they did know but chose to ignore it. It was nothing nourishing, candy bars and stuff like that, and if we were lucky milkshakes. If we were really, really lucky king-size milkshakes and cookies.

Shelving my thoughts of food I concentrated on my mission.

I got off the dirt road, tentatively making my way along the bushy terrain, the idea to dart behind a bush should the van or any other vehicle come into view. Every few feet stumpy little trees stood proud providing good cover. I knew I couldn't make as good progress having soft sand underfoot, although the upside was the sand was kinder to my poor feet.

Trudging down that gritty dirty track had done a real number on my feet which were becoming sorer by the minute.

The moon was doing a superb job in allowing me just enough light, however it was pretty dark and spooky. I couldn't see too far in front or worryingly what I may step on as I pushed any thought of snakes and other critters out of my mind.

Keeping myself in check was not going too well, my yelping and cursing not abating. I used language I didn't know I knew. It was tumbling out at every turn and when my foot came into contact with something horrible or sharp an "f" word or double "f" word came rushing out.

There was nobody here but the wildlife so I guess I can moan and swear to my heart's content. "Suck it up," I whispered to myself. I would rather be trudging through the wilderness feet cut to smithereens than being pawed by walrus features. The vision caused me to come out in a cold sweat and tremble. Besides, us Yorkshire people aren't quitters however tough the situation.

The whinging to myself was constant as I pressed on, my emotional energy on the prize which I hoped lay ahead. Freedom.

Maybe I was being a tad optimistic but I figured I was doing quite well. Sore feet or not, I was progressively moving forward. Turning to look back now and again, I had put a fair bit of distance between myself and my former prison.

There was no sign of the van or any other vehicle which I took as my second slice of good luck tonight, the first one being getting out from that hell hole in one piece without that bloated brute doing what we both know lurked in his vodka-soaked mind. Maybe even worse had been in store for me as my mind scrolled back to the screams which came before Fiona disappeared.

I must have been trekking along for well over an hour when suddenly in the distance I could see a road. Not the interstate, more a main road possibly leading to or running through a small town. I sighed heavily with the realisation help could be within my reach.

"So far so good," I muttered. Although Lady Luck had been kind to me thus far, I had to remind myself there's a long way to go before I am safe.

My tenacity had brought me here, what to do next remains a blur. Who am I to trust? Are there people in the vicinity, folks who know what's going on in the scruffy little house? Are they being paid to look the other way, ignoring the whole thing, scared to get involved? In cahoots?

Talk about being out of my comfort zone. Come to think of it, I don't know what my comfort zone is anymore.

If, or should I say when, I am out of this mess, will it be possible to slot back into normal everyday life? I suspect I no longer have a job. I don't suppose you can go missing for six weeks and turn up as if just returned from a backpacking holiday in Thailand.

How am I to explain this? Do I want to explain it to people? Could I take the shame?

"I'm getting ahead of myself again," I whispered to whichever bit of wildlife is taking note. Just one step at a time, I'm nowhere near the finishing line, I thought.

Another half an hour or so went by and my sore feet were barely doing what feet are designed for, tenacity pushed me forward and a brief tinge of excitement as I edged my way closer to the main road, streetlights lining the road in the distance.

My hope was this road would take me to a small town, and I could only hope in this town I've conjured up in my head there will be a sheriff's office.

I know there are small towns out in the desert as I had on occasion travelled through them on road trips with friends. The road ahead afforded me a slight glimmer of hope, although knowing full well I need to keep myself in check and not become too excited for fear it could backfire.

It's imperative I'm vigilant and I keep a lookout for the vehicles coming this way. Suddenly out of the corner of my eye I caught sight of a vehicle by the side of the road. A truck. A double cab or crew cab whatever they're called.

A surge of excitement and apprehension engulfed me in equal measures.

My mind racing, heart beating out of my chest, and my brain in overdrive, I was conjuring up a plethora of different scenarios. Good scenarios. Bad scenarios. Good people. Bad people. Mostly the latter. That's how I saw the world we inhabit now. Two different worlds, them and us. Good and evil.

My stomach tightened again and hurt, probably nervous tension. However, it could very well be pure hunger.

Questions bombarded my hungry brain. Could this person be my saviour? A good Samaritan. Would he or she take me to safety?

Total bewilderment engulfed my senses. After everything, to just happen upon a parked vehicle out here in the middle of nowhere. Suspicious or what? I said in my head.

Everything so far was strange. The truth of the matter was I didn't know what to call normal anymore, my mind was simply all over the place.

In the first instance I couldn't see anyone, not a soul.

Weird, an empty truck sitting there, headlights on. I surmised the owner must be in the bushes adjacent to the truck. Spot on with that one.

45

A guy appeared. From what I could make out he was mid to late thirties. He was zipping up his trousers. Caught short maybe?

I was eagerly watching his every move as he scrambled back into the truck, and for whatever reason he didn't start up the engine. A moment or two later I caught a glimpse of him making a call on a mobile. Or at least that's what it looked like from my vantage point.

I stayed crouched behind a large bush in an effort to stay hidden.

The streetlights were not fully operational, some of them out. To my way of thinking this should work in my favour.

I could see him but hopefully where I'm hiding I'm totally inconspicuous. I watched with bated breath him slugging something from a can. It was too far away to determine exactly what. Beer, soda maybe?

My gaze fixed, I didn't want to let him out of my sight. Curiosity and suspicion ran rampant through my brain. Could this Diet Coke man be part of their crew?

I was intentionally evading his line of sight, at least I hoped I was, anxious and fearful knowing in all probability this soda drinking guy could well turn out to be on Jake's payroll.

How would I know short of jumping out and asking which even I knew was a stupid idea. Hundreds of things were going round and round in my head, picturing the scene if he's part of Jake's circle.

I was also picturing and considering how I would feel if the opposite was true. That he's kosher and willing to take me where I want to be right at that moment. Specifically, the Las Vegas Police.

Do I take a leap of faith and ask for help? My body wound up tight with apprehension. I'd had the stuffing knocked out of me and I had little if any trust. Everyone in my mind is up to no good, a wrongdoer. I guess this is to be expected after what I'd endured.

To my mind he looked out of place as if he shouldn't be there, sitting quietly knocking back that drink. My stomach in knots, my mind darting back and forth, I didn't know which way to go. Could it be that he had engine trouble and was waiting for the rescue service or a friend?

I stealthy edged my way forward towards the back of his truck, crouched, almost at a crawl.

It pays to be a small, I thought as I manoeuvred forward, taking tiny, stooped steps unsure of what I ought to do next. Short of laying on the ground I positioned my body as low as I could, hopefully out of his sight.

I knew I had to do something, be decisive, be brave. Make a move one way or the other.

Cold, hungry, my feet killing me, my head all over the place, any minute now the hotel van will come hurtling in my direction. The idea came to me that maybe I could be sneaky and climb into the back of his truck without him noticing.

"I'm agile, I can do this," I whispered as I struggled in vain to pluck up the courage.

Surely to God there had to be a good chance I would end up in a safe place. At least I would be out of immediate danger.

Wrestling with the uncertainty of which way to go I knew in my heart I had to make a decision, and quickly. If I didn't make a move soon he'd be gone leaving me with no decision to make. It'd be out of my hands.

"Put your big girl pants on and do something, Vicky," I chastised myself.

Me out on the edge here, ripe to be picked up, locked up again, or worse.

As I'm eyeballing him I caught him bounce out of the truck.

At this point "Diet Coke guy" stood at the front of the vehicle, his arm raised as he's waving his phone in the air. I guess he must be losing the signal.

He was losing his marbles too by the sound of him, constantly yelling, "hello, hello," over and over again peppered with a barrage of effing and blinding, his tone brimming with frustration.

"At least you've got a phone, mate," I whispered to myself. To possess a phone to wave in the air would be like a dream come true. Not for the first time I was wondering what had actually happened to my phone. One word came to mind – Jake.

In my fragile state of mind I'd concluded what I'm about to embark on is a huge if not crazy course of action. But hadn't I taken a huge risk in doing what I'd done tonight? The question I had to ask myself was is this is a risk worth taking? However dicey and stupid I considered darting into the back of a vehicle of a complete stranger, I deduced it had to be a more viable option than waiting around here. I don't expect there will be a bus along any minute. Men yes, buses no!

My primary goal from the moment my feet touched that gravelly dirt road was to get the hell away from there. But being realistic I knew I was out of options.

Short of me tapping him on the shoulder, offering up a sob story and asking for a lift to the sheriff's office, sneakily hitching a lift to my mind was the safest route out of there.

That's it, decision made. Hopefully, I will end up in civilisation where I am able to sneak out the back the same way I intend to climb aboard.

I made for the back of the truck. "Here goes," I said to myself.

I surprised myself with my nimble moves, what with my backwards jumping jacks earlier I'm on a roll.

Without making a sound I proceeded to manoeuvre myself over the edge. Fortuitously sitting there was a tarp so I carefully tugged it over my small frame. With any luck this would help me stay hidden. I had done it. Dare I hope I am now on my way to being free and taking my life back?

Chapter Seven

Bat out of Hell

I couldn't help but allow myself a small moment. Here I am nestled in the back of a stranger's truck, me a real-life stowaway reminiscent of something you'd see on television or in a film. Really, you couldn't make this stuff up. I had hopefully moved on from being a real-life kidnap victim.

The downside of laying under this tarp, apart from the obvious, was where he is heading and the fact I couldn't see a damn thing.

My deep thought interrupted, the truck shook, followed by a loud noise. I presumed this to be the driver side door banging shut. I waited eagerly for him to start the truck. He obliged. We were off.

Again, I prayed. "Please let me be out of imminent danger."

Clearly way off the mark thinking engine trouble, I couldn't help but wonder what and why he had been hanging about in the middle of nowhere. What or who had the Diet Coke man as I had named him been waiting for? Worryingly, I hadn't the slightest notion where this thing was heading or where I'd finally end up.

His behaviour was peculiar to say the least. He was mooching around, maybe like most of the guys I'd had the misfortune to meet lately, a weirdo, an oddball. A nutter who considered this as down time, taking the weight off. All on his lonesome sipping a beverage at the side of the road in the Nevada desert swearing at his phone.

A secret rendezvous with a married lady perhaps? Maybe she saw sense and stood him up. As is usual with me, my imagination was hell bent on taking me to nefarious places.

My Diet Coke man took on a new persona, that of a racing car driver. Just when I thought I'd escaped death I found my slight thin body chucked around in the back. Naturally, not knowing our exact location I hadn't a clue of the speed limit, but clearly he didn't give a hoot. You'd have thought the cops were on his tail. Talk about gunning it.

Maybe my assumption was correct. He'd been stood up. His driving was that of a man on a mission alright. An irritated if not angry individual. Oh boy, of all the parked vehicles in the middle of nowhere to climb in the back of I had to pick this dude.

"What have I done now?" I asked myself whilst being tossed around like a crouton on a caesar salad. The pain on my sore limbs was exasperated by all the bouncing and jerkiness. I prayed and willed him to stop or at the very least curb it a little.

My thought process being what it is gleaned a hell of a lot from the way he drove his vehicle. At least it served the purpose of giving me something else to focus my mind on, briefly taking my mind off my predicament back at the dungeon.

A different take and a more logical explanation. The roads are not exactly bumper to bumper with motor vehicles at this hour, so I guess if fast driving's your thing you can go for it on these roads.

And for all I know this could very well be his usual everyday way of driving. How would I know? I thought to myself. I purported to see all men as wrongdoers, up to no good, on the make. Undoubtedly, my experience had clearly tainted me. I questioned if I would I ever get the old me back and allow myself to feel a modicum of trust for any man.

Having picked up no sounds from other vehicles as yet, I surmised we were still out in the boondocks.

I had a burning desire to lift the tarp and sneak a glimpse of where we were at. I thought it prudent to make a note of roads but this proved a non-starter. As ever, my intention to bring law enforcement back to that hovel was my goal. The guilt on leaving the others, especially young Susie, was insurmountable.

Forty minutes later give or take the road gradients changed bringing me to the conclusion we were now entering a ramp and joining a freeway. As I didn't know which one it didn't help matters, I'm still none the wiser. I could hear traffic either side so I figured spot on with that one, plus a much smoother road surface. His speed eased off a little as well. Much to my relief he'd quit driving like a bat out of hell allowing my battered body a moment of relief.

I'd nothing else to do but think, and as the traffic whizzed by I weighed up my new and latest quandary.

Lost in thought, all manner of scenarios were playing out in my head. Moreover, where Diet Coke man could possibly be heading.

Home perhaps seeing as he's been stood up? A bar to find a replacement for no show lady? A store for more Coke or beer? Wherever we're travelling to, it's not going to be worse than what I've just left behind, that's for sure.

"Luck's on my side, I'm on a roll, right?" I said under my breath.

Suddenly, I'm jolted. The truck had come to a stop, a sharp stop shaking me out of my thoughts.

This wasn't the plan or supposed to happen. Oh hell, this isn't good. I could be anywhere. More to the point, how far have we travelled and for how long? Not being in possession of a wristwatch granted me absolutely no sense of time.

The truck is moving slowly towards a building. My guess is that we were about to enter a garage or some other outdoor structure. The vehicle brought with it an echo. My ears then caught what I believed to be automatic doors coming down on a concrete surface.

I lay frozen, not even daring to scratch my itchy nose. Fear gripped me and my stomach tightened again. The next explosion to dominate the silence was a bunch of keys jangling together with the shaking of the truck as he abruptly jumped out.

I lay motionless, not brave enough to show my face or do anything for that matter.

I couldn't escape the notion he could possibly know I'm here. But did he though? The wisest thing to do for now was to be still, quiet and wait. I would make a move only when I'm sure the coast's clear.

Bleary-eyed, cold, hungry and emotionally drained, I waited nervously.

My mind and body had been battling with everything which has been chucked its way lately, it didn't leave much room for patience. Though I'm keen to be out and see where I'd finally ended up I lay as a fallen statue, fixed to the spot. I didn't so much as flutter an eyelash.

Seconds turned to minutes. Nothing. I'm going to be laying here for hours, I just know it, I thought. I was consciously trying not to shake though it was difficult to adhere to under these cold conditions.

Cold and afraid, my frazzled brain was going ten to the dozen. No way can he still be loitering round the truck. The quietness and silence was almost deafening. My ears were straining to hear something, anything. The sound of him walking, opening a door with the jangling keys? Nada.

He must have gone wherever he intended without me catching it. I'm tired and confused. Have I simply missed it? My ears like rest of my body I suspect are not firing on all cylinders. Allowing a few more minutes won't make much difference. I lay there under that tarp, eyes closed and hardly daring to breathe.

Suddenly without warning the tarp flew over my head. The suddenness of this action instinctively made me scream out loud. It was more of a wail than a scream, then the man took a step back clearly startled.

"Oh shit," were my first words.

Up close, a foot or so away, I could see him clearly for the very first time.

He was a tall muscular man in his late twenties maybe early thirties. His wavy hair was blond-gingerish in colour. His skin was quite pale, unlined and clear. Mr Diet Coke man dressed smart but casual. It gnawed at me for a second but I couldn't quite place who he reminded me of. An old boyfriend perhaps?

From out of nowhere, it hit me.

A clear vision flashed before me.

My memory had not deserted me. It suddenly dawned on me who he was.

Dexter Morgan from the TV series of the same name! Then came the punchline. In my recollection of this show Dexter killed people, lots of people. He was a serial killer.

52

Guessing his ears were assimilating to the shrill of my big mouth, he paused before addressing me. His voice was even and calm giving the allusion of a chilled individual. His precise and measured tone was scarily similar to that of the TV character.

My half-arsed logic was thinking what have I gotten myself into? Again!

Grinning smugly with what I took to be a conceited expression, his voice although not loud echoed in the huge garage.

"Well, well, who do we have here?" he asked rhetorically.

He was smirking, his eyes boring into me as he spoke, taking in every inch like he'd never seen a girl before.

He reached out with his right arm beckoning me to get out of the truck. I cowered in the corner. I must have looked like a scared rabbit caught in the headlights. I couldn't help but think there was something menacing about the way he spoke and the way in which he scrutinised me.

Had I jumped out of the frying pan and into the fire? I had to wonder. How could I not?

The Dexter lookalike appeared to have an air of confidence tinged with a hint of arrogance. In some weird way which I couldn't put my finger on he reminded me of Jake. How was I going to navigate my way out of this?

Perhaps I am reading him wrong. After all, my only crime to date was to hitch a ride in the back of his truck. No harm done. He can't be that put out, can he? I couldn't quite figure out if he had been aware all along he had a stowaway. "Come on," he beckoned.

"Why are you so scared? I don't bite. Are you hungry? You look like you could use a good meal, and what's with the clothes?" he queried, in almost a mocking laugh as he quizzed me.

Making use of the overhead lighting of what I'd established was a garage, I glanced down at myself. Embarrassment swept over me and I blushed.

"It's a long story," I offered, feeling like I should explain or say something.

"Well, I've got time if you have," he went on.

Again, he was reaching into the back with outstretched arms motioning me to come on out. I realised I had no choice but to comply. Assessing my options, which at that moment were non-existent, I climbed over the edge of the truck taking his arm to steady myself as I did so.

I stood unsteadily on the cold concrete floor of the garage. Without warning and in a formal sort of way he stretched out his hand and introduced himself.

"I'm Simon, pleased to meet you."

"I'm Victoria," I replied meekly.

I was naturally anxious being in this garage with this strange serial killer lookalike.

Not having an inkling of where we were wasn't helping matters. Not brave enough to ask, I swiftly gauged my surroundings. I looked for an exit door but to no avail. As weak and frail as I had become, my gut was telling me to run and run fast. If not run walk away and give him some crap about needing to be someplace else.

He advanced towards a small wooden staircase which led to what can only be described as a steel door. I assumed the other side of this door was his residence. Or an office maybe? It is an unusual way to enter a home. What is this place? I wanted to ask, but daren't.

I had to acknowledge the threat I felt minutes before was dissipating slightly, but I'm still on my guard.

Maybe my first impression is way off the mark.

Walking in front, allowing me to follow rather than be insistent and pushy, I followed as at that point there seemed no other way out.

It wasn't evident how the garage door opened, so I figured he must have one of those automatic fobs. I could hardly make a run for it. Besides, my body at this point was powering down as I was weak and faint, desperate for food and, more importantly, water.

Chapter Eight

True Intentions

Standing before me my serial killer impersonator proceeded to guide me along a small hallway leading to what my eyes told me was a kitchen. It was a very large, modern, open concept room situated just off a small anteroom a couple of yards from the solid internal garage door.

As if he could read my mind and thoughts he proceeded to pour me a large glass of water from a filtered water jug. I gulped it down way too fast, almost choking.

"Steady," he said pouring me a second glass. "Boy, you were thirsty, weren't you?" he remarked, followed by, "Hungry?"

It occurred to me I must have looked pathetic in my drab, scruffy clothes that clearly didn't fit properly. By now I was knocking the water back like there was a drought.

He started in the direction of a large refrigerator.

As he opened one of the stainless steel doors I could see food and lots of it. I was trying my upmost not to look eager, although I think it was a bit too late on that score. I simply couldn't take my eyes off the wonderful sight of food glorious food.

As he's reaching for various items out of the refrigerator I waited for questions, obvious probing questions. Questions any normal person would be curious to know the answers to.

His inquisitiveness must be ramped up or getting the better of him. I know I'd want to know why a strange-looking individual like myself was hiding under that tarp.

He hadn't even asked where I had come from, or when or where I had clambered into the back.

What's with the waif and stray routine? Why am I dressed like a homeless person and of course there's my entire demeanour?

His only conversation centred on what would I like to eat. Am I a vegetarian? Had I been I wouldn't have barked at a bacon butty, steak, sausage, you name it, I'd have devoured the lot.

Thankfully, at this point, he was not giving me the third degree. Showing curiosity would have been a natural reaction in my book, but I was in no mood to divulge anything to this guy who'd gone from the Diet Coke guy from the advert to a serial killer in one fell swoop.

Besides, I wouldn't have known where to begin. I felt sure at some point I'd have to spill the beans and tell the whole sorry story, informing the police being the first on my to do list.

My Dexter lookalike began to take sliced beef and ham out of an airtight container. He put it on the two plates he had set out followed by cheese cut into clumsy chunks.

Pasta bake in a rich tomato sauce was spooned into a bowl and into his microwave oven. The smell was like nothing I had smelt in my life. It was amazing.

Mr Dexter then awkwardly spooned the food onto our two plates. To my surprise he hadn't finished. He then opened the lid of another receptacle. I got a whiff of fresh salad. He set the container down on the countertop along with wooden salad servers.

This was insane. It had been so long since I had seen so much food, let alone been offered it. The whole thing was preposterously civilised.

"Tuck in," he prompted, passing me a knife and fork. Real silverware, not the plastic rubbish I had had to learn to get used to. The weirdness of someone offering me a metal knife was not lost on me.

To taste a simple meal of fresh food was unbelievable. All this was too good to be true. I kept thinking I'm going to wake up at any moment and find myself back in the dungeon and this will all have been a dream.

At this point we were both seated a few feet apart on leather backed bar stools. Simon was eating his food with just a fork, glancing at me every now and again. Me, well, I'm trying to eat with a bit of decorum. I suppose on reflection I was not succeeding.

I couldn't work out what he was all about, his motive, or indeed what he was thinking.

The whole situation felt surreal.

On first discovering me in his vehicle I'd have said he showed signs of being put out, perturbed. Annoyed even. Perhaps a little amused at the same time.

To then be so hospitable and invite me into his home with no questions asked and offer me this lovely food knowing absolutely nothing about me was more than a little peculiar by anyone's standards.

Lonely? Desperate for company? I pondered trying to make some sense of the situation.

A good way of meeting girls. Park up in the middle of nowhere and wait until one surreptitiously climbs into the back of your vehicle then off you go.

It could catch on. It's more honest than putting a fake profile online I ruminated.

In a soft tone he glanced at me and told me to leave what I couldn't eat.

I paused giving myself a few valuable seconds thinking time.

Being particularly careful before I opened my mouth, I didn't want to seem ungrateful, or ungracious.

My get out of the door speech began.

I stood up.

"Perhaps I had better be going," I said impassively, inching my way back to the door we'd walked through before the food fest. "The meal was lovely. You've been very kind and hospitable. Thank you for not creating trouble for me sneaking a lift without asking permission. I know it was out of order. You've been really good about things. Really, I can't thank you enough."

He listened. Now it was his turn to speak.

"Here's the thing, you don't need to leave. 'Yet' is what I meant to say. Clean yourself up a little. There's towels and shower products in the main bathroom."

Worry and anxiety aside, I couldn't deny the mere mention of a hot shower was more than a little tempting.

Undoubtedly the circumstances I find myself in are unsettling and troubling, not to mention bizarre. I couldn't grasp the reality of the situation. What is he all about? What does he want from me?

Oh yeah, I could take a guess.

The memories flooded back about the last time I took a guy at his word, though this Simon character does appear genuine, albeit a bit suss. Still, I'd been burnt and treated like garbage by the last guy I took at his word, the vision in my head of that charmer's smiling mush as he made the offer of a lift home.

That warm friendly smile.

I stood my ground but at the same time weighed up my options.

As is becoming a habit, I began seriously overthinking this, my mind in turmoil. Should I? Shouldn't I? I guess it's only natural a tiny part of me really wanted to trust my host.

Is this me being gullible? Again? Why is Simon being so nice? What did he want? I couldn't figure him out.

The silence is broken by his friendly voice.

"Look, you seem like a nice girl who has most likely found herself in a bit of trouble. Things happen, and there's no judgement here," he remarked, gesturing with his hands in the air. "You've clearly been through something horrible."

Pausing for a second he pointed a finger to what appeared to be dried blood on the side of the grey hooded sweat top, the inference that the blood must be mine. Bringing up my hair I could now see it was matted with dried blood. No surprise there, I thought, recalling how the brute yanked at my ponytail with his knuckles digging into my skull.

In a soft tone he persevered with the offer.

"The offer's there. Take it or leave it. Please, see for yourself, third door on the right. I'll stay here while you go suss it out. Take a look, there's a lock on the inside of the door. You can take me at my word, I won't hurt you I promise. I'm just offering help."

My resolve began to evaporate and my defences were slowly going down the plughole. For obvious reasons my cloudy mind was doing anything but thinking clearly or making informed decisions.

I conceded due to the premise I'd feel more human after washing the dried blood out of my hair, plus giving myself a good scrub wouldn't hurt. I would wash the dirt and grime from that wretched man and wretched place from every part of me.

The dried blood smatterings on the clothes were nothing to do with the injury I'd caused my jailer. My sore scraped legs were bloodied and underneath my clothes I felt bruises forming. Simon brought up my scalp which I knew had bled, none of which could result in what I see before me. I shuddered at the thought of whose blood this might be. A cold chill ran down my spine as I struggled to keep it together.

In my heart I'm dying to take him up on the offer but I daren't move. Simon began to walk down a long hallway beckoning me to follow and passing a couple of rooms which I assumed were bedrooms we came to a bathroom. Picking up on my nervous demeanour he gave the door a gentle shove to show no one was sneakily hiding. I peeked round the other side of the door and saw nothing untoward. He hadn't lied, the door did indeed lock from the inside.

He walked away leaving me standing in the doorway.

The bathroom, as with the rest of the condominium, encompassed a contemporary look and feel about it. Stylish but cosy at the same time. It felt luxurious, everything so white and clean. I was wallowing in the whole experience.

Now to the task in hand. I had to get myself cleaned up and give my long dirty hair a good wash, hopefully without hurting my tender sore scalp any more than it already hurts.

I disrobed slowly.

I stood in this beautiful glass fronted shower allowing the steaming hot water to spray and run all over my frail body. The sheer ordinariness of this small thing triggered confusion.

Anxiety and terror washed over me together with the water. My mind wouldn't stop racing. Here I am standing naked in a stranger's shower when out of the blue it hit me. I had a pivotal moment while thinking about the horrific and degrading things that had been done to me and what I had been forced to participate in. I had put up a front, boxed it all away.

Without warning it began pouring into my mind. I had lost the power I'd held on to week after week. I couldn't shake the images.

My whole body began to slide down the wet tiled wall and I curled up in a foetal position allowing the water to drench me as I sat curled up on the shower floor hugging myself tightly. I began to cry, silently at first then louder and louder. Before I knew it my sobbing became uncontrollable. I could hear the guttural sounds emanating from my mouth. I wanted to scream.

Utter despair engulfed me and took over my very soul and at that moment I was lost in absolute misery.

As with the water all calmness and self-control floated away. The reality of what I'd endured these last six weeks was suddenly bombarding my mind. Pictures, visions of events, faces I'd buried broke through the safe place in my head, my thoughts flooded with disgust and horror of the situation of how I'd been forced to live.

I was what I'd fought so hard not to become. I was broken.

Unable to curtail my hysterical crying, I'd momentarily forgotten where I was until I was brought back by Simon's knocking and concerned voice at the bathroom door.

"Are you alright? Can I get you anything?"

"No, I'm fine. I'll be out shortly."

I was doing my level best to sound composed but it was not working.

I was consciously aware I must have sounded pathetic knowing full well he probably wouldn't believe me.

I rinsed the shower cream and shampoo before carefully stepping out of the shower. The grazes on my legs and hips were stinging and bleeding a little, and in the hope they'd dry up I dabbed them with dressings and gauze I'd come across whilst rooting around in a cabinet. I smeared the steam from a large mirror with a towel. I couldn't help but be a little shocked at the sight of my face after my forced captivity.

My curvy physique had disappeared and I had lost so much weight I had taken on a gaunt appearance.

On the back of the door hung a white thick velour dressing gown complete with a hood reminiscent of those from a plush hotel. I put it on and cautiously ventured out into the hall tentatively making my way back to the open-plan lounge diner where I'd previously eaten the scrummy food. I was hyper aware that I was in a shaky if not dangerous position.

I caught a glimpse of him nonchalantly sitting in an easy chair, my fear becoming exacerbated. The uneasy feeling and stomach churning continued as I slowly entered the room.

Now what? I thought. What were his expectations? Did he expect something in return for his generosity? Am I in the company of another monster?

As I entered he got to his feet, looked me squarely in the face and proceeded straight for me. The tension surrounding us could be cut with a knife.

Instinct and fear prompted me to take backwards steps. Barefoot, I almost tripped on the long robe.

The neutral look on his face gave nothing away and sensing my nervousness he backed off, at the same time giving a subtle hand gesture towards the couch indicating for me to sit opposite him.

Hugging the bathrobe tightly I slowly made my way to the couch choosing to sit the furthest point from his chair. He settled back into the easy chair.

He got up and padded across the room, heading for what I assumed was a drinks cabinet on the far wall.

"I think maybe you could use a brandy," he offered.

After pouring what looked to be treble shots he carefully set my drink down on a small coffee table in front of me, plonking himself back in the chair opposite. Drink in hand he took small sips.

Feeling weak and a little dehydrated, I concluded drinking alcohol was the last thing I ought to be doing.

I sat cross-legged on the couch ensuring the huge gown covered every inch of my body. Only my head and hair were exposed. My long hair straggled messily over my shoulders and back and was in desperate need of attention. I began finger combing it and pulling it straight, thus having something to focus my mind and occupy myself.

"I'll bring you some water as well. We don't want you becoming dehydrated."

At that he got up again and headed for the kitchen area.

Lost in the moment, and thinking about Claire, Susie and my other friends, I froze.

I didn't even see it coming. I felt a sharp sting on the back of my neck then I slipped away. My mind went blank.

Chapter Nine

Back at the Ranch

Derrick's blurry eyes darted back and forth in a vain attempt to at least capture something. Somebody. He was not quite grasping where his stupidity had taken him, and he could not believe he'd been outsmarted by a girl.

His booze addled brain did its best to process the unfolding scene as he felt the wetness of blood on his throbbing head, catching sight of his chubby red fingers covered in fresh dripping blood. Sick and dizzy he attempted to manoeuvre his huge frame from the floor into an upright position. Steadying himself, he used the side of the sofa for leverage in a bid to bring himself to his feet.

"What's up with 'ma head? What the fuck have I 'bin hit with?"

The pulsating, painful injury coupled with the sight of the blood had him in tears. A wave of self-pity washed over him as he caught sight of the bright red blood trickling to the floor forming little red pools.

"This isn't right," he ranted. "Where's that fucking bitch? I'll fucking kill her when I get hold of her," he yelled.

Like a bolt out of the blue it hit him that Vicky could, would, most probably be long gone.

"This ain't good, I'd better give them the heads up." On that note, and not having Jake or anyone else's number, he rang the number provided in case of an emergency. Having rung it before he knew it to be a downtown motel. He didn't think for one minute Jake resided there, from what he'd garnered it was a sort of message service.

The overcautious Jake gave no one his number, certainly not him.

He gazed around struggling to assess the mess he found himself in.

Music blasting from the CD player compounded his sore head. Staggering over to the unit holding the player, he harshly pushed the stop button almost launching the player into the air.

"Fucking Boney fucking M," he muttered out loud as he brought the music to an abrupt end.

The open door enabled the cold air to sweep through the small, dishevelled dwelling, and the air fanning him was bringing him round.

Panicked, he glanced over at the cellar door and a brief sense of relief flooded his mind. "Thank fuck for that," he said under his breath. The door appeared exactly as he'd left it, firmly bolted shut.

Placing his hand in his pocket, he was overwhelmed with relief at finding his keys were where he had put them before all this. This being another little debacle to add to the list he'd begun to compile whilst working for Jake.

For a nanosecond he flirted with the idea that Vicky may have precipitated an escape of the other two and dropped the key back in his pocket, which of course would be a dumb thing to do.

It wasn't logical and made absolutely no sense, but the way things were going nothing would surprise him.

At least they've stayed put he snorted.

For now at least he held on to his feelings of superiority. King of the castle. Master of his own little universe, conceding he's still in charge and had total control over the captives, albeit they were now down to two. At least until the others were dropped back at the ranch he mused, the enormity of his blunder as yet not quite sinking in.

Why did he have to choose that Vicky to have his bit of fun with?

Reflecting back to having her straddle him, boobs almost hitting his face, he closed his eyes briefly reliving the fantasy.

It was looking good for a minute, he thought, conjuring up the lap dance for the second time in as many minutes. This wasn't the first time he had let a girl come upstairs for a bit of fun only for it to end badly. Talk about fucked up, he thought. Why me? Why does it always happen to me? He recalled Jake's reaction at not being happy at having to "clean up my fucking

64

mess" as he so eloquently put it last time things went pear-shaped.

He couldn't help replaying over and over in his head the fun he'd had with that one. More than once. Of course, he lied to the boss man inferring it to be a one off.

That Fiona girl was a real feisty one. Pity about her. His warped mind was going into overdrive imagining all manner of perverted scenarios. Oh yeah, lost out on some good times there, he sniggered. To him the fact he'd killed her was of minor importance compared with him not being able to get his rocks off.

The talking out loud to himself resumed.

"Wouldn't be a good little girl and take it. Oh no, the psycho bitch just had to get nasty. Kicking me ferociously where it hurts, she did, the slut. Twice. Real bloody hard too."

The imagining of the sex stuff was now replaced by something completely different. Anger. Violence. Followed by carnage.

"Why couldn't she just take it and play nice like she'd done before? And the time before that. The other girls did. They knew better. They know who the boss is they do."

Obviously, these incidents only occurred on nights like this, nights when he'd been left on his own with only the TV and booze for company.

The most recent, Fiona, sprung back into his filthy mind again. And again. He just couldn't let it go. It was like he harboured a grudge against her for not letting him rape her, for dying after he beat her senseless. He simply couldn't drop it. "How the fuck did she think I'd react?"

Screw you, Jake, he thought defiantly. The cheek of him saying I'm not one of the paying Johns. So what if I get a freebee once in a while? Perks of the job. Who am I hurting?

He'd had them dropped here barely able to stand or walk. Some of the others were barely conscious, including that Vicky one, so he can get off his high horse before he even starts. Justifying his behaviour in his own head, his ranting ramped up a notch. He rationalised if Jake could do what he wanted then why the hell couldn't he.

Reflecting how Jake reacted last time, Derrick guessed he'd better get his thinking cap on and come up with a plausible lie to explain Vicky's departure, knowing full well the guys were most likely on the way back from tonight's drop off.

What made it worse this time, however, was that for some unknown reason he knew Vicky to be one of Jake's "special girls". Evidently, he had her down as a real money maker, remembering she was only ever sent out to the high rollers. He'd heard Jake mention once she had that cute girl next door thing going on. Probably a British thing. He liked her and Jake didn't like a lot of people.

Feeling grieved, the muttering and swearing in no way eased up. "Don't suppose he'll class tonight's little escapade as looking after her."

Another of Derrick's gripes in relation to Jake was that he could get any girl he wanted. Better looking than that Vicky one I'll bet, he thought. And younger. Snap his fingers, smile with that gob of gleaming white teeth, he don't even buy them a drink half the time.

It'd cropped up in conversation with the other guys, well, more like he'd caught snippets when they'd been gabbing. Jake had a girlfriend. More than one by the sounds of it. Real stunners is what he goes for, and by all accounts they fall at his feet. Real pretty and young. Oh yeah, right snazzy dressers by the sound of it. Classy too, can talk proper and everything. Most of them are up for anything from what he'd caught listening in on conversations, although how they'd know beats me, he thought. Jake didn't strike him as the bragging type. After all, he'd no need to.

Having trouble shaking the image of pretty girls doing all manner of things to Jake, the injured pervert said out loud, "What's all this about then?"

In Derrick's criminally wired up brain it made perfect sense to kidnap, torture and hold girls against their will. Just don't get caught, he thought, as the memory of his most recent stay in the penitentiary zoomed into his head.

Insanely jealous, his hideous rambling about Jake and the girls who he saw as his for the taking carried on for the next few minutes.

He was sick of being ordered about and sick of their stupid rules.

In his head he could hear it now, Jake's tone, sprouting the same old tune as if Derrick were thick.

He knew his job didn't entail a whole lot. Basically, keep them under lock and key so as not to let them escape and trot off to the cops. You don't say! he thought sarcastically.

That Vicky coming on to him like that, she might well have cost him his job. He'd had it drilled into him countless times what he was supposed to do and not supposed to do. Top of that very long list was to leave them down there and no touching.

His dilemma at this precise moment was how to explain this one away. He hadn't the foggiest. His head hurt even more, straining his brain in an attempt to concoct a credible story.

As far as he's concerned he does what he's paid to do which is to dish out the painkillers and first aid dressings when needed. Oftentimes it gave him the excuse to have one of them up here. Blindfolded at that. Though he couldn't do much if one of the other big gobbed drivers were around. Or Jake which on occasion he was.

Suddenly his ears caught something. Rambling about the boss man would have to be shelved albeit temporarily.

The sound of a vehicle gave him pause.

Bummer, the van's back already.

He was taking in the sound of the van edging nearer and nearer, the crunching of the gravelly dirt on the tyres as it made its way back up the dirt road. The rickety sound of the vehicle brought with it anxiety and apprehension.

Then again, it might well be the cops for all he knew, eliminating the need for a story.

Five, ten minutes, maybe a little less before he had to give his account of why they were now one girl down.

"Oh, shit," he couldn't help but blurt. He'd had no time to concoct anything, at least anything plausible which would make a modicum of sense and not make him look stupid.

Of course, his main fear was the boss man, Jake. He'd heard things about him. Scary things. Without a doubt he'd go ballistic.

I should have left well alone. That Vicky is too cunning by half and smart. More trouble than she's worth. He'd have been better off choosing the young 'un. If he ever clapped eyes on that bitch again he would make her pay big time.

"I'll have 'ma chance if we catch her," sniggering like only he could at such a thought, his face contorted like a rubber mask, the kind wore by bank robbers.

His mind rampant with twisted logic, he reasoned that it was obviously her fault he'd wound up in this mess.

Jake's deriding tone was ringing in his head over and over like a broken record.

"Rule one, basement and main door always to be kept locked," emphasising the word "always".

Chirping up with "are you listening here? I mean no exceptions." He also stated the girls were to be blindfolded and their wrists tied. According to the slave master these ritual assists were important to mentally break them down and making an escape a thing they can only dream about.

"Oh well, guess I've failed on something else in this lousy life," he shrugged, grunting to himself.

Taken aback as if it was a complete surprise, he caught the sound of the van coming to a stop outside the main door. In walked Pete, one of the drivers, tutting and shaking his head disparagingly as he took in the sight of the empty booze bottles and beer cans scattered around, clocking Derrick half standing, half leaning looking agitated and pitiful. Rolling his eyes sarcastically, he immediately picked up something had gone badly amiss, again.

Derrick's appearance was even more unkempt than usual if that was at all possible. Adding to his overall unruly scraggy look, a wound was clearly visible on the side of his head. Fresh blood was dripping over the seemingly dried blood on his forehead and the side of his face.

"I won't even ask. Here we go again, couldn't keep it in your pants, could you?" came the rhetorical observation. Instantly recognising what he took as a repeat of the catastrophe of a few weeks ago, he said "You got a death wish or what?" He went on looking around the room.

Derrick swallowed hard and glared at him. He was wise enough to know that getting into it with Pete was a complete waste of time.

Damage control was the best he could hope for at this juncture. A little bit of sympathy wouldn't go amiss either, he thought. For some weird reason he was surprised none was offered. After all, he's the wounded party here.

"I need to go to the emergency room. I was out cold. Think I've a concussion, my head hurts, I probably need a couple of stitches. It hasn't stop bleeding."

For a split second it occurred to him the sympathy card could just work. Then maybe not. He was grasping at straws here, and as he knew from previous exchanges Pete was not exactly a fan of his.

"You'll need more than the hospital when Jake gets a hold of this. Why the hell does he keep you around? You're nothing but a pissed up screw up," the driver shot back completely exasperated. "Now spill."

"It was that Vicky one. Said she'd real bad stomach pains. Woman's problems, that kind of thing. I brought her up here to check her out, and when I turned round to look for the painkillers, bang, she walloped me on me head." Derrick prodded the wound as if it wasn't evident.

Pete studied him intently, a look that Derrick interpreted as he could very well be buying into the fairy tale.

Eyeballing the massive brute standing before him, he began with the questions.

"How tall are you, fatso? And Vicky, five four give or take, maybe 100 pounds wet through?" Not expecting a response, he carried on with the insults. "I can see why you'd avoid looking in the mirror, but in case you haven't noticed that gash is at the side of your head. I take from this it's a repeat of the other week's fiasco. What have you done to this one, where's the body?"

Not computing the point with regard to the injury, Derrick wanted to make it clear he was the injured party.

"She's fine I guess, not a mark on her, it's me needs the help. She's gone. Bitch must have done a runner while I was out cold."

"How long?" Pete shouted.

"An hour, maybe longer. I dunno, I've only just come round," replied Derrick sheepishly.

Pete took two phones out of his pocket, his own phone, and the other one, Derrick guessed, a burner.

He began speaking on the burner turning his back on Derrick as he did so.

"Jake, it's me. We've got a problem. A big fucking problem."

He couldn't hear Jake's side of the conversation but got the bones of it hearing Pete's responses.

"Yeah, you guessed it, he's fucked up again. No, this one's not dead. Injured maybe. You're not going to like it though, it's the Brit, Vicky. He's let her escape. Yep, I hear you. Oh yeah, tantamount to putting the fox in charge of the hen house all right," glaring at Derrick in disgust as he imparted the last comment.

Derrick was wondering what the hell foxes and hens had to do with anything.

Pete listened for a minute or so, ended the call and dropped the phone back in his jacket pocket.

"Jake's got some calls to make then he's on his way. Says he won't be long as he's only the other side of Dolan Springs," said Pete, who was shaking his head in disgust as he spoke.

70

Chapter Ten

The Wrath of the Slave Master

Without a single word of explanation to the injured man Pete promptly walked outside to the parked van where the other girls sat.

Determined to have his say, Derrick shouted after him, "So, this is how it's going to be, is it? After all I've done for Jake and those girls. Toss me aside like a piece of garbage. My head's still bleeding and I need medical help. Are you listening?" Incensed at being ignored he continued hollering.

Pete walked back in with one of the other guys who'd hung around outside near the van. He had most likely stayed put to guard the girls and shoot off with them if need be, both sensing a potential threat upon catching the door wide open.

Derrick recognised it to be Dave who he'd previously had banter with.

Dave and Pete had a similar look. They could almost be twins if not for the slight age difference, thought Derrick, but refrained from voicing this observation for fear of offending them.

Maybe it was the way they dressed, always in plaid shirts, jeans and boots which Derrick thought of as cowboy boots. Pete was probably the older by a couple years. Mid-forties he thought.

I bet both of them have a bird, he thought begrudgingly.

"How 'yeh doing, Dave?" came the upbeat greeting, hoping to play down the magnitude of the fuck up, thinking a little chit-chat would relieve the tension between the men.

"A lot better than you by the look of things," replied Pete's plaid shirt chum.

Clearly irritated by the whole situation, Pete promptly started with Jake's orders.

"*Certain measures required. Things to be done to ensure no evidence could be linked back to any of us should the police or FBI come calling.*"

"Open the basement then give me your keys," Pete directed at the bleeding man sharply. "Get down that basement and bring both girls up here sharpish. Jake needs them in the van with the others before he shows up. It's important the youngster doesn't see him."

Derrick chirped up enthusiastically, "What about the blindfolds and zip ties?"

"Drop the act, fatso. If you'd used your one brain cell and done just that then we wouldn't be here having to clear up your frigging mess again. Or better still left that Vicky chick down there like you were supposed to. Besides, it don't matter what they see now, thanks to you. They're not gonna be around much longer," he spat venomously at Derrick.

The last remark brought a cold shiver and made him want to puke. If what was being said was what he thought, he didn't fancy his chances of making it to his next birthday.

Girls equalled money and if they could be gotten rid of to save their skins it didn't bode well for him.

Clearly pissed at the situation, Pete continued to fill Derrick's head with more worrying scenarios.

"Do you for think for one minute Vicky won't go to the authorities? Apart from what you probably did to her, she has enough ammunition to send all of us down for life. Not forgetting the dead girl Fiona. Remember her, you halfwit?"

"I didn't do nothing to that Vicky one, she's the one who whacked me leaving me for dead," came the feeble response.

"Well, she didn't hit you hard enough if you ask me," Pete snapped.

Just then the sharply dressed Jake appeared at the door. All the rushing around and commotion prevented them from hearing the BMW pull up.

Wasting no time Jake did what he did best. He mouthed orders and reiterated the instructions he had given his underling on the phone.

"Pete, Dave, crack on with getting rid of evidence, we need to be out of here pronto."

Pointing a finger at the worried-looking Derrick, he spat, "And you, Casanova, in here, I want details."

Derrick slowly followed Jake into the lounge part of the house.

"Let's have it, bulldog features, what did you do this time? The shortened version if you don't mind. I don't want to be in this dump any longer than is necessary. Oh, and before you come up with the usual bullshit, just so you know the two girls who didn't go walkabout are my witnesses. You can bet I'll take their version over yours if it doesn't tally."

Knowing it to be futile but nevertheless concluding it had to be worth a shot, he sheepishly began trying to blag his way out of the shit storm he'd again gotten wrapped up in offering the same rendition he'd given Pete.

"Stop, enough already. Is that the best you can come up with?" said Jake.

Glued to the spot, Derrick stood there like a naughty child waiting for permission to move. For the moment Jake chose to ignore him.

Turning to Pete he probed, "All the stuff in the van? And the two girls?"

"Yeah, all loaded. The new girl Susie's in a bit of a state though."

Jake looked incensed. "That bastard hasn't touched her, has he?" glaring sideways at Derrick.

Feeling cornered Derrick opened his mouth. He managed a few words before Jake gave him the look. "I never touched the mouthy bitch, if she says otherwise she's a lying fucker, and another thing–"

Ignoring the outburst Pete spoke. "No, it don't look like it. I gave her and the other one water and sandwiches we'd brought back. They were complaining of hunger and being thirsty."

"Nobody lays one hand on her. Do you hear me? She's to be kept clean and fed properly. I have bigger plans on the horizon for pretty little Susie. Big, big money plans."

Noticing Jake's gaze firmly on the quivering Derrick, Pete rolled his eyes. Child kidnapping was not exactly what he'd signed up for. Things have changed, this a whole different kind of ball game in his book.

"Chuck me those zip ties will you, Pete?" the boss brusquely requested.

Willingly he obliged.

Consumed with fear, the wounded man was shrinking by the second. He didn't know what was heading his way but he knew it wouldn't be good. The stories he'd heard about Jake while doing time in Folsom on a bogus rape charge were nothing short of blood curdling. Really bad stuff.

It was well known in their circles that Jake possessed not an iota of remorse nor had a conscience.

Without warning Jake harshly grabbed Derrick by the wrists, zip tying them together tightly at the front of his body, cutting them for good measure.

Given a taste of what the girls have to endure was not nice, though he daren't open his mouth in protest. Pathetic and scared, his fear went into overdrive.

In a brief moment of reflection, picturing the girls blindfolded, he caught a glimpse into their world.

His stomach knotted and bile began to rise up his oesophagus. At this point it took everything he had not to vomit.

His one and only recourse was to plead for his life.

Derrick cleared his throat essentially swallowing what had started to rise inside him.

Praying it would work, he began with the pathetic excuses and platitudes. Desperation engulfed him, a dead man talking was the only way to describe the scene.

Absorbing the tension and anger from the man who stood a couple of feet away, the pleading ramped up. Standing stoically before him, Jake seemed to be listening.

Derrick's only concern earlier was getting the boot. Recognising this was the least of his problems, he thought about how he was going to get out of there in one piece.

Clearly deriving pleasure from the man's fear Jake began to grin mockingly. Without a word he reached inside his jacket and pulled out a small gun.

Glowering, unwavering, eye to eye with the frightened man, Jake fired at point blank range hitting him in the upper arm.

The babbling from Derrick's lips was replaced by a shrill-like scream followed by, "You shot me! You shot me!" as in a broken record over and over again.

Wincing in pain, he dropped to the floor like a brick. The restriction from his tied hands meant he had become completely helpless; he couldn't even put pressure on the wound. In tremendous pain he remained on the floor rolling round and whining like a baby.

"What did you call Susie? And Vicky? What did you have in store for her? Like I need to ask. I hope she hurt you good and proper. She should have finished the job. Who's the bitch now, 'eh? Kiss my feet you no-mark."

The injured man knew better than to respond or move.

Jake directed the gun at him again waiting for the snivelling man to make eye contact before pulling the trigger, intentionally hitting him squarely on the other shoulder.

"No more Mr smart mouth now 'eh, Dumbo? All you had to do was sit here and read a book or watch your soap operas for a few hours. But oh no…" The rhetorical insults just kept coming. Glancing at Pete he added, "He can read, can he?"

Jake considered this his right, one of his guilty pleasures. Hurting people. It was usually young, vulnerable, attractive women, but he didn't discriminate. Derrick would do for now.

Of course, he had no intention of killing him. As usual this was a job for one of his lackies, a way of keeping them in line. One step ahead, as cunning as ever, he liked to have as much dirt as possible on the guys who worked for him.

Returning his gun back to the holster in the inside of his jacket, Jake turned to Pete. "Everything ready? We need to get the hell out."

"Yeah, we used gloves, there's no fingerprints from us. Guess there'll be prints on beer cans and other bits of crap from lover boy here," he offered, looking at the man writhing in pain rolling round on the floor.

"Everything? The shovel used for the little outside jobs?" enquired Jake.

75

"All taken care of," said the ever loyal but equally irritated employee.

"Dave's ready for the off with the girls. I've given him the new location, I guess the sooner we get the girls relocated the better. This place is probably compromised thanks to that idiot," added Pete.

The revving of the van starting up, followed by the crunching noise of the dirt track becoming ever distant with every passing minute, the girls disappearing into the night, the great unknown in front of them.

Jake shifted to look at Pete face on. In an almost sardonic whisper he venomously announced, "You know what, Pete, she's not as clever as she thinks she is our little British wanderer. She'll be begging to come back here when I've done with her."

Pete didn't want to know what he meant by that, he could only imagine. As long as he wasn't involved that was fine by him. Besides, he'd had enough for one night cleaning up this mess. Knowing Jake for as long as he had, he'd the distinct feeling he had some real finishing up to do.

It was odds on since Dave's now on the road it would be left to him to get rid of the gormless Derrick.

No loose ends Jake had said on the phone. Of course, elaboration not required. They'd all been down this road before and knew what was expected of them, it's what they were paid the big bucks for.

Ferrying the girls round and looking out for them was obviously risky, though that side of the job Pete didn't find so bothersome.

Money for old rope he deliberated. That idiot had to keep messing up, just couldn't keep his hands off the girls.

One mistake after another, well this is one too many, he pondered, reeling from the image of seeing the state of poor Fiona a couple of weeks back. Her face looked like she'd been in a prize fight, and the rest of the body was not much better. Pete shuddered, mentally picturing the image of the dead girl.

Most likely Vicky would have ended up the same way if she hadn't lamped him one. For obvious reasons he wasn't glad she'd got away, but he sure as hell felt glad he wasn't burying her at the back of the house with the rest of them.

Derrick had it coming, Pete reasoned.

For once he'd have welcomed not being the one left to "take care of the big fat loose end" as Jake so eloquently put it.

Glancing at Derrick who was bleeding on the floor from the bullet wound, Jake turned to Pete. "You got your weapon?"

"Always."

"Well, I'll be off then. Dave will be back for you when he's done what needs to be done. I'll see you back on the strip for a drink if you fancy. Call me when you're near, I'll let you know where we are," said the boss calmly, treating this as an everyday run of the mill occurrence.

Earlier Pete had caught site of Derrick's beat-up truck round the back. He decided to use that and call Dave on the burner as soon as Jake had done a bunk.

Common sense dictated this the best way forward. His plan was to leave the keys in the ignition, wipe his prints and dump it in one of the rougher parts of town.

"Oh, and get rid of that little lot. Burn the lot of it."

Jake turned and pointed to the heap of women's clothes and other items that were clearly on display for all to see.

Pete knew as much as the next guy about DNA.

Something else on Derrick's list which he had omitted to do, thought Pete, glaring at the cowering man and shaking his head. "Bloody useless," he uttered.

Having given the final order, Jake walked purposefully out of the door.

The two of them alone, Pete glanced over at the petrified man on the floor.

Derrick knew at this stage of the game the curtain had fallen. His life was about to end.

Chapter Eleven

The Full Package (Jessica)

"Thank goodness they weren't fussed when I left them all too it. They barely noticed I'd snuck off to my room. Some of us need our beauty sleep and have an image to uphold," Jessica muttered to herself.

The hours before she'd finally hit the sack she'd had enough and heard enough. Her parents were still up and pacing when she'd tiptoed up the winding staircase. They were pacing and sniping at each other from what she could hear. Playing the blame game.

This is how it's bound to play out, Jess concluded feeling narked. The golden child had disappeared, done a bunk. A few hours and all hell breaks loose. I've been out clubbing in Vegas longer than Susie's been gone, I didn't see the shit hitting it for that one.

Failing to pick up when called, that'd got them rattled. That stupid sparkly phone welded to her ear 24/7. Sure, she'd been at school, never played hooky my sis.

Apparently, she got lost on the way home after saying "bye" to her daft giggling little chums. That's the version they're sticking with.

"Boo hoo," Jess whispered to herself scathingly. She never got that reaction or fuss when she hadn't come home from school. Well, not after about the hundredth time anyway.

Puff! In a cloud of smoke the prodigal daughter had vanished. Clever, studious, straight "A" Susie, her future all mapped out, medical school, the whole caboodle, just like Daddy. Who'd have thought it, Daddy's little girl being rebellious.

Jess had her own clear set of values, aspirations and goals. Not that they were privy to her thoughts. She told her parents very little about anything. Nothing in her future was going to involve hard work or much in the way of effort. Unless you counted the work she put in at the gym or time spent getting her hair and nails done.

Over the years she'd become pretty apt at playing the game, their game, being clever enough to know just how much work was required to fly under the radar, thus keeping the light shining on their bright little star.

No one could deny Jess certainly had other attributes, the most popular, not to mention coolest girl in school for one. She never tired of being told she could follow her mum into the modelling world with her looks.

As far as she was concerned school was a place to pass the time, socialise with the cool girls and flirt with the boys. Flirting and teasing was fine in her world, playing games with people is what she did, excelled and revelled at.

Jess wanted a man, a real man, someone with a flash car, money and who'd meet her standards in the looks department. Standards which no boy in her school could possibly match.

She counts the hours, then minutes for the end of the school day. Excitedly waiting. Not every day of course, due to what Jess took to be work constraints, though as often as humanly possible. There her beau would be waiting. Waiting for her.

Jack, her delectable older boyfriend, a real man.

The man who finds her irresistible and never tires of telling her so. His primary goal, according to the young girl, is to shower her with attention and adorn her with gifts, attention a girl such as Jess so rightly deserves.

What business he's in eludes her. She hadn't the foggiest despite attempting to worm it out of him on more than one occasion, eventually kicking to the kerb the notion she'd ever be party to what brings in the dosh.

"Whatever he's up to during the day sure does pay well," adding, "Oh, and occasionally he dashes off at night after he takes a call," she offloads to her bestie.

"Oh yes," she told Crystal, "one thing's for sure, he's definitely the full package. He can fully meet my needs but do I cut him a bit of slack when there's an emergency or there's something his minions can't manage."

This, what they have, is enough for her. For now at least.

Jack, who drives along the Vegas strip in his flashy white BMW, his young girlfriend seated proudly by his side looking every bit the twenty year old glamourous young women, a supermodel, or a seventeen year old schoolgirl pretending to be a twenty year old supermodel.

He sure is smitten, she oozes to her friends, as he periodically fires off little messages during school hours, intimating he'll come to pick her up when school finishes and where he will be parked, and where they will go and what they will do when they get there.

What he will do to her that is and what he would like her to do in return, offering little snippets just to keep them guessing.

He inauspiciously parks the beamer a little way outside the school gates, waiting for his "little sweet thing", sitting patiently looking every bit the rock star.

Unbeknown to Jessica he would eye up young girls as they sauntered past the car. Girls of all ages.

Then it's back to his place.

Jack's condo is situated just off the main drag, the first port of call for the glamourous pair. As is their usual routine, they hit his place, shower, change and glam up as Jess puts it.

As it should be, an extensive wardrobe is at the ready at her boyfriend's gaff. A walk-in wardrobe no less, bigger than the one at home she boasts to her friend Crystal, not failing to leave out the Victoria's Secret lingerie he regularly purchases leaving the cute little pink bags on the bed for her to open and of course model for him.

"Oh, I love that shop," chirps her envious friend.

"Oh yeah," Jess crows, "Jack loves me to wear the sexiest underwear under my outfits. That's 'cos he enjoys stripping them off me," she offers in a naughty tone. "Got it off to a fine art he has, using his teeth so sexily, the teasing, breathing hot breath and putting his tongue to good use in all the right places..." She trails off in her soft giggly little voice, not saying what places, just putting it out there. "Anyway, that's just one of his little games," her tone quickly reverting back to the everyday Jess tone. "Jack has lovely teeth," the naïve girl offers wistfully, overflowing with praise for the love god she's managed to bag. "Then again he has lovely everything," she says, giving her friend a knowing nudge in the ribs as she raises her eyebrows with a knowing smile.

"You know, well, I imagine you don't, he's got this other game he likes to play requiring a tie or silk scarf. He can't resist a little teasing. We can be on the bed or someplace else, he'll blindfold me, then quite forcefully flip me over. It's as though he thinks I don't know what's coming," she laughs naughtily. This is a common theme amongst Jess and her girlfriends, she regularly drip-feeds them little antidotes about her nights out knowing full well most of her friends hadn't got past second base. And forget hot nightspots, they hadn't seen the inside of any club on the strip. More to the point were not allowed. None of them, including Jess, were old enough to gain entry to the clubs or drink.

As usual on a roll about their escapades, Jess had plenty more she wished to divulge.

"There was this one time we're on a date on the strip at one of our regular haunts. We were sitting real close in the VIP area, nothing out of the ordinary, enjoying the music, having a drink, chatting away. Well, I'm doing most of the talking having got his full attention for once. Yeah, the champers was flowing freely." Feeling the need to embellish further, "Jack only likes the good stuff." She then says, "He's kissing me, tenderly at first, delicately, growing real passionate, again nothing new. Jack's not one to be afraid of public displays of affection. Then, out of the blue, he put his lips to my ear. Nibbling and breathing faintly he whispered three little words."

"What three little words?" asked Crystal excitedly.

Jess whispered, "Take 'em off."

Crystal gawked at her, bewilderment etched across her face.

Simply dying to tell, Jess whispered, "Take off my panties is what he meant."

"Jeez, Jess, you didn't?" was Crystal's shocked riposte.

The effect was exactly as she'd hoped, and gleefully eyeing her shocked friend Jess shamelessly enthused, "I sure did."

"How? I mean, surely you mean in the bathroom?" Crystal showing more interest than perhaps she should have.

"Nope," came proudly from Jess's lips.

"Wow, Jess, you're so bad," Crystal responded jokingly, thinking wait until the rest of them get a load of this. That said, she thought Jess would probably give them chapter and verse herself.

"It's easy. No biggie really." Having got Crystal's full attention, not to mention shocked her into silence, she was unable to resist regaling the whole scenario for her friend.

"We were sat at the back as I said, in a booth in the VIP area. In case I'd not mentioned, I wore that clingy red Versace number, the dress that has the zip running almost to the bottom of the dress. I knew he had something on his mind when he forked out for that pricy little number. Remind me to show it to you. It has a built in bra thingy so no need for one. Oh yeah," she laughed cheekily, "that guy's got his finger on the pulse when it comes to shopping."

Continuing with episode two of the Jess and Jack show Jess said, "There we were kissing. I can't deny things were heating up, hot and heavy or what? Then those long piano fingers got to work, doing what they do best. His hand had sidled down to my thigh, caressing, probing, I'm sure it don't need spelling out. You get the idea? To be honest it was not the first time with the wandering hand routine," bolstering in an unashamed tone, "in public."

Augmenting the story further, she continued. "The beauty of it is we weren't alone. There were people everywhere. Some of his employees I think, loitering around nearby drinking bottles of Bud. I guess they were either drunk or ignoring us." Divulging more juicy revelations Jess rabbited on. "One hand gently stroked my neck at the back under my hair. He took hold of the zip and began unzipping me slowly, very slowly, careful not to snag my hair which I had down that night. He began to unzip the dress. The dress stayed put, the front of it I mean, and luckily the booth was positioned in a corner so we had our backs to a wall. He slipped his hand inside the back, moving it slowly down to my bottom squeezing with his hands inside my panties. Moving his hand to the front, he put his hand between my legs and gave a little tug of my white thong. I jerked, thinking he was going to rip 'em off. He didn't though. His command was whispered in the most seductive tone. You know

82

me, I had no hesitation in complying. There's only one winner in this little game was the way I saw it. I think it was a little test, him daring me to see how far I'd go. You know what I mean?"

"Actually, no not really," voiced Crystal.

Jess had more to tell and Crystal was clearly rivetted on hearing the latest exploits.

"I had my left elbow resting on the table holding the champagne flute, and with my right hand I bent slightly under the table and slipped them down my leg and over my heels. Sort of bending as if I was picking something from the floor."

"Then what?" Spellbound, Crystal's imagination was in overdrive, half expecting Jess to say they'd got down to it there and then in the club.

"I screwed them into a tiny ball and dropped them into his hand. He just couldn't resist with the touching of my inner thigh. You know, close between my legs, fingers going... well, you don't need drawing a map."

"My god, Jess, has he got a brother?" Crystal laughed.

"I think he has actually. Never met him, although I've caught snippets of phone conversations," she replied, her voice changing into a more measured tone.

"But how do you know it's his brother?" Crystal asked curiously, seriously wondering if she dare ask her to set her up.

"For one thing he answers, 'what's up, bro?' and he uses a more, well, different tone. That's not Jack as a rule, he's businesslike on the phone. Quite brusque. I'd use the word curt if I had to describe how he addresses people at times if I'm being honest."

"Then what happened?" asked Crystal, clearly hooked at this point and feeling insanely jealous.

"We finished the bottle of champagne."

She knew exactly what her friend meant but was enjoying watching her squirm and clocking her reaction as she reeled off what was more or less a normal night out for her and Jack.

"He zipped me back up and we headed out. We had to wait for one of his cronies to come pick us up seeing as we'd drank a fair bit. Plus, it meant we would be sitting in the back seat where he would have his hands free, if you know what I mean.

Then back to the condo where we made good use of that massive bed."

Returning to the rest of the night's events and ending the story on a flippant, jokey note, Jess says, "Then of course I have to make tracks and get home before my clothes turn into rags and the beamer turns into a pumpkin. Careful is Jack's middle name," she informs her best friend. "He don't take chances taking me home, no parking close to the house, just near enough for him to see me through the gates, caring and thoughtful boyfriend that he is," she enthuses with pride. "Can't have the neighbours snitching like that time Dave my ex got eyeballed doing just that. I guess you remember when all that kicked off? Was not pretty," she added. "Dave nearly had an accident when the neighbour banged on the steamed-up window."

Reflecting back and knowing Jess was only sixteen, Crystal wasn't at all surprised Dr and Mrs Simmons reacted as they did.

"And did they go ballistic? Mum blew a gasket with Dad not too far behind. Talk about an overreaction. Mind you, if you saw what I was wearing I guess I should have expected it," she said, sniggering like a naughty little girl whilst in the throes of repeating the incident.

"Would you believe it?" she ranted, carrying on with her unjustified gripe, "Just 'cos of that, my dad threatened to cut up my credit cards. AND ground me."

"He wouldn't?" Crystal feigned shock.

"Oh yeah, he would. It's a common theme in our house when he's pissed at me. He deprives me of things, things I need as well. He's done this on more than one occasion," the grieved teenager reflected. "That's enough to bring on the waterworks. Snivelling and crying is my default mode, the poor me act, typically followed by the promise I will get my act together."

She then explained to her friend she had to be on the ball and not drop herself in it by bringing up something they knew nothing about. "Done that before," she said, shaking her head. "That's where the wealthy older boyfriend comes into his own. Am I onto a winner or what? A cool boyfriend who cares, looks out for me, panders to my every need. And I mean 'every' need," smiling like the cat that got the cream.

Jess revered Jack and took on board his advice and little suggestions of how to keep off their radar, cumulating with her not being in the bad books with regard to her "night activities".

"Night activities is a clever anecdote Jack came up with, one way to describe what we get up to," Jess smiled smugly. "Never fails." This girl knew how to exact whatever she wanted from her boyfriend. Her emotional, physical and material needs were met and then some. She thinks back to the early days of their relationship.

The young girl gazes longingly into her man's eyes, and in a soft sweet girly tone extended only to him, words come freely and easy. Emotional blackmail. Not that it is at all necessary, or emotional. But it's fun. Oh boy, is it fun. A game he could, no doubt, and would willingly play over and over until the end of time.

What is it her mum used to say to her when she was little? "Use your words, Jess." Oh yeah, she does that alright. Words don't elude her no more. Oh no, she's got the words off to a tee.

It begins with the look, then she uses her words. Gazing at Jack longingly with her big blue eyes and pouty lips, let the game begin.

"You want me to look all pretty, all grown up like one of those sexy Vegas women, don't you? Not a little girl?" pleading in her most playful tone and sticking her bottom lip out as she does her thing, watching every inch of his body while he hangs on to her every word.

She watches him watching her.

"I can't go clubbing or out on the town in this get up, can I?" pointing to her school attire which she purposefully wore.

"Really, Jack, just look at me," peeling off her school uniform slowly in her well-practised tantalising manner.

She was standing there in her tiny, plain, white cotton panties and bulging out of her sports bra. All tanned, toned smooth brown skin. The full works, even down to the little white socks and pumps. Her eyes don't leave his as she puts a finger in her mouth and sucks.

No prompting, no hesitation. Works like a dream every time, always. This is her time, she's the one in charge. She wallows in the moment and willingly takes the lead. Until it's his turn, then she plays innocent, the shocked expression at his demands and forcefulness.

The young girl clearly embraces the power she holds over a grown man.

Chapter Twelve

The Good versus the Bad

Quite early in the relationship Jack set the ground rules.

Her ever attentive boyfriend presented her with a phone. There was one stipulation. He made it abundantly clear she must only ever use this particular phone when contacting him. He told her she must never use her own phone and that he would pick up immediately, urging her to get in touch with him any time, night or day, especially if things get too fraught at home or if she just wanted to blow off some steam and have a good old moan.

He'll always be on hand to talk and offer advice. A rather ingenious idea thought the grateful young girl, rather cunning too she admitted.

Typically, one of her dad's top grievances were phone charges.

Well, problem solved. This put paid to that little indiscretion, plus the argument that usually followed.

Mindful of the age gap, she was guessing Jack to be mid to late thirties, although she didn't really care. It went without saying she could do without her folks getting the wrong idea. Not that it would be the wrong idea. She was certain it would lead to a boatload of trouble for both of them if they caught on, though she suspected primarily for him, Jess being a teenager.

Then of course there is the credit card Jack furnished her with that they hadn't a clue about.

"Anything to help with life's little luxuries and beauty treatments," he offered. It was gratefully received and she was more than happy to return a favour.

"Ask and you shall receive," was one of Jess's favourite little mottos as she whispers into Jack's ear suggestively, her hot breath having the desired effect as she sits straddling him on the sofa, bra undone at the ready, waiting for his gentle probing fingers to do their thing. She never tires of playing the role of the naughty ever so grateful little schoolgirl.

"We don't always go out," she tells her friend. "A night in the condo can be just as much fun if you see where I'm coming from," she giggles.

Crystal simply rolls her eyes and says nothing.

She'd become quite the covert operator since taking up with Jack and became quite apt at sneakily finding different places to hide the phone, credit card and other expensive items he willingly bestowed upon her.

The designer clothes, including underwear, jewels and other the expensive gifts stay at his condo for obvious reasons.

Jess is clearly smitten with her "older" boyfriend who, for the most part, is a sweet and loving person to be around.

All that being said, she'd become deeply conscious of another side to him, a dark side. A weird almost nasty hidden persona. It doesn't often rear its ugly head, but it's there all right, lurking beneath that golden exterior. Being the loyal, dutiful girlfriend she considered herself, it wouldn't do to dwell on such a thing. So long as he's a good, kind, giving boyfriend then that's fine by her. The good definitely outweighed the bad, she concluded.

She often wondered if she's seeing the real Jack or if he's playing some kind of game with her. Jess might be blonde but she's anything but stupid.

Studying people was her forte. She knew how to read people, pick up on their moods and idiosyncrasies. There was no denying the fact, there were many faces to Jack Jones. It hadn't escaped her notice that his mood could change on a dime, an example being the manner in which he speaks to people who work for him. Nasty, condescending, arrogant, another word evoked when on the subject. It could be said at times he's a rather egotistical if not narcissistic individual.

To her way of thinking there's a trade off if you want to be successful and make money in this life, this thought a kind of get out clause to assuage her misgivings.

Knowing only too well what grown ups can be like with regard to work stresses, the last thing she wanted was for them to fall out. No way would she precipitate a row.

Making a zipping action across her closed lips, she told Crystal, "I just keep shtum when he goes off on one. I'm sure as hell not gonna poke that bear," she joked half-heartedly.

Take a step back and keep it buttoned was her default position. Let him blow off steam and lose it with whoever was fine so long as she's not in the firing line.

When he's in that sort of mood it's usually targeted at the person or persons in the vicinity. More often than not though he spewed his venom to the person he's on the phone with.

He'd made it abundantly clear that under no circumstances should she converse with his business associates. No problem, she'd articulated.

"Once, and it would only ever be the one time, I picked up his phone. Have I told you this? I can't quite remember." More revelations were heading Crystal's way from her indignant friend.

"I was at the condo in the lounge. Lover boy was getting dressed in the bedroom having just taken a shower after we'd been all romantic. Well, when I say romantic…" her face lit up briefly before taking on a "pissed off" look.

"His phone began vibrating, dancing round the glass coffee table like it'd end up flying off. I shouted for him. No answer. Again, no answer. Where's the harm? It could've been an emergency. I pulled out all the stops, utilised my posh telephone voice 'an everything. I could have been his secretary for all they knew. If he has one that is. I offered to take a message for Mr Jones as he's unavailable at the moment. It's not like I said he's in the shower 'cos he's just shagged his schoolgirl girlfriend. The door swung open and he came bounding out of the bedroom like a racehorse out of the paddock. Naked. I've never seen him move so fast, and let me tell you I've seen what he can do in the fast-moving department. One minute I'm his sexy sophisticated girlfriend who's the best thing since gluten free bread, the next thing he's treating me like a naughty child. His venomous tone really got to me. You'd think I'd have asked the caller for a date or to meet up later for a quickie," Jess tells her best friend. "Well, all I will say is if any other boyfriend spoke to me in that tone, dumped is what they'd be. Well and truly dumped. No messing."

Crystal was about to jump in and agree with the dumping part but her friend didn't seem to draw breath. Plus, she clearly had a lot more she wanted to get off her chest, some of which was old news.

I wish she'd talk more about the sex stuff, it's more interesting, Crystal thought to herself whilst Jess continued venting.

"But Jack is Jack I guess. Love him or hate him, he is who he is," Jess added, following the dumping statement.

Never one to let anything go, Jess continued serving up more of Jack's character flaws as if her friend would be interested. The few occasions his mask had slipped had really impacted her, "shocked and scary" just two of the words applied in describing various incidents, pointing out to her friend that for the most part he can be the sweetest and coolest guy you could ever wish to meet, let alone want to sleep with.

"Then there were times he acts like a complete jerk, like he's better than everyone else, even me. Can you actually believe that?" Jess continues, rolling her eyes. "It's like he has an air of superiority about him. Talk about split personality, he takes on a different persona whoever he is with at the time," she said. "This other Jack is pompous and arrogant. I know which one gets my vote. I'm for the generous charming Jack. And another thing, don't get me started on his work cronies. Not that I'm allowed to have a conversation with any of them or I'd want to for that matter. All a bunch of weirdos."

"There must be names for people like that," her friend butted in.

"Yeah, sociopath," said Jess laughing.

The friend, trying to be of help, had an idea. "Maybe therapy is worth a shot?"

"Well, I sure as hell am not suggesting that, I can tell you. There's a price to pay for everything," she laughed.

There was no getting away from it, she was young and naïve but the girl was learning.

Chapter Thirteen

How it Came to Be

For only a few very short years Jess had been their one and only child, Dr and Mrs Simmons' pride and joy, a beautiful curly, blonde, green-eyed baby girl, a cute little princess made to feel special and treasured.

Then suddenly replaced. In her mind at least. No longer the baby of the family or the centre of their universe. Baby number two had entered the world. Susie, the latest of the Simmons clan, just as cute and just as loved.

To outsiders the perfect family.

An eminent surgeon with a beautiful model wife and now two adorable daughters.

This perception of how she's viewed was deeply embedded. It felt as though she had to act in a certain way to get their attention.

Jess caught on fairly quickly. Oh, this is how it's going to be, is it? but never actually came out and voiced it.

Not like she does now.

That constant feeling at being the nuisance problem child. After a while you take on a new persona, a new identity without realising it and make it work for you. And there bestowed upon her a label: "the problem child".

It didn't take her long to realise that a title had to be lived up to and Jess being Jess, though still a youngster, sure had fun with this. The stories she could tell about her childhood were legendary. And she did constantly making everyone laugh. Even Susie.

"I'll say one thing for your sister, Jess" said Crystal, "she sure is a good sport. Anyone else would be running off home crying to Mama."

Thinking about her sister brought to mind a recent conversation she'd had with Jack. In a roundabout way he'd paid Susie a compliment.

It came out of nowhere. "She's a cute girl your little sister."

In her mind "cute" was most definitely a compliment. She tried not to make a thing of it but it had rankled her somewhat.

Appreciating it was her fault although unable to recall why, one evening whilst chilling in the condo she showed him Susie's Facebook profile.

But then thinking about it later, he knew their family name so could have easily put in a search at any time. She probably just wanted to gauge his reaction.

He expressed openly, "Susie has a lot to live up to being your sister."

Is that what he really thinks though? Or is this him buttering her up for what would most likely come later, she asked herself silently.

Yeah, he's definitely in full buttering up mode. "Keep going," she said to herself. And he did.

"There's no getting away from it, Jess, you've certainly got it. Oh yeah, model mum, model daughter," he announced with an adoring smile.

Looking at her with those come to bed eyes he knew exactly what to say and how to keep her from straying. More importantly, to keep her just where he had her.

"There would be nothing stopping you following your mum into the modelling world if that's the road you want to venture down. After you've graduated, of course, as you are smart. Real smart. Beauty and brains," he added fondly.

He was on a roll, staring lovingly into her eyes, showering her with compliments.

She was his prize.

He lifted her chin and kissed her tenderly on the lips making her go all tingly inside. That sealed the deal for Jess, that's all it took. She never tired of hearing the compliments which fed her blossoming ego.

For sure she'd got the make-up down to a fine art, complementing the glamourous dazzling look she effortlessly pulled off. The sophisticated look. With those big green eyes, long eyelashes, slightly chubby cheeks, blonde, almost waist-length hair, she could be who and whatever she wanted to be.

"For my eyes only," whispered Jack suggestively on one of these occasions whilst he took his reward.

As with all couples they had the odd date which didn't quite go his way. The mood dampened, not so much dampened as got drenched.

He just had to say it again and ruin the vibe saying nice flattering things about Susie. He couldn't help himself.

Jess, clearly taken aback, was slightly perturbed at the utterance. Out of nowhere came the innocuous little statement. "Susie sure is growing up. Becoming prettier and prettier. Turning into a lovely young lady."

Jess threw him a cutting stare.

Thinking about it, as she had done on more than once occasion, he'd been perusing his phone when he offered this blatant little insight into Susie's future.

Smiling and sniggering mischievously as the words left his lips, he was clearly expecting some response.

Jess just couldn't help but throw it out there. Rather cuttingly, her tone was as sharp as a razor.

"What're you doing checking her out online?" Before he'd had chance to respond she carried on with the snide remarks. "Please," she said, hurt and a little disgusted all at once, "what is your problem?"

Reading between the lines she didn't care for the implication.

Those few little words out of her boyfriend's mouth meant a hell of lot, implying in a few years when she is roughly Jess's age there is a possibility she could be on a par with her. A rival. A rival for Jack's affection.

Incensed, she promptly shot him down, insinuating Susie would never entertain him or any boy for that matter. Dating's way down on her agenda, enlightening him on the fact Susie and her little buddies are saving themselves for "the one". The one they'd marry.

What made its way out of his mouth next was even more galling.

"There's a first time for everything and that's not such a bad thing. She's obviously a smart kid who knows what she wants and has firm values."

Recounting the incident for her best friend as she often did, she said in a stroppy pissed off tone, "He almost ended up wearing that glass of wine. The only thing that stopped me and made me think better of it was the fact that he'd just ordered the most expensive bottle of champagne. Plus of course we were in the VIP area in a top Vegas nightspot. Despite who's guest I was I couldn't risk being chucked out in the early hours of the morning. That would've precipitated a call to the hospital for a lift and my dad was being called in for an emergency operation that particular night. I'd overheard a conversation between him and Mum as he was darting out of the door after dinner. Mum doesn't budge once she's settled for the night. It would have taken me being attacked or a car accident. Even then she would have said call 911." Her whining was in full swing. "I can't imagine my dad would have been too pleased after finishing up surgery and having to pick up his wayward daughter from the strip on a Friday night. Make no mistake, that would put be me back in the bad books for sure. Especially being half cut, wearing heels and the shortest little black dress I could get away with. The last time he saw me in such attire he said I looked like 'a hooker'. And that particular dress wasn't nearly as short or figure hugging. I did wonder how he knew what a hooker looked like. If only I hadn't said as much. I just can't keep my mouth shut at times."

"Some of the things you do and say are so out there," Crystal laughed.

"I'll say one thing, this Susie business aside, he genuinely takes an interest in all the family. He listens and remembers," Jess offered.

What she'd failed to mention to Crystal or anyone else was Jack's desire to see Susie in the flesh.

Taken aback, Jess was hesitant. Showing interest in family members is one thing, a face to face meet with her sister another thing entirely.

All the compliments he'd thrown up lately regarding Susie added to her angst.

94

Another concern, although Susie was no grass, was a possibility she might let it slip out in conversation.

Not sure if this point needed to be made, she did so anyway. Jack took her concerns on board and made a suggestion. "Surely we could arrange a covert meeting, thus Susie would be none the wiser?"

After cajoling and a lot of coaxing, Jess conceded and threw up an idea.

Jessica concocted a "tea date" for Susie, stating they do this from time to time when they're both free. It'll accrue brownie points with Mum if nothing else, she thought wistfully.

Susie was brimming with enthusiasm when Jess suggested the little after school outing to their local Starbucks.

"You'd think I'd have offered to take her to Bloomingdale's for a Gucci purse," Jess told her friend Gail at school the next day.

"She needs to get out more," came the glib comment from Gail.

"Ain't that the truth," Jess said in agreement.

"Maybe this is the start of things to come," Susie had enthused to her best friend Beth.

She looked up to her big sister and felt really proud she'd made the offer, even if it was just a coffee and cake date. She thought of Jess as funny and interesting. Sophisticated and sort of worldly is how she described her sister to her friends.

Most, but not all, had a completely different take on Jess, but were much too nice to dwell on it or make waves between the two sisters.

Tuesday, the day of the arranged tea date was soon upon them. For Jess a degree of anxiety took hold. As innocent as this is, she couldn't have anything go wrong.

Sitting and chatting away, suddenly out of the corner of her eye Jess caught sight of Jack.

They'd agreed he shouldn't make eye contact, simply "look and walk on by".

Casually he proceeded to walk by their table, respectably passing the two young girls.

Without a doubt he'd caught a good look at her. That's what they'd agreed. Enough to satisfy his curiosity.

95

Oh no, he just had to do it, it had to be more. A pretty girl in his sphere he couldn't resist, even if it is his girlfriend's little sister. Curiosity got the better of him and he did an about turn. Smiling, he ventured where he'd promised not to go.

For a split second something told Jess he'd taken a photo. No, he can't have. Can he? Surely not. Why would he? I'm being paranoid, thought Jess.

With a warm friendly smile he began to speak and deviate from the plan. The agreed upon plan.

Sweetly, the ever charming Jack began enquiring if they'd knowledge of a business he was looking for. Pressing further, he showed them his phone which held a map.

A bit lame. Is that all you can come up with? Jess thought bitterly.

Making small talk all three chatted congenially. Susie being the naïve friendly girl that she is proceeded to chat away sweetly, having no problem holding up her end of the conversation.

Maybe she's feeling confident 'cos she's with me, thought Jess. Perhaps her way of acting all grown up. It was all Jess could do not to get up and drag her sister out of there, her suspicious teenage brain going ten to the dozen. Did she like him? Did she see what I saw in him? No, Susie didn't think like that, that much she knew.

Jack on the other hand, his lecherous eyes bore into her.

Susie's intelligent, a good conversationalist and can talk on any subject quite articulately. Beautiful and intelligent is what Jack will be thinking. Jess knew him so well.

For a minute it appeared as though he intended to pull up a chair and join the girls.

"Jesus. Just go, Jack, will you?" Jess said with a look in her eyes. Enough already.

Apart from anything else, all the smiling and chatting had Jess feeling a little jealous.

She watched as Susie conversed pleasantly with the handsome stranger. She'd decided not to engage in the hope he would get the message and back off.

Glancing at Jess periodically as he spoke to Susie, finally he took the hint.

The penny's finally dropped has it? annoyance and sarcasm in equal measures gliding through her pretty head.

Jack could read Jess like a book and aptly tuned into his girlfriend's moods, her face indicating her annoyance. Of course, he knew he'd overstepped the mark. He also knew it was worth it.

Not happy about the deviation from the plan Jess vowed to make him pay, though she was not sure how yet. "I'll come up with something," she said to herself.

Then it hit her. The bastard. He's ogling her like there's no tomorrow.

All at once it came to her, it was what Susie was wearing. Having come directly from school she still wore her school uniform!

Just as this thought hit her, he shook both their hands and headed for the door.

"He seemed nice," said Susie in her usual polite Susie tone.

With the rolling of the eyes "whatever" was the only light-hearted thing Jess could think to say.

Her mind at this point was plainly elsewhere.

Susie's response began her usual girly giggles.

Now here we are a couple weeks down the line and Susie is missing. Abducted, possibly kidnapped for ransom, to hear her mum and dad talk.

The opinion of the local police couldn't be more different.

This is a frequent occurrence in their world. "They usually turn up," said one of the detectives, Detective Baldwin I think his name badge said.

They weren't being nonchalant as such, all pretty routine, all in a day's work to them, that much was evident.

"Best thing you can do is to wait. Stay home by the phone." Dad fumed when he heard their platitudes. "Sit it out, she'll come home when she's good and ready."

Both cops had a number of theories.

She had most likely crashed at a friend's house, fallen asleep. Then hesitant to come home for fear of being in trouble. Drinking, partying, she probably ran off to prove a point. Did they fight, is Susie argumentative? A rebellious teenager? Has she a boyfriend? Have her grades been slipping? The questions were endless and went on and on.

No, no and no, came the frustrated reply from my dad, becoming more frustrated by the second.

Shoving, and I mean shoving, one of Susie's school photos in the detective's face, Mum's protestations at the implication that their youngest is the sort of child who may be staying away from home in an attempt to push the boundaries was simply absurd.

Jess was half expecting her to point the finger in her direction just to show them what a wayward child really looked like.

A well manicured finger pointed at me as she yelled, "Look no further if you want to see an argumentative, spoilt, rebellious brat of a teenager, too busy with her latest boyfriend to worry about slipped grades or her sister."

It didn't happen though. I might as well not have been in the room, Jess concluded.

All this took place the previous evening.

Jess, having slept like a baby, thought she'd better show her face, cautiously making her way downstairs.

Of course, before doing so, for the twentieth time since all this kicked off, she had another go at calling Jack's mobile. Surprise, surprise, no answer.

Another one done a disappearing act. Go figure, it's catching. What the hell's he playing at? Some boyfriend he's turning out to be. Yeah, he's busy making loads of dosh, I get that. Never leaves me hanging like this though, Jess moaned.

Realising she hadn't eaten dinner the night before, Jess felt ravenous. With all this Susie business she remembered her mum hadn't prepared anything. Also, keen to know if the police were still around, she crept downstairs. Tiptoeing quietly into the lounge, out of the corner of her eye she caught sight of her dad. Their house was now eerily silent as her dad appeared in an almost trance-like state.

Turning to acknowledge her, without a single word he offered the thinnest of smiles. Appearing tired and haggard, a double shift at the hospital doesn't give him that look thought the teenager. It ran through her mind that maybe they wished it were her instead of Susie, but she opted to keep that firmly in her head. No good would come of announcing that little snippet. It would come across as self-pity as if trying to divert attention from Susie to herself. That was something she had never done and wasn't going to start now.

"Any news yet, Dad?" she asked sombrely.

"No, nothing. The police are supposedly doing what they do, though what is anybody's guess. They mentioned something about an amber alert for all the good it will do."

"Why don't you go and get your head down? I'll man the phone," Jess offered, wanting to appear helpful and concerned.

Probably for the first time ever Jess felt for her parents, crushed, both weighed down with fear and anxiety, frustration and pain etched on their faces.

In that instance Jess felt lost and alone as she ached for her man. A desperate craving to hear his voice overcame her, and the urge to vent and moan like never before. "Where are you, Jack?" she said with a sigh.

Chapter Fourteen

Jess

Mystified, Jess couldn't comprehend this latest saga, this simply doesn't happen to her. Unfathomable was one of the words that sprung into her frazzled brain accompanied by several expletives.

"It don't make sense, where is he and why the unanswered texts?" she muttered to herself angrily.

Nevertheless, despite everything the yearning for her man intensified. The anger remained but the yearning slowly overshadowed it. The longing to have him near her for the feel of his touch.

In all the time she'd known him she'd never gone this length of time without speaking, or at the very least receiving a text. Day or night.

These last couple of days felt like forever, lost and alone, having no communication with her beau gnawing at her.

To hear his raspy voice, that saccharine tone warmed and soothed her.

"Hey, what's up, my little sweet sexy one?" That phrase, that voice, bounced into her head as if part of a song which had irritatingly taken up residence after singing along in his car.

For more than one reason her once cosy, ordered life had taken an unexpected turn, an unexpected and grossly unsettling turn. Jess wanted comfort. Wanted life back to normal. Normal as in last week's normal.

Only one person held the power to make it happen. Jack. She didn't kid herself, her boyfriend was nowhere near perfect, but for all his peculiar little idiosyncrasies he was hers and hers alone and she adored him.

Her mind took to snaking off to places it really had no business venturing. Dubious thoughts and scenarios seeping through randomly, her suspicious imagination was conjuring up images involving Jack with her cute sister.

If only he'd pick up the phone, text, e-mail, whatever, she silently prayed. The plan was to cleverly concoct one of their secret rendezvous. A little way from here, a couple of blocks, that'd play out nicely. No question he'd be charging in on a white horse to her rescue, replacing the white horse with a white beamer in her moment of escapism.

The image of that tanned Ray-Ban adorned face gazing adoringly, ready and eager to whisk her off for a bit of daytime fun was all too tempting. To a world where there are no adults watching her every move or telling her what to do.

Granted there were not so much daytime shenanigans "'cos my guy's gotta make the dough, plus me being still at school 'an all." Oh yeah, no messing. Keen as mustard with the hint of an impromptu clandestine little tousle, the teenager inwardly sniggered.

The neighbours suddenly sprung to mind. Her neighbours. The very nosey neighbours who according to Jack ought to get an effing life. The enemy. Enemy number one as far as Jess was concerned.

"Dad's probably got them on the payroll," she'd moaned to more than one of her friends. "It's as though they've got nothing more interesting going on in their lives. Hence the need to spy on me."

Having been grassed up on several occasions over the years, her dalliances with Jack were completely under the radar. One step ahead, our Jacky boy. Oh yeah, he's got flying under the radar off to a fine art.

"Been there, done that, got a stack of T-shirts," was his whimsical comment early in their blossoming relationship.

"Clearly been down this road before me thinks," metaphorically speaking of course.

No response from Jason Bourne as he made a speedy getaway.

Neighbours aside, a completely more ominous problem presented itself today.

If it's true that officers of the law are meandering around the neighbourhood going house to house and knocking on doors like worker bees, then this sure could throw a monkey wrench into the works.

Jess concluded the detectives were inclined to make out they were actually doing something other than hassling them and guzzling their tea and coffee.

The idea lodged in her head that just maybe her folks would buy the notion she needed to get out, stretch her legs, go for a jog. Having been cooped up in the house there's a slight chance this one might fly, recalling her mum going on about endorphins, stress and such. Not such a stretch, they'd believed a whole bunch of crap more out there than this in days gone by.

If her folks bought it, and why wouldn't they, she'd make the excuse she'd bumped into a friend and they were off on the great Susie hunt, using a somewhat less flippant tone naturally.

It'd be a suitable ploy albeit not the most creative, but needs must, thought the despondent girl.

On the upside the outfit she'd leave the house dressed in was cute running attire, cute according to Jack that is. Cute or not, designer gear which like everything else she wore looked cool and showed off her figure to the max.

Jack had a thing for her "little gym clothes" as he referred to them, pulling up the memory of his face with the wide eyed grin, ogling her as she walked enthusiastically towards the parked car that very first time. The first, but by no means the only, occasion she'd thought to use this as a ruse in the daytime hours. Without a doubt he'd be on board with this not so original bit of role playing, smiling as she imagined the ensuing moments when they'd finally end up back at his place.

Her thoughts floated off elsewhere. Baldwin. Baldwin the police detective tasked to bring Susie home. When his face flashed into her head her stomach was reminiscent of the dryer in their laundry room. The churning took on a whole different meaning.

Clasping her hands together in silent prayer, she frantically mouthed, "Please, please, allow Jack to take me away from all this. Let it be before that cop Baldwin shows up again."

This Baldwin character irritated the hell out of her yesterday. That intense glare and those piercing brown eyes drilled deep into her core like he possessed special powers and could see what she was thinking.

Her dad had given her the heads up following a chat with the detective first thing. All agreed, wrapped up in a pretty red bow long before she'd climbed out of bed let alone brushed her pearly whites.

She recalled the exact words out of her dad's mouth as she made her entrance into the lounge still half asleep.

"The detective would like another chat with you if that's OK."

The inference it was optional meant she had a choice, but him agreeing to this without checking really pissed her off. Righteous indignation in full flow, Jess aimed her annoyance at her dad rather than the cop, grumbling quietly but not too quietly,

"Wow, I'll look forward to that. He had my life story yesterday, so I don't know what he expects me to divulge today that he ain't heard already. Heh, that's OK, I can make something up if it'll get him off my back."

Embroidering further in a slightly cheekier tone, "People are not usually inclined to listen to what I have to say, so I guess it makes a welcome change. I'll just give him a different version of the bullshit I offered up yesterday." Her tangent was in full flow as she slowly edged her way from her dad, playing the game, ensuring this snippet was out of earshot.

She was vocal in her agreement with her father on one thing, the police ought to be more proactive and be out there doing police work and quit speaking to family members. "Wasting precious time," being one of her dad's voiced criticisms. Of course, Jess nodding in agreement with that one.

Another thing perturbed Jess. Clearly something was simmering between her parents. She took on board that there was bound to be tension in the house especially under these circumstances, but garnered there was more to it than that. Jess couldn't quite put her finger on it.

She wouldn't have called it a rift as such, but they'd definitely been fighting. Friction and tension hung in the air, a smouldering ash cloud on the verge of swallowing up everything in its path. Including her.

It could be something kicked off before her sister's disappearance, she really had no notion.

In retrospect, she wasn't in the house long enough to be clued up on what was going on with anyone, including Susie, adding to her puzzlement regarding what she could add to her statement.

So now here she sat in limbo. Hanging around. Waiting for "Denzel" as Jess had named him.

About right her sis gets the attention of probably the only cop in the whole of Vegas, maybe the whole country, the spitting image of the actor on her case. He could double for Denzel Washington, and Jess wondered if she'd be the first to bring this to his attention.

If the conversation dries up she intended to put it to him and ask him if he'd ever thought about a career in the movies. A bit of buttering up might just keep him off her back.

Glancing in the direction of her father, Jess figured he'd been rooted to that spot all night. Undetected, she craftily made her way to the sanctuary of her bedroom leaving him alone with his thoughts. Dark disturbing thoughts by the look of him.

Fixedly staring out of the window his forlorn eyes channelled straight ahead, scrutinising the view along the gravel drive leading directly to the huge front door. The long slightly winding drive which by way of crunching gravel indicated the presence of a visitor long before coming into view.

He was stoically standing, watching, staring hard with the occasional deep sigh, willing his missing daughter to miraculously appear.

Jess breathed in the aroma of freshly brewed coffee as it wafted in from the kitchen. It wasn't lost on her a cup hadn't been brought to her dad, at least not since she'd been sat there.

The kind, dutiful daughter she considered herself to be, she flew into action. She made a rare trip to the kitchen returning with hot coffee and buttered toast, placing it at the side of her dad on a little table.

"You need to eat something, Daddy," offered Jess in an unusually sweet tone.

"I'm OK, sweetheart," he replied, acknowledging the gesture.

"Sweetheart". Her dad hadn't referred to her in such a soft-hearted way in as long as she could remember. "It was almost unnerving, definitely teetering on the edge," she said to herself.

She settled into one of the comfy leather chairs.

Feet lifted from the floor at an angle, scrunched up, weight resting on her thighs and ankles, she settled down. Her knees were supporting her coffee cup and while dipping a granola bar she was periodically glancing between her dad and her phone to check she'd not missed a text.

Her dad shifted slightly once or twice never actually vacating his adopted spot, hardly allowing his gaze to wander from the view of the drive. His demeanour was pitiful, forlorn. The confident, controlled eminent surgeon, Jess couldn't recall ever seeing him looking so down.

For a split second he shifted to a different angle. Catching a glimpse of her out of the corner of his eye, he glumly expressed concern at the way she sat scrunched in the chair.

In a soft fatherly voice the words were barely audible. "Why don't you place your feet on the floor, sweetheart? Sitting that way will hinder your circulation and will do you no good at all."

Without so much as a back word, for once Jess did as she was told. There it came again, "sweetheart".

It wasn't that he spoke to her harshly all the time. In the main their everyday conversations were commonly peppered with requests to do something, or more pointedly not do something.

Today however things were different as the command came in a soft, warm tone.

Could this be him recognising what he had in her and how special she is? Appreciating his first born? As though he had to hang on to her now as she is all he has? Contemplating silently, her gaze rested on him.

Nah, I'm being an idiot. Where's my head at?

Talk about reading too much into things, Jess chastised herself.

Only one person really cared about her and he'd gone AWOL.

"It won't be too long before I'm back where I belong, in the doghouse. The bad books. Digging myself out of a hole as usual. Another misdemeanour under my belt, I can bank on that one," Jess said to herself pessimistically.

Through the kitchen door, which she'd omitted to close behind her when returning with the coffees, she viewed the garden terrace outside the vast open concept kitchen. Her mom and Auntie Jean could be seen pacing back and forth along the patio.

It wasn't lost on her that not so much as a, "How 'yer doing, Jess, you managed some shuteye? Do you want some food?" came her way. Nada.

Her rationale, the police bods received more consideration. Barely a nod from the both of them as she'd precariously entered earlier to perform the part of "the dutiful daughter".

The rancid smell in that area hadn't escaped her either. Stale cigarette smoke. More recent smoke drifting in from outside adding to it. She was guessing her mum was back to partaking an old habit with Auntie Jean keeping her company.

Knowing her dad hated cigarettes, she wondered if this was at least one of the reasons why they were keeping clear of each other.

As a general rule Jean only pops round when her dad's at the hospital. More often than not, they'd make an arrangement to meet at the Mall or elsewhere, her mum frequently popping round to her aunt's for a gossip often taking Susie and any of her friends who were at their home.

Auntie Jean, Mum's older sister, most likely added to any hostility if there had been fighting. Jess got the impression Jean wasn't her dad's biggest fan and vice versa.

One thing for sure, her auntie loved Susie. Then again, didn't everyone? I'm surprised we don't have a house full of people. Still, there's time for that, she thought. The landline had been ringing on and off from the minute they'd begun to contact Susie's friends.

Naturally, there were suggestions of coming round to offer well-meaning support. Thankfully, her dad had declined all offers which was more than fine with her.

At the same time though there were equally as many unhelpful offerings, the majority bordering on the ridiculous.

"You know what kids are like, they lose track of time. Always trying to see what they can get away with, push the boundaries. My Johnny did this, that and the other when he was her age. Susie's got a level head on her shoulders. I wouldn't worry, she'll be alright. She'll turn up with her tail between her legs wondering what all the fuss is about."

She understood why her dad had his snappy head on after listening to the constant drivel out of the mouths of those cops. The bullshit. Things they said or didn't say far from instilled confidence in them.

Their missing daughter will likely as not saunter through the door exclaiming, "What's the problem?" purported Denzel, in his experience claiming this is the most likely outcome.

"Utter nonsense. Total garbage," voiced her exasperated dad, his tone fraught with fear and anger.

Pondering on Denzel's boldness at conveying such a statement, she began ruminating about a past conversation she'd had with her invisible boyfriend. How did his leery insight go again?

"Girls go missing day in and day out. Especially in this town. How often do you hear about them turning up?"

Aren't we full of the joys of spring, a scrappy morsel she'd refrained from imparting at the time.

She couldn't exactly recollect when he actually came out with the weird creepy insight, but she had an idea what triggered it. For no real reason other than perhaps a little bored, she'd read aloud an article in the *Nevada Star*.

Jack was plonked on the other end of the sofa, glass of Chardonnay in one hand all chilled, ears pricked impersonating Mr Spock at the ready to impart his extensive knowledge of all the nefarious goings on in Vegas.

The article stated, *Again, shockingly another young girl has gone missing. Blonde, attractive, petite frame. Very similar in appearance to the previous girl who disappeared a couple of weeks earlier.*

Reflecting back to the news article, it said this girl was a grown women in her twenties.

She was not quite sure whether he had any basis for the abysmal statement which followed his last bit of expertise on the subject. To her reckoning there was nothing new here. Simply put, it was Jack being Jack knowing everything about everything and everybody as usual.

Halfway to being pissed, it was as if he couldn't resist imparting his next offering.

"Girls go missing on a regular basis day in day out here in Vegas. No one normally bats an eyelid or gives a shit. The town's full of people who want to disappear. What makes this newsworthy?"

This was just one of the instances where she outwardly curbed her emotions and revulsion. All the same, a shiver ran down her spine when he voiced this little gem.

It was probably the delivery of his pearl of wisdom as much as anything, smiling effusively with a dirty little snigger tagged on the end.

That got to her, made her think. And remember.

There was a time way back when it occurred to her that maybe he made shocking comments and sprouted this kind of stuff for no other reason than to gauge her reaction. Pure entertainment value to see what it takes to ruffle her feathers.

She'd got it into her head it was all a game to him and he took pleasure in shocking her, coming out with dodgy stuff to push her buttons.

She'd resumed reading the lengthy article choosing to keep it zipped. According to the journalist, this girl was last spotted in a top Vegas nightspot, naming the actual hotel and rooftop bar and club.

Recalling this particular instance, she'd very nearly blurted out to Mr Know all, "we've hung out there on a few occasions, haven't we?" halting her tongue pretty sharpish.

The newspaper reported:

when prompted for information, the friends of the missing girl informed the Vegas police she'd gone on a date, a first date but weren't absolutely positive. A date with a guy she'd met online or so they assumed. Again, they weren't sure so couldn't swear to it. Work colleagues reported her missing as there was no family close by. Simply GONE, vanished into thin air, disappeared.

It was a complete mystery to the police and people who knew her according to the news report.

The "date" had not yet come forward despite repeated requests from the police and there was a distinct lack of witnesses according to the cops. Assuming that's if what had indeed occurred according to one detective.

Adding to his previous statement, when probed by the journalist the cop indicated, "Every day adults choose for whatever reason to simply take off. They are perfectly within their rights to do so and make new lives for themselves without informing friends and loved ones."

He was highlighting the fact this is not uncommon and not against the law, emphasising that as this lady has been reported missing they are obliged to follow up and make enquiries. "Every effort is being made to locate her and make sure she is safe and well."

The news media was ostensibly stating again this girl had simply vanished.

The police only agreed to a point she'd been taken, Jess concluded after reading the piece, wondering at the same time if she'd been the only one to be perplexed why any of the cameras hadn't picked up footage. The strip was teeming with them, she reflected, saying as much to herself in a whispered tone. "About the only thing you can do in Vegas without being caught on camera is go to the bathroom," she chuntered.

"A dangerous city we live in," more insightful knowledge from the all-knowing Jack, the cadence of his voice a tad too creepy for comfort. Jess shivered and a cold bead of sweat ran down her back and dissolved into her designer T-shirt.

Smirking, he swiftly snatched the paper out of her hands, and without so much as a word dropped it into the trash can. He was throwing more of his scary inferences at her as he beckoned her out the door. "You can bet this town is full of chancers out looking for the opportunity to grab some little hottie."

The way he came out with that one made the hair on the back of her head stand up. A bit of a night owl herself who spent a lot of time on the strip, as much as she could get away with anyway.

She'd never use the term soul mates but her and Jack had a hell of a lot in common, especially taking the age gap into consideration. They had a good laugh and the physical side of things were bordering on perfect, but there were moments she'd told her best friend when she had to wonder about him. Really wonder. Weird was one word to describe his attitude, darn right scary a more apt portrayal.

Chapter Fifteen

Chocolate Chip Muffins

All this lounging around waiting for Baldwin was impacting Jess in a big way. The detective irked her like no one else. She wanted the interview, whatever it's called, over. Over and done with. Kaput, finished, firmly put to bed.

She hated talking to the cops, especially him.

The mere thought of it, him, made her anxious. And not much made her anxious, the waiting ramping up her boredom barometer.

She might be unaccustomed to the feeling of anxiety, but boredom, that's something she suffered from in spades.

Killing time in this silent stale cigarette smelling domain was allowing her too much time to mull things over and ponder on things she knew little to nothing about.

Jack being at the forefront of her mind prompted her to pull up one of their other weird discussions from a few weeks back. She didn't have to dig too deep to bring this little gem up. One of the many occasions he'd ventured to stick her with more "goings on" he professed to know all about.

This however was firmly lodged in her head and had stayed put.

Maybe it had been triggered by the newspaper episode or a TV report, she couldn't quite recall, but she remembered the words which came rolling out of his mouth:

"Missing young women in and around Nevada and Arizona." The inference by Jack as he openly declared, "Of course, girls will disappear in these areas. The area's huge. They most likely take off on their own accord most of 'em. Probably getting up to things they don't want their mamas getting wind of. Too shame faced to go home I'll bet. It's hardly worth a mention in the media, you can bet half of 'em are not reported."

His tangent was in full flow, offering up more of his expertise on the subject:

"The world, especially Vegas, is full of people who are only too ready take advantage and use people. Exploit the weak and vulnerable. Predators is what they are, predators ready and waiting to pounce. The police don't take it seriously. They've got enough on their plates with crime brought here by visitors and outsiders."

All this stuff was whirring round and round and wouldn't leave her pretty little head.

She could hear the ticking of a clock in the hall from her comfy chair in the lounge.

As if time had stood still.

She sighed while contemplating the sudden change in the setting of their once vibrant home, now filled with tension and dread.

Jess had had enough of the silence and that ticking clock.

She wanted out of that chair, that room, that house.

She'd decided to go up to her room for reasons she couldn't figure, though she daren't make a move.

In keeping with the pretence of the good daughter, she sought approval from her dad.

"Do you want me to stay down here with you, Daddy?" The sheepish request came wrapped up in the sweet tone she'd adopted.

"No, you're OK, go do whatever you have to do. I'll call you when the detective shows up. If he can be bothered that is," came the reply.

"OK, if you're sure then," endeavouring not to come over as too eager. She bounced to her feet and made her way towards the foyer, passing the noisy ticking clock.

Retreating to her bedroom, the idea was to continue her quest to get hold of Jack.

She sat on her bed and stared at her phone speaking out loud, "Ring, please ring," hoping her words held the power to conjure up a response. Then, just like magic, it sprung to life.

"That's it, I'm done. One more go, then that's it," she said to herself as she tapped redial. "If he ain't getting it by now that

I'm in need of his undivided, well, he's not the boyfriend I thought."

What happened to "if you need to talk day or night?" she thought bitterly.

How could he do this, abandon and be dismissive of her?

"I'm gonna make his sorry ass pay. He's gonna have to have a pretty good reason for treating me so abysmally," she said under her breath. "He'll have some serious making up to do, make no mistake. This will cost him dearly."

In an effort to wean her mind off the conundrum surrounding her, she did as her dad had suggested and cracked on with her homework, after which came a bit of channel hopping in the hope of finding something watchable.

And there, just like that, it hit her. The very reason there is next to no television watching going on in this room.

Swamp people, bush people, hoarder type people, entitled, spoiled, rich housewife people. Reruns of *Law and Order*, bad people. She settled for *Judge Judy*, a woman after her own heart.

"You go, Judy, give the stupid idiots the sharp end of your tongue. You tell 'em, girl. Nothing better to do than sue their own family!"

Mind you, they could be onto something with that one, seriously giving it some credence. She was lost in thought and wondering if anyone had ever sued their parents for ignoring them. Better still, for losing a sibling.

Suddenly the silence in the house was no more. She pressed mute and momentarily shelved her scheming, ears straining to catch the voices speculating why and who.

Curiosity won over. Tiptoeing along the landing, making her way to top of the stairs, quietly, gracefully taking small steps in her stocking feet, she listened keenly to the raised voices. Straining to hear what and with whom her dad was conversing, she gingerly made her way to the top of the long winding staircase.

Oh no, spotted.

"Oh, there you are, Jessica. I was just about to call you," strangely a slightly more upbeat tone from her dad.

113

Two detectives walked in her direction meeting her at the bottom of the stairs.

Baldwin spoke. "Hello, Jessica, this is my partner Detective Mike Simpkins."

He was roughly the same age as Baldwin, early forties maybe, only white with a thin black moustache which matched his wavy black hair. Not quite matching his partner in the snazzy dresser department, he wore a beige-coloured long raincoat over his suit. Bizarre, her first thought as she looked him up and down.

Simpkins held out his hand for a formal handshake. "I know what this is, good cop, bad cop," she said to herself as she shook his hand.

Simpkins playing the part of good cop.

The warm friendly smile further added to the fatherly look he owned, a tad different to his African-American counterpart, Jess thought.

Baldwin turned to her dad. "Have you a room we could commandeer for a few minutes? We'd like a private talk."

Dr Simmons beckoned them towards the dining room. Jess followed slowly.

Baldwin, or Denzel, as Jess had secretly named him, motioned to Dr Simmons stating he'd prefer to speak to her alone.

"You know she's a minor?" Back to the familiar testy tone he'd adopted when speaking to the detectives.

"I'll be fine, Daddy, don't worry," shaking her head casually in a "I can handle this" kinda way.

"Alright, if you're sure," said Dr Simmons as he backed off.

The two detectives and Jess entered the dining room. Parking herself in one of the easy chairs by the window she took up a relaxed cross-legged pose.

She was intentionally facing the large window which offered a good view of their lush green sprawling lawns and a side view of the patio in front of the kitchen area.

Hitting upon the idea if she became bored or irritated, which didn't take a whole lot, she would clock how many cigarettes her mum and Jean smoked between them.

114

Denzel took a seat opposite and fixedly glared into her big green eyes. Jess took this to be his version of a scare tactic.

Dream on, buddy, she thought, struggling to muffle a smile.

Was it to determine if she is telling the truth? Good luck with that one, she mused.

His sidekick was pacing and surveying the room as though looking for something worth stealing.

She was cheekily tempted to blurt out, "You won't find anything worth stealing in here, nor Susie hiding behind the furniture."

Thinking better of it she kept it buttoned. After all, she didn't want them getting the idea she was something of a smart mouth. No, sir, Jess had every intention to stay on point vowing to be on her best behaviour, the overriding factor she wanted them gone.

Denzel spoke decisively, his tone coming off like a real police person. "Right then, Jessica, can you tell me what you know about the man you and Susie had a chat with at Starbucks a week last Thursday?"

Without a thought the word "What!" burst forth from her lips, a touch louder than intended or warranted.

"Do you want me to repeat the question?" he asked in a slightly scathing voice.

Taken aback, she needed to gather her thoughts and quickly pull herself together.

"No, you don't need to repeat the question," she shot back. "I'm not stupid, I'm simply not sure who you're referring to, that's all. It might be news to you, Detective, but I talk to a lot of people. Or should I say a lot of people talk to me. Where are you getting this from anyway? Don't tell me they have CCTV in Starbucks?"

"That's a strange question, Jessica." Raising his eyebrows Baldwin glanced over at his partner.

"Well, there's plenty more where that came from," the words exploding from her mouth like an out of control freight train.

Oh, here we go, I've done it now, she thought.

Her smart mouth never let her down and led her into more trouble than she cared to own up to. Her promise to herself to tow the line was down the pan on the first question.

Baldwin, clearly taking a dim view of her attitude, rebuked her firmly.

"We are asking the questions here, Miss Simmons. This is a very serious matter. Your sister is missing and we intend to do all we can to locate her. When we ask you a question we don't expect smart mouth comments. We expect honest, concise answers. You comprehend?"

The cadence of his voice had gone up a few notches, and his face had changed to an even badder bad ass cop puffing up in the process.

Despite the fact she wasn't used to people speaking to her in such a tone and didn't particularly appreciate it she thought she'd better comply, if only to see where he was going with this surprising morsel of information.

Eyeballing him sporadically as he glanced at the notepad in front of him, her logic was telling her there was more on that notepad coming her way.

It could have rather worrying consequences if the truth got out. She didn't see how it could. All the same, she had better set about doing a little digging of her own.

Appearing vague and dipsey, she began with the version she thought would fly with the cops. More importantly, would get them off her back.

Her index finger was tapping her full red lips, and her eyes were jotting back and forth eyeing the ceiling decor attempting to at least appear as though rousing a memory.

A long empty pause came before her response.

"Let me see now."

A little more hesitation.

"Yeah, that could be it, the last time me and Susie had coffee. Well, not coffee exactly, hot chocolate to be accurate. You want me to be accurate, right?" She was directing her skit at both detectives as his partner had joined him. He obviously had not found anything worth stealing. "There was this tall oldish guy." She paused for a second in attempt to summon up an insult or two. The whole thing had well and truly pissed her off. "Yeah, old if it's the one you're referring to. I wouldn't say as old as you. He approached our table and started up a brief conversation with both Susie and me." She contemplated adding the word haggard but considered it to be a step too far.

Baldwin ignored the "old" comment.

As he paused the friendlier-looking cop took over.

"Now then, Jessica, do you think you remember what you talked about?"

"Not exactly, it was a while ago."

She wanted the questioning over. After this it was imperative she speak to lover boy.

She'd decided to ring him from her OWN phone and not the covert phone he had given her. He would pick up then, even if it's because he's annoyed.

"Right then, Jessica, we've established you remember the incident in Starbucks. Do you recall Susie mentioning seeing this same man on other occasions. Perhaps asking her if she wanted a lift home?"

Overwhelmed with disbelief, shock was replaced by nausea.

It was probably the one and only time words got stuck in her throat. The young girl was momentarily stunned into silence.

After a long pause she spoke, the parlance of her voice changing dramatically. The upbeat cocky voice was replaced by a more subdued quiet tone.

"No, I don't think she mentioned seeing him again. In fact, I'm pretty sure I would have remembered and told Mum. Is that what she told Mum?"

"Actually," said the detective, "speaking to Susie's friends we have reason to believe the man you conversed with in Starbucks approached her on at least two other occasions. It is our understanding that on one of these occasions he asked her where she was going and if she would like a lift."

Incredulous on hearing this, and hoping beyond hope the detective was not as good at reading people as had first crossed her suspicious little mind, she took a breath and tried her best not to come across as nonplussed.

All's becoming clear why they wanted this second interview. The penny had finally dropped, bounced back up and hit her on the head knocking her sideways.

Jess sat there with the look of someone deciphering and contemplating a problematic question. Folding her arms across her chest, her eyes darted from Baldwin to Simpkins then back again as if taking their question seriously.

"She definitely hadn't brought it up to me. I guess you're aware she only has a couple of blocks to walk. Same routine day in, day out. Walked with the same crowd. I can give you their names if it'll help," knowing full well Detective Simpkins had already spoken to the usual suspects.

"Oh, and by the way, I didn't see what car he drove if that's what you were gonna ask," offered Jess a little too smugly.

"That would've been my next question," said the bad ass cop, in a tone she didn't care much for but was becoming all too familiar with.

"Obviously, we were sat inside, not facing the car park."

The emphasis on the word "obviously" was as if it would be clear to the detectives where the best place in the coffee shop would be to sit.

"Susie liked to sit in those comfy armchair-type seats near the back. I think they're called bucket seats or something on those lines. Oh yeah, we were tucking into those huge chocolate chip muffins. Have you ever had one of those? They're yummy and sooooo filling. That gooey sweet chocolate stuff oozes out when you bite into the middle of 'em. Susie had come straight from school and said she was ravenous. She wanted another bun but I said no way, trying to get a raspberry white chocolate out of me. I said to her 'no way Mum will kill me.' She had a banana instead if I'm remembering correctly. Or maybe it could've been the other time we went to Starbucks she had the banana. I'll tell you something for nothing, for a tiny little thing that girl sure can put it away. Guess it's all the sports she does. Me not so much, one muffin is enough for me. Oh yes, I couldn't eat more than one of those bad boys. Cheekily, Susie kept spooning cream from my hot chocolate into hers, she loves the stuff. I remember getting my phone out to take a picture when she had a coating of it above her top lip. It looked like a big white fluffy moustache, hilarious. I intended to put it on Facebook. Didn't though. I forgot about it. I can get my phone if you want to see the picture. I don't think I've deleted it."

"Enough already, we get the picture," said the clearly irate detective. raising his hand indicating for Jess to cease with the rambling.

For a split second she had visions of the notebook flying in her direction.

The other detective completely bamboozled was hiding his face Jess figured, stifling a laugh.

"So, Jessica, the man clearly must have had to have gone out of his way to talk to you both. You were sitting at the back of the coffee shop, correct? He had to make his way past groups of people's tables to reach the both of you?" Denzel persisted, like a dog with a bone.

"Yeah, I guess so. I didn't say at the back, just near. I never thought about it really to be honest. Have you asked anyone else seeing as they've CCTV, maybe you'll be able to locate the other customers, right?" she enthused.

"We're asking the questions here, Miss Simmons," said Denzel, clearly narked after Jess's suggestion. His tone was bordering on offensive. Jess concluded he didn't have a lot of patience considering his profession.

Baldwin glanced at his watch then at his partner who'd averted his eyes, evidently finding the whole thing amusing, the young girl suggesting to him how to do his job.

Teenagers, he thought to himself, the worst kind of people to interview. They either sit there silently chewing gum or ramble on about irrelevant crap. I'll take interviewing drug dealers or mob bosses any day of the week. They are easier to read with a hell of a lot less rabbiting. Chocolate chip muffins, milk froth!

"As it happens there is no CCTV, Miss Simmons. Therefore, we need pertinent information from you. And I emphasise the word 'pertinent'," said Baldwin ramping up the narky voice.

"Oh, that's a shame," she replied, struggling in tempering her glee.

One all she thought.

I've got that little nugget from him and he now knows where we were seated.

Why the hell did I let that one slip? Me and my big mouth. I clearly didn't think that one through. I'll have to be more careful and think before I open my trap.

Jess pressed on with more detail of the ominous meet.

"For sure, he may have approached other people. I really have no idea, I can't say I noticed. Maybe he did, them not being as nice as me and Susie hence he talked with us," she said, hoping this would count as co-operating and be enough of an answer.

Baldwin fought on, he was nowhere near finished.

"By your reckoning you had the suspect in full view for a few minutes, therefore I take it you got a good look at him? We will require you to give a detailed description," he said purposefully.

Rankled by the word "suspect" and of course wondering which of Susie's friends had furnished the detective with this, she contemplated a little fact-finding mission.

Not for one minute did she think her boyfriend had anything to do with this but, and it was a big but, by arranging that impromptu meet in order to gawp at Susie in the flesh, ostensibly he had made himself suspect number one.

Thank god there wasn't any CCTV in the vicinity. Or was there? She didn't trust the cop any more than he trusted her.

"Wow, you have a suspect already?" enthused the young girl, her tone reminiscent of someone who had just been informed they were going on an all-expenses paid trip to Hawaii and had better start packing.

"A person of interest. We're running down all our leads and this came to light," offered the friendlier-looking detective.

"You haven't answered the question, Miss Simmons." Again, Denzel was crazily persistent.

By the sound of it what little patience he had had gone the way of her boyfriend. Vaporised.

Wrestling her angst, she felt the way which he addressed her topped with his tone really disrespectful.

He said "Miss Simmons" in an almost derogatory fashion. It crossed her mind maybe his tone wouldn't have been as derisive had her dad joined her. Then again, was her dad party to this? She thought not. Playing the dizzy blonde Jess said she had forgotten the question.

"Could you give us a detailed description of the man you and you sister conversed with at Starbucks on the day in question please, Miss Simmons," the emphasis this time on the "please" as well as the "Miss Simmons". The delivery was sharper coupled with a more precise tone.

Grappling to pull up a detailed description, Jess reverted back to the jotting eyes, a serious expression and lip tapping, completing the look with total bewilderment.

"Well now, let me see. I suppose he wasn't bad-looking for an older guy. Had the look of a pharmaceutical rep or a rather flash used car salesman if you ask me."

Offering up that she knew what a pharmaceutical rep looked like as when his dad's secretary had an appointment, she occasionally manned the office and did her job which, incidentally, she was very good at, much more efficient than the secretary herself.

More long-winded garble for the detectives to digest followed.

"I don't mean one of those grey haired or bald cheap suit salesmen," looking both Baldwin and Detective Simpkins up and down as if on the verge of saying something inappropriate about their attire. "I'd say the suit looked Armani if I'm being honest. I know a bit about Armani as Dad wears Armani suits. When he's not in scrubs that is. Plus, Mum's got a few Armani threads."

This is heading down the same path as the earlier muffin anecdote, only replacing it with designer clobber. Jess knew damn well this wasn't the sort of detail they were hoping to glean from her. So far she thought she'd told them precisely nada. She prided herself on the fact she could talk endlessly about absolutely nothing. It usually had the desired outcome as they, whoever they were, gave up and left her alone.

Less than enthused Detective Baldwin butted in halting her in her tracks, having no desire to hear about all the designer gear the family owned.

"I think we'll have you come down to the station and have you sit with one of our sketch artists," he said, clearly at the end of his tether.

"I have to say you don't seem very worried about your sister. I deem from this you don't like her. You're not exactly coming over as wanting to help."

121

Baldwin felt compelled to offer up his somewhat acerbic observation.

"Is that a question?" Jess countered sharply.

Equally as biting and before he could respond, Jess gave her opinion on his observation. Her tone was more uppity than it had previously been, if that was possible.

"Of course I like her. Everybody likes Susie. You ask anyone. I doubt anyone has a bad word to say about her. She's pretty, smart, thoughtful, sweet, one of the nicest people you'd ever want to meet. She hasn't been gone twenty-four hours, I just don't know what the great hoo-ha is in aid of, that's all. She's smart, real smart, she wouldn't do anything stupid. I don't like your inference."

Her answer was expressed hurried and sharply.

"Why do you think we're here making enquiries?" said Denzel's partner. "When we have a young person who goes missing like your sister we take it very seriously. We have to explore all avenues and speak to people they associate with, to find out if anything, or anyone, stands out."

The detective got to his feet. As he did so he handed her his card. "If you can think of anything, however small, please ring me. Meantime, we'll arrange for you to meet the sketch artist as soon as possible. Preferably today."

Both slowly took steps to the door leading to the hall. As they did so, Jess thought she heard Denzel mutter something under his breath, words to the effect, "Well, she'd have to be smarter than this one, don't you think?" There was no answer from his partner, just a wide grin sufficed as a reply.

"Cheeky bastard," was her silent retort.

She was smiling inside as she thought, Never fails, the dumb blonde act comes through for me every time. It's not let me down yet. Not that dumb, am I? I got a sight more out of them than they got out of me, she smiled to herself.

I'm glad that's over, for now at least. Her primary objective had to be to talk to Jack and give him the heads up regarding the questioning this morning. She wanted to clock his reaction to her sister missing. This would determine if she revealed to him the cops had him down as their prime suspect. Maybe that

would scare the shit out of him. Then maybe not. She figured
it'd take a hell of a lot to put the wind up her fella.

Chapter Sixteen

Groundhog Day (Vicky)

"Ows keeping?" Knock, knock, knock. "Ows keeping?" These words were expelled over and over.

This unfamiliar but nevertheless welcome voice roused me from a deep disturbing fog like unconsciousness. Frozen with fear, I strove to assimilate what had happened. Where the hell am I? What is this place?

Terrified, here was another daunting predicament to navigate my brain around. Disbelieving this could be happening, I strove to compute the horror I'd somehow been propelled into as my heart registered one hell of a low moment.

As opposed to my past life I now inhabit a monstrous evil world, a world where I'm forced to adapt and accept the crimes that are perpetrated against me. Accept that I'm powerless to control anything that these nasty evil individuals do to my body.

Snapping my head back to the here and now, the doggedly persistent voice is in no way easing. I'm slowly transporting my mind back to the land of the living. My senses that are gradually unfurling are becoming clearer, the synapses surrounding my brain firing up like tiny nerves being switched to the on position.

Now I get it, that term brain fog. I'm totally disorientated with the ability to think straight stripped from me. Places and people are grappling for a place in my head, my mind overloaded.

Unnerving blackness envelops me and I'm unable to see. Had I gone blind? Snap out of it, I rebuked myself sharply. Get a grip, it was duct tape or some other blindfold if I were a betting woman.

Persistent to a fault my noisy new friend, I'll give her that. She was not willing to abandon me for some weird, unknown reason. The voice was unrelenting, the volume amplified and a slightly more irritated tone adopted.

Some unknown person recognises I'm here, wondering at that very moment where exactly here is. Wherever I am, my heart and soul is praying silently to be rescued.

On the upside, if anything could be considered an upside, my head is coming round a little with each passing minute.

Short term memory not so much though as my thoughts are jumbled, but they're heading in the right direction. The clearer they became the more unanswered questions bombard my head.

Where the hell am I now? Back in the basement? I suppose the why requires no explanation. The who throws up questions, I suppose the list is widening on that score. After all I've been through, what's in store for me now?

Thoughts, questions, dilemmas are ricocheting around my pounding head, the thumping indicative to having been whacked with a mallet.

Figuring out where I am is a challenge in itself. One thing's for sure, I'm not in that condo. For reasons unbeknown, the condo flew into my head piercing my messy ponderings. The mystery surrounding how I got out of there and who I came into contact with to bring me to this point is baffling and frightening. It's quite evident to me I'm experiencing gaps of lost time.

As if struck by bolt of lightning a vision flashed into my head. Then a question. Could it be my memory is returning? Then a second question. Do I really want to remember?

Simon, a needle. Oh my god, what had that slippery bastard done?

I figured I'd blacked out with his face seared into my head. Other than that everything was woolly.

I had to think and think quickly. Be proactive, take the bull by the horns and get out of here.

It doesn't take a rocket scientist to acknowledge I'm in a whole heap of trouble. Again. Whoever had the audacity to do this to me possesses nothing in way of humanity or scruples and means business. Evil, perverse business.

The unknown doer clearly had no intention of allowing me to do a runner. Painful as it is, I slung all my efforts into shifting my position. I'm hardly able to move due to the restraints. I come to realise I'm well and truly stuck and I'm going nowhere.

My brain endeavoured to grasp the enormity of my plight. I was incredibly uncomfortable as I lay tethered in pain. My laboured breathing was pulling in the damp smell which had lodged firmly in my nostrils and seeping slowly into my lungs. The noisy one continued ten to the dozen, hollering and knocking for all she's worth. I'd already concluded it to be a female and she knows I'm here alright, not me personally but someone. Perhaps she saw me brought in and has an inkling of what's going on.

Having no intention of letting up my mouth did what it's been known to do, make an almighty racket. I could taste the nasty tape which hindered my speech somewhat. Duct tape had been forced tightly into my mouth as well as round it, painfully cutting into the corners of my lips affording me no possibility in enunciating actual words.

Jeez, what had gone down for me to end up in this state? Is this how it all ends? Notions on how I must be the unluckiest girl in the world ran parallel with my fearful ramblings, pitiful, morose, obscure ramblings.

This, my newest predicament, is reminiscent to the very first night I was taken, my initiation into the world of torture, sadism and utter humiliation.

It always reverts back to him in my head where it all began with that sadistic sexual deviant.

Is that what this is, the road I'm heading down? A repeat performance of that torture? I shuddered at the memory. I'd rather die than go through that again, I thought defiantly.

My mouth and throat were tremendously dry. The only thing I do know for certain is I'm in dire need of water.

Although I'm no expert on the subject, I'd put money on me having been drugged. I was nauseous and dizzy, compounded with hearing what can only be described as a whirring sensation. I had a distinct feeling if I were to stand up I'd drop like a stone.

It occurred to me I might possibly be able to manoeuvre my torso into a different position, ideally pull my body upright to allow me to assuage my nausea and dizziness. The fear of choking if I vomited terrified me. However, the angle and manner I'd been placed afforded me no leeway for manoeuvre whatsoever.

The time was endless and my whole body was consumed by the most incredible dull throbbing pain.

The way they'd positioned me, whoever they are, knew what they were doing. My wrists were squeezed tightly together with what felt like reams of thin rope, my arms raised above my head.

Even shallow breathing in this position hurt. My ribs were bruised and sore. I'm doing myself no favours tugging and pulling but I have to do something. In pure survival mode, the choice along with everything else taken from me, I'm pulling, wriggling and using every ounce of strength, but my endeavours were fruitless.

Far from evoking the desired result, it's evident I'm making matters worse. My position is perilous. I sensed the wetness of my own blood as the rope cut into me. I'd thought since my wrist was so tiny I could maybe pull them through the bindings.

I deduced this rope was fastened to a bedpost. My body was kind of twisted, essentially angled on my right side, my ankles secured in the same way, fastened to what I hadn't a clue. My arms and torso were secured in such a position my limbs were tantamount to being stretched. I figured the way my body and muscles hurt it's likely I've been in the exact same position for hours, maybe days. Who knows? I don't know anything anymore. This in itself is torture.

This had Jake written all over it. He's found me or the delectable Simon delivered me to him on a silver platter.

Metaphorically speaking I put my best foot forward and made the loudest noise possible, the scream suggestive of the roar from a lion or other beast, exuding a loud desperate noise giving my persistent friend a run for her money. I concluded if I had any chance at all then making an almighty racket would be the way to go.

If I've got it right help could be within my grasp. I had to hope and pray. Hope is all you have to cling to in the grimmest of situations, and I'd been in a truckload of those lately.

My throat was sore and dry, nonetheless, I ventured to keep up the commotion. After all my efforts I'm down to generating throaty hoarse sounds. It'll have to suffice I said in my mind as I gave it another almighty shot literally scraping my voice box. I'd every intention of sticking at it until I elicited a response, or my voice packed in.

And that's exactly what I did.

As the seconds turned to minutes and the minutes passed, my resolve was slowly melting.

I'm losing it, losing all control. Frustrated and hysterical, my screams are now replaced by uncontrollable sobs. The cries grew louder and louder, tears welling up and stinging my eyes as they'd nowhere to go.

My only recourse was to lie there and wait. Wait and think. And fret and worry. But there is no question in my mind of me giving up or giving in, especially after I had come this far.

My friends needed me. I have to do for them what I know they'd do for me, namely be strong, tenacious and bring about their freedom.

I wouldn't have thought it possible, but in a last-ditch effort my woeful cries hiked up a few decibels.

From the moment I'd come round the banging and shouting was constant, then I noticed it ceased abruptly. Stopped altogether. Nothing. Complete silence. I could only conclude the person making the racket had left.

Is this it now? The opportunity lost as my tormentor returns?

I couldn't eradicate the notion the tormentor could be on the way back this very minute, maybe he was outside the door.

My imagination was fraught with all manner of scenarios, my mind going in a million different directions. Perhaps he'd popped out for supplies or had brought punters back.

Whilst lost in the depths of despair thinking about all the horrible things and people I had encountered on this horrendous journey, I pulled myself up. I could hear footsteps and chattering. I was spot on, both male and female voices gradually growing louder and nearer.

Could it be my wretched animal noises yielded results?

Chapter Seventeen

My Knight in Shining Armour

A loud masculine voice resumed where the lady had left off.

"Police! Open up!"

Again, more pronounced with added volume.

"POLICE! OPEN UP!"

Oh, thank you, Jesus, I said in silent prayer, hankering to say the words out loud.

The lady clearly sensed something afoot and had smartly called the cops, all this going some way in comforting my cotton wool brain.

Deluged with pain and scared out of my wits, the sarcasm still made a break for it bubbling to the surface and lodging firmly into my brain space. Of course, that's all they were at this point, sarcastic thoughts.

The no nonsense Yorkshire girl that I am was itching to open her mouth and sprout what ran rampant through my head as I caught his demand, specifically to open up the door.

Do you think I want to lay here trussed up like a bloody turkey at thanksgiving?

The officer pounded again, forceful and with more purpose.

The only offerings from beneath my duct taped mouth at this juncture amounted to a total illegible racket. Even I couldn't make out the words and I'm the one making the row.

Despite my noisy exasperated cries I caught the sound of what I took to be a key card in the door. And just like magic, it flew open.

Sarcasm aside, with every cell in my body I ached to cry out and express my gratitude, the words careering out like a foreign language.

Amazing relief washed over me and with it came fresh air. A wonderfully soft warm breeze fanned my aching limbs. My hearing was indicating at least one person entered, footsteps heading my way.

"Police, miss. Are you alright?" The voice that of the same police officer.

Close now, I could feel his presence, his nearness, coupled with a slight whiff of aftershave.

He was inches away, shielding me from the breeze.

Again the most ludicrous of questions.

"Miss, are you alright?"

Maybe they have a script to follow I theorised not wishing to make a big deal of it.

I guess he's speaking to me as who else could he be addressing? This is all too ridiculous considering my mouth along with the rest of me is duct taped, trussed up.

Am I expected to respond?

Oh, and by the way, do I look alright? hurtled into my head.

I'd vowed to keep my sarcasm button well and truly switched to mute.

The last thing I needed was to get on the wrong side of the cops. To me, along with the Spanish speaking lady, they were my saviours.

I exuded more of the guttural sounds from under the plastic tape hoping he'd got the message, my tongue going ten to the dozen enunciating my anguish.

"Help me please," were the words being expelled from my lips. In reality I could have done with a translator.

The cadence of my voice was stepping up a gear, my sorry cries becoming more vocal. Thankfully, the daft questions ceased.

Finally, they're getting it, my police friend is getting it.

The only dialogue from his end was his intention to free me of my bindings as quickly as possible.

The desire and longing to be released took over every inch of my body. Instead of struggling I shuddered with anticipation and hope.

Listening attentively and absorbing every word out of his mouth, the tone of his voice took on a quiet soft tempo. The words and tone were immensely soothing compared with the stern demands delivered minutes before.

The reassurance and elation at having him here with me were indescribable. Simply knowing I'm not alone. The comforting declarations were from what I visualised to be a relatively young policeman. I hung on his every word.

"This is going to hurt but I'll do my best to be gentle," his voice authoritative but at the same time reassuring.

Slowly, he steadily peeled the tape from my face, sensitively walking me through each action step by step, apprising me of his every move.

I felt his fingers gently unpick the tape from around my mouth. I gasped as the final strip left my face, appreciating the deep solid breaths. Somehow that familiar musty smell was exaggerated, a split second later it had taken up residence in my parched throat.

My policeman friend allowed me a few seconds before continuing with the task in hand.

I think he was fully grasping how much this meant to me.

This tape would no doubt be bagged as evidence, the premise it could yield fingerprints. He took great care in loosening the tape which had been wrapped around my head akin to a tight bandage covering a head wound.

"Nice and gently does it," he murmured, unwrapping the horrible stuff from my eyes.

At that moment relief engulfed me accompanied by a dash of hope. Could it be salvation is within my reach? Saved from my hellish nightmare, my unknown tormentor.

The light blinding, my eyes adjusted slowly. Blinking, I shook my head in an attempt to expand my normal vision. At last things were beginning to come into focus triggering me to scan the room. By the look of it I was in a motel room, a rather low rent motel room.

Accompanying my affable cop friend I spied another cop. I guess they come in twos. This guy was his partner, an older guy, a little portly though I wouldn't say chubby.

He stood nonchalantly in the doorway more out than in, assuming the role of guard duty.

I briefly glanced in his direction. He slid me a look, rapidly averting his eyes outside the open door. I could be way off the mark but I sensed he'd rather be anywhere else than where he stood.

He's probably seen it all over the years, everything there is to see as a Vegas beat cop.

From my perspective it was a sense of relief having the two of them there. If the perpetrator is lurking, waiting to pounce, Mr grey hair cop holding up the door would hopefully have the desired effect.

Then something else hit me like a bolt out of the blue. My clothes, or lack of. Embarrassment shrouded me. I was barely decent wearing only my underwear. I could feel my face colouring.

I was gobsmacked that I could actually react in such a way after what I'd been put through.

It was strange that my state of undress alluded me when I initially came round, not forgetting the headache akin to a volcano erupting in my head which still caused me to wince. I guess all things considered it overshadowed the feeling of being semi-naked.

Had I been raped? Sexually assaulted in some way? Maybe I'm in denial, but it didn't feel as though I'd been touched in that way.

My imagination ran riot with all manner of crushing visions. Anything could have been done to me whilst I was out cold. I recoiled and shook at the thought of what most certainly would've been my fate should the police have not shown up.

I'd undoubtedly be done for had the lady ignored this room and gone on to the next. Something inside me couldn't help but find this slightly baffling as to why she persisted and didn't simply move on.

As I'm trying to apply logic to the whole thing my policemen friend continued in his efforts. It appeared the wrist ties were proving problematic. The blue plastic gloves he was decked out in were not helping matters, hampered due to the way the rope had been fashioned. Tremendously tight, and knotted, both wrists were brandished snugly together, palms facing. My wrists that were wet and bloodied continued to bleed as he fought on to free me. I didn't say anything but I guess he knew I'd done this to myself in an attempt to wrestle free.

Observing his colleague going all out and seemingly fighting a losing battle, the older one left his post.

Scared, I caught the sound of my own voice as I instinctively shouted after him.

"Oi, where're you going? Please, please don't leave."

In a calm, friendly tone the rookie cop did his level best to reassure me, clearly sensing my fear. Fear which lurked vehemently near the surface of what remained of my former self.

"You're OK. I'm not leaving you alone. My partner has just nipped out to get something from the squad car. He'll be back in a minute," he said reassuring me.

A minute later he's back with what I recognised to be a cutting implement. Passing the device, he informed his colleague an ambulance was a few minutes out.

He then took root back at his post. Same spot, same pose, arms crossed high up on his chest. Eyes trained on the outside.

"Thank you for coming back." Five little words of gratitude left my lips rather sheepishly.

Tilting his cap in acknowledgement, I caught the kind sentiment, "You're welcome, miss."

The rookie cop didn't look up as we spoke.

He was methodically sawing the rope and I eyed him fixedly noting the care he took in ensuring the blade stayed clear of my bloodied, tender skin.

After a short while he said, "Steady does it, here we go." With that my hands suddenly sprung free.

That moment, that joy.

Free from that hideously stiff rope surpassed the sight of the blood and rope burns. It wasn't going to faze me, that sense of freedom at being afforded the use of my hands. Incredible.

Sheer relief triggered a flood of tears. The fact I'm one step closer to getting the hell out of there. No doubt about it, I was overflowing with gratitude.

At last freedom was within my grasp. Daring, hoping, I could be out of harm's way edging back towards some semblance of normality. All of this new terror was yet to sink in, reflecting normality will have to remain a future goal.

My ears suddenly filled with the sound of sirens. The ambulance was edging nearer. Double the people. This thought fuelled my minor contentment.

As he released my feet I thanked him. There was no escaping his deductions, evidenced by his facial expressions working me free. I'd say he was notably shocked by my disposition.

Mr grey hair not so much.

His counterpart was not jaded. Maybe he was more perceptive with a different take on things, exhibiting all the signs of a sincere, empathetic person oblivious to the facts and murky details. Moreover, absorbing my fear and hurt.

Just then my new cop friend thoughtfully grabbed a towel from the adjoining bathroom, carefully wrapping it around me to cover my modesty. A welcome gesture which I appreciated after which he beckoned me towards a chair. A rather out of place high backed chair. I was assisted in getting my aching limbs onto the seat, placing one of the pillows behind me for support and handing me a small bottle of water. Another welcome gesture. I whispered my thanks.

Apart from me sipping the water an unnatural quietness hung in the air.

I began to mull things over, recycling the same thoughts and questions.

What would've transpired should the cops have not come a knocking? Where would I be now?

Bet he, they, or whoever did this to me are none too happy. Maybe they were lurking in the car park watching. Watching and waiting. From the chair I could see past the cop on guard duty, noticing the car park was quite full.

A lady who I took to be the maid stood behind grey hair in the doorway. She looked scared and shocked. He beckoned her not to come any closer. The words "Jesus, Mary and Joseph" could be heard in broken English.

In broken Spanish I caught him asking her if she could bring a coffee from the reception.

134

I get he's not fazed or shocked by my predicament, this is Vegas after all. But coffee?

Guard duty returned to his post contentedly sipping away at the free coffee.

His colleague smiled, rolled his eyes and shook his head from side to side in a disapproving but light-hearted fashion.

I felt a hint of the "old me" return for a second.

My voice was barely audible but the nonetheless the words left my mouth. "Why doesn't he go the whole hog and pop down to Dunkin' donuts? Don't mind me."

My forthrightness brought a grin from the younger officer, who was no doubt well versed in regard to his partner's ways and mannerisms. It was one of those "anything for an easy life" partnerships.

Unexpectedly, he softly caressed my cheek with the back of his hand, his gentle touch warm and affectionate. I took this as him expressing his agreement with my sentiment. Still, it was a strange gesture if not a little forward on his part.

Grey hair having addressed him earlier told me the younger cop's name to be Andy.

Andy my saviour.

Andy the kind caring Las Vegas police officer.

I sat in the worn scruffy armchair waiting, waiting for the ambulance to take me out of this dreadful place to safety.

Looking at me attentively, Andy broke the silence.

"I need to ask you a couple of questions in order to get a bit of background information, primarily to pass to the detectives who'll be meeting you at the hospital. You'll see a doctor first so don't worry." It was spoken in the same soft caring tone he'd adopted since he'd set foot in here. He got out a notebook and a pen to take my details. "Can I have your name please?"

"Victoria Walker. I go by Vicky," I replied, wondering why I'd offered the last part.

"How old are you, Vicky?"

"Twenty-three. I was twenty-two when all this began." Although not requested I gave him my date of birth.

"Married?"

"Nope," came my response a little too readily.

He paused, clearly apprehensive asking the next question.

"Now, Vicky, can you... do you remember how you came to be here? Were you restrained?"

Trepidation swept over me. Where to begin? At the very beginning just over six weeks prior or my most recent encounter with Simon? Which although I wouldn't say torturous, was equally unnerving.

Without expressing as much, all I could think at the time was this is gonna be one hell of a long convoluted story.

Silence hung in the air.

Vague jumbled recollections of these last few weeks were running back and forth in my head. I paused as I stared at the grubby carpet.

My kind, young policeman was sensing my trepidation, and clearly not wanting to rush me kindly allowed me a moment to gather my thoughts.

He obviously wanted to make speaking about my ordeal a little easier.

He spoke before I could conjure up any words.

"There's no need to be embarrassed."

"I'm not. Well, I am," I replied, my tone unnecessarily sharper than it ought to have been.

In a rather doleful tone I came forward with something to start the dialogue. I didn't want to reel off the whole last six weeks here in this seedy place, plus we hadn't time before the ambulance showed up. I started with my recollection of the last thing I do remember.

"I don't know how I got here or even where here is. Some bastard did this to me. Sorry for swearing. I think, no, I'm sure I've been drugged. I kind of remember a sharp stab in my neck."

Instinctively, I pulled my long hair to one side so he could take a look.

He leaned in slightly to survey the damage.

"Yes, definitely a needle mark. Oh, and swearing's permitted," he said, presenting me with a warm smile as he imparted this, at the same time writing on the notepad.

His coffee drinking partner glanced over as Andy delivered this comment, his interest piqued.

Just as we were having this conversation two paramedics appeared at the door.

One of the paramedics put an arm around me for me to lean on, placing me firmly but gently on the stretcher. Andy explained I would need blood work done, rationalising this request by pointing out I have "two" needle marks on my neck along with a little dried blood.

Embarrassment came rushing back for the second time in less than thirty minutes. I imagined how they'd view this, how it'd look from their perspective. The scene in its entirety: semi-naked young woman tied to a bed in a lower end motel, rope burns on her wrists, duct tape and rope clearly visible in clear plastic sealed evidence bags.

Knowing I'm on route to the hospital is comforting, viewing this as a place of safety, sanctuary.

Surprisingly, and not sure if normal for an incident such as this, Andy purported he'd be along later after his shift to check on me.

Chapter Eighteen

Shining Star (Jess)

Increased anxiety levels notwithstanding, Jess felt incredibly relieved. Relieved Baldwin had quit glaring at her, and more importantly firing stupid accusatory questions her way.

Listening to that condescending tone had become tiresome, disrespectful to say the least. His words were ringing in her ears including the way he used her name, "Miz Simmons".

Bloody charming. She'd a good mind to put in a complaint and see how that went down with his superiors, she thought on leaving the room, the room he'd commandeered as his own personal interrogation room.

The two detectives had made tracks but left one of the uniformed officers in the house, drinking coffee and snacking as had become the norm.

Their home reverted back to the same deathly silence it had before they'd shown up.

Mum not speaking to Dad. Dad not speaking to Mum, and neither of them conversing with Auntie Jean by the look of things. Not a single person wheeling out the sympathy wagon for her. Not so much as how did the "interview" go?

Is she OK? Does she need to talk? Nada.

Really, Jess thought bitterly. Am I invisible? Reinforcing her belief that this is how it'd always been in her family.

"Bottom of the totem pole that's me," she moaned quietly. "It sure is a good job we haven't a dog, I'd be way below the mutt. Nobody gives two hoots what I have to say or think," she went on under her breath.

As not one of them had taken the slightest bit of interest in Jess's police talk, interview or whatever it purported to be, she'd decided not to volunteer anything. She was sure as hell not prepared to go through the whole meaningless Starbucks escapade again.

If only her parents knew what she knew, she sniggered to herself a little too smugly. It'd be a different story. Oh yeah, then they'd want to talk to her, feeling more self-assured at her ponderances than perhaps she should.

She was mulling over Denzel's assumption that the same man we talked to in the coffee bar was the same one who offered Susie a lift as ludicrous.

Evaluating the situation in her head, no way could this guy be Jack, if at all there was a guy.

"Gotta get out of here like yesterday or I'm gonna go nuts," she muttered under her breath heading upstairs to her room.

The anger she'd felt earlier was beginning to dissolve as he flooded her daydreams.

Only good things were roaming around her young brain now. Good things they'd done together and more importantly good things he'd done to her. A sharp tingle ran through her body as the memory of the last time they'd slept together surfaced. She blushed as it played out in her head.

She knew she could never stay mad at him for long. She knew he knew it too.

Jess reminisced about the Starbucks meet, admonishing herself at her thoughts. Ridiculous thoughts that were clamouring for room inside her head.

In those early days of their relationship Jack had readily agreed to drop her more than a block away from the house, as the last thing he'd want to get her into hot water. He had never relented and taken her near to the house however much her feet were killing her due to her three-inch heels.

It wouldn't make sense to offer to drop Susie at the house.

Although she never brought it up, in her own mind she knew his motive to be self-serving. She'd got his number clear as day, look after number one. Common sense dictated he'd be in a shit load more trouble than her if their relationship came to light.

There isn't a person in their right mind who'd agree that it's OK for them to be boyfriend and girlfriend, the age gap putting him up there with her folks.

It was certainly not in his interest to be spotted talking to a fourteen year old schoolgirl.

Changing tact with her thoughts it was a complete mystery why he hadn't been in touch or texted.

Another more ominous scenario flashed across her mind. Maybe he'd had an accident on the freeway. She shook her head to eliminate such thoughts, she didn't even want to go there.

She was pausing to gather her thoughts and contemplate her next move. Out of loyalty she felt duty bound to at least give Jack the heads up. She didn't want him getting caught up in all this. Worryingly, she came to the conclusion that this might end things for them if he got dragged into this drama. All this was bad enough without losing the man she loved into the bargain.

No, she had to delve deeper and do her due diligence and do some investigative work of her own. She would speak to her sister's friends to find out which of Susie's pals were furnishing Baldwin with the details he had in that notebook, feeling certain the detective was keeping something from her.

Mind you, by the way he squinted his eyes and glared at her, she'd an idea he had her sussed and knew she was spoon feeding him a load of garbage.

Invisible to her dad, mum and Auntie Jean, she sneaked upstairs back to her room, wanting to dress in more suitable attire.

In the main Jess knew all her sister's friends. She would start with her best friend Beth, then onto the twins, killing two birds with one stone. She'd work her way from there. All three lived in Henderson only a few minutes apart.

Now for the hard bit. How to get out of the door without getting an earful.

Grabbing her purse, Jess put her covert phone in the pocket she had secretly sewn into the lining of her jeans, also being careful not to forget her "proper" phone. She tentatively made her way down the winding staircase to the hall, then she picked up the keys for her mum's Range Rover and headed towards the outside door.

"Won't be long, Dad, just nipping to Beth's then on to the twins' house to see if we can make a poster and get a Facebook page going or something. Bye."

The words were out before he'd noticed who'd spoken them let alone what was said.

"Wow, that was easier than I thought," she said out loud as she climbed into the car and closed the door.

Three minutes and she's pulling into Beth's parents' drive. Before even climbing out of the vehicle Beth came rushing out. Flinging her arms round Jess it was evident she'd been crying, her parents looking on just inside the door.

Jess gave her a gentle hug and walked with her to the front door.

Beth's parents were genuinely good people who Susie was very fond of. The feeling mutual, they thought the world of her. But then who didn't like Susie? Reflecting back, it hit Jess that Susie and Beth had been friends right back to kindergarten.

"Come on in, Jess," prompted Beth's mum Anne.

She told Beth how she'd spoken to her mum and Auntie Jean that morning and of course last night after they'd heard the shocking news. Also, that Detective Simpkins had called round in person to talk to Beth. Naturally, he'd had a barrage of questions, explaining this is normal procedure and talking to everyone involved in Susie's life.

"Take a seat, let me get you some juice or do you want a warm drink? Have you eaten?" came the friendly tone from Anne.

"I had a granola bar earlier," Jess offered pathetically.

For a split second she nearly put forward the fact her mum hadn't cooked last night or this morning. She checked herself quickly realising it would sound insensitive at a time like this, not to mention she should be doing her bit with regard to domestic chores.

Anne tutted and shook her head. "You poor girl. That's no good. It's not enough for a growing girl like yourself. If you're anything like Susie…" her voice trailed off.

Jess could see the anguish written all over her face. The mere mention of Susie's name put Anne close to tears, putting her arm around Jess's shoulder and giving a gentle squeeze.

"Is it alright if I go with Beth to her bedroom to have a little chat, Anne?" she asked in the sweetest tone she could dredge up. Beth was clearly upset and guessing she was even more so after speaking to the cop about her bestie last night.

This was Jess at her best.

Acting, speaking in that cute soft girly tone, she trusted this would be enough to swing it, knowing full well she couldn't say what she had to say and more importantly ask in front of the grown-ups.

She planned to stay put until she had squeezed every bit of information out of Beth that she'd given that detective last night.

Pausing briefly Anne glanced over at her daughter as if seeking approval.

A slither of a smile at her mum saw Beth rise from her seat. She eyed Jess quizzingly as if wondering what she could possibly want from her.

Beth beckoned her into an adjacent room.

Jess took this to be her dad's study. Apart from a couple of chairs and a large wooden desk by the window, the floor to ceiling bookshelves dominated the room. Adjacent to one of the book filled walls was a small ladder.

Fleetingly, Jess had an image of Beth as a youngster climbing that ladder. Gosh, I'd have had fun with that, came the second fleeting thought, almost breaking out in a smile visualising the books flying through the air.

"Your dad OK with us using his study?" she enquired.

"Yeah, he's cool," came the sombre reply.

"My dad's a stickler about his office," said Jess, surveying the room, wondering how to broach the subject of the dodgy guy in the car who'd supposedly spoken to Susie.

Making small talk about how precious her dad is with regard to his office was an opener.

"Anyone would think he had something in there we weren't allowed to see. It wouldn't at all surprise me if he were hiding something or someone in there," she offered jokingly.

At that instant, the very moment it left her lips, she realised what she'd said.

That flippant comment was wrong in so many ways. Every kind of wrong especially in light of why she was there in Beth's home. I'll have to start thinking before I open my big gob, she thought, hoping she could skate over her latest faux pas.

She sincerely hoped Beth was too caught up in her grief to be listening properly to her inherent chit-chat, and if she'd caught it simply take it as Jess being her usual gregarious self.

She decided it's imperative she get to the point, having decided if Beth doesn't pan out she'd get back in the car and go on to the "Olsen twins" as Jess called them behind their backs. Then she'd go back home before they got the cops on her for being missing. "Oh yeah, like that would go down," she said to herself mockingly.

Overhearing the dialogue between the cop and her folks meant she'd better get her skates on. It had been decided she would meet with the sketch artist while her parents were at the station for an update on the investigation.

"What's on your mind, Jess?" Beth asked sweetly.

She took a breath and hesitated.

Hesitated and hoped. Hoped that she chose the right words. Here goes, the great reveal.

"It appears that, and I'm not sure when, some guy approached Susie and offered her a lift home. The police mentioned it this morning. I wondered if she'd talked to you and revealed any details. A description, or the car maybe?"

There it was, words spoken, out in the open. Her heart fluttered in anticipation.

One down, twenty or so more friends to go.

Beth stared at her, pausing for what seemed like forever, contemplating the question as if it related to quantum physics.

Bewildered, Beth began with her recollection of what had passed between herself and her best friend.

"Yeah, there was a guy. I'm not sure why you're asking me about it though. I thought you knew all about it, sorry, him."

"Why would you say that?" Jess asked more than a little perturbed.

"Cos Susie said he was the person who you'd both met and spoken to at length in Starbucks the other week. I'm only going by what she said mind you. I don't have first-hand knowledge of course as I wasn't there at the time." Beth continued. "He was an acquaintance of yours or at least somebody you know."

143

Fuming inside, this was all she needed. This is what Beth had told the cops.

"And he offered her a lift to where?" Jess continued, questioning Beth in a tone that had the makings of a police interrogation.

Appearing anxious as though she'd done or said something out of order, or that she shouldn't have said anything at all, Beth said, "Well, if I'm remembering correctly, Susie bumped into him a couple of times. One time he offered her a lift, or was it a coffee, or both maybe. I'm saying bumped into, it was more like he pulled alongside her in his car. I could be wrong but that might be when he gave her the impression that he knew you. Something he dropped into the conversation I think." She rattled on as Jess's mind computed the enormity of what had been disclosed. "Mind you, people say that, don't they? That they know someone you know, sort of implying they know the family therefore you're safe with them. As if that makes them trustworthy. You follow what I mean? A sort of ruse to get you in the car," Beth said rhetorically.

"Yeah, they say that. I guess that's how it came about. I certainly didn't know him. There was this guy in Starbucks but he spoke to Susie more than me. You know how chatty she can be? Talk the hind legs of a donkey that one. We didn't see his car as we were sat at the back so wouldn't know if he had a flash car, truck or arrived in a taxi," Jess offered by way of explanation.

"I hear you," Beth said in agreement.

She gave Beth a meaningful look.

"You and I both know Susie is too clued up to get in anyone's car. Especially a stranger's, right?" Jess said desperately needing confirmation Beth wasn't going to make a big deal out of this. She was having the distinct feeling she was adding bits each time she told the story. She needed to know what Beth had actually told the police, hoping but guessing she hadn't reeled off the bit about Susie purporting the mysterious flash car driver was an acquaintance of hers.

If it had been thrown into the mix she deduced the detectives would have hauled her ass down to the station for more intense questioning. How could she broach this without coming across as though she had something to hide? Or more importantly attempting to hold back vital information from the police, she deliberated uneasily.

Jess studied the young girl's face wondering if there was an easy way to say what she wanted to say.

"Look, I don't know how to put this, Beth. Without sounding selfish or that I'm more concerned about myself or what people think of me I don't want this misconstrued, but you didn't bring this up to the police did you?"

Beth met her gaze but said nothing.

"I mean that you think Susie might have assumed I knew the guy who offered her a ride, coffee or whatever?" Jess asked in a worried tone. "Because obviously I don't know him. I'd say he appeared to be bit of a jerk if my recollection's correct. A bit too suave and sure of himself," continuing on with what she hoped was damage limitation.

Beth listened carefully. Not wanting or daring to interrupt, she was wishing she had kept schtum with regard to Susie suggesting Jessica had knowledge of the dodgy guy.

Beth liked Jess and didn't want this to be something between them. After all, there was no evidence that Susie's disappearance was anything to do with the flashy car guy or that Jess did know him. It was all supposition she thought and not worth wrangling Jess with. Clearly, she had enough on her plate without this.

The young girl came forth with an explanation she thought would appease Jess.

"The police, Detective Simpkins primarily, came to speak to me as I'm most probably the last person to see Susie yesterday. His questions got around to, 'had I any knowledge of anyone bothering Susie.' He used the word 'stalking'. In as much as I didn't think she was being stalked, the guy in the car came to mind. I thought it pertinent to bring it up, that's all. Susie said he looked like she'd seen him before. I think it was the day after at lunch period. Without prompting she blurted it out, 'Starbucks with Jess.' I didn't get what she was talking about at first then she filled me in. She said it had been playing on her mind where she thought she'd seen the guy before," she offered tearily.

Shucks I've set her off, Jess thought.

Any minute now Anne is going to come dashing in and end the conversation.

Worse still, Beth will probably make known my overwhelming desire to allude to the knowledge I might be party to who the dude is who drives the flash car. Which of course I don't, she thought slightly panicked.

Jess had visions of the visit going sideways. Forced to change tact she decided she'd better get her thinking cap on and begin smoothing things over.

Putting her arms around Beth to give her a hug, she beckoned her to sit in one of the high back leather seats, kneeling in front of her to make direct eye contact. In her mind this gave the impression of sincerity and genuineness.

"Look, sweetie, nobody's blaming you. Everybody knows you love Susie like a sister, you're more like a sister then I am if I'm honest. I'm not blind or stupid. My parents know you love her and are the best friend any girl could hope for. Most importantly, Beth, Susie knows this too. Wherever she is it will be her family and her close friends like you who keep her going and her spirits up. She won't falter, Susie's strong and resilient, we all know that. You said it yourself, she's too clued up to take a lift from anyone, even if she thought I did know them. Which of course I don't. People lie, it is as simple as that. Susie wouldn't go with anyone willingly."

Jess instantly regretted the last bit of this pep talk. Oh boy, she thought she'd done it now.

Beth was sobbing silently.

"That came out wrong. I didn't mean to imply anything. We don't know. The police don't know. They say this sort of thing happens frequently with teenagers, more often than people are aware. They come toddling back safe and sound. What I was referring to earlier about the guy in Starbucks and Mr flashy car being one of the same is mute really. We, not to mention the police, don't know either one of them or if they've any connection with Susie. It was as if I was doing their job for them this morning when we had a catch-up. I was the one who made the suggestion they look at CCTV in Starbucks. If that's the road they are going down of course. I get the distinct feeling they weren't getting excited about it though and didn't welcome my input. My dad said they focus on the wrong things and ought to be out there pounding pavements and knocking on doors, that type of thing."

Having spotted a box of Kleenex on the desk Jess got to her feet, grabbed a handful, knelt in front of the distraught girl and gently dabbed Beth's cheeks, patting lightly around her eyes.

"Come on, you need to be what Susie would want you to be, the gutsy spirited friend you've proven to be to her for all these years. She'll be brought back to us before you know it, just you wait and see."

In an effort to lighten the mood, she commenced filling Beth's head with future images of happier times to come.

"You'll still both be bridesmaids at each other's weddings and be there for each other when little Susies and little Beths come along. You mark my words. I can see it now, my mum admonishing me for not producing grandchildren. You and Susie showing me up as usual."

The imagery implanted by her friend's sister brought a smile to her teary face. Jess's intention to lift the mood appeared to be working.

Even at her own expense she didn't care. Beth wasn't blind or deaf, she'd got the measure of the Simmons family.

Being around them as much as she had been, she knew Susie was the one who brought smiles to her parents' faces. The shining star.

Beth had a hint of a smile between tears now.

Hope was regained with a few simple words, the implication being Jess had been aware of their girly talk about their future hopes and aspirations.

Changing the subject, the scheming girl added, "Dad mentioned you being good at art and the computer an all. Maybe you could create a poster? We would get a few hundred copied and stick 'em on trees and them out in the Mall later or anywhere else that comes to mind. The twins could help too."

"Yes, that sounds like a plan. I'll get straight onto it as soon as you leave. Gosh, that sounded bad. I didn't mean it like that, Jess. I meant to say I'd contact the twins straightaway. Sam,

Joelle and a few of the others we hang with as well. They'll all want to help. I'll rally the troops so to speak."

Patently recovering from her self-pity mood with enthusiastic zeal, Beth was clearly on a mission.

"Thanks, Beth, I knew I could rely on you. I'll pass this on to Dad. I'm sure it'll give him a boost knowing what you're all doing."

She was going a little overboard with the compliments knowing full well posters, Facebook and the rest are the last thing on her father's mind.

"I'll be heading home. Dad's coming with me to the police station this afternoon. That is if we haven't heard anything. Who knows, Susie will probably come walking back through the door any minute."

Her tone was a little too bubbly all round.

"Why do you need to go there? They've already spoken to you this morning from what Mum said," curiosity getting the better of young Beth.

Taking a breath, Jess began with her torrent of big fat lies.

"Well, to be honest it was my idea. I made the suggestion to the police. Namely, that I meet with a sketch artist. I asked if it would be of more benefit if I gave a more detailed description of the chatty dude who couldn't resist talking to Susie in Starbucks. I say fresh in my mind but I can't remember much as it was a couple weeks ago."

Already on her feet Beth made towards Jess, putting her arms around her waist and hugging her tenderly.

"Susie is so lucky to have you as a sister," she enthused.

Manipulation one oh one, she thought, patting herself on the back, delighted at having achieved her goal. Talk about having the gift of the gab and knowing exactly what to say and when to say it.

"I'll give you a text if we have any news. You've got my number?" said Jess, making her way to the office door as she spoke, possessing a strong desire to get out of there quickly. It was one thing telling porkies to a fourteen year old, a different thing entirely spinning it to the grown-ups.

They'd most probably be speaking to her parents in the not too near future, and she could do without the shit storm which

148

would come hurtling down from a great height should this come to light.

She knew for now Beth would be focused on rallying the troops as she called it and moving forward with practicalities. Hopefully, mission accomplished, she thought to herself as she climbed back into the Range Rover.

Having no desire of producing her "other" phone at Beth's, she retrieved it from the hidey place before starting the engine.

Shaking her head in annoyance and disbelief, again there was nothing from her boyfriend. "Tut tut," she muttered, rather pissed off.

Chapter Nineteen

Hope at Long Last (Vicky)

The journey to the hospital went by in a haze.

My brain, if not the rest of me, was awash with whichever drug that sneaky bastard Simon had stuck me with.

Although the fuzziness was slowly dissipating, I simply couldn't get my head around this horrendous mess I'd gotten myself into. Again, through no fault of my own. I've had more than a lifetime's worth of shit heaped upon me. I'm below zero, depleted emotionally and physically.

As with Jake, I've no real idea of who this needle stabber is.

My predicament at this particular moment in time is dare I believe my nightmare is over? More accurately, nightmares. I now had no faith in anything or anybody. Could it be Jake was waiting in the wings to drag me back?

An emotional tsunami was whirring round my fuzzy brain, I couldn't get my head around any of it. No way do I intend to rest on my laurels or become complacent. Not today, not tomorrow, not ever.

I hear that little voice in my head loud and clear. Lesson learnt, trust no one. Be on your guard.

Mindful I'm an individual who rarely took an aspirin, let alone any drugs, it'll be a relief to be looked over by a doctor and receive a blood test. I'm desperate to know what kind of poison is bombarding my system and killing my brain cells.

Scrutinising my thoughts and racking my brain for answers resulted in keeping me awake. Although barely. The desire to drop off to sleep is overpowering. The drugs I guess. On and off during the journey I fell into a weird, fretful sleep, jerking myself awake periodically.

Sheer exhaustion was taking its toll on my body. Could this be the reason I'm having difficulty staying awake? My short-term memory is frazzled, my thoughts lost in a flurry of a maelstrom. My shrinking demeanour as it stands now, I couldn't help but feel it's a miracle the maid woke me at all.

My once vibrant mind is replaced by a slower, dazed version of me, and at times almost trance-like my brain switches to a different channel.

Is the correct and sensible thing to simply give in to my body and sleep? I really had no notion.

The upcoming visit from the police drifted into my head, pulling to the surface a further quandary. It may very well be they don't consider this worthy of an in-depth investigation. I couldn't escape the possibility I'm unable to articulate the frightening journey me and my band of sisters had been forced to live through.

Unquestionably, seeing my recent injuries should add weight to my case. I've got myself down as a piece of evidence now. A case. What else did I have to back this up?

The mere fact I've resorted to thinking along those lines, sad, pathetic, not to mention scary. "Be prepared," I said to myself, "this could quite easily turn out to be anything but the outcome I'm anticipating." Anticipating and hoping. Desperately hoping.

In my mind there ain't a snowball in hell's chance I'll accept my freedom, simply plod on with my life and forget the rest. My friends, my adopted family.

And certainly not young Susie. Yeah, I'd only just made her acquaintance, but by God I fully intend to fight equally as hard for her, incensed that those evil toerags had snatched a child off the street.

Lost in my own world, my drowsy fuddled mind came to the realisation we were coming to a gradual stop.

This is it I thought. A momentary rush of salvation washed over me then dissipated before I'd a chance to wallow in it.

Wasting little time, the paramedics made for the door. Out they jumped, opening both doors, the idea by the look of it to take me out on the stretcher. In my view it was a little unnecessary but I guess they follow protocol, wheeling me straight through huge glass doors, past a reception desk and down a corridor.

I'm back with the weird smells and noises. I'm suddenly nauseous.

We were met by a doctor and nurse who walked by my side, the nurse informing me I can call her Joy. She reassuringly patted me on my arm as she spoke offering a warm smile.

All the while one of the paramedics was imparting shards of information about my vitals. The only part that registered with me was my blood pressure was dangerously low. According to the paramedic who was reeling this off I had been drifting in and out, something which was gobbledygook to me about my pupils and a possible partial seizure.

I caught the statement regarding drug use, well, lack of. Evidenced by my lack of needle marks it was unlikely I'm a habitual drug user apparently. You don't say, I thought to myself, slightly perturbed anyone would think such a thing of me.

I also caught the "two needle marks on her neck. Left side. Adding a tox screen will be necessary."

Taking a wild guess, they concluded from the positioning I hadn't done this to myself. I also take from this that junkies, drug taking people, have certain areas they shoot up.

I hadn't thought about it whilst they had their mitts on us, or at all really if I'm honest. The mentioning of drugs and needles brought a shocking revelation home to me.

Reflecting back to my ordeal, I suppose in retrospect we were damned lucky they hadn't pumped us full of drugs. Up to now that is.

Who knows what's going on since my escape? At this thought I struggled to hold back the tears. There was no question they would come, if not with relief the awful realisation that I could have made conditions harsher for them. Equally as sickening, I'm unable to dredge up information, cold hard facts, in order to precipitate their freedom.

We'd only been here for a few minutes when I found myself in a closed off hospital room. I was grateful to have a room all to myself. A fleeting serene feeling came and stayed for a while.

The doctor introduced himself. Wasting no time he got straight down to it. Eyeing a chart I assume the paramedic had given him, he proceeded to run through what I guess he considered necessary in terms of tests and procedures.

"A little discomfort but nothing to worry about," informing me in his most professional and compassionate tone and that they will do their upmost to be gentle.

That was the least of my concerns after what I'd tolerated ran through my head but didn't make it out of my mouth.

All in all, after vials of bloods were taken, the doc proceeded to examine me from head to toe.

Completing his initial exam, he gestured to the nurse with the request, "We need to do a rape exam." Apart from the obvious involved in such an exam, scraping underneath my fingernails was to be incorporated in the test.

Before further tests my sore wet wrists were gently cleaned.

The antiseptic wipes applied to clean the blood was soothing, followed by gauze, then a soft white bandage wound round and round. The nurse assured me the gauze wouldn't stick to the wound and would be checked and replaced in the morning, adding if the blood seeped through during the night not to hesitate and press the buzzer.

Although my head was still woozy I overheard the part about my ribs. Bruised and tender, possible fracture beginning to heal, instructing the nurse to arrange for a trip to the X-ray suite.

I felt thankful for their expertise and kindness and their gentleness as they performed the intimate test. They fussed and got on with it without question. At no point did they make me feel I'm to blame for the state I'm in or pass judgement.

As the doctor took his leave he explained he had put a rush on the tests and would be back forthwith. Nurse Joy followed him holding a small tray with the vials of blood.

Again, with a comforting smile she stated she'd be back imminently, and if I needed anything at all not to hesitate in pressing the buzzer. She also informed me she had ordered me some food from the cafeteria.

I was not sure I could eat anything but I thanked her all the same. I was grateful for her kindness and not shy in imparting this.

Now I really am alone and it granted me a moment or two to collect my thoughts.

One of the first things to pop into my head was the fact that I was high up. I was not sure how many floors this hospital consists of, but this particular ward was clearly a few floors up.

I gazed out of the window. A spectacular turquoise sky was peppered by the odd white cotton wool cloud.

Talk about a beautiful sight. I drank it in and embraced the peacefulness, the tranquillity. The serene feeling I felt earlier returned.

Here I am in my quiet sterile hospital room peering out at a view which in past weeks I could only dream of, remembering how they'd stolen daylight from us along with our freedom and dignity.

My eyes were adjusting slowly to the brightness as I took in the view. Coming to terms with the notion I'm located on one on the higher floors gave me a tinge of safety, as if I'd somehow be safer here than on the ground floor. The thinking behind this logic was I am further from the entrance therefore out of reach of the bad guys. I knew it to be a totally illogical hypothesis.

The door was slightly ajar affording me a view of a busy ward.

From my own little safe place I could see doctors and nurses milling around just outside the door.

My reasoning was a sense of safety and comfort achieved. For the first time I can remember in a long time I felt protected, secure and safe. Safe in their hands.

Chapter Twenty

Two of Vegas's Finest!

I was flung out of my daydreaming by a sharp tapping of the door.

I quivered slightly, glanced over and saw two smartly dressed men in the doorway.

One of them took it upon himself to close the door a little, leaving it slightly ajar.

Both took a couple steps forward in sync, pausing a little way from the bottom of my bed.

Instinctively I pulled back and for a split second my posture shifted.

It was ridiculous but having them stood there created the illusion of me being stuck, trapped in that confined space. Caged.

However tempted I was to bolt past the suits through that slither in the door gap I stayed put, irrationally tugging the bedclothes and concealing as much of my torso as possible.

"Sorry to startle you. I am Detective Pratt and my colleague here is Detective Carp. How are you feeling?" asked suit number one in a soft, fatherly voice.

My doom and gloom cloud was evaporating little by little. A split second took me from the cusp of an anxiety attack to cranking up my inner strength.

I gave a short to the point answer. "I'm fine now," but for some reason added, "but still frightened."

Terrified was nearer the mark but I was holding off on that one. Maybe another British trait, the need to be perceived as strong, composed and in control whatever the circumstances.

"That's good to hear," said the detective. Detective Carp if I'd caught it right.

The other one proceeded to pull out a notebook, his pen poised at the ready.

Pratt eyed me keenly and wasting no time he began to speak. "We've spoken to the officers who were called to the scene. Obviously, we have your name and a few minor details, Vicky. Do you mind if we call you Vicky?" he asked.

"No, go ahead, that's fine."

"If at all possible I'd like you to give a detailed account of how you came to be at the Spring Motel."

He paused, raised his thick eyebrows and took a deep breath. He then added, "Tied up."

"In your own time, take your time now," the prompt from the slightly rounder and balder of the two named Carp.

I hesitated for what seemed like an eternity, in reality it was a few seconds.

Figuring out the precise words to articulate the atrocious depravities I'd lived through was no easy feat.

As a matter of urgency my goal, my duty, was to furnish the cops with information. Namely, the sordid rendition required to fire up an investigation. To trigger them to move forward in a timely fashion as in now, today.

So much had transpired, the whole spine-chilling debacle tremendously difficult to process. How to navigate the different layers of torment.

I swallowed hard and tried to breathe evenly. Here goes, now for the difficult part.

Here I sit, recounting the worst few weeks of my whole life for two complete strangers. The murky life I'd been sucked into, the betrayal, the acres of anguish, suffering and degradation I'd somehow managed to survive. I cleared my throat and began to give an emotionally charged account of the frightening world I'd left behind.

Now of course there was an added segment to include, the mysterious Simon. I did my best to be as candid as possible, knowing it imperative I supply the detectives with as much information and detail as my brain would pull up.

Fear and anxiety augmenting in my gut, it was as though I'd developed a speech impediment. The knowledge was there, the difficulty was finding and speaking the words.

Most unlike me, my speech was jumbled. I concluded the drugs were doing their thing, swimming from my gut to my head and back again.

I had to admit that me, a level-headed Yorkshire girl, had stupidly climbed into the car of what was essentially a total stranger. Willingly at that. How I and the other girls had been caught hook line and sinker. Hoodwinked for want of a better term.

Through blind ignorance or sheer stupidity we'd all taken the bait, a night on the tiles courtesy of Jake.

As difficult as the process was I was unearthing details locked in a box somewhere at the back of my mind. I proceeded to quietly voice what that man and his accomplice unashamedly wielded upon me, the unknown but equally sadistic accomplice.

My delivery ceased, I stared out of the window for a second or two to gather my thoughts and allow my brain to catch up.

An unnatural quietness dominated the room.

I was mindful in choosing my words carefully for plausibility, curb the sarcasm, the hatred, though why I thought this necessary eludes me.

The last thing I needed was to come off as not credible. For reasons unknown to me, I felt it down to me to convince them of what those bastards had done to me and my friends. The way I looked at it, it could very well come down to my word against theirs.

I knew it vital I bring them to a place of understanding and to paint a picture of the enormity of this horrendous crime. I had to hammer home to these two suited and booted cops standing before me that it's not primarily about me. Far from it. Other girls are languishing in this nightmare as we speak.

"Continue," prodded the detective, betraying nothing in the way of emotion.

My voice quivered as I went on to illustrate how it all started, that very first night. The first night six weeks prior. How I'd been assaulted with a taser within seconds of seating myself in that car.

My tone was demure as I painstakingly pulled details from memory.

"As I've indicated, tasered. Rendered unconscious. Whilst out of it my hands were duct taped as were my eyes. Then I was transported to an old, dilapidated building. Against my will you understand?" I stated. "An air of oldness and dampness permeated the air of this building. A warehouse maybe? I dunno." Further nauseating details poured out of my mouth. "When I came to I was disorientated and strapped to a beam, hands tightly fastened above my head. There were two of them. Two guys. Jake and some other guy. I didn't stand a chance."

Momentarily I stopped talking, the embarrassment at having to speak of such things unbearable.

Finding the strength and courage from deep within I slowly took up where I'd left off, my tone quiet, shaky, bashful.

"Then they launched into their game. The torture. The rapes. Mauling. It went on and on for hours. I passed out, came too. Then out again. I lost all track of time."

I took a deep breath, closed my eyes and recounted more of what had poked through my brain space. There was no stamping out my pitiful subdued tone, it was here to stay.

"Beaten, whipped and burnt, carefully avoiding my face. Everywhere, and I mean everywhere, but not the face. I coughed up blood for about a week after."

My ramblings ceased. I had to take control of my emotions, my mind. And breath.

"My only recourse had been to switch off, close down. Bring the shutters down on my mind. I tried to pretend it wasn't me they were touching, hurting, penetrating." The same soft subdued tone brought with it more material for them to digest.

I was battling so hard to eradicate the visions which had surfaced, other pictures filtering through unceremoniously. Image on top of image. Faces on top of faces.

The rancid smells, the bodies, grunting, slapping. Absolute cruelty for the sake of cruelty. All of it in my head waiting to explode from my very core as in a volcano erupting after years of remaining dormant.

I was reeling it all out for two men which was utterly mortifying and distressing. I could feel their eyes glaring at me, burning into me. I didn't want them to see me. See me as I saw me.

It was clear to me I was on a ledge and on the brink of losing it big time. It was all I could do not to scream, shout and become hysterical. The tightly gripped bedsheet was shielding me from their gaze. I clutched it for all it was worth.

I was recounting how whilst semi-conscious I was transported to a second location. Blindfolded, tightly bound, drifting in and out of consciousness, I vaguely recollect being in the back of a van stating, "eventually waking in the basement of a ramshackle house in the middle of nowhere only to discover I'm not alone in this dungeon-like basement. What's more, I discovered the depraved, twisted purpose of why I had been abducted. Me and the others."

I proceeded to provide them with the whole vile routine which had become our daily existence, divulging things I never thought I could. I wanted to be sick laying it all out. I was trembling as I spoke and a moment came when I nearly bolted for the bathroom.

I chose my words carefully as I spoke of the vile, atrocious, demeaning exploitation we'd all been forced into.

"Under their control. Held at gunpoint. Threatened, punched and kicked should we dare to protest. Locked in the rooms." I added, "Without fail cable ties were applied to our wrists when moved from A to B. And blindfolds, eliminating any thought or possibility of escape."

I told the listening, more pointedly stunned, detectives how a window of opportunity had opened up and I took it. I made my escape.

Full of trepidation, I continued painting a picture of the day I'd seized the moment.

"We were all well aware the basement door was permanently bolted. Apart from the fact we could hear the heavy bolts slide across, we routinely crept up the steps and tried the door. It was a little ritual of ours, we each took it in turn. Futile as it was, in our minds it was worth a shot. I don't suppose any of us had an idea what we'd do should we find it unlocked. It didn't seem likely the main door would be unlocked either. It made absolutely no sense. I could only conclude on the night I hightailed it outta there that it was a fluke. Maybe the fat, brainless lump guarding us that night thought it no big deal. After all, he'd secured the cellar door. Or it was my lucky day, him having knocked so much booze back it'd slipped his mind. This particular night it was just him. Well, him and me. Me having been yanked up the concrete steps to be his plaything for the evening. The unlocked door was probably my only bit of luck to come my way."

Nauseous and embarrassed, my nervous prattling was going full throttle.

Part of me was wondering why I was going into so much detail, like it mattered we did this, that and the other. The floodgates had been released and having plenty to say I couldn't stop, hoping the incidents playing out in my memory and coming out of my mouth came over as brutal and heartless as in actuality. To my mind no words fit the pictures roaming free in my head.

I alluded to the fact several of the girls were drugged and snatched from bars and clubs, as I thought it essential they're made aware of this practice.

"These girls were snapped up by persons unknown. Opportune kidnapping? Stalked? They were taken for one purpose, to participate in things no girl should ever have to. Essentially, used as sex slaves." There it was, out there. I'd said it out loud. Sex slaves.

As an alcoholic has to say the words out loud, I spoke those two emotive words "sex slaves" for the first time. Somehow saying it out loud made it real and brought it home bestowing upon me shame which should not be mine to own.

I also brought to their attention the girls who were randomly singled out then dragged out of the basement, the motive patently obvious. The fact that once taken we never clapped eyes on any of them again led us to only one conclusion.

Crucial in my heart and mind I bring to their attention my friend Fiona. Her life mattered. I was pointing out that we were powerless to do anything, just watch and take in the brutality as she was whisked away.

I attempted to conjure up words without exaggerating to paint a vivid picture of what took place in that room above our very heads, further adding when it was my time to be plucked from the basement an opportunity presented itself and I took it.

I was impressing upon the cops it was probably a one in a million chance and in no way am I suggesting the others escaped.

While they listened I relentlessly talked and talked telling them of my exploits with regard to hitching a lift in the hope I would end up somewhere safe. Which led to phase two.

"This is gonna sound out there. Corny even. The guy driving this truck I'd sneaked into the back of, I swear to God he was the spitting image of that guy Dexter Morgan from the TV series."

I revealed how exhausted I was and how I'd fallen asleep, then jolted awake while hidden under the tarp and how he'd furtively yanked it back.

"He stuck me with a needle, what drug I've no idea. I've never used drugs. The next thing I know I'm tethered to that bed in that grotty motel. I'm not sure how long I was out of it in that place, it was the maid knocking and hollering that sort of brought me round. The girls are still being held captive and suffering. Claire, young Susie, the others, they all need rescuing quickly."

The cadence of my voice raised as the pleading intensified. I carried on in the same hurried tone.

"They urgently need help. Your help. Please save them. I feel real bad for leaving them, I really do. I couldn't help them at the time but I can now." My incessant pleading took on a life of its own. "You need to stop all this and bring them home," I begged. Fighting back tears I said, "This is all so messed up."

Begging and pleading had the effect of ramping up my emotions. I had been feverishly doing my upmost to remain calm and refrain from overshadowing my message with emotion. On that score I'd failed miserably.

Drawing on my experience, talking and laying it all out had become too much. For every word out of my mouth I experienced gut wrenching pain, making me feel sick at reliving the horror and opening up wounds that were still raw. I was hoping beyond hope I was being taken seriously and all this was not in vain.

Clearly taken aback the two cops traded glances.

At this point the note taking had stopped. They were transfixed yet appeared to be digesting what they'd been told.

Was that a good thing or a bad thing? I couldn't quite figure that one.

After a few minutes I quit with the jabbering. A mound of information still needed to be brought to their attention, I also knew my account thus far was pretty long-winded. I felt slightly perturbed as I simply wasn't sure this was coming out how I wanted it to.

The way in which I'd laid it all out differed to how I'd played it over and over in my head.

Both detectives hadn't moved an inch and had hardly said a word.

Emotionless, the pair of them perched a little way from the door, my perception was ready for a quick getaway.

Could it be they saw themselves in and out in five minutes? The end of the shift, a quick nip into the hospital to take a statement from the bimbo who managed to get herself tied to a bed in the Spring Motel of all places. Take a few notes, write a report over morning coffee tomorrow and job done.

I had been spewing it all out for about twenty or so minutes. Thinking back, it seemed like an eternity.

My words had been replaced by mind ramblings.

I glanced over at them and asked my inner self if I should I go on. Neither displayed any emotion, their expressions offering nothing in way of empathy.

I just couldn't gauge or work them out. Maybe this was normal. Were they trained to show no emotion? Am I expecting too much?

I'm guessing this wasn't what they were expecting to hear by the look of them.

My smart-alec radar was well and truly fired up at this point, and I was just getting started.

Time being against us I'd only touched on the hotel van, the guys acting as drivers, pimps or whatever their job description entailed. Plus, there was a whole manner of other vital things that ought to be thrown into the mix; half starved, having to beg for water. More significantly, my belief that maybe these goofs are possibly targeting kids, Susie being only fourteen 'an all.

Neither detective spoke, there was not a question from either of them. There was a look of bewilderment on Pratt's face as if he'd never heard anything like it in his entire career.

Of course, I hadn't at this phase in my life but I'm not a cop, I'm a normal everyday girl going about her business. Well, I used to be.

I ventured these Vegas detectives know a thing or two about what goes on in the underbelly of a city such as Vegas, but I'm flabbergasted by their reaction or lack thereof.

The silence which stood between us was unnerving. I didn't know whether to keep it buttoned thinking maybe it's a case of too much material to digest in one go.

I had done the hard bit by laying it all out, the majority of it anyway. Certainly, there was enough for them to get the ball rolling.

An important factor in all this which had never strayed far from my thoughts from the minute I'd bolted was time. Time is not a luxury we are blessed with.

"Say something then," I blurted. I don't have much control over my mouth when I'm anxious.

They traded looks, simultaneously glancing at me.

I couldn't make out if they were shocked by my forthrightness. They had evidently not come across a Yorkshire girl in their time as Vegas cops.

"Surely you have questions? One question?"

My eyes are playing ping-pong back and forth searching their faces.

I became more and more agitated. Pissed off if I'm honest. I had to check myself. I held serious misgivings on how this was going and I was having trouble holding my tongue.

I caught a conferring look pass between the two of them as though it was necessary to verify they were on the same page.

At long last Pratt responded.

"We'll need a little more to go on to advance the investigation to collaborate your story. Just to verify a couple of things, Miss Walker." His riposte came easily but awkwardly.

It's Miss Walker now, is it?

Dispensed with the pleasantries have we? It was all I could do to stop myself screaming at both of them to get out.

The word story got me right off the bat.

"How's about going back to that motel and checking if they've CCTV then enquire who booked the room? Credit card details that kinda thing? A description of this individual? I sure as hell never checked myself in, I can tell you that. Sound like a plan, heh?"

I heard my mouth barking orders in a somewhat cutting tone.

Annoyance and sarcasm bubbling to the surface was washing away my otherwise calm sensible demeanour.

"We intend to do our due diligence, Miss Walker, please be assured of that."

Pratt was outwardly displaying his annoyance seeing how I'd took to suggesting how he ought to be doing his job.

His partner weighed in with, "What's your thoughts on this Dexter Morgan lookalike character? Did he sexually assault you and make you do things you didn't want to?"

His finger did air quotes when the name Dexter Morgan came out of his mouth. To me this was not only rude but patronising.

One of his questions was easy to answer, the other complete conjecture.

They had both pushed the wrong button now. "Oh shit," I said to myself as I began to speak.

My tone was peppered with antagonism. I was off, there was no stopping me now.

"His name is Simon by the way. I made the point he looked like the TV character in order for you to have a better understanding of his description. An easy way to describe him that's all. In answer to your question, he never laid a finger on me or suggested anything untoward. Nothing adds up. I've really no notion of his intentions either back at the condo or the motel. I could hazard a guess..." I offered, my voice trailing off retaining a hint of aloofness.

"I need to tell you, Miss Walker," said Carp, "this is quite a remarkable version of events, certainly intriguing. Truth be told, it is not something we hear every day."

Pratt was nodding in agreement.

164

On hearing this I'm on the cusp of losing my composure and confidence.

This is not going the way I'd anticipated or hoped. Far from it. The opportunity in facilitating the release of my fellow cellmates was fading rapidly. Going down the swanny as we say over the pond. In my heart I knew I had to press on and give it one last shot. I was desperate for them both to be on the same page and acknowledge the urgency and the dire situation for those I'd reluctantly left behind.

My voice was breaking as the words tumbled out. I spoke as precise as humanly possible, being careful not to become hysterical as I felt pretty close to the edge. "Please, I know this all sounds far-fetched and hard to digest. It's hard for me too, it's breaking me just talking about it. It's paramount I know you'll do more than look into this. I have to know you will move forward with an investigation, not for me you understand, for the other young women who as we speak will be forced to take the pain and abuse doled out to them. If not worse. Please, please," I pleaded.

Desperation oozed out of every pore.

The detectives looked at each other as if they wanted to bolt from the room. I could tell they just weren't getting it.

I readied myself for what I had a feeling would be their parting words. Both of them had inched away from the bottom of the bed and were now nearer the door.

It was Carp's turn to speak now. "We'll need to have more solid information before moving forward. There appears to be a myriad of things to check out. Quite a few gaps in your timeline. We have our forensic guys back at the motel room as we speak. The tape is a good piece of evidence which is on the way to the lab. I can say with a degree of certainty that we will look into your complaint. Of course, CCTV will be checked, that goes without saying."

He offered a bemused half smile as he imparted the CCTV statement. I guess it was a little comeback directed at my earlier outburst.

Expounding further, "We've spoken to the doctor in charge of your care who we've asked to keep us informed with regard your test results. It'll be interesting to see what the labs come back with."

No sooner had the detective given his little speech Nurse Joy appeared with an orderly pushing a wheelchair, almost pushing the cops out of the way.

I couldn't help wishing at least one of them had suffered a bang on the heels as the wheelchair passed them.

"I hope you've finished," the nurse said to the two detectives in a rather school marmish tone.

"Vicky is going down for an X-ray now, after which we want her to be left alone so she can get some rest. If that's OK." Again, with the exact same tone, more a statement than a question.

I could tell from the moment I first clapped eyes on the nurse through my fog filled haze that I was going to like this lady. I was right.

At that the detectives left the room, though not before exclaiming they would see me at some point the next day.

I'll look forward to it, sneakily crept into my brain. And that's where it stayed. I said nothing.

Chapter Twenty-One

A Family in Crisis (Jess)

Jess hadn't gone into detail with regard the police request for the composite drawing. The only explanation she had offered her mum and dad was a big fat lie. Not that they had an inkling.

She'd said that when Susie and she had their last coffee date a couple of weeks back an older guy passed their table and started up a conversation. It had slipped her mind and should the police not have brought it up she wouldn't have given him a second thought.

Illuminating further she said nothing about the guy stood out, stating of course she did her best but barely remembers him as he didn't make much of an impression.

She was mindful not to bring Beth's name into it, her parents knowing full well how close the two girls had always been. They also knew from past conversations they told each other their most private secrets. In fact, pretty much everything.

She determined it only a matter of time before Beth and her parents landed on their doorstep. If there was any reluctance on Beth's part it was probably because she'd expressed how bad she felt having been the last person to speak to Susie. Guilt was a powerful emotion, thought the scheming teenager.

Her real feelings with regard to "assisting with a composite drawing" were anything but casual. Apprehension and trepidation were just two of the feelings running through her.

She had lied to the police now as well as her parents, the information she gave to the nice sketch artist lady a complete fabrication.

If her parents, let alone the detectives, had any suspicion her boyfriend was the "person of interest", she was screwed.

Although she hadn't been rescued from the state of complete boredom she'd had to endure these last few days, she had at least had a text from Jack.

His excuse was in her mind complete baloney. He'd been out of the country "taking care of business".

"And?" sharply sprung from her mouth in the privacy of her bedroom as she'd read the text.

Although her anger was slowly waning she was still mightily pissed at him. His pathetic excuse didn't help matters. Before it wore off altogether she needed to make her point.

Sending him the one-word text, *AND?*

"They don't have phones in that little country called England?"

The upside for Jess was duty free and expensive gifts were mentioned in his follow up text. He was feeling guilty and buttering her up she guessed. But she'd take it.

Her decision to tell him about Susie and ask him about the stalking would have to be put on the back burner. How to broach the stalking without actually using that word would take some thinking about, she thought.

The whole Simmons household had been thrown out of kilter.

A situation such as this was obviously all new to their family. They had been well and truly forced out of their comfort zone and catapulted into a new one. Here no comfort or peace existed.

The presumptions levelled at the Simmons was all too much. Drugs, boys, bad grades, arguments, this couldn't be further from their youngest daughter. Either of their children. Dr Simmons felt revulsion at their questions and was sick of reiterating Susie's not your average teenager.

They had always considered themselves lucky to have Susie as their daughter.

Now their world had forever turned upside down. Their home not as it was, everything out of sync.

As ordinary as the standard lamp in the corner of their living room, or any other furniture for that matter, Dr Simmons was permanently rooted to the same small section of floor by the bay window. His adopted position afforded him a clear view of their drive where in his head he visualised her walking after first entering through the wrought iron gates in the direction of her home. The only home she had ever known.

He was praying and imagining any minute she'd come marching down the drive, school bag slung over her right shoulder, eyes glued to that sparkling phone wondering what all the fuss is about.

Gnawing at his psyche were more ominous notions, thoughts he dare not voice for fear of making them real. Ponderances which were slowly stifling his heart inch by inch, breath by breath.

Was this their new reality, what they'd been reduced to?

Reflecting back to the year she entered the world, it was a rocky year for the couple brought to an end with joy. The Simmons had celebrated and embraced having such a sweet, beautiful, healthy child.

Pulling up a scene in his head, he was in the delivery room when the newly born Susie was placed into his arms. His love palpable, the bond unbreakable, he knew this baby was special and vowed to love and cherish her forever. This baby marked a new beginning for the family.

Had they enabled this? Is this down to them? Shielding, wrapping her up in cotton wool? He'd questioned this on one of the few occasions he and his wife dared to voice their thoughts to each other. Could it be they'd cosseted her and made her vulnerable thus making her a target for a predator?

These thoughts jostled with the complete opposite. Common sense had been instilled in both their children.

This had gone from a nightmare to something utterly indescribable. More time had elapsed since those policemen had stood in their home sprouting what amounted to nonsense with the odd platitude thrown in. So much for their expertise on the subject, nothing, no notion of her whereabouts, not one piece of good news. Any news.

Trying to stay strong was harder than anyone could possibly know. It was all they could do not to go to pieces.

Time had stood still yet simultaneously had speeded up. How could this be happening to their family? What had they done to deserve this?

They were recalling one of Susie's little mantras, counting sleeps. She would do this in the lead up to a special event or a trip away. Even now at fourteen she jokily uses that term.

Could she be somewhere counting sleeps until she's back home where she belongs?

Chapter Twenty-Two

Missing the Point (Vicky)

I couldn't shake the anxiety.

The stomach tightening left me briefly only to return when my mind went back to the hell I'd escaped from. And to the visiting cops.

Is this going to be how it is for the rest of my days?

So much had transpired as I was striving to come to terms with the car crash that is my life. The stress was hurting me physically and emotionally and I couldn't shake all the irrational thoughts bombarding my mind.

I took to taking deep breaths in the hope it would dispel the anxiety welling up from deep within.

Here in this busy hospital ward I should feel safe. But I don't. I struggle to shake the fear which for all intents and purposes is engrained deep within me. My thinking is irrational and stupid.

I suppose in laying it all out for the cops I'd the notion I would feel a huge sigh of relief, a ten ton elephant lifted off my back. I had to resign myself to the fact that I'm only one step up from where I'd been earlier today.

It also occurred to me there's a strong possibility I'm fighting an uphill battle with the cops.

On reflection, considering the limited information I'd been able to bring to the table, I'd better hold back with the high fiving. Apart from anything, I'd deduced those cops sent to interview me weren't exactly Tubbs and Crockett.

Here I sat propped up, all cosy in my nice clean hospital bed, fluffed pillows 'an all unable to shake the feeling of disquiet. It's like I know deep down something is about to happen. Historically, that's because it usually does. That's the way things tend to work out for me these days. One tiny step forward, two gigantic steps back. This appears to be the world I now inhabit, I thought, feeling rather sorry for myself.

And then it hit me right in the mush. Why the hell shouldn't I feel sorry for myself?

At that moment, coupled with all my other worries, I felt alone. So very alone.

I was full of thoughts and daydreams and completely lost in the moment and entrenched in all the stuff I need to get my head around. I hadn't noticed a knock on the door of my room.

My eyes darted to a figure at the door.

Andy the rookie entered without waiting for my response.

He took a few steps into the room and approached my bed.

"Sorry, I didn't mean to startle you."

It was the same soothing tone I recognised from when I had been blindfolded and tethered in that awful room.

Surprise and I suspect bewilderment adorned my red blotchy face.

"No, you didn't. Well, you sort of did. I just didn't expect to see anyone, let alone you," I said in a rather apologetic tone. "Sorry, that came out wrong," I continued, digging myself out of a little hole.

"How's it going anyway? You looked miles away," he asked.

To find my affable friendly cop, my rescuer, appear there at the foot of my bed was the last thing I'd have expected. I think I'd been so lost in my own little world thinking about my poor friends, having him visit briefly flummoxed me. A very welcome flummox nonetheless.

He was looking very different out of uniform.

In a good way.

I hadn't really paid attention to his features back at the "Bates Motel". I felt my face begin to colour and I blushed, my whole face and neck taking on the colour of a rosy red apple. There was no need to see it, I could feel myself heating up and it popped into my head what I must look like.

I'd clocked my image earlier when I'd used the washroom. Evidently, the duct tape had left marks on my sensitive skin, pink tramlines where the thick wide tape had been strategically placed, one on the top of my face the other above my top lip

171

and chin. The same width and colour. I looked ridiculous and I knew it. Talk about awkward moments. Then to top it all off it hit me what I was wearing when he'd found me. Well, more like what I wasn't wearing. Oh boy, I thought, do what you do best, Vicky, crack a joke. Break the ice. After all, he didn't have to come and visit when not on duty.

"Don't be put off by the look. I'm in dire need of a top lip wax, I've just had a visit from the beauty therapist," I offered.

A little chuckle came my way. "She's done a sterling job."

"I guess you know the detectives have paid me a visit?" I offered, my irked tone inadvertently giving me away. It wasn't easy to mask the sarcasm in my voice.

He met my gaze.

Pausing for a second the astute officer appeared as though figuring out a response, choosing his words carefully I suspect. Surprisingly, he'd picked up on my uneasiness regarding the visit with that one question.

"Not go so well I take it? Pratt, and I forget his partner's name."

"Carp," I said sternly.

I was careful in not giving too much away for fear of coming over all stroppy. Getting on the wrong side of law enforcement was certainly not my intention, though I think that ship had sailed.

I smiled nervously before continuing.

"They listened, took notes, then inexplicably ceased with the note taking. They glared at me as if I were exaggerating, making it up, beamed down from another planet. It was as though it was down to me to convince them of the horror I'd had the misfortune to be party to, more pointedly lived through. And escaped. I felt duty bound to justify myself."

My eyes glistened over as I spoke to the young police officer.

Andy looked at me sympathetically not sure how to respond to my outburst.

"Well, so long as they have the key facts then I'm sure they'll do the necessary. From what I can gather they're both seasoned professionals. Both been on the job a long time. Pratt

172

partnered with my dad for a short time. He's a highly thought of detective. I don't know a great deal about Carp but I gather he got transferred in a couple of years ago."

I suspect the purpose of the glowing endorsement was to placate me, or at least to make me feel better.

It wasn't working.

"I don't care how long they've been cops or who they've worked with. I'm not buying they are going to get to the bottom of what is without question an organised criminal enterprise. Even I'd worked that much out."

Tired and feeling physically wrecked, I neither had the inclination or the emotional energy to argue or explain myself. I was grateful he'd made the effort to pop in to see me but I was sick of talking about it.

I was desperate for some shuteye and rest, feeling the aftermath of being pumped full drugs. My head hadn't got rid of the headache and fuzziness.

A little bit of small talk then hopefully he'll shoot off. I wanted him to go. I felt obliged to come forth a little and make an effort. It was stupid really after what I'd been through and the way I felt emotionally and physically. Why should I?

"Your dad's a detective then?" came my weary retort.

"Used to be. He retired off the job last year. Spent the best part of twenty-five years running down the dregs of society, making sure to get as many locked up as he could before he went. Life of Riley now. Spends his days on the golf course," he stated rather proudly.

"We could do with him now. I know a few who could do with locking up. Dregs of society doesn't cut it, sadistic, depraved sociopaths more like." At that I felt something harden inside me. "You've obviously been through something distressing and I don't blame you for taking that tone. I am not the enemy here. We're not the enemy." He paused for a second before adding, "I share your concerns. You need to know the police will do everything in their power to find the perpetrators and bring them to justice. Just allow a little time and we'll do just that I can assure you, Vicky. You will get your justice."

My posture straightened and I'm simmering inside. The light mood of earlier had dissipated. I needed to say this one last thing and for him to hear it. Then for him to go.

I took a deep breath and started my retort, hopefully keeping my tone in check.

"I am grateful for the kindness, truly I am. Obviously, you're one of the good guys. But you and the other detectives are missing the point. REALLY MISSING THE POINT. It's not me, I'm out of there, I ran for all I was worth, it's the others left behind. My friends and the new girl Susie, she's only fourteen. From listening to her I gathered she was literally scooped off the street in broad daylight. She was on her way home from school is what she said. They've probably added her sister Jess to the mix, her name was banded about. The stakes are very high. Somebody, when I say somebody, I mean the police need to step up and stop all this."

I spoke hurriedly in a panicked tone, hoping beyond hope he got the urgency.

"How'd you know about this Susie's sister and friends?" he asked in a measured tone.

"Because when they took Susie she had her phone in her possession. All this came to light the very evening I made a break for it. By the grace of God I fortuitously got the hell out of there. Unfortunately, as I told your colleagues, I was unable to rescue the others."

I'd said enough. I stopped talking and waited for him to respond. Hopefully favourably with something constructive.

I had difficulty gauging his reaction.

No words came, no questions, aside from the one already asked and answered.

Andy stayed rooted to the spot, more or less the same spot he'd occupied on entering my room. He was standing at the bottom of the bed as if not daring to come any closer.

Saying his goodbyes as he reached the door, he turned a half turn smiling that sweet smile of his, informing me he would come by before I was discharged. He said I would be here a day or two.

Ah, checking up on me now, I thought. Interesting.

"OK," was all I could think to mutter.

Chapter Twenty-Three

Andy

Andy left the hospital room a tad disillusioned if not disappointed. It hadn't exactly gone how he'd hoped. Moreover, how he had anticipated.

The sole purpose of popping in was to offer the hand of friendship and support. Practical or otherwise, a shoulder to cry on if that's all she needed.

It was a little misguided maybe, but he thought a kindling of rapport had sparked between them back at the Spring.

He couldn't help but find her intriguing, likeable. Different. And yeah, pretty. But it wasn't just that, he likened her to a deer caught in the headlights. Vulnerability and terror exuded from those big blue eyes when she spoke, and when she stayed silent.

The joviality woven in amid the serious content of their chats was clearly an attempt in masking the pain lurking beneath the surface.

That look all too familiar in Andy's world.

He'd certainly no intention of giving up and leaving it there, inwardly admitting she's having the benefit of his support whether she knows it or not. He'd far from given up on her.

His mind flashed back to the scene in the motel as the door was flung open, the image in front of him, her tied to that bed. Towering above her he'd paused momentarily, contemplating where to begin with the unpicking of the thick silver duct tape.

Feeling his face reddening and other parts starting to throb, the mere recollection of the image flooded back into his mind. Her laid on that bed semi-naked. For a split second he'd absorbed every tiny detail.

A screenshot of an image jotted back and forth in front of his eyes, an image which had taken root. He was shaking his head from side to side as if by this simple motion the picture would evaporate into the great wide yonder.

His sauntering was replaced by a more purposeful gait as he headed for the lift.

Truth be told there was no erasing her from his memory. She'd pulled him in without even knowing it. Another word had entered his head out of nowhere: Enigmatic.

His head was swamped with scenarios and questions, and her words echoed back and forth as he made his way along the long busy ward towards the lift.

Andy had only been on the force a couple of years but quickly realised this wasn't a run of the mill call. It was a weird one, make no mistake. Even his partner said as much, and not much gave him cause for comment.

And then there's the maid. She was a little too involved. Maybe she caught sight of something or someone else why call the cops? She could have simply moved on to the next room. Nothing quite added up. Rankled by the whole thing, he possessed a strong desire to play detective and dig deeper. After all, who could it hurt?

Entrenched in deep thought he continued on. Pictures, people, incidences scrambling to the surface.

The area surrounding the Spring was at the forefront of his mind; part of their beat. It was familiar territory to him, his partner and fellow officers. Unremarkable in its appearance, the motel fitted in with the other low rent establishments situated at the bottom or a couple of blocks north of the strip.

From the moment he'd gained entry into the room he was hit by a charge in the air, an unexplained aura. This scene didn't fit. She didn't fit. This girl was too put together, too pretty, too clean cut. Too ordinary if that's the right word. Probably not the only word his weary brain was able to conjure up.

Ordinary in a good way, he added to his last thought, unsuccessful in his attempt to suppress a smile that ran across his tired face. Speculating inwardly, he concluded it wasn't beyond the realm the perp scarpered the minute they pulled into the parking lot. He caught sight of them and did a three sixty. There were too many unanswered questions to wade through on this one.

The words of his partner were ringing in his head. "Leave it, Andy, just leave it. We're not social workers, it's not our problem. We've done our job." His mind bounced to her demeanour after he'd taken off the last of the bindings. She was undeniably frightened. Trembling. Shaken to the core a more fitting portrayal.

Nonetheless, she showed little in the way of self-pity. She was visibly distressed, teary and teetering on the edge, but she embodied calmness and steely determination, the like of which was very rarely found in victims. If ever. Judging by the spiky tone she was plainly underwhelmed and frustrated by her interview with Pratt and what's his name. He concluded from their questions or lack thereof they weren't getting it, getting her. Had it been the same for the visiting detectives? Is it possible she'd read them wrong?

I've met my share of cynical cops, he conceded, but surely to God they can't have taken this as a falsehood or a fabrication. What's in it for her? He quashed that notion sharpish.

Undoubtedly the girl's intense. Even he had to admit a little odd on the behaviour front, smiling as he recalled the insinuation with regard to the coffee drinking and donuts.

Despite his partner's words Andy wanted, no, needed, to delve deeper. He had a gut feeling and wanted to share it with a detective. At least feel 'em out.

Although not on duty, he saw no harm in popping back to the station. He would clock which of the detectives were milling around the squad room. It was commonplace for there to be several of them finishing paperwork at that time.

He was ruminating to when his dad was a permanent fixture in that place, a second home which only had good memories, he mused.

He was recalling with a smile how he'd spent many an evening after school cracking on with his homework at a spare desk, cops ruffling his hair as they strolled past. There was teasing by the truckload, regaling tales of the "odd bods" they'd encountered during their shift.

Andy pondered the odd bods reflecting how he frequently falls upon a few of the same poor sods out and about now and again. Not that they'd recognise him.

Full of contemplation as he went about his mission, thoughts bounced from Vicky, the cops and the poor unfortunates who'd crossed his path as he went about his day. Having grown up around most of the detectives, he had listened to stories and on occasion caught the tail end of things maybe a young boy shouldn't have. Andy had not been put off. If anything it had steadied his resolve. All he'd ever wanted was to become a cop and take after his dad to help people and put away the bad guys.

He retained a clear vision with regard the career he wanted to pursue, hoping one day to be a homicide detective, maybe even rise higher in the ranks. No doubt about it, he had aspirations.

His mind wandered back to Detective Pratt. If he knew anything at all about the detective he was well aware how he'd view his interest. One word: interference. Well, maybe two words. Another thing he knew about Pratt, he definitely wouldn't be in the detective squad room at this hour. Paperwork or not, Pratt and his buddy were most likely holed up in the nearest bar.

Keen to share his qualms, Andy eagerly drove the short journey back to the police station.

Chapter Twenty-Four

Back at the Squad Room

Andy made an off the cuff decision to use the back stairs to the detective squad as opposed to trudging past the desk sergeant and the guys on the opposite shift.

His breathing tempered by the time he'd reached the third floor, and he stood a moment before proceeding to open the door to the large open-plan office.

Taking a few steps into the office he spotted the first set of booths were vacant. Another few rows further back were occupied. Detectives were randomly positioned engrossed in paperwork, on the phone or glued to a computer screen.

On hearing voices at the far end of the office he spotted Detective Baldwin and his partner. Baldwin was a long-time friend of his pops and a frequent visitor to his home. Not so much now, but in his youth.

Striving to pull up Baldwin's sidekick's name he approached.

Detective Baldwin greeted him warmly on catching sight of him.

"What's up, young Andy, we don't often see you up here?"

Baldwin's partner was scrolling through a database on the computer. He effortlessly acknowledged Andy with a nod as he neared.

Sheepishly Andy spoke.

"I don't want to step on anyone's toes or interfere with an ongoing investigation…"

Before he could elaborate further, Simo ceased what he was doing and looked Andy square in the face.

"But?" he questioned.

Andy didn't directly respond but proceeded to ask his own question, wanting a clear path to divulge his thoughts and of course his hunch. Having no clear facts at this point it was just that, a hunch. Well, a little more than a hunch after Vicky's outburst. Her outburst not withstanding, he had to concede from what he'd gathered hard evidence was a little thin on the ground.

"Pratt and what's his name aren't working late then?"

Eyes were scouring the squad room and sensing something afoot, Baldwin proceeded to speak.

"What's going on? More to the point, who's got up your nose, Andy?"

"You heard about the call me and Willard responded to at the Spring Motel?"

"Yeah, I heard Pratt talking to Carp. Some hooker got jammed up wasn't it?" Baldwin replied.

"Not even close. That's the road they're going down? Ah, that makes sense and explains a lot."

Andy shook his head disdainfully as he spoke.

"Let's have it then. What's your gut telling you? Is there more to it?" Simpkins chirped up.

"This girl Vicky, the victim. And make no mistake she is a victim, she's not on her own. I'm not sure if Pratt and his partner took her to be credible and fully grasped the enormity of what they'd been told. More to the point, if they intend to proceed with this as an investigation. My senses are telling me this is big. It's more than her, the one victim. From the impression I got let's just say they were a tad dismissive. Glib even. She took from their attitude they had her down as a time waster, an exaggerator of the truth. Even after laying it all out for them they're not looking at it seriously."

Andy had more to say but for the moment had ceased talking. It was the way the detectives eyed him, wide eyed, silent.

The long empty pause gave Andy an uneasy jolt.

There was not a word between them and he was unsure how to take this forward.

Had he overstepped the mark? Essentially, he figured he was pointing out Pratt and Carp were doing a half-arsed job.

His dad had been a good detective and had imparted a lot of wisdom and knowledge to his son.

One of his mantras which he'd heard time and time again was, "Go with your gut, son. If something's telling you it's off and doesn't feel right then more than likely there's more to it. You get to the bottom of it until it feels right, until you're satisfied you've unturned every stone. Only then you can put it to bed and move on." Another solid piece of advice was thrown his way. "You owe it to the victim and the job to delve further, this is what good police do. Never ignore a hunch. It could save a life."

Oh yeah, Andy had all this stuff and more firmly imprinted to memory.

Another thing firmly imprinted to memory was fear. Her fear. Vicky the girl who Pratt had down as a hooker. Her anguished, tear-filled face the moment when he'd finally freed her from the tape and rope.

His take was she'd endured torment on another level. She had really suffered. Aside from what he himself had witnessed back at the motel. There was no denying she'd shown remarkable resilience but that shouldn't cloud the judgement of the investigating detectives.

Baldwin made swift eye contact with his partner then back at Andy, then began to speak for the both of them.

"Well, you sure are your father's son," he sprouted light-heartedly. "Nothing's gonna get past you that's for sure," he continued.

Still eyeing Andy, Baldwin probed further.

"I'm taking it you've seen her since handing her over to the paramedics? I also take from this you've built up a rapport and got more out of her than Pratt and Fish? Sorry, I mean Carp," Simpkins sniggered. "Otherwise, I guess we wouldn't be graced with your presence."

Andy's retort followed after what he took to be a somewhat patronising observation on Baldwin's part.

"Nope. That's not it. From what I gather, plus the pain stamped across that poor girl's face which was hard to miss, she'd laid it all out. She gave them chapter and verse. No doubt about it, she's been through the wringer, put through hell. Laying it all out and talking through her ordeal took balls. It

181

doesn't take a brain surgeon to see she's genuine. Or a detective," Andy snapped, but didn't mean to.

"I can see she's got to you. There's a missing girl too, Susie Simmons, though we expect she will probably just turn up. Tell you what, we'll have a word with Pratt in the morning to get a broader view of the case to see which way they're going with it."

Baldwin hoped this would placate the inquisitive cop.

Andy took a breath. He was struck by the information divulged.

"Missing girl you say? How long's she been missing? I guess you've spoken and met the family. Siblings? It wouldn't be she has a sister roughly her age? Jane, Jess, something or other?"

Silence hung in the air.

An unspoken aura passed between the two detectives. They glanced at each other, simultaneously turning to the young officer not quite believing the words coming out of Andy's mouth.

Baldwin was the first to speak.

"You're telling me your little hooker friend has information about Susie Simmons' disappearance?"

Andy began with his riposte, the tone louder and more deliberate.

"I'll tell you what I am telling you and I'll say it again, 'cos you obviously missed it the first time. She's no hooker. I don't give a shit how Pratt and that fish guy read the scene. This girl's been coerced, threatened and she's in fear for her life. She's been drugged and held against her will for weeks by the sound of it. She's the one going all out to get somebody to do something. Moreover, we need to help this youngster. Susie Simmons you said? If it is not your missing girl it's someone's missing daughter. And there are others, she'd made that clear. You need to speak to her. Urgently!"

Rigid with his delivery, he knew he'd overstepped the mark. His tone was sharp and disrespectful but at this juncture he really didn't care. He was pissed off at Baldwin's attitude.

"Wow, I've got your attention now, bringing up the fourteen year old and her sister. Perhaps your missing person, eh?"

Cynicism was oozing with every word and Andy still wasn't done.

Maybe in hindsight he should have been less bolshy and quit while ahead. He'd possibly done more harm than good. It hit him for a split second there must only be so much attitude an ex-cop's kid can get away with.

Throwing anxious glances his way the detectives both listened in stony silence allowing him the floor to say his piece.

Unable to gauge their reaction to his little tangent, Andy's eyes hopped from one detective to the other. He had a lot of respect for both cops who now wore the same bemused if not stunned expression.

The best move I can make is to beat it, he mused. He then thought it was probably wise to attempt to minimise the fallout. In a tone less ardent he addressed the two detectives.

"Well anyway, I've said what I came to say, it's up to you now to do what you think needs to be done. I don't want to be seen to be crossing boundaries here if you get my drift. Enough said, I'll catch you guys later."

Andy did an about turn and walked back the way he'd entered.

After he'd disappeared out of sight Baldwin and Simpkins turned to each other in astonishment. They were clearly taken aback with the little flurry from Andy.

Baldwin was the first one to speak.

"That's a turn up for the books, heh? Something, or should I say someone, sure got him all bent out of shape. I can't work out if it's fish face and Pratt or the girl. One thing's for sure, it's worth a chat. What'd you reckon? A quick trip to Mercy on the way home?" the detective suggested, one hand closing down his computer, the other rooting in his pocket for his car keys. He looked over at Simpkins who'd not shifted except to glance at his watch. He was tapping it repeatedly intimating it had packed up.

Simpkins slung his jacket over his shoulder as he spoke.

"Sorry," said Mike, feeling a little guilty.

If it was a toss-up between his partner and his wife there was no contest, knowing he'd be in a world of hurt missing another one of Angie's family get togethers.

"Alright, alright, no sweat. We don't want to upset the prom queen," Baldwin mocked gently, fully aware Mike had done more than his fair share of late-night visits to crime scenes. "We are only talking about a quick chat, it don't take two of us," concluded Baldwin.

Plus, unlike him Mike had a life outside this place, a pretty good life at that. The prom queen thing was a long-standing joke between them stemming from banter about wives and ex-wives years earlier.

Simpkins had announced proudly, "You do know I married the prom queen, right?"

Mike was one of the rare cops who had balance in his life which brought his thoughts back to young Andy. And his dad. Now there was dedication.

The cogs were whirring ten to the dozen. He'd known Andy most of his life and had watched him grow into a man. A cop, a good one at that. What is it they say about the apple not falling far from the tree? he ruminated in deep thought.

That fire. That passion rarely exhibited in a beat cop. And to go out of his way to bring this, her, to their attention was definitely worth a follow up. He could very well be onto something with his suspicions, cop's instincts and all that.

It was a long shot, yes, but there's always the possibility Andy just might have fallen onto something big. His attention had peaked on hearing a sister mentioned. Point being, he'd take the leads any way he could get them.

Baldwin proceeded to push open the double doors to the corridor leading to Lieutenant Dalton's office to appraise her on this latest development.

Chapter Twenty-Five

An Unexpected Visitor

His boss brought up to speed, Baldwin wasted no time. Minutes behind Simpkins he headed out to his car.

This girl already had the benefit of the Keystone Cops, Pratt and Fish. He was guessing the last thing she would want is to talk to more police. Nevertheless, he felt it incumbent to find out what she knew.

Going over the whole thing for the second time since he'd got into his vehicle, he was hopeful she'd be willing to talk.

Figuring it late for turning up unannounced at the hospital, it was early enough for a half decent evening if things played out. Glancing at the clock in his vehicle he realised it was after seven.

His ponderances turned to the next day. He'd formulated a request to gather the local Henderson boots to do a recanvas of the area around the Simmons home, experience telling him it's commonplace to miss people due to work commitments or vacations first time round.

Five minutes later found him entering the hospital car park.

Due to the late hour, plus him thinking doing this was a courtesy, he didn't intend to be more than fifteen minutes tops.

Deciding to park near the front entrance of the hospital, "easy for a quick getaway," he said out loud, he pulled up in a parking bay meant for dropping and picking people up.

He promptly rummaged in his glove box for his parking permit and placed it firmly on his dashboard.

"A quick chat, get the lay of the land, see what shakes, then I'm gone, outta here," he chuntered to himself while climbing out of his car.

Thirty seconds later he was strolling across the foyer advancing towards the lift having already learned from Andy she was on the fifth floor.

About to reach the lifts, his eyes caught sight of an unexpected glitch. On the floor in front stood plastic yellow barriers. Attached to both lifts were sheets of A4 paper comprising the words "Lifts out of Order".

"What both?" he barked openly in a slightly irritated tone.

The word "shit" shot out without warning.

Right then, no problem, I'm not decrepit, I can climb a few stairs. Call it a workout. It'll do me good and get the old ticker pumping. Who needs the gym?

There was no easing up with the silent moaning as he made his way to the door encompassing the word "Stairs".

His vow to remain calm and friendly was dwindling with each breath. Each breath and each step.

The hope he'd be in and out in the time he'd allotted for the trip was evaporating, grumbling something about gonna kill Andy with each step. A little breathless and wheezing slightly, he eventually arrived on the fifth floor.

A fire door comprising the floor number in big bold lettering stood directly in front of him.

Hand clutching the door bar, he pushed it open.

Baldwin had an uneasy feeling entering the ward. It appeared deserted. His eyes took in the nothingness, scouring the corridor for signs of life. White coats, nurses, family members?

"It's like the *Marie Celeste*, where is everybody?" He was breathing heavily and hoping someone would appear out of thin air.

His position afforded him a view of the whole length of the long corridor of a ward.

Doors adorning the right-hand side were all closed. There were curtained areas opposite but still no signs of life. Uneasiness was replaced by an eerie feeling.

He spied a commotion at the far end of the ward.

Blue uniforms. Not cops, he was guessing they were security personnel.

While his eyes were trained on the people at the other end of the ward, from one of the curtained areas darted a female, a nurse, the first person he'd encountered after trudging up to the fifth floor.

Without hesitation she dashed past heading straight for the lift.

"Where's the fire?" he shouted, having regained his composure.

"No fire," she replied as she took steps to enter the lift, the door slowly closing behind her.

Flabbergasted, he watched the lift door close and the lit numbers above as it descended.

"What the...? This day just gets better," he ranted, him quickly cottoning the lifts were in working order all along.

He walked quickly in the direction of where it was all happening. Curiosity was gnawing at him, his mind focused on why he was there. Andy's victim.

Something within him told him the fracas up ahead had something to do with the girl.

Seeds of anxiety began to take root evoking a weird feeling in his stomach. Another feeling told him his fifteen minutes had whizzed by just like that nurse, as was a relaxing evening in front of the box watching reruns of *Hawaii Five-0*. "Book 'em, Danno," glibly left his lips.

Nearing the commotion up ahead, a security guard strode purposely straight for him.

A few feet from the detective the man forcefully stretched his arm revealing the palm of his hand, an attempt in preventing Baldwin moving any further.

Taking not a scrap of notice, he ignored him and kept up the pace.

Brusque and loud, the guard hollered his demand for Baldwin to heed his warning.

"Sir, stop. Stop right where you are. You can't go any further. We are waiting for the cops."

"I am the cops," offered Baldwin, retrieving his badge from his pocket and waving it in the air, resuming his quest to see the girl.

"That's quick, must be some kinda record," scoffed blue uniform loud enough for Baldwin to hear.

"Oh, we can be quick when we want to be," Baldwin shot back in his usual sarcastic tone.

187

His flippant tone aside, his gut tightened as his hand went to his holster, a default move on his part.

A second security bod was now eagerly vaulting towards him.

Maybe I'll save my breath and just shoot this one, he thought brashly.

"You can't come any further. There's been an incident. We are waiting for the police. Stop right where you are," he went on without taking a breath.

"I've heard it from your mate," offered Baldwin, pointing to the other security guy further down the corridor flashing his badge as he spoke.

"Sorry, my mistake," came the doleful response.

"Would you please tell me what's gone down?" asked Baldwin.

The security guy went on to impart the sequence of events as reported to him, making a point that he was getting it second-hand from nurses on the scene. He had not seen the perp though was told he was dark skinned.

Glancing at Baldwin, he quickly changed the last bit to African-American.

Baldwin began putting the pieces together in his head.

By now they were standing with the rest of the onlookers outside the room. The room which held a recently admitted patient. A young woman.

The name of the patient on the door of that room was clearly visible: "Miss Victoria Walker".

Synapses were going back and forth in Baldwin's brain as he tried to figure this out.

Had he got the full story from Andy?

Baldwin naturally had a hundred questions. The first, and the one which took precedence over the other ninety-nine, was is she alive?

"Is she badly hurt? Is that her blood?" he said, gesturing towards the blood splatter visible a little way inside the room.

"Yes, not sure and don't think so," came the sheepish response from Mr blue uniform.

"Elaborate," snapped the detective sharply. He'd lost what little patience he'd clung to whilst clambering up the stairs.

Breaking his thoughts, his phone came to life. It was the lieutenant and the words "Oh shit" again flowed freely from his lips. This time he'd an audience and felt a little embarrassed. Turning his back on them the word "Lieutenant" sped out of his mouth. "Yeah, I've just got here. That's right, fifth floor." There was a slight pause while Baldwin heard his boss out. "Yeah, the same girl. Someone tried to off her from what I can make out. I'll update you as soon as I have more." With that he hung up.

He hoped she wouldn't ring back wanting a more in-depth update, at least until he had more details. At this precise moment he had nada.

Baldwin surveyed the girl's room, the crime scene as rent a cop had effusively pointed out.

Turning to him he enquired pointedly, "Where is the girl?"

"Oh, she's OK. Well, I suppose OK's stretching it a bit after what's she's been through."

Just for once it would be nice to get a straight answer were the words itching to hurtle out of the detective's mouth.

Clearly sensing Baldwin's frustration he offered the first bit of relevant information, the first bit of good news.

"We, well, me really, thought it best to move her. We have a wing on the fourth floor not in use at the moment so I instructed a couple of porters to wheel her down there. Two of my guys were standing guard until the cops show up." Meeting Baldwin's eyes with a smug smile, he was clearly eager to pass on the baton. "Well, you're here now so over to you. Do you want me to take you to her?"

"Yes, that would be most helpful, Mr Piper," Baldwin said, having just spotted a name badge on the blue uniform.

"It's Joe, no need for Mr Piper. What's your name again? Don't think I caught it." The guard was having visions of a working relationship forming with the detective.

Keeping pace with his new friend, Baldwin did a sarcastic roll of the eyes and shake of the head as he ignored the question, both traipsing through a door at the furthest part of the ward, a door which read "Danger. Do Not Enter".

On reaching the floor below the guard produced a key card and slid it in the door.

Continuing down a corridor the detective spotted the two security guards "Joe" had referred to.

"Any problems?" Joe asked. Without allowing either of them the opportunity to open their mouths, he pushed through a set of double doors and took steps into a room on the right-hand side.

Entering what appeared and smelled like a newly decorated white walled room he caught sight of a bed smack bang in the middle, the room reminiscent of a psychiatric ward from one of those classic horror films.

Baldwin sighted a figure on this lonely out of place bed.

A small outline which could almost be that of a child was curled up in a foetal position shrouded beneath the covers.

Chapter Twenty-Six

Shock and Disbelief (Vicky)

I'd dared to believe my brush with misery could be in my rear-view mirror. I'd paid my dues, done my time, surely enough bad shit had come my way for two lifetimes.

Now I find myself in the middle of a new kind of shit storm. New but no less terrifying. An appendage to my non-stop prolonged nightmare.

At this juncture, I'd describe my existence as a never-ending bad dream. I wake and am afforded a glimpse, a moment of reflection, then wham! I am catapulted into a different more dangerous set of circumstances.

Jesus, keep me awake. Don't let me sleep. It's sheer luck, a miracle, I hadn't drifted off back in that room. My mind had perceptibly remained on high alert.

No longer a mere concept, that which I feared had without warning suddenly become a reality.

This fear meshed deep inside my psyche was ingrained and here to stay. From the second I'd legged it barefoot out of that ramshackle perverts' lair it had crawled inside my head.

Lurking amongst all the other crap swimming around in my head I had a strong feeling an attempt would be made on my life, though thinking it and coming face to face with it was a whole different ball game.

I'd done the inconceivable and escaped and given one of them a parting gift, a taste of his own medicine. I am also a living, breathing, talking witness. I was expendable as there were plenty more where I came from. They didn't want the big mouthed troublesome English girl mucking up their moneymaking venture.

My mind was doing somersaults and I was on the cusp of spiralling into madness. I was constantly questioning how much can one person endure before losing it completely. I'll be knocking on the door of the nuthouse if there was any more of this.

Recalling this morning laying on that skanky mattress in one of Sin City's delightful little establishments, the identical notion zigzagged through my brain. Then this, a knife wielding dirtbag coming at me with a blade.

Trembling and fearful, here I lay ducked under the covers in a state of shock. I couldn't get my head around what I'd witnessed or been party to.

The picture of the knife glistening from the downlights was firmly etched in my memory, together with those dark, dead eyes of that sneaker wearing psychopath.

Suddenly, I was thrown out of picturing knife wielding maniacs by the sound of footsteps, heavy footsteps plodding along the hard tiled floor.

I was tempted to re-enact the break the sound barrier hollering and screaming I'd perfected earlier. The emptiness of this bare room bounced each step off the wall, the heavy footsteps getting closer and closer.

Laying here wound up as tightly as a spring I deduced the footsteps were unfamiliar, different to those of the security people. The guards to my new prison. By now my ears were accustomed to any sound emanating from within these walls and beyond.

Whispering voices, the treads of their feet, rustling newspaper, the jingling of keys, my amplified hearing missed nothing.

I'd been informed I am now in a secure location. Secure? It's an empty ward awash with the stench of paint. If I didn't feel nauseated already then I darn well do now.

I'd also been informed by one of the security guards that two of them had been tasked to stand guard over me until the cops arrived, adding they would "keep me safe".

I wouldn't bet my lunch money on that, I thought, as I lay frozen on this bed here in this stinky paint smelling domain.

The shoes now had a voice. The decisive voice of a police detective according to his greeting.

I remained cocooned in my makeshift hidey place.

As yet, the police had instilled me with little if any confidence.

I heard him ask one of the security bods if he could bring him a chair. Well, when I say ask it was more of an order.

I gathered they jumped to it as seconds later I could hear the feet of a chair scrape the hard floor nearby inching closer to my bed.

Chair deposited, I took it that he being the detective positioned it himself near the head of the bed.

Again he spoke, his voice even, pronounced and calm. With an air of extreme confidence came words of reassurance. I'm assuming he hoped, if not considered, these words would count as convincing and sweep away my fear and trepidation.

"I'm here to help, Miss Walker, but in order to help you I need you to assist me. I understand you've been through one hell of an ordeal, and I'm not just referring to the harrowing incident in the ward above. Primarily, what you'd been put through before you ended up in hospital. My mate Finn prompted this visit and told me a little. I was actually here already on my way to see you immediately after this latest shocking incident. I'd like you to tell me if you recognise the person who tried to harm you, but more importantly I need you to know something, Miss Walker, something very important. Nobody, and I mean nobody, is going to lay a finger on you, that I promise."

To hear these words expelled in such a resolute manner and voiced with tremendous purpose had a profound impact on me.

Indeed, it was a moving statement from someone who doesn't know me from Adam. The sentiment was delivered in the softest of tones in a voice which oozed sincerity and promise. For the first time I'd been offered a little hope, but it was hope nonetheless.

Maybe, just maybe, I have finally got someone's attention, a cop to take me seriously.

It had taken me close to getting sliced and diced, but hey, at least I've got them to sit up and listen. I decided to make a move and expose my duct tape stripey face.

And if I'm honest curiosity had won me over. Plus, I had questions of my own.

I slowly edged my way out of my cocoon to a sitting position, both hands clutching a blanket securely positioned all the way up to my neck.

In a kindly way the face matched his voice, and although I couldn't place him he held an air of familiarity.

He politely extended his hand to make my acquaintance.

"I'm Detective Baldwin, nice to meet you. Sorry it's under these circumstances," the friendly greeting from the friendly sounding cop.

"I'm Victoria Walker. Vicky's fine."

"I want you to feel at ease here, Vicky. Before I get down to the questions I urgently require answers to, is there anything you want to ask me?"

It was my turn to speak and ask a question, a little irrelevant if not flippant under the circumstances but heh, he did ask.

"Yeah, there is actually. Who's Finn?"

His eyes twinkled as he offered a smile.

"Ah, sorry, I think you know him as officer Andy Finnerty."

"Yeah, him," slotting it together in my mind.

"Finn was the nickname for his dad. He's retired off the job, worked in our squad for years. We all took Andy under our wing after his mom passed. He grew up in the squad room. Andy's so like his dad some of us refer to him as Finn. Or little Finn. I shouldn't think the lad takes offence," Baldwin said.

"Yeah, he mentioned his dad earlier when he showed up here."

I was well aware what the irrelevant chit-chat was in aid of. His attempt at putting me at ease before the onslaught.

"Please can we just get on with it?" I urged.

"No problem. To the point, I like that," came my newest cop's keen observation.

Baldwin pulled out a notebook, pen and a small tape recorder from his jacket pocket.

"Do you mind if I record our conversation, Vicky? I'd like everything down on the record if that's OK."

"No, that's fine," I uttered, wanting it over with. I was emotionally exhausted with adrenaline almost depleted with each repeat of my horrendous journey.

"OK then, we'll take things one at a time. Do you know who attacked you tonight and why?"

"Nope. Never clapped eyes on the knife wielding toerag in my life. It all happened so fast. I was half awake when I heard squeaky sneakers drawing closer and closer. All at once the shoes came to a halt at my door. Instinctively I darted up. We locked eyes and I froze momentarily. There was no movement and no words. I screamed and hollered as fear overtook me. I needed help. Then as they say, all hell broke loose. I dived out of the bed. Talk about the Duracell bunny. I finished up the opposite end of the bed to where he stood. I'm still making an almighty racket as he pulled out a knife. I don't know why but I picked up a metal food tray, to shield myself or whack him I'm not sure. You've probably been told my screams brought two nurses. A male nurse tackled him, he's a hero. I feel bad, I think he was the one got stabbed. One thing you can do for me please, detective, is find out how he is."

I closed my eyes in an attempt to bring specific details into focus.

"He wore a blue work type overall and blue baseball cap, Mexican if I had to make a guess. He had a tattoo on the wrist he held the knife, but I couldn't make it out. Sorry, I meant to say the left hand. I guess he was left-handed."

My head spinning, I ceased with the rabbiting for a minute. My rendition had flowed freely, almost on autopilot.

The detective remained patient and refrained from interrupting my frequent pauses, listening closely and digesting every single word. The vibe projected one of understanding.

If I had to make a snap judgement I'd say my new cop friend was unflappable.

I was unsure if I ought to come forward with my theory that this could possibly be down to my original kidnapper Jake.

I forced myself to keep on talking and allow him a glimpse of the terror I'd had thrust upon me whilst in the hands of those evil men.

My hesitation was prompted by my earlier encounter with Vegas's finest and Andy who in my mind hadn't grasped the enormity of my ordeal.

That said, I must have hit a nerve otherwise why this visit?

Still smarting and daunted by the way I was received by the last pair of detectives, I had to hope that this time round would yield better results.

This was different, this cop genuinely listened. Listened intently.

I dived in deciding on a shorter watered down version, emphasising on vital chunks of information.

I opened with how I was taken and held against my will and what me and the others were made to do by Jake and his fiendish friend.

The van, the girls, the food or lack thereof.

My serendipitous escape from a rapist.

Simon, his role in all this.

"It was as though I'd landed in the twilight zone, one inexplicable bad thing after another. Though I had my suspicions, I never determined if this Simon character was in cahoots with the other lot."

I made it clear I'd given chapter and verse to the other detectives who at best appeared to be paying me lip service.

What was it Pratt said again? "Some version of events and not something they hear every day," or words to that effect. I felt like adding, "Guess what, neither do I, buddy, but it sure as hell happened."

As I'd done with the other police officers I brought to his attention the last girl kidnapped. My tone was laced with urgency as I worked my way through the Susie story articulating my disgust and revulsion as I informed him of her age.

I extracted every detail I could from my woolly brain concluding it could be they'd changed tact and decided to use youngsters. More profit, easier to handle, who knows how their sick minds work. Worryingly, her sister's and friends' names had been brandished about.

Baldwin stayed close lipped and allowed me talk. He was openly transfixed and absorbed every word, a different kettle of fish from the last two, and though recording my unfolding torment he'd also taken to jotting things in his notepad. He listened and wrote while I hurtled out potential clues. Hopefully they were potential clues, conveying the sequence of events as they'd unfolded.

I was expressing how I felt the need to protect the youngster. "I'm no hero or anything but I did all I could to shield her. If what I'd experienced was anything to go by she'd got enough bad shit coming her way. I'm telling you, her nightmare hadn't got off the starting line, poor girl."

Again I paused, attempting to maintain my composure and struggling to veil my mind from picturing Susie and Claire. "We were down to three that night. Three including the new girl. The others were taken to a motel, it was a fluke I was not shipped out."

Glancing at Baldwin I noticed he'd put the notebook to one side. I ceased with the incessant prattling. He began to speak and I sensed the urgency in his tone. Finally, they're on the case. He'd allowed me speak and absorbed the information. Now for the questions.

"Am I correct in the belief you're unable to pinpoint precisely where this house with the basement is situated?"

"That's the point, I don't think I'm able to, I haven't a clue. I wish I could. I'm sorry, I feel terrible I can't guide you and take you to the others. I feel real bad leaving them but I didn't have a choice, I had to run and keep on running. Then I found a place to hide. I cowered under that tarp scared to death he might rumble me. I'd no idea what or who I was dealing with."

Tears pricked my eyes as the words tumbled out pitifully.

"Don't beat yourself up, Vicky, you're doing good. Everything you've told me and the other detectives is tremendously helpful. It is vital you know this. There'll be knowledge and facts you've repressed, but it'll all come back. Behind the grisly images engulfing your thought process your brain is striving to assimilate everything. It'll return eventually. Trust me. It is evident you're a bright girl, but time is shrinking rapidly so it's vital we get our skates on and find them. I'd like you to close your eyes and transport your mind back to the van. That trip back and forth to the motels. I know it's hard after what those bastards put you through."

I closed my eyes, squeezing them tightly shut in the blind hope this action would tease the information to the forefront of my brain. All I'd ever wanted was for someone to listen and take me seriously.

I was not quite with it as I was probably still riding the wave from some drug or other. However, I'm definitely on board and willing to give anything a go.

I attempted to visualise the journey in my mind. It wasn't easy. Recalling any of it wasn't easy.

I'd boxed it off in my head as I didn't want to relive it.

That journey we'd been forced to take so many times, collectively crammed like sardines side by side relying on each other for comfort, warmth and sanity. We were pulling up words of solace from deep within in the hope we'd make a difference in helping each another.

That scruffy, cold, hard seated, blue rickety van.

Tears trickled down my cheeks as I silently cried.

The soulless faces of my friends unceremoniously seeped into my head, desperation and fear etched onto their bleak tear-filled faces as they bound us.

Huddled together we all had the same thoughts and questions. When will this all end? Will the day come when we'll be allowed to take our lives back?

My eyes were firmly locked while reliving those moments, those thoughts. I felt his strong hand touch my shoulder. He was clearly sensing my pain and distress. To my surprise, just as with Andy's touch, I didn't recoil.

Pressing forward he continued, his soft tone reminiscent of Andy's voice when my world was full of blackness, blackness he had released me from.

"What would you say was the approximate timeframe from Vegas to where you were held?" I could hear him breathing anxiously. "Did you get a sense if the van drove on the freeway? If so, can you recall for how long?" He paused momentarily before easing into further questioning. "You'd probably, but not necessarily know if you entered a ramp. Are you there in your head, is the journey becoming clearer? Don't worry if it doesn't come, it will." Probing delicately, his tone reeked of empathy and understanding.

"Yeah, I'm not absolutely sure how long from the strip. The bottom end of the strip. There were cars either side of the van, we were on a freeway, probably for close to an hour. There was some traffic but we usually headed back during the early hours."

My memory was flooding me with visions, catching a glimpse of the van as we were shepherded into the back. There was a view up ahead of the bright lights at the end of the strip a few blocks below Fremont Street.

My eyes remained firmly closed but I pushed on racking my brain for details. My aim was to pull facts from that compartment in my head, that compartment where I'd stored horror, disgust and revulsion. Horror I found impossible to eradicate.

Words free flowed as I tried to keep my emotions in check.

"Fremont Street, lights and signs. A dingy blue van. One of those with the door on the side which slides open. There were bits of white paint around the rim of the sliding door like maybe it was white once," I enthused, gleeful at recounting this small detail. "I remember Susie referred to a blue van, and old tatty thing. She said it was out of place in her neighbourhood. She was waiting on a corner for the walk sign when this same van pulled up at the side of her."

"That's good. Real good, kiddo. You're doing real good." Baldwin's calm voice was full of praise. "Names, Vicky? Are there any names you can recall?"

"Yes, I've a few names. Mostly first names apart from the guy I told you about who snatched me from the strip. White two-door BMW. The same person that took some of the others too. The psycho's name is Jake Brown. If you go online you'll see his dating profile. He's probably schmoozing some poor sucker as we speak," I added indignantly.

It was his turn with the dialogue, eloquently and purposefully filling me in on a few things.

"This Susie you met. Her name is Susie Simmons. She was reported missing about three days ago. We weren't sure if she'd just took off. The sister, Jess, who may be in danger is older than Susie, at seventeen. Myself and my partner Detective Simpkins are on the missing girl's case. Now, Vicky, I'm going to request another detective come down here to write up specific details such as names and descriptions. If anything else jumps out at you please be sure to pass it on. However small the detail it all adds up. Think of it as a jigsaw. All these little pieces come together to make a complete picture."

The detective rose from his seat clicking his tiny recorder off as he did so. Pulling a sheet from his notebook he handed it to me along with a pen.

"Also, jot down anything you'd like me to bring you. Food, toiletries, anything you need. I'll pick it up when I come by later or one of the officers will drop it off. I'm going to make a brief visit to the Simmons residence, then on to secure a safe house where we'll be able to provide you with comfort and safety. There'll be uniforms here soon as I leave so try not to worry, Vicky," Baldwin informed me gingerly.

Leaving the chair by my bed and talking ten to the dozen on his phone, he walked with purpose out of the big white room. For sure I thought, a man on a mission.

Chapter Twenty-Seven

Jess

There it goes again, that knock. They have this certain knock the cops.

I knew it was him before I heard that dulcet tone. Why so late? Has the chosen one made an appearance? Oh, I don't want to miss this as I sneaked down the stairs doing a good impression of the Pink Panther walk without the music.

"Yeah, I'm right on," she muttered as quiet as a mouse. Baldwin with a sidekick.

Not the original sidekick, a newer, better-looking version. Younger, early twenties.

From her hidden position the vantage point offered a decent view, a decent view of the newbie.

He was slim though quite muscular. I bet he works out, she mused. His hair was dark blonde in colour and he was handsome in a cute baby-faced way. Not my usual type, but hey, if it goes south with Jacky boy he might do as a replacement. You never know which way the wind's gonna blow, she sniggered.

Inching her way to the kitchen area where they'd all congregated, her mum was doing her best barista impression offering coffee and tea. For once her dad had vacated his position by the lounge window.

From her position in the dining room Jess could just about see Baldwin. See him and hear him.

She was stunned by a sudden loud clatter, breaking crockery hitting the hard tiled floor of the kitchen.

An instantaneous shrill cry followed, more of a wail than cry, immediately realising it had come from her mum. The crying developed into sporadic snivelling as she struggled to form words.

Hearing this, Jess was tempted to gatecrash but pulled back. Her dislike of the detective superseded her desire to get in on the action or get acquainted with Baldwin's sidekick.

"It's good, Chrissy, somebody having seen her. It means she's still alive and we can get her back," declared Auntie Jean earnestly.

Her dad strode purposefully toward her mum. Taking her in his arms his fingers gently brushed away the curly blonde hair speckling her puffy bloodshot eyes. He lovingly kissed the top of her head as he held her, and gently rubbed her shoulders as he spoke.

"We will get her back. Mark my words, we'll bring our daughter home."

The tone had notably changed when he said the words "our daughter".

It was a rare shared moment of togetherness by her parents. Jess was momentarily gobsmacked, surprise tinged with jealousy mixed together.

Keeping a firm hold of his wife her dad had more to say.

"And you say this girl is at Mercy under guard? And she'd been taken by someone she met online? A date on the strip? What has she got to do with my daughter, Detective? What did you say this guy's name is? Jack? I'm pretty sure Susie doesn't know anyone like that. She wouldn't get in a BMW, blue van or any other car for that matter. She knows better." Dr Simmons was directing his irritation at the detective, ignoring the young officer. "Oh, this gets better and better," came the exasperated voice of her dad clearly pissed at what he took to be insinuations by the detective.

Jess listened keenly unbelieving of the words fired angrily from her father's lips. Her thoughts darted first from one thing then another. She was tempted to reveal herself and find out more but was terrified of what she'd already been privy to.

Silence hung heavy in the air for what seemed like an eternity.

She guessed Baldwin was allowing her dad to cool his jets before dropping another bombshell. On tenterhooks and waiting with bated breath for the next instalment of the Susie saga, the sneaky young girl stood firm.

He then began with what Jess considered damage limitation, choosing his words carefully by the sound of it.

"Dr Simmons, you're not hearing me. In no way am I implying your daughter knew this guy or would get into his car nor meet up with him for a date. I'm informing you of this in the event that you may know a Jake Brown or on the off chance your daughter has mentioned him or the car. Vicky has given us information which is credible. Evidently, she met your daughter on the day she disappeared. Without giving too much away as I do not wish to jeopardise an ongoing investigation, Miss Walker, along with several other innocent girls, met this individual online."

Pausing as if not daring to impart the rest Baldwin continued in a more subdued tone.

"Miss Walker met this Mr Brown just the once, the same evening she was taken. As did the other victims. After accepting a ride home in a white BMW she was snatched, apparently taken from the strip roughly six weeks ago. The name's quite possibly false but it's the description we consider relevant. The information she is able to provide will hopefully result in bringing your daughter home."

Jess was glued to the floor. A shiver ran down her spine, did a U-turn and ran all the way back up to her neck.

"Oh God," she said to herself, "is this really happening?" She tiptoed backwards until she was out of the main living area, almost taking a backwards tumble over a coffee table as she did so.

Turning around quietly, she sprinted two, now three steps at a time until at the top of the stairs, ending up on the wide landing.

Her mission was to gather her things and get the hell out of there. She grabbed her purse, jacket, a couple of changes of underwear and her phone. Both of her phones.

Her purse on her shoulder and boots in one hand, Jess crept back down the long winding stairs in her stocking feet, through the lobby and slowly out the main door. Baldwin's Crown Vic or whatever they are called was parked in the drive. She'd heard the heated conversation whilst making her escape, her dad doing most of the talking as usual. Good, she thought, keeps them occupied.

For a brief moment she thought about letting the tyres down on the Crown car. Then it came to her that she wasn't sure how to do this. The deciding factor was she might get her hands dirty or, God forbid, break a nail.

In her peripheral vision she spotted a cop leaning on a patrol car, a young guy who was cheekily stomping on the end of a cigarette in their drive.

Easy pickings, she smiled to herself.

"Hey, Jess, you alright? Should you be out on your own? Does your dad know you're out?" the questions erupting from the mouth of the cigarette smoking cop.

She didn't know him by name. Although she was introduced to him three days ago when all this kicked off she simply wasn't listening. She didn't know any of their names apart from Mr cantankerous Baldwin. Some people are so not on my radar, she thought, wishing Baldwin wasn't on her radar either.

She ignored all the well-meaning questions.

"Your shift finished?" she asked in her little girly voice.

"Yep, going for a couple of beers then get my head down. Maybe watch the game on TV. I'll be back here at 5 am to relieve my colleague Wes," offered the young cop.

I didn't want your life story. A yes or no would have sufficed, thought Jess.

"I don't suppose you can give me a lift to Mercy? I need to get some files for Dad, might help him occupy his mind for a bit."

"Sure. Hop in. No problemo," his enthusiasm brimming over.

Jess thanked him and got in at the side of him.

In full friendly banter mode, he talked about his life, family and why he'd joined the force.

This is gonna be a hell of a long journey, she thought. Some people just never know when to button it.

Trying not to encourage him, finally she gave in.

"I don't want to be rude or seem ungrateful, but do you mind if we don't talk? I'm a bit tender with my sister being missing 'an all. I'm sure you get it."

"Oh yeah, off course. Sorry, didn't think." Apologetic words stumbled out of the mouth of the friendly cop.

They drove the fifteen minutes from Henderson to the hospital in silence. There was the occasional smile on catching each other's eye.

Dropping her at the entrance of the hospital he said goodbye then drove away.

Right then, to find the correct ward. Out the corner of her eye to her right she spotted the reception desk.

"How 'yer doing?" she asked in a casual upbeat tone, hoping she wouldn't be recognised having been a stand in in her dad's office from time to time.

A lady probably in her forties looked up from her computer. She said nothing and simply continued staring at the screen and tapping the keyboard.

How people think they can pull that look off over a size twelve is totally beyond me, Jess thought, as the clerk bent down to put a file in a drawer. Disparaging little nuances were floating around her head as she watched the admin lady do her job.

Eyeing Jess suspiciously, she completed what she was doing, looked up and spoke.

"How can I help you?"

"I know it's late and visiting hour has passed, but I've just heard my cousin has been admitted as an emergency today."

"What is her name?" asked the receptionist.

"Vicky Walker," replied Jess, craning her neck in an attempt to peer over the desk at the information on the computer screen.

The lady fidgeted and appeared a little agitated. Without taking her eyes from the screen she began to speak.

"Well, we do have a Victoria Walker. Hmmm, yes. I'm not sure what ward she's been moved to though. Hmm, let me see now, yes, there was an incident on the ward."

Continuing to digest information from the screen, she seemed totally mesmerised. Mesmerised and a little perturbed.

"There's a notation stating the police were called."

She breathed in and seemed to take forever to release the air, clearly enthralled by what appeared on the screen in front of her.

"Someone was hurt. No, more than one person was hurt. They've moved your cousin to a secure ward. A ward by herself from what I gather reading the notation. I wasn't here, I have just come on duty so only know what I am reading. Anyway, you won't be able to see her. Patients need their rest you know and visiting is over."

By now Jess had both elbows on the raised reception desk and was gawping at the lady. She was ready with plan B if she doesn't play ball. Her intention was to get in and out quickly, momentarily wondering if her dad had any clout with personnel so he could get dodgy hair the sack.

I'll bore her into submission, that usually works. Jess's mouth took over and began with what she does best, the onslaught of total crap hurtled right at the receptionist like a frisbee, utter garbage secreted at full speed.

"You don't look busy. You don't mind if I wait here for my pops, do you? I can't be sure when he'll show up though. He'll just assume I'll be gabbing with Vic, he knows what we're like when we get our heads together."

It worked like a dream. The woman was ready to have an incident of her own. Her face changed colour and seemed to be puffing up by the second.

"Tell you what, what did you say your name is again?" the exasperated tone from a woman on the edge.

"I didn't but it's Cassie," Jess offered with great ease.

"You should be OK to pop up for a bit. Don't be too long mind. As she's in a ward by herself you won't be disturbing any other patients. It's the fourth floor, south wing. If she's asleep you'll have to come back tomorrow. And don't tell anyone I gave you permission, do you hear? I like this job."

"Scouts honour," said Jess smiling as she put her fingers to her head, did a salute, turned, and strutted smugly out of there.

No words, a simple disapproving shake of the head watching Jess flounce out of there and head for the stairs.

Taking the stairs two at a time she soon found herself on the fourth floor.

As Jess entered through a door ahead of a corridor, she immediately caught sight of two security guys standing at the far end in front of a double door. Common sense dictated that's where she would find who she'd come to see.

She strode with an air of confidence up to where the two guys stood. Looking her up and down, they immediately stopped talking.

"You with the police?" enquired a gormless-looking chubby guy in a blue uniform.

As tempting as it was to say, "Yes, I am with the police," and add, "Detective Simmons," as it had a nice ring to it, she said no.

As quickly as they asked the question, she wondered how many years she would get for impersonating a cop. Not worth the hassle, Dad's got enough on his plate, she deliberated.

"No, I'm here to see my cousin Vicky. I thought after everything she's been through she could use a friendly face."

"Well, we're not supposed to let anyone in. We're waiting for an officer of the law to relieve us," said the not as round one purposefully.

Smiling she began with her usual bullshit.

"You know, I would have figured you two for cops," pointing her well-manicured glossy finger at the slightly slimmer one then back to the other. "Maybe it's the uniform. I bet you could really carry the police uniform off. Yeah, I mean the two of 'yer."

Her arms crossed on her chest and pushing her boobs out her eyes went from one then the other, smiling effusively as she imparted this piece of crap while watching their bulging eyes giving her the once over.

"Quite frankly I'm surprised you don't know this. Come on, someone must have said as much, surely? I bet that's why they chose you pair to guard my cousin. One look at you two, vavoom! Bad guy outta there sharpish. I'm glad she's got you two on the case anyhow."

Sprouting the nonsense which never fails to pop into her pretty little head, it serenely made its way from those full pink lips in the direction of the intended targets.

The two guys began chatting away. How they'd thought about joining the force, comparing what that would entail as opposed to what they did as security. One of them said he had his sights set on going down that very route, joining Las Vegas police.

It's like they'd forgotten or lost interest in the job in hand. Good job I'm not a knife wielding bunny boiler, thought Jess.

"I'll only be five minutes," she said, upping the girly tone as she pushed past them gesturing in the direction of the door.

"I guess you're not a danger to anyone, and being a relative 'an all it won't hurt. OK, five minutes, do you hear, young lady?" said the guard.

Jess was halfway through the double doors before the words were expelled from his lips.

She found herself in a huge white walled ward. She entered Vicky's room and sat on the chair next to the bed.

She was visualising Baldwin, notebook in hand and pen poised at the ready seated on that chair.

She shifted her thoughts to the task in hand, knowing the police could be right behind her. "Here goes, now for the hard part," she whispered under her breath.

Chapter Twenty-Eight

A Revelation and a Half (Vicky & Jess)

After running through my nightmare for the detective, plus speaking to another cop, my emotional energy reserves were running on empty. I was out for the count, not completely, but certainly dozing. Dozing and thinking.

As quickly as he'd said his goodbyes the other detective appeared. And the best bit was I'd recalled a few more details. Pertinent details.

Specifically, at the end of the dirt track I recall two road names and a sign for a petrol station a mile to the left. I'm hoping these details bear fruit. My soft-spoken detective friend was correct. Random bits did pop into my head. It could be the drugs filtering out of my system that assisted in unravelling details which I guess I hadn't realised had registered.

Sleepy and a little out of it, something or somebody caught my attention.

A young girl's voice. A familiarity about the tone. Is it my imagination conjuring up voices?

I manoeuvred my torso to where the voice stemmed from, my escape route. I'd sussed the route out of here just in case the shit rains down again.

I peeked above the blanket and caught sight of a young girl heading my way. The familiar voice had morphed into a familiar figure.

I instantly got it. A sister or relative of young Susie. Wow! It was surreal how alike they were in appearance and tone of voice.

A few feet from the entrance of my "secure" white room, the young girl walked purposefully in my direction. Inches from the chair, she took a deep breath and opened her mouth to speak.

"I'm Jess, Susie's big sister. How are you doing, are you OK?"

"Do you want platitudes or the real answer? You genuinely interested?" I shot back sharply.

"Sorry I didn't mean to…" her voice trailed off.

"No, it's me who should be sorry. No doubt you've had an update from the detective and you're concerned about Susie."

"Well, there's that. But I need to ask you something."

The girl went silent for a moment, outwardly nervous, apprehensive.

It got me worried. Giving the cops chapter and verse was one thing, the last thing I wanted was to open up to family members.

"This thing I need to ask, well, it's a bit delicate really," revealed my mysterious visitor.

"This Jake, Jack, whatever he calls himself. Baldwin said he snatched you after you'd been on a date. A first date. And the car. You'd brought up to the cops it was a white BMW, right? Sorry to go over this stuff again, I guess you're sick of rehashing it all. Is there anything else that comes to mind?"

No way had I been expecting this.

The hesitation and angst in her voice was patently palpable. Now I'm getting it. The real reason I found her stood in front of me looking like the cat that lost the canary. Or her sister.

"You see," said the pretty blonde teenager looking like she'd rather not disclose what was on her mind, "I think I know him, and worse still I introduced him to Susie a few weeks back," came the sheepish confession.

Perplexed, I had to ask. "Why are you coming forth with this now? Here, to me? More to the point, do the police know?"

"I heard the description the detective gave my folks. I'm a bright girl, I'm not stupid. I worked it out and put two and two together." The reply came easily but awkwardly.

The misty-eyed Jess looked at me with terror in her eyes.

"I think you'd better tell me the whole story, Jess. Your sister and friends of mine are in serious danger. They need help.

Your help. Girls have been killed, murdered, raped. Do you want me to go on? You need to know the truth." My voice was blunt but to the point.

She sat on the chair and sobbed. For her sister? Herself? At this juncture I hadn't the foggiest. Maybe the thought of dropping the ball and introducing her sister to that slimeball or what her parents would think of her. I really didn't know. I know if I had a sister and this was me I'd be bloody wailing, but I'd want to do the right thing.

"Here, blow your nose and wipe your eyes," I prompted, passing her a handful of Kleenex.

"Look, Jess, I've no desire to see you in trouble. We're talking about an older guy here. He probably tried to groom you into introducing your sister. I get it. I was young once. Let's face it, he had me fooled and us Yorkshire girls take some sweet talking."

The crying ceased. I even managed to raise a little smile from that blotchy, nonetheless pretty face.

Words flowed from her lips. It was like she'd been itching to tell someone to unburden herself.

"I can tell you where he lives, where his condo is and what number. Also, where he hangs out. He will be in the casino lounge right now. If not there I can offer several other places he is likely to be."

"Do you know what he does for a living, where he works?"

"No, not really. I tried to wheedle it out of him but he just changes the subject saying he's a businessman. He always has tons of money though. I know he has a brother but I don't know his name."

The air of confidence she'd trotted in here with had dissipated. She was in pain. Or trouble. Probably both in equal measures.

"I shouldn't be here," came the pitiful mousy voice from the side of me.

Here we go. I'll let her ramble on and get it off her chest, then remind her again it's her sister who's in grave danger.

"This is all gonna come down on me. A mountain of crap all heaped on top of me, I just know it. It's always the same. That cop Baldwin hates me. Hell, my whole family hate me, and when they get wind of me having dated this psycho for nearly a year…"

She paused, sighed and blew air from her lungs so sharply I thought I was trapped in a wind tunnel.

"God, some of the texts that went back and forth. Oh, the pictures. Jesus." She closed her eyes at that one as if praying to the Lord or hoping to be beamed up, one or the other.

At that she carried on with the self-deprecation.

"If they find out I told him things about Susie. Never mind the meet and greet. I'm screwed. I'm one sunny day away from finding a rock big enough to crawl under and die. Dead girl walking, that's me. I can't go home. Not that they'd notice if I weren't there. This is all so twisted. Talk about screw the pooch."

If feeling sorry for yourself was an Olympic sport this gal would be gold medal material. Boy, could she talk. She didn't stop to breathe. If I'd have wanted to chip in I'd have no chance.

Finally ending the one-girl pity party she shut up.

I didn't want or intend to lose it with her but I couldn't help what came next.

"Get a grip, will you, you need to step up. This is more than likely the most important decision you'll ever have to make in your life. No, scrap that, it shouldn't be a decision. It's a no brainer. You have to put your big girl pants on and do the right thing. I think you know this. Like you said, you're a bright girl. Although I've yet to see any evidence of that. I guess a member of your fan club came out with that one?"

"Yeah, my boyfriend tells me all the time." The stupidest statement thus far that flew out of her mouth.

"Oh, well then, you must be smart. I don't suppose he's trying to get in your pants by any chance?"

"He don't need to flatter me to get in anything. We have a connection. Chemistry. No matter what, I know he loves me. He treats me good and buys me nice things. Expensive, designer things."

"I get it, I totally see where you're coming from," in a tone that said, "Yeah, I really do get it but do you?"

"You don't understand," was her pathetic retort.

212

"You got that right," gushed from my lips.

Does she actually believe what she's saying? I had to ask myself. Then it hit me. She really does. Naïve and bananas all rolled into one. And I thought I ought to be knocking on the door of the psycho ward!

"Hah, it's all falling into place. I see it now. You're a self-serving little madam who wants me to do your dirty work for you. That it?" I scoffed.

"I'll lose him if he thinks I grassed him up to the cops."

"And if we don't get behind who's fronting all this you'll lose your sister and my friends. And that, young lady, could be on you. Do you want to live with this on your conscience? For the sake of some nice things and a shag with an older, rich guy. A man who should know better. Imagine what your family life will end up like if you don't get your sister back into the fold. Do I really need to say these things? OK, you lose a boyfriend. I can tell you something, sweetheart, he ain't worth it. Your sister is a good kid. A decent kid."

Her cogs must have been whirring as the next thing to come out of her gob was even more astounding. I had to clutch the side of the bed as I could have quite easily tumbled off.

Her tone had changed to what I can only describe as upbeat and real chipper.

"I think I've come up with a plan. A real good plan. I have got this feeling that maybe it could work if I lure him and make him tell us where Susie and the other girls are. You know, tempt him, use myself as bait."

It had it all this "real good plan". Make him strip, blindfold and tie him to the bed, then torture him by burning him with cigarettes and waterboarding. It unravelled like the plot of a B movie. To my reckoning this was revealing some sort of fantasy of hers. I was not quite sure at this point.

I shook my head from side to side incredulous that she would think she had the powers of persuasion to lure him into such a vulnerable position. And if she did manage to lure him, tie him to a bed, sit on him and do the dirty, it would be a given that he would let her in on where her sister and the others were being held.

213

"Sounds to me like you want one last shag before he gets twenty to life," I said flippantly. "I take it Susie's got your share in the brains department. Seriously, Jess, and this is about as serious as it gets, you need to open up to the police. I'm picking up you and Detective Baldwin haven't exactly hit it off? There are other detectives you can talk to. I know some of them aren't the best, and believe me I've dealt with some that are lacking in the empathy department."

My desire to probe her further was curtailed.

I'd barely got one word out when a blue uniform poked his head through the door.

"Baldwin and his partner are on the way back," enthusiasm brimming over as he made the announcement.

"Oh shit," came out of the young girl's mouth.

"I'd better be off. He, well, they actually don't know I'm here. Nobody does." The panic-stricken voice matched her face.

"Where the hell do they think you are at this time of night?" I enquired curiously.

"That's just it, they don't. They don't know or care. How do you think I've managed to date a guy nearly as old as my pops for a year?"

The bitterness oozing from that pretty mouth was tangible.

"You're going nowhere, Jess. Stay right where you are," I said in the most authoritarian voice I could pull up.

"I'll deal with Baldwin so don't sweat. He needs me, I'm a witness. Jesus, Jess, you're a witness. Are you getting it? You could be the key to the whole thing. Surely you can see that. I get that you and Detective Baldwin haven't exactly hit it off, but he has to acknowledge you're still a minor and you were scared. This guy Jake, well, he took advantage of you. Grooming is what it's known as. He targeted you because of Susie maybe, I don't know."

Just then Baldwin appeared. At his side, to my surprise, was Andy. Or more precisely patrolman Andy Finnerty.

214

Chapter Twenty-Nine

Catch More Flies with Honey than Vinegar

Detective Baldwin's jaw nearly hit the floor on catching sight of Jess.

I came to learn that according to her parents Jess is at home tucked up in bed! It seems that her mum had popped her head in her room and caught sight of sleeping beauty out for the count.

"Let the poor girl get her rest," said Mrs Simmons.

For a brief second Baldwin was visibly dumbstruck. Flabbergasted.

"Can I ask what exactly you are doing here, Miss Simmons? And how do you know Vicky?"

There was no hiding his tone was patently unhappy, if not pissed off.

I'm cottoning on to why Jess appeared reticent to see him and divulge what she knows. Surprisingly, considering the way he handled me he came off quite curt when addressing her.

Evidently there was no love lost between the charismatic African-American cop and the pretty blonde teenager.

Almost cowering, she said nothing. I couldn't help but feel a little protective towards the vulnerable-looking girl who shrank at the mere sight of him. Was her shrinking wallflower demeanour genuine or for my benefit? I had to ask myself.

I felt the need to speak on her behalf.

"Look, Detective, Jess overheard you and her parents talking and sought me out in an effort to find out what I know about Susie. What shape she was in, that kinda thing. I could be crossing a line here but I'm guessing she hasn't opened up to you. I think she knows more than she realises, especially since she overheard you talking."

"How so?" came the reply.

"I think young Jess here holds vital information. I'm pretty sure, in fact I'm positive of it. Information which will go some way in tracing the perpetrators, well, the ringleader anyhow. She's disclosed things to me, and I want you to know this, Detective, it's not easy for her. Jess, to my mind, is another victim in all this. I think the word used by you professionals is groomed."

I was hoping my little dance on her behalf would help smooth the waters and get her back on track with the detectives. His eyes never left me. He'd listened and let me have my say which was something.

Then he spoke.

"Do you hear this, Andy? My questioning Miss Simmons here this morning yielded zilch. Nada. Don't know nothing about nothing. All of a sudden Miss Simmons knows everything about darn well everything."

Looking squarely at Jess, the detective announced quite sharply, "You, Miss Simmons, are going down the station. Withholding evidence is what we call obstruction of justice."

Turning to Andy, Baldwin enquired, "Got your cuffs on you, Andy?"

With that Jess began to sob.

To my thinking it was at best an overreaction, at worst a scare tactic. A needless scare tactic.

No way was I letting this slide. Nor was I, for reasons I hadn't assimilated, allowing them to take her anywhere.

"This is a fine way to handle a witness I must say. If handcuffs go on her I'm gone."

It was worth a shot, but at the same time I knew he could just as well haul us both down to the station.

Not surprisingly she'd stayed put.

I had more to say and was wasting no time in saying it, pointing out that precious minutes are evaporating. I wanted to move forward in terms of making tracks and be gone from this place. This place, the hospital which I'd viewed previously as a place of safety.

"If they, you, haul her ass over the coals you'll get nothing. She'll clam up. It is evident she is intimidated by cops and I'm beginning to see why. How is it you think she told me stuff and you zero? Has that occurred to you?"

Ignoring Baldwin for the moment, I turned my attention towards Andy and began with demands of my own.

"Can you take Jess out into the corridor please? I need a word alone with Detective Baldwin. A private word if you don't mind."

My bossy nature was out in full force and I intended to have my say, no matter that I was ordering around officers of the law.

Baldwin nodded at Andy in compliance.

Jess ceased whimpering, smiled sweetly and ambled gracefully in the direction of the double doors. Andy was right behind, cuffs staying firmly where they were.

Baldwin added as I would've expected, "Keep a close eye on her, don't let her outta your sight."

I hoped, though wasn't banking on it, that he would hear me out. It could be that he'd tolerated my behaviour up to now as he held a degree of sympathy knowing what I'd been through.

Plus, the pendulum was now swinging in his favour with this case due to me drawing the cops' attention to my conundrum. The Susie Simmons missing person case.

My own motives aside, I'd surely bolstered the investigation and was helping to move it in the right direction.

I think I'd earned five minutes and a little leeway.

At the same time I doubted he'd afford Jess the same courtesy. Her behaviour thus far could be described as questionable. A spirited girl yes, but her recklessness overshadowed the real Jess.

Spoilt, selfish and entitled was the face she puts out there, knowingly or unknowingly.

I perceive her to be a girl who for whatever reason has lost her way, clinging to driftwood, clinging to her man.

When the two were the other side of the door Baldwin spoke stating he would allow me five minutes. I assented that was fine and all I required.

I began with my only recourse.

"I was stunned if not more surprised to see Jessica than you, Detective. Curiosity won me over and I decided to hear her out.

217

She's not a bad kid, a little misguided maybe. I think she came here in the hope she could establish that her boyfriend, and make no mistake this is how she sees this guy, is the same guy I met online. She hasn't said as much but I think she's deduced he is involved in her sister's disappearance."

"Boyfriend?" spat Baldwin. The word pinged in my head and echoed in my brain. "Boyfriend?" More pronounced, louder and prickly.

Shock, outrage and disbelief matched equally in his tone. Placing the palms of his hands to his face, he shook his head in exasperation.

I half expected him to dive out of the room and drag her back by the scruff of the neck. He took stock, straightened his posture and surprisingly after my revelation did as he'd vowed. He heard me out.

I began to regale the account Jess had poured out.

"And you are probably correct she should have been more forthcoming and spoken to her folks. Naivety, who knows? Stupidity, yes. She's got it into her head she is able to sort this out herself, and believe me it's a good job she opened up with what's rattling around in that head of hers otherwise you'd be looking for two Simmons girls. Talk about an off the wall plan!" I said rolling my eyes. "And here's the clincher," I offered. "She has his phone number as they are in constant contact. Apparently, and this is completely out of character according to her, for the last few days he's gone AWOL. Incommunicado, completely vanished. Whereabouts unknown as you'd say. He told her he'd been out of the country. She'd gone on to say in the year in which she'd being seeing him he'd never been out of contact for more than a day, even when abroad. In her view it was unusual and suspicious. And yes, you heard me right."

"So she'd be sixteen when this all began and Susie thirteen," said Baldwin speaking quietly, though loud enough for me to catch the inference.

"You're getting it. It sounds to me like this pervert groomed her. And another thing while I'm offering up my opinion, I don't know where her mum and dad were while their sixteen year old is dancing the night away on the strip. Is it any wonder she has attitude, it's the people she's mixing with if you ask me."

"What are you, some kinda teenager whisperer? How'd you get her to open up in the short time she's been here?" he asked curiously.

"Well, you could knock the 'Miss Simmons' bit off for a start. Tone it down a little," I suggested only half-jokingly. His answer to my suggestion flew out before I'd barely finished speaking.

"Miss princess grumpy pants it is then," his tone less testy.

His mood lightened a tad, he stood having perched himself earlier at the side of me on the chair.

"Back to why I'd come here tonight, late as it is. I've got the OK from my lieutenant with regard to securing you a safe house. Actually, a hotel. A suite to be specific. This particular hotel is one of several we use from time to time. I've asked Finn if he wouldn't mind babysitting you. At least the first shift. I've cleared it with his boss. I thought a friendly face would put you at ease."

Hesitating and taking a deep breath, he began to offer the first bit of good news. A glimmer of hope.

"I could be getting ahead of myself here, but those details you gave to my colleague could have quite possibly come up trumps. One of my detectives has an inkling he knows the little town in the desert which could be close to where you were held. He possesses a photographic memory. He has been recalling street names after a visit to that 'Skywalk over the Grand Canyon' with his better half. Apparently, coming back they were nearly out of gas when out in the middle of nowhere he caught a glimpse of a sign for gas. I'm pretty sure he recollects catching the street names you spoke of in the same vicinity. Needless to say we're on the case. I'll be heading to the area to see what we can turn up. I'll let Andy know if it pans out and he'll keep you in the loop. I guess you're itching to get out of here. Apart from the obvious, the smell of paint must take some getting used to."

His comment couldn't have been more spot on.

219

"I hear you on that. My one qualm, well, worry really…" I took a long breath wondering how my next request would go down. "Jessica," I said meekly.

"What about her?" asked Baldwin.

"Well, for one thing, you don't think she intends to go home from here, do you? Not many people leave home with a change of clothes and a phone charger stashed in their purse if they're only going to be gone a couple of hours," I enlightened him. "The charger will be useless, as little does she know I'll be taking that phone on the way out. As for the rest of it, who knows what lurks in the confines of a lady's purse?"

I felt compelled to voice something that had lingered inside since she'd turned up here.

"Before you rolled up I had full-on waterworks. She was talking about harming herself. I'm not sure how well she gets on with her folks, but she's of the opinion that she's surplus to requirements. Jess is just a daft kid underneath all that bravado. You said yourself they thought she was asleep in bed. She's a bit too canny for them if you ask me. Couldn't you tell them she's a material witness and you have her in the safe house with me? At least there would be two of us keeping an eye on her. Just maybe she'll disclose new info, who knows? When you were here earlier and we talked you were on the money with the notion I would randomly recall bits and pieces. It got me thinking that more than likely I could garner more from her in a more relaxed setting. If she skips out on her parents you might not see her again. You said yourself I've built up a rapport with her."

"Enough already. I get it. Fine. You're concerned. You can stop talking now. I don't know what it is with you and her but you've hit on something. You'll get her to open up if anyone can. Flies and honey spring to mind. She'd probably clam up and ask for a lawyer or her pops will if they get wind of her being questioned. It's either that or down to the station. Her phone's coming with me though. That's non-negotiable."

"Thanks."

"I'll wait outside the door while you slip something on. You win. For now at least. After I've taken madam's phone she's your house guest. It's either that or down the station."

And there, unpredictably, was the beginning of a friendship. Me the English girl who escaped from hell on earth and the pampered surgeon's daughter.

Chapter Thirty

Desolate Terrain

Baldwin reflected on everything that had come to light these last few hours.

In face of the mounting maelstrom he sure had a lot to digest.

Most definitely, if not for Andy this case would be dead in the water.

Thanks to him they now had a lead, and with a bit of luck they could still bring the girl home alive and hopefully unharmed.

Having listened and absorbed every detail Vicky had disclosed which was far from pretty, it really would be a miracle.

Correct in her deduction, she'd been held by a well organised gang who had been at this for years. Unbeknown to her she'd ended up in the clutches of the Mexican gang "El Torres".

Baldwin ruminated the whole thing as he drove along US 93.

A trade off maybe? Drugs? Drugs was their usual MO. Although he had heard the rumour from his informer that they were branching out. By no means an expert in gang culture, he knew enough to know the rumours usually had a modicum of truth weaved in somewhere along the line.

Mulling over the events of the last few hours everything had skyrocketed. Not a sniff one minute, the next minute all systems go. Having been informed by Dalton he had called in off duty cops and was assembling a task force. This case had snowballed like no other.

In full contemplation mode, his phone suddenly sprung to life.

Jolting his mind back to the task in hand, he noticed the call came from Lieutenant Dalton.

"Speak, I'm driving," said Baldwin brusquely.

"I should hope so," came the reply from Dalton in her usual no-nonsense tone.

"I know you're sleep deprived but concentrate on the road ahead while I bring you up to speed. Cars will be waiting for you when you get onto US 25. We can't have you poking your head in without backup. It took a bit of sweet talking to get them to hold their horses as I didn't want them going in all guns blazing before you show up. The last thing we want is jurisdictional issues."

Dalton was half expecting one of Baldwin's glib comments, knowing how fractious he can be. Plus, he doesn't play nice with cops in other jurisdictions, nor take kindly to the lieutenant calling him on it.

Another twenty minutes or so and he'd left US 93 and was onto 25. Driving down a long unremarkable road, surveying his surroundings, he pressed on. "Now what?" he chuntered, "and where's my escort?"

He saw a sign "Welcome to Dolan Springs". "Hah, at least I'm heading in the right direction," he muttered.

It can't be too far, he thought. It was a small town from what he'd been told. Slowing down further, eyes darting left then right, he kept his eyes open for road signs, the names of which were jotted in his notebook and firmly fixed to memory.

A couple of pick-ups passed on the opposite side almost blinding him with their full beams. Driving through the small town he took note of how sporadic the streetlights in this area were.

"When they said this place was off the grid they weren't kidding," he said out loud shaking his head.

His tired eyes strained to see the road in front. Suddenly, in the distance he spied what he'd been on the hunt for. Can hardly miss 'em really, he thought, venturing in the direction of the police vehicles with their flashing blue lights.

By the look of things at least four police vehicles clustered together were announcing their presence to the world. "Is this for my benefit or to give the bad guys a heads up?" he muttered to himself.

"Here we go," he said to himself. "Why not go the whole hog and break out the sirens? Can't have them miss us rolling up on 'em now, can we?"

One brave uniform had the gall to step out into the road gesturing for the Vegas cop to pull over. Not a good move after day I've had, thought the tired and irritated detective. I'd better comply, either that or run him over and I don't suppose that'll count as playing nice.

Baldwin brought his car to a halt.

Exiting the car, warrant in hand, devoid of words, he simply drank in the complete picture visualising a terrified young woman here in the middle of nowhere praying she'd find help.

After venturing down the dirt track and reaching the end of the road Vicky must have taken a right. Out of his peripheral vision he caught sight of Lost Mine Road further along Pierce Ferry Road. An arrow on a sign in big red lettering was indicating "Gas two miles" pointing left precisely as the gutsy Vicky had laid out.

This was the road where she'd come across a pick-up by the roadside. Was the driver in league with the kidnappers as Vicky had intimated? A reasonable assumption, thought Baldwin.

After checking the spot for tyre tracks, discarded cigarettes and anything else, he didn't see it as a popular parking spot for the locals.

Baldwin turned to the cops who were eyeing him fixedly, their eagerness evident.

A big bear of a man with a long wispy moustache which curled up at the ends took a couple of steps in his direction.

"How 'yer doing? I'm Sheriff Jackson, I'm guessing you're Baldwin?"

Baldwin hesitated for a second. The long grey moustache had him transfixed. Snapping out of it he swiftly responded, "Yeah, that's me." His hand met Jackson's for a formal handshake.

He took it this was the entrance to the building where Vicky, Susie and other girls were being held. Hopefully, the only entrance. Observing the scene, he wondered if it had occurred to the sheriff to check if there's another way in or out.

"You got your search warrant?" asked moustache's deputy shattering his ruminations.

"Sure have," Baldwin offered, passing it to the deputy for inspection.

"Let's get this show on the road," said the sheriff brimming with eagerness as he reached for the door of his car. Dropping into the seat behind the wheel, the weight of his body was having a detrimental effect on the car's suspension.

His window wound down, he beckoned Baldwin to follow.

Buzzing with urgency and suspense he did as prompted. Starting up his own vehicle, he got in line behind the sheriff who shared his car with his deputy.

In a convoy the police vehicles proceeded to drive the short distance to the house. Dust and dirt was thrown up spraying each car in turn as they rattled along the road. What lay ahead? What and who? They were on high alert wondering what they would find and speculating what nefarious deeds had taken place right under their noses in their little town.

All at once the building was spotted. One by one the police vehicles came to a stop, all taking their lead from the sheriff, his deputy and Baldwin who had all pulled up a little way from the house. The state police cars hung back.

If Vegas police intel was correct they'd driven into a dangerous situation. The state police followed protocol to the letter and wasting no time they exited their vehicles quickly.

For cover they crouched behind their open car doors, weapons drawn. They waited for an order from the men in front who were now out of their vehicles and creeping stealth-like in the direction of the scruffy house adorned with what looked like blacked out windows.

Baldwin's inner self questioned the scene. It was too quiet. Are they being watched or walking into an ambush?

Instinctively taking his weapon out of its holster he drew closer to the door of the dingy building. At this point the sheriff was standing back a little allowing Baldwin to be first to make contact with the occupants. A small flashlight in his left hand provided a clearer view of the door.

Closing in he observed the door slightly open. The small gap offered up something horrendous, a foul odour, a smell familiar to law enforcement officers. The smell of decomposition.

"I'm going in," mouthed Baldwin.

The state police and sheriff nodded in agreement allowing their visitor to make the first move.

At that Baldwin took a couple of steps into the house into what he took to be a kitchen area.

"Police, I need you to show yourself!" yelled Baldwin loudly.

Nothing. Not a single sound.

Gun at the ready, his eyes quickly scanned what looked like a two-roomed open concept dwelling.

His eyes widened as instinct and adrenaline surged through his entire body. Ready for anything, he inched forward nervously, and although prepared he was aware he could be walking into danger. The lion's den.

Eyes searching, he was hoping to come into contact with the victims. A perpetrator even. From his angle he could see the door of the cellar Vicky alluded to.

It was a huge wooden door furnished with two sets of sliding bolts and a lock. A proper dungeon door. Purpose built maybe? If there had been any doubt they were in the wrong place they were quashed at that moment.

Clearly this is where the girls had been held captive. Worryingly, this door opened a slither, and on seeing this an unsettling feeling engulfed him. "Please God no," he whispered.

The room, or hovel, he'd entered was empty. An arch to his left afforded him a view to room number two. Taking a couple of soft steps forward allowed him to see where the smell and blowflies emanated from.

A body was sprawled out on the floor, a huge hulk of a man, obviously dead. Blowflies were circling and doing their thing and several wounds occupied by maggots were adding a coating of nastiness to the horrific scene.

It was nothing Baldwin hadn't seen before. His first thought was he was glad it wasn't Susie or one of the others. "He's going nowhere," Baldwin whispered at the same time wondering where the hell the other cops were.

Taking no risks, gun and flashlight firmly gripped in one hand, he pushed on carefully. Undeterred, he opened the cellar door. All his senses were on high alert as he made his way one step at a time, hitting each step with a beam of light before planting his foot down. His objective was to avoid destroying precious evidence.

His eyes caught sight of clumps of hair, dried blood and broken fingernails. In no time at all he'd reached the bottom. With presence of mind not to contaminate evidence, his feet remained firmly on the bottom step.

His flashlight revealed a foul-smelling commode on the left of this large windowless room. The cold concrete steps behind him, he stood spellbound by the vision in front of him. A dungeon. He repeatedly shone his flashlight back and forth. Nothing. No Susie, no girls, no bad guys.

As he'd done earlier at the entrance to the dirt track, he tried to imagine the sheer terror Vicky and the others must have felt. Shuddering, a coldness ran over him. The degradation and horror of waking here must have been terrible, and the feeling of camaraderie between them had to be the only thing holding them together.

His fellow officers were a no show. He was guessing their enthusiasm only reached so far.

"Keep it together, Baldwin, at least you've got backup should you need it," testily attempting to reign in his sarcastic thoughts.

He was pretty certain the place was deserted but following police protocol he called out, demanding anyone there to make their presence known. There was always the possibility a scared victim was in hiding. The other side of the coin was one of the perpetrators was waiting. Waiting with a weapon to ambush him. Take him down.

Time was not on his side so he shouted again. "Police, show yourself! Make yourself known!"

He repeated the request with less vigour before allowing himself to accept whoever had been here had long since done a runner. Most likely shipped out upon realising Vicky had flown the nest.

The place was creepily silent, empty but for the dead man in the room above along with the scuttling rats and blowflies.

Heading back towards the light above the basement steps he caught sight of the sheriff and deputy.

"There's a corpse in the other room," proclaimed wispy moustache.

"Not much gets past you," Baldwin whispered, not caring if the two cops got wind of his sarcasm.

Moments later Baldwin joined the two men in the grubby kitchen area.

"Well, what do we have here? Do 'yer think your girl got it wrong?" asked Jackson waving away flies which were showing great interest in his bushy facial hair.

"No, I don't think my girl got it wrong. Or anything else wrong for that matter," Baldwin replied sharply. "I'm guessing after she made a run for it they cleaned the house or had a good go at least. There's dried blood and hair on the cellar steps alongside other material. Down there, as with these rooms, is off limits. I don't want uniforms trudging down there with their size nines. Got it? Crime techs are gonna have a field day when they get down there."

Unequivocal in his delivery Baldwin declared, "We'll find them, the doers and the girls, make no mistake we'll find them."

He was clearly annoyed at the whole scene and what had taken place here, and at not finding what he had come all this way to find.

Without a doubt this place will hold a mountain of useful evidence, he thought. From the information garnered from Vicky he was confident that these jerks were holding the girls.

Clue number one, leaving a dead man smack bang in the middle of the floor. Bodies equal evidence. And then there's all the crap laying around here. With a little luck they should be able to garner fingerprints from some of the empties. Hopefully DNA.

Taking in the whole sorry scene it crossed his mind any criminal with a brain cell would have set fire to the place. Were

228

they confident it wouldn't be found maybe? Assured in the knowledge Vicky was taken care of? Baldwin's lobes were entrenched in thoughts and questions.

Enough time had been squandered already. Bulldozing forward his mouth took over and he was now doing what he does best, barking orders. The first one was fired at Jackson and his sidekick.

"I need you to gather a team and start knocking on doors. Oh, and before you bring it to my attention there's no need. I'm well versed in the fact there's some distance between dwellings. It doesn't rule out the possibility someone has sighted vehicles going backwards and forwards, so get all descriptions of vehicles you can. Granted the probability is low but it's still worth a scout round. Get more of your people up here, we need to search the perimeter. Do a walk round. They've been sloppy inside so let's see what's outside, shall we?"

Without waiting for protestations he continued with his commands.

"Oh, and the liquor store or whatever it is I passed on entering Dolan Springs. Any CCTV cameras? Any other places come to mind such as gas stations? They got their alcohol and grub from somewhere," said Baldwin, gesturing with his hand at the empty food containers and beer cans. "While they're making enquiries at the store I'd appreciate a coffee. Black no sugar. I'll settle up upon their return."

"Anything else?" asked the sheriff in a tone that oozed pissed off.

"Yeah, get outta my crime scene. I need you out before my crime scene lads show up. They're not a happy bunch at the best of times so finding individuals trampling over and touching their evidence will annoy them big time."

As they all started for the door they'd entered one of the state cops suddenly poked his head in.

Although Baldwin was not familiar with his usual look, the young cop looked grey. Grey, anxious and nervous. His face was affirming he had something to divulge but the words were clearly stuck.

"Spit it out, Kev," said the frustrated sheriff.

229

"You gotta see this," he answered sheepishly, eyeing all three men.

Baldwin, Jackson and the deputy walked eagerly behind him with not a single word uttered between the three. Most likely they were all of the same mind, wondering and dreading what had rankled the young cop.

While the sheriff had followed Baldwin into the building, the two state police officers had made the decision to do a cursory search around the property, in particular the back of the house and surrounding area to see if they could uncover a back door or perhaps a vehicle, neither of which were found. But their search did prove fruitful in the worst possible way. As the cops scouted round a gruesome discovery was unearthed.

"Is this what I think it is? How many do 'yer reckon?" directed the sheriff at the cop who'd guided them to what looked like a grave site.

"At least four by my reckoning," was the doleful reply from the young cop. Clearly shocked, he had questions of his own which freely flowed out of his mouth.

"What the fuck is this place? What's gone down? Is this your missing kid?" directing the questions at nobody in particular, although the last one was fired at Baldwin.

Again, Baldwin felt the need to take charge of this which was now undoubtedly a crime scene.

Addressing the bewildered-looking cop he instructed him to tape off the area also informing him to keep everyone back. A few feet from the furthest body a shovel stood in the ground as if marking the area for what it was, a burial ground.

"Bag and tag that," the Vegas cop ordered, pointing his finger in the direction of the shovel. "I guess it don't need saying but glove up and don't touch the handle. It's important to bag both ends. Got it?"

This order was directed at any one of the cops who'd gathered and was staring blankly at the scene. His colleagues looking on from behind the yellow tape, the rookie had wasted no time in following the order.

The deputy had taken a roll of the yellow police tape and began zigzagging it across the door of the house while muttering expletives loud enough for his colleagues to hear.

Along with the other officers Sheriff Jackson was looking on in astonishment.

Baldwin considered this a good moment to update the lieutenant. Surprisingly, he found he had a signal. Dalton picked up after two rings. Baldwin walked a few feet from the other cops and the makeshift grave site.

His call was brief and consisted of appraising her of what they'd found so far. And, of course, what they hadn't found, namely Susie and the others. Baldwin made a mental note as his boss filled him in on who is on route to Dolan Springs to assist explaining they will be out there with him as quickly as possible.

Listening without interrupting as still trying to get his head round everything, he ended the call. Before doing so he'd informed her he would be back at the office for a debriefing, although he was unclear when this would be.

He was walking purposely over to the shocked onlookers, most of whom were standing and eyeing the mounds of earth behind the yellow tape and muttering to each other in disbelief.

"Listen up," he said in a loud, firm voice. "My lieutenant has notified the M.E. and crime scene technicians are on the way as we speak. A couple of detectives are en route to assist with the processing of the crime scene indoors. I'm going to need as many officers as Sheriff Jackson can spare," his gaze meeting Jackson as he imparted this.

Jackson began dishing out his own set of orders to his men.

Physically and mentally exhausted Baldwin listened.

The sheriff appeared to have got on board with what had now become a crime scene of colossal proportions, articulating what will be required from each of them and how they can assist Baldwin's counterparts when they show up. He impressed upon his subordinates that it is their job to preserve the scene, thus ensuring vital evidence is not lost.

"It don't need saying that this is big. Girls have been killed, murdered. Young innocent women need our help and are relying on us. They are still out there most likely transferred to a different location, and after what we've seen today in grave danger. These young women are people's daughters, sisters, children. We've all got families. They need you." He paused as

231

he took a deep breath and continued. "They need us to follow through. Come on now, get to it and keep your radios on."

Given that the sheriff and deputy hadn't done anything close to police work so far, Baldwin was impressed how the sheriff had sprung into action and had begun to co-ordinate his men with vigour showing enthusiasm and emotion in equal measure.

Quenching his thirst with a bottle of water, he sat for a moment. Maybe he'd got him all wrong, he reflected, watching and listening from the comfort of his car.

Allowing the sheriff to do his stuff, Baldwin took a breather. He contemplated how this thing had mushroomed in such a short time.

Dead bodies. Sex trafficking. Sex slaves. Gang involvement. And still a missing teenager. What next? Baldwin thought to himself.

Just then his phone lit up. It was the lieutenant. Baldwin flipped it open.

Chapter Thirty-One

Jess, Me and Andy Make Three

I think we were all struggling with tiredness by the time we hit the hotel.

It was quite impressive and was more of an apartment. There was a kitchen, a couple of bedrooms, each with their own bathroom, coupled with a generous lounge area leading to a decent size balcony. This offered a side view of the bright lights overlooking the top end of the strip.

"Sweet," was the first word from my young friend's mouth, followed by, "Where am I sleeping?"

Before making a quick exit Baldwin had confiscated her phone. Without fuss she'd willingly handed it over negating the need for him to go rooting in her purse. My take on it was she didn't want him to see the bra and knickers I'd caught a glimpse of earlier. That's understandable, I thought. It wasn't lost on me she had these things with her along with a toothbrush and other bits.

I settled her in one of the bedrooms. I was grateful we each had an en-suite as I did not fancy sharing a bathroom with a teenager. A pretty stupid thought really, taking into account the quality of accommodation I'd had to endure lately.

I sat on the sofa and Andy sat in an armchair. I think we were both too tired to have a full-on conversation though I did feel the need to offer my thanks. After all, if it weren't for him taking the lead and prompting the detectives into action I don't know what I would've done or where I'd be now.

There was no escaping the charge in the air and this whole set of circumstances felt decidedly uncomfortable. Perhaps it shouldn't have done but it did. Having Jess in the room created a different mood. A lighter mood. A barrier.

"Talk about making yourself at home," I mused.

I jokingly called after her to remind her to brush her teeth. She hollered back in that sweet girly tone. "No problemo, I'll see you two in the morning."

A spontaneous roll of the eyes accompanied Andy's knowing smile.

"Teenagers," he said. "But she don't seem like a bad kid."

I took from Andy's demeanour he was just as uneasy being alone with little 'ole me for company as I was with him.

Just as I was about to break the uneasy silence he beat me to it.

"Here we are then," offered my cop friend in the friendly tone I'd become accustomed to.

"Yep, here we are," for once feeling a little lost for words.

"Before I say anything, Vicky, I want you to know how sorry I am about what happened back at Mercy. I couldn't believe it when Baldwin touched base and filled me in on what went down just after I'd left you. Thinking about it, it must have been minutes after I'd left your room. Crafty bastard. I was shocked. I should have cottoned on to the danger you were in. I could have stuck around and requested a detail outside your door. I'm sorry you had to go through what you did," his voice cracking with each sentence.

I guess he was as tired and exhausted as I felt. From what I'd heard on the drive over here he'd been on shift from six that morning. I'm tired and emotionally drained but that was part and parcel of my new world. A good restful night's sleep was a distant memory for me.

The last thing I wanted him to feel was guilt, especially since there was no need.

"It's hardly your fault, Andy. Sure, you and your coffee guzzling partner were first on the scene, but you're not responsible for me from here on in. Besides, if my memory serves my big gob played a major role in you shooting off!"

"Talking of big mouths," he said lightening the mood a little, "when that intruder entered your room you could be heard the other side of Las Vegas Boulevard. Oh, and that tray was a serious misuse of hospital property." Laughing quietly to himself he seemed to be enjoying the teasing. "It could catch on though, sturdy things those trays," he scoffed.

"Ha ha, very funny. I'm glad you found it amusing. You do what you have to do with what you've got to hand. That much I've learnt during my forced break to what was once my boring life. My interrupted life," I batted back to him glibly.

Andy wasn't going to let me have the last word, and looking directly into my eyes he said, "So, I'll be here drinking coffee on this sofa for what's left of the evening. Therefore, no trays required. You and the cereal munching princess in there can hopefully sleep soundly. And just to be clear, I take full responsibility for any blonde Brit chicks I have the job of freeing from the Spring Motel. Every single one on 'em. Full liability until they get back on their feet and my services are no longer required. Even the noisy ones who can clearly take care of themselves. Got that?"

There was no retort or witty comeback from me on that one. Stunned and completely taken aback, I bid him good night, went into my perfect little room, showered and crawled under a duvet. And under the watchful eye of my newly acquired protector I slept like a baby.

Chapter Thirty-Two

A New Day, a New Revelation (Vicky)

I glanced around this totally foreign room the quietness slightly unnerving, and my heart began beating hard on my chest wall for no other reason than I'd woken up and remembered.

That little voice hadn't deserted me. Brace yourself, be guarded, be ready, it said.

Without shifting an inch, I assessed my surroundings.

To my left there was a room with a tiled floor, wash basin and loo. Obviously the bathroom. I was reflecting back to the last time I came round in unfamiliar territory. The noisy Mexican lady. The zealous banging. Thank the Lord for noisy, conscientious maids.

At the side of the bed was a digital alarm clock. It was seven ten. I felt refreshed, as refreshed as I'd felt in a hell of a long time. At least I was not doped up and incapacitated as in the previous day. That's got to be a bonus. "Things are on the up," I whispered flippantly.

I began to ease my way out of the bed. Sore and stiff from yesterday's little fiasco, I shuffled as if I'd suddenly aged thirty years.

I entered the bathroom where I came across a toothbrush and toothpaste. I brushed steadily, scrunched my hair on top of my head, then scooped handfuls of warm water onto my face, although I soon wished I hadn't bothered as I caught sight of myself in the mirror above the sink. My cheeks were hollow and I hated the way I looked. One more thing to hate those bastards for, I thought bitterly.

Then something else took over that superseded my vanity. I'm safe. In that instant Claire and the others popped into my mind, and my thoughts and visions bounced from one

236

horrendous scenario to another. In that moment I wanted to scream.

My self-recrimination and torment was punctured as I'm catapulted back to the here and now. There was a knock on the door and then a voice.

"Vicky, are you up? I heard running water."

"I'll be out in a second," came my quivering response.

I dabbed my eyes, took a deep breath and grabbed a gown from a hook on the bathroom door. I tied the cord snuggly around my middle, this simple act highlighting how thin I'd become.

I opened the door to find Jess standing there with a coffee in her hand. The aroma was like nothing on earth.

I thanked her and plonked myself on the sofa. She sat in front of me cross-legged on the floor.

The open balcony door gave way to a lovely soft breeze as the cool morning Vegas air swept across the room.

"Thanks for the coffee," I said gesturing with the paper mug.

A few sips of the lovely brew and I realised it was from that patisserie place in the Aria Hotel. It wasn't that I recognised the coffee, the logo on the paper cup gave it away.

Bemused, my eyebrows squeezed forming a frown. "Jess, have you been out?"

"Oh no, don't worry. Scouts honour. Andy brought it when he went off shift half an hour ago. In case you're wondering there's another cop outside the door. He's not as nice as Andy or as good-looking but he's OK. I think I scared him as he didn't want to come in. He said he might when you get up. Weird if you ask me."

Not that weird, wafted into my brain.

"I bet you're wondering how the coffee is still hot," she enthused.

"Me and Andy had a good old chinwag before he zoomed off. He's quite chatty isn't he? He said to pour the coffee in one of the enamel mugs, put it in the microwave for forty seconds max then pour back in the paper cup and put the lid back on. He wrote it on a pad at the side of the microwave in case I got distracted. Oh, and there's a croissant left if you're hungry. Coffee OK is it?"

"No worries, it's fine," I acknowledged while unwrapping the delicious smelling croissant, melted cheese oozing from the inside as I carefully peeled away the wrapping. He'd had it double wrapped so it was still warm.

Thankfully, she kept her exorbitant prattling to a minimum while I ate and sipped the coffee. I savoured every morsel.

I didn't say it but I wondered if her verbal diarrhoea contributed to Baldwin's posture when in her presence. No wonder Andy had toddled off for coffee.

Curiosity getting the better of me, I had to ask. "Have you spoken to your folks?"

"Nope. I should get my phone back today according to Andy. Baldwin informed them I have to stay here in witness protection until they have that asshole in custody. Andy said they put a tail on him and are watching his every move. They have been since last night when you gave them the information that I gave you," she said rather smugly.

"Oh, that's something I guess." The only unoffending words I could offer at that precise moment.

I made a mental note to ask Andy exactly what was going on with regard to Jake, visualising him behind bars with the rest of the criminals.

I then got a pot of coffee on the go. Before going into the shower I opened the door to enquire if our guard wanted a cup. No way did I want to inflict Jess on him.

Stepping into the lounge area he thanked me for the coffee. I beckoned him to take a seat as I gestured to Jess to allow him to have his coffee in peace. Backing out of the lounge she curled up on one of the chairs on the balcony. The cop gave me a half smile which I took as a thank you.

Twenty minutes later I was dressed. Dressed and bored. Itching to simply do something or go somewhere.

A couple of hours went by when we heard a knock at the door, startling both Jess and me. The cop got up nonchalantly and peeked through the spyhole. Without a word he opened the door.

In walked a middle-aged detective, and garnered by the way her face dropped Jess had previously made his acquaintance. He approached me smiling warmly and extended his hand to

238

shake mine, at the same moment offering up his name. This friendly faced detective introduced himself as Detective Mike Simpkins making it known he is Baldwin's partner.

He nodded in Jess's direction.

His smile evaporated and was quickly replaced by a look of concern. A look that spoke volumes. Even Jess kept quiet and stared. We waited for him to speak.

The silence in the room was deafening.

I willed him to divulge his thoughts but at the same time I was scared. Scared to know what he knew.

"I think you should sit down," came the sombre request.

Choosing his words carefully, he began filling us in on what the police had been doing so far.

A hell of a lot by the sounds of it, much to my astonishment.

"We have a suspect in custody. The bad news is he's not playing ball. He's denying knowing anything about Vicky's or Susie's kidnapping. We have taken his phone. We asked and without so much as where's your warrant he handed it over. It's with our tech guys, nothing gleaned as yet. I've put a rush on it. I have to admit, he's no criminal mastermind."

"Oh, that's about right, that's what he'll want you to believe. Ted Bundy could learn a thing or two from this guy, I can tell you." Clearly narked by the look on her face, Jess couldn't resist voicing her opinion.

"And?" I heard myself say out loud. In my heart of hearts I knew there was more simply by the pained look on his face.

"Well, Vicky, the information you gave regarding the house, the street signs at the crossroad, the petrol station, it all tallied. We found the house."

There was more hesitating from the detective.

Relief engulfed me and I broke down. Oh my god, I just can't believe it.

Jess sprung to my side and hugged me.

Something was clearly amiss. I looked at the detective with my tear-soaked eyes, his face crestfallen.

There was obviously more, much more, and this cop came here with the intention of laying it all out.

I gave him an out taking it upon myself to ask the question. The most important question.

"What's the bottom line here? You've found the house, now what?" my aggressive tone unintentional.

"There's clear evidence you and the other girls were held there. And Susie. We found her phone and schoolbag," offered Simpkins.

At that Jess broke down, her face filled with fear and anguish.

It was my turn to offer comfort and I gave her a hug and a cuddle. Me, I was hanging on by a thread.

Simpkins allowed us a moment to digest the information then began to speak.

"And there's more. I can't get into specifics but there's evidence that more than one person has been killed. The evidence does suggest one of the bodies is one of the perpetrators. A man. A large guy who we're hoping to be able to identify. I don't want to go into particulars but we should be able to get prints. He's probably in the system."

The detective paused.

He didn't look at both of us, just me. My stomach tightened and I felt instant nausea. Jess put her arm round me and held my hand tightly. I caught a sideways look at her and could see the tears welling up again.

Simpkins pressed on.

"Vicky, I need to tell you something which I know you're going to find shocking and alarming."

Once again a pause. Then he spat out what he'd been holding in and I guess dreaded telling me.

"We've unearthed at least two bodies buried behind the building. Bodies of young women about your age. Our crime scene guys are slowly and methodically excavating the site."

While I remained silent and tried to be strong Jess pulled away from me and put her hand over her mouth.

Simpkins turned to Jess making it clear it wasn't Susie, that much was evident.

She sat motionless wearing the same perplexed look she'd had earlier.

My emotions had retreated somewhere deep inside my body and were eating my soul. My stomach knotted and I was unable to shake the nauseated feeling. On top of that my voice abandoned me.

Breaking the silence, the other cop asked if he could get me anything.

I heard him but words wouldn't come. My thoughts were running rampant imagining what all this could mean. Imagining the very worst.

The room was still with the eerie silence apart from the sound of the cop making another pot of coffee.

I had an abundance of questions for which I demanded answers.

"How many bodies? Do you know who they are? Did you find Claire and the others? The big guy, how'd he die? I hit him, you know, I told the detectives as much. It's how I managed to escape. I stunned him, I think. Yes, definitely stunned. He was alive when I darted out the door. I heard him mumbling swear words at me on the lines of he was going to kill me when he gets hold of me. I didn't doubt he'd carry out his threats. You see, his intention at the time had been to rape me. He had a penchant for the rough stuff..." my voice trailing off as I imparted the last bit.

I had been with Jess less than twenty-four hours and had begun to sound like her. It occurred to me I hadn't drawn breath. It also occurred to me I just might be a murderer. Or do they class it as manslaughter if you've endured what I had? I had more questions which at this point would have to wait.

The cop whose name eluded me made the rounds with the Italian brew. I felt bad not remembering his name. He had a fatherly look and presence about him. I thanked him and took the coffee out of politeness.

Simpkins was soon back to business.

"When you're ready, Vicky, I want you to look at some photos. My colleague is as we speak in missing persons bringing up photos of girls who've been reported missing. Don't be alarmed if you can't pick out any faces, we'll have dental records."

At that both me and Jess recoiled.

"I'm OK. I'll look at whatever you need me to and answer anything you need answering. I'll be OK, it's just the shock and the visions floating around my brain of what took place back in that hell hole after I'd bolted. And by the sound of it long before I landed there." My voice was filled with absolute determination.

"Good," said Simpkins. Taking his eyes off me he glanced at the cop who was sat close by.

"I have an image of the face of the guy you described as the perp who tried to rape you and held you against your will. I must warn you it's not a pretty sight. It's just that if we can get an early identification we can see who he associates with, the vehicle he drove, maybe another residence in Vegas. Oh, and before you ask as it might be of concern to you, you didn't kill him. He was shot. And more than once at close range. I'm taking it you didn't have a gun?" he said.

The part about the gun was a little more upbeat than the bit about Derrick not being a pretty sight and the rest.

"I can tell you now, the son of a bitch was an ugly lump of lard when he was breathing so he's not going to be a pretty sight now he's dancing with the devil. Let me see it, I want to make sure he really is dead."

My little rant, and make no mistake it was a rant, brought a slither of a smile to Simpkins. His colleague looked away but I think he concurred.

Jess being Jess made some comment about "orange being the new black" and me looking good in orange.

I eyed the photo and agreed he was dead. I also agreed he was who I'd said he was, Derrick the gatekeeper.

I confirmed I'd no notion of his last name. I refrained from adding to my early rant as I didn't want to make light of the situation or for them to think I was that person. I was far from that person. In my mind I was glad I didn't have to use more violence on him, although how could I not be glad that the brute is dead?

Chapter Thirty-Three

Revelation Part Two

Simpkins drank his coffee then began with the what's next. Next for me and Jess that is. He went on to say he would like us both to come down to police headquarters as soon as we were ready. Me to look at photos of girls. Jess apparently because they had a few more questions for her and wanted a firm ID on the man they had in custody, a request which for reasons known only to her put her on edge. Clearly rattled, she asked if she could she wait here.

Simpkins either didn't hear the soft-spoken question or chose to ignore it.

The detective brought to our attention the fact that they had the suspect in custody but as yet no charges had been levied. They could only hold him for so many hours then either charge or release him. Depending on what we brought to the table it could possibly make all the difference. Clinch the deal, so to speak.

The dialogue from Simpkins only added to Jess's perturbed manner.

He briefly gave the gist of the identification process explaining it would take place behind one-way glass, therefore Jake, Jack as Jess calls him, would not be able to see us, directing this at the both of us.

Naturally, there was no hesitation on my part which is more than I can say for my new roommate.

She appeared positively unwilling and I envisaged waterworks starting up any minute.

After finishing our coffee we got ready the best we could and headed out of the door.

With Simpkins on my right and the other cop on my left we walked to the elevator, Jess trailing a few feet behind. Her pallor was evident, her gait that of an individual walking to the gallows.

I turned, smiled and allowed her to catch up. As we silently rode the lift down to the reception area I contemplated my misgivings about the young girl. Her apprehension more than likely stemmed from knowing she'd given up her one true love.

She'd come clean and divulged she'd introduced Susie. To me at least. It's not like she'd said, "Here, she's yours for the taking!" At least I was hoping not.

Recalling the request from Baldwin with regard to commandeering her phone, there was no argument on her part. She had willingly handed it over. Changing tact with my thoughts, how could I forget Susie's attitude when walrus features brought Jess's name up. It was pretty clear Susie thought the world of her sister.

Ten minutes or so and we were in the safest place we could be. Las Vegas Metro Police Headquarters.

Again, all four of us entered a lift, quickly reaching the third floor.

A small corridor led to a huge open-plan office. The whole place was buzzing.

"Wow, this where it all happens? Busy place," rolled straight off my tongue. I couldn't help making a comment.

Jess stuck to me like glue, sombre faced, and hadn't said a word since she'd left our safe house. Pondering on it briefly, it was very un-Jess like.

Taking steps into the office Simpkins informed us that we were in the squad room.

Along the wall to the left was a row of small rooms. The detective beckoned us into the one in the middle with the number "4" on the door.

It was a gloomy room consisting of a table and several chairs. The table took pride of place in the middle of the room.

The room consisted of two long windows, the one overlooking the office adorned with vertical blinds. The other on the back wall resembled a huge glass mirror.

Jess dragged her chair a little closer to mine. I gently squeezed her hand.

"It'll be OK, Jess. Just tell them what they need to know. Remember, you've done nothing wrong. Keep in mind they wouldn't have that pervert in custody if it weren't for you. We're here to slot all the fragments together, join the dots so to speak. The primary goal is to get your sister and my friends back. You know this and I know you want to help."

Clearly listening and absorbing my words, Simpkins smiled at both of us.

The other cop came back with our drinks, telling Simpkins coffee was being brewed and that he would bring it before he scooted off.

A little knock startled us. Jess almost jumped probably thinking it was her favourite cop. It wasn't. A slim, smart suited lady I took to be in her late forties walked in announcing in a voice which reeked of authority, "I'm Lieutenant Dalton. Nice to meet you both. I'm sorry it's under such dire circumstances, Victoria. And I'm sorry to hear about your sister, Jessica," turning politely to each one of us as she offered her sentiments.

I took it this lady's rank was above the detectives, my assumption being that she was "the boss".

"I want you both to know we're using all the resources at our disposal to bring Susie and the other girls home. As we speak my team are scouring CCTV footage. The footage retrieved went some way in marching the investigation forward. We consider this an enormous breakthrough. In particular the CCTV from a house two blocks from your family home, Jessica. Vicky had thankfully remembered things Susie had told her, a key piece of evidence being the exact location Susie stood as the van pulled up. This van was used to snatch and transport her, and remembering the colour and description of said van was also vital in helping to locate it. On the back of the information you provided, Vicky, things are moving rather quickly. The occupants of the house where the CCTV cameras are located only arrived back from a vacation yesterday. On seeing a police presence they came forward with the footage."

"Oh yeah, they would do," exclaimed Jess quietly.

We all glanced in her direction but opted to ignore her miniature tantrum.

There was not so much as a ripple from Dalton as she continued imparting where they were with the enquiry.

"My officers have extracted vital clues from this surveillance equipment. From the footage I've seen, the blue van is clearly visible."

She was smiling as she keyed us in on their progress. The lieutenant seemed pleased with what they'd achieved.

Inwardly I felt a little pleased myself, recalling the stuff Susie had poured out considering the brief time we'd had together. I was glad I had approached her and had that moment to talk as we did. I was doubly thankful for the fact she shared at least one trait with her sister. Talking.

Dalton had more to say.

"The motel. The Spring."

Then a flurry of deep breaths.

What about it? I said in my head, reluctant to interrupt due to my keenness to hear her out.

"From the information we've gathered and the intel from one of our C.I.'s, that's confidential informer, the place is a known hangout for gang members called El Torres. From what we've been able to ascertain you were sold to them for a purpose I wouldn't have thought requires an explanation. I'm sure I need say no more apart from I'm glad my officers responded as quickly as they did, Vicky. Not forgetting the maid who has been spoken to by a translator, it transpires she was approached by a man who paid her fifty dollars to gain entry to the room and most importantly call the police. Having seen two guys leave she made straight for the room, heard you, and thankfully called the police. The rest as you know is history."

I couldn't grasp this new revelation. I was stunned.

"I guess I owe the maid a bigger thank you than I first envisaged. I just can't get my head round all this. Who was this man?"

Dalton hadn't finished.

"It's a hell of a lot to take in I know. I also know you've already been through a hell of an ordeal so could have done without hearing this. The maid's recollection is vague. He was tall, slim and fair skinned. Oh, and he wore a beanie hat and sunglasses. We're just grateful for his involvement. The attempt at Mercy was either revenge for fleeing or in the event you could recognise them. Either way, due to a tattoo caught on camera when he pressed the button on the lift we can see he is one of them. The gang that is."

Dalton paused momentarily. Maybe to give me more thinking time. I'm not sure if I've got enough days on God's green earth to come to terms with what I'd just been told.

My words rang out in the little closed off room.

"Sold? Sold? For crying out loud I thought I'd heard it all. Every inconceivable bad thing that could have come my way has. Now this! I'm either the luckiest girl in the world or the unluckiest, I've not quite got the measure of which."

"I hear that," said Jess who had for once listened and kept it zipped.

The lieutenant had more to add.

"I'm sure it doesn't need to be said but it's clear you've bumped up against some pretty loathsome excuses for human beings. But I think I speak for all the police who've come into contact with you, Vicky, in saying you're a remarkable young woman. The determination and resilience you've displayed, well, all I can say is we've never encountered it in an individual who's been put through the horror you have. I could go on but I won't. As you're both aware time is a luxury we don't have. Talking of the dregs of society, ladies," she said looking from me to Jess and back to me, "I know Detective Simpkins brought to your attention it is vital you both make a formal identification of the individual we have in custody. The guy who snatched you, Vicky, and groomed you, Jess, and we suspect targeted Susie and other young girls. Formal identification will go a long way in building a case. More importantly, giving up where the others are being held. As is usual in these cases it might be that we offer a deal in the hope he does the right thing. As yet nothing has been written up, but we're in the midst of working with the District Attorney. Nobody's going to walk on this, please be assured. We can go over the nuances when I've more time, but at this point identification is crucial. We need probable cause for a search warrant of his residence."

247

"What do 'yer mean search his residence?" came the little voice from the side of me, which again we all ignored.

"Yeah, let's get on with it shall we, Jess?" I urged.

Catching her expression anyone would've thought I'd offered her up to the El Torres or whatever they're called.

I got up, she stayed seated.

I put my arm under her right arm to manoeuvre her into a standing position.

Considering her sister is still out there, why wasn't she diving in to make the identification? I don't suppose I was the only chump in that room thinking what I was thinking.

"Jeez, Jess, what the... come on, you need to step up to the plate for Susie and for the others. Time is getting away. You've heard the lieutenant, we haven't got time for all this."

Unwilling and teary-eyed, I managed to get her to come with us to another even smaller box-type room two doors down from the last one. I followed Dalton and Simpkins, arm around the snivelling young girl. Dalton who was taking little notice was talking on her mobile.

All four of us entered the room simultaneously.

Without warning a smartly dressed man in his fifties joined us. Taking his place next to Simpkins he nodded to both me and Jess.

"This is Mr Jones's lawyer, he's here to observe," said Dalton. "Just to reiterate, ladies, the man behind the glass cannot see you."

In a well-practised manner Simpkins began to confirm the procedure to Jess.

"Now, Jessica, I need you to confirm that this is the guy who contacted you on Facebook. First, I am going to ask Vicky to step outside for a moment. It wouldn't be correct procedure for you both to be here at the same time. Vicky will have her opportunity as soon as you're finished here. I'm sure you both understand."

He was straight to the point without giving her an opening to throw a wobble.

"Right then, to clarify a few things you've made it known to us you've been in a relationship with this man for the past year. The man who you are going to see through this glass either directly or indirectly expressed an unhealthy interest in Susie whilst in your company. This is the same person who, for whatever reason, you introduced Susie to in the coffee shop just over two weeks ago."

After hearing all this spelled out to her I took it upon myself to make a quick getaway without making eye contact.

I said nothing, walked out the door and left her to it.

Having got to know Jess a little it wouldn't be a stretch to say Simpkins' statements will have pierced her uppity ego. If she thinks her integrity is called into question she'd simply refuse to co-operate.

I'd assisted in getting her to where she now stood but hadn't the emotional energy or patience to deal with one of her moods.

Jess stood facing the window. Facing the window and shaking. Dalton kept her gaze firmly fixated on the young girl along with a firm grip. I think they'd got the measure of how unpredictable she could be and I think they half expected her to bolt out the door.

The button at the side of the huge window was pressed to reveal a bored-looking man sitting behind a table. Jess covered her mouth with her hand and gasped loudly as if she'd seen an alien.

"Yes, that's him," she offered in a church mouse tone.

Simpkins asked her to repeat her words a little louder. Jess did as prompted, her eyes never leaving the smartly dressed man sitting at a table in the next room.

Simpkins thanked her and indicated it was OK for her to leave, pointing to the officer waiting outside to take her back to the other room. She insisted on waiting with the cop while I played my part in helping to put that evil jerk behind bars.

I stood in the same spot in front of the window.

Simpkins placed his hand gently on my shoulder.

"Vicky, I need you to take a good look at the man in the room. Can you please confirm if this is the man who abducted you nearly seven weeks ago?"

His question came in a quiet soft tone.

My ears caught the sound of the switch at the side of the window. The great reveal button.

I daren't look. Although I'd always hoped this day would come, I now dreaded it. The thought of seeing that man again made me shiver and want to vomit.

I averted my gaze from studying the laminate wood floor and the detective's shoes to the image before me. The room behind the glass was now fully lit.

A man I had never set eyes on before was seated behind a table. A smart, smarmy-looking guy sat facing the window as if looking straight at me. A guy who I assume Jess had just identified.

I adjusted my torso away from the detectives to get a closer look. I couldn't believe what I was seeing. They'd got it wrong. So wrong. How could this be? They hadn't found him after all. I felt sick to my stomach. The build-up, the anticipation, now nothing.

"Who the fuck is that? I've never clapped eyes on him before in my life." I unintentionally raised my voice, my shock evident for all to witness. My worst fears were realised and my eyes bored a hole in that glass, that dude's face.

Dalton and Simpkins eyed me uneasily.

"You sure? Do you want to take one more look, Vicky?" questioned Dalton.

"No prompting the witness please, Lieutenant," the lawyer spoke in his haughty, toffee-nosed voice.

Ignoring the snooty lawyer I looked Dalton square in the face and said what needed to be said.

"I don't need to look again. I'm positive. Don't think for a second I will ever forget that face. That face will haunt me for the rest of my days. This is not the guy I met up with who raped, tortured and sold me. Yes, there are similarities, the guy sitting there is probably ten years older for a kick off. I couldn't be more certain that's not him. I want out of here, I can't breathe."

I darted out of the little room almost knocking Jess over in the process.

"Let's get back to the interrogation room where we can iron a few things out," Lieutenant Dalton said to the both of us.

"Interrogation room?" Jess repeated sharply as if Dalton had said "gas chamber".

"It's just a term used for an office in the police building," I stated, a tad curt.

"I'm going with you. In fact, I'm going nowhere until I find out what's going on here," I added desperately wanting answers. Needing answers.

Jess followed behind looking perplexed.

All four of us were back in our interrogation room.

Turning to Jess, I couldn't stem what was roaming through my mind, nor the harsh words.

"Your description, Jess? I know you said he was nearly as old as your dad, but really? Really? I didn't think you meant literally. You said he was no spring chicken, a good ten years older than you give or take. Everyone over thirty is old to kids these days, right?" My question was directed at Dalton and Simpkins who both nodded in agreement. "Talk about crossed wires," I said, shaking my head.

Chapter Thirty-Four

What Came After

"Holy crap. You're not kidding are you, Vicky, you really don't know him? That's good then? You can't charge him?"

"Seriously?"

The one-word question zoomed from my lips, struggling to contain other words which weren't as polite.

In unison the police and I displayed our thoughts with identical disbelieving looks.

All three of us were taken aback by the words that came tumbling out of Jess's mouth, coupled with her perked up demeanour and enthusiasm.

I think that was the most we'd heard from her since we'd left our safe place.

"I'm gone. I want outta here. I've done what you've asked, we both have," said the young girl haughtily.

I grabbed her wrist firmly, not tight, just enough for her to stay put.

I guess the cops were powerless to step in, moreover manhandle a witness. Even one as irritating as Jess. I guess they were pretty damn tempted though as I for one felt like giving her a good old shake.

"You're going nowhere, Jess. We need to get to the bottom of this," I heard myself berate her.

I was in shock, crushed, my hopes well and truly trampled over having convinced myself with the help of Jess that the two guys were one and the same.

From my perspective I have to acknowledge we were no further along in finding this sadist or my friends. Jake is free to do his worst.

I'm guessing Jess had it in her head I would be the one identifying him, leaving her free and clear. It takes a whole level of stupidity to think they can just pick up where they left off. The word "delusional" very nearly ran from my mind to my mouth.

The detective who'd been here with us earlier asked if we'd like more beverages. I politely asked for a strong coffee and more water. It didn't sit comfortable with me having people run round after me, it's not something I'm used to. Jess on the other hand...

"Another soda please, with ice. Is it possible to get something to eat? Pizza would be great."

I rolled my eyes at the lieutenant feeling slightly embarrassed. Why, I've no idea. After all, she's not my kid.

I put my hands up as if to say "Don't look at me." But I didn't want to poke the bear.

I figured Jess was still holding back and knew more than she'd come forward with. She'd told them absolutely squat. Even the grassing up of lover boy had to come from me. Why she couldn't, hadn't, opened up to the cops was beyond a mystery.

I was theorising the cops concurred, evidenced by the way they were treating her with kid gloves.

Clearly something was amiss. Why else conclude him being missing for a couple of days equates to him having taken Susie? She'd had suspicions he was up to no good before that though not come right out with it, but certainly implied as much.

Wasting no time Lieutenant Dalton opened up the dialogue.

"Right then, let's get down to it, ladies," looking at us both as she imparted this.

"While we wait for the food we can make a start. It goes without saying time is our enemy here."

"Fine with me. What else can I tell you which I haven't already?" I responded eagerly.

The lieutenant wasn't the only one concerned about time elapsing. I cracked on with what I thought I could bring to the table which at this point was next to nothing. I'd previously given a comprehensive outline of everything known to me.

Although unable to furnish them with certain facts the police had done their homework filling me in on things they'd uncovered. I then added more.

"For sure this guy Jess knows has a similar appearance to Jake, but I can't stress enough that this is not the guy I met on the dating website and went on a date with." I couldn't help adding, "That bastard who took me from the strip is still out there," the cadence of my voice revealing my disappointment, anger and frustration. And I suspect fear. "One step forward and two back," I muttered to myself.

"Now, Jess," said Dalton who'd seated herself at the table directly across from the young girl. "As I believe Vicky laid out for you yesterday evening, you're not in trouble. You are after all a witness. Clearly, you'd no idea when introducing Jack to your sister she would go missing. The harsh reality is you were played, used. Possibly to target Susie or her friends. We have tech people who are able to do what we refer to as 'dump a phone'. That is to say search for things previously deleted. We found pictures of Susie, some of which strangely enough hadn't been deleted. Evidently, he's been following her on Facebook for quite a while. It has to be said we have absolutely no concrete evidence linking him to her kidnapping, none whatsoever. Another anomaly, Jessica."

Dalton took a long breath.

Jess said nothing which came as a surprise to me. She was probably digesting the things put to her by Dalton or wondering what was next.

"The findings unearthed by our tech guys tells us that this phone contains only one call from you. The call in question was made the day after Susie disappeared. There's no return call. Nothing in the history. You state you've been going out for a year? This throws up inconsistencies. As you quite readily gave Mr Jack Jones up things aren't making sense. It is our understanding from the interview with Mr Jones that you refrained from telling him your sister was missing. For whatever reason, it never came up in that conversation. Until we brought him in for questioning yesterday he was completely in the dark, the shock on hearing this clearly palpable. I would go so far as to say he took the news badly, which all things considered is strange and not what we'd expected. Can you see where I'm going with this, Jess? There are too many contradictions. Nothing adds up. It's clear you know more,

254

much more. Is there anything you are not telling us, Jessica? What are you not telling us? I don't need to reiterate how important this is. It is imperative that you do not waste police time. Is it some kind of vendetta, a ruse to get your own back for some misguided reason? Did you finger Jack because he's wronged you in some way? We just need to know so we can rule him out and switch our focus elsewhere. Anything you tell us will not leave this room."

Probably shocked by Dalton's facts and innuendos having been launched at her, she remained mute. Surprisingly, up to now Dalton had spoken in a rather congenial tone. It could be worse, I thought, Baldwin could be doing the questioning.

As with the police I'm eager for answers to get to the bottom of this.

Knowing her as I do, I thought I'd better stick to the "softly softly" approach. I held her hand and gave her a half smile. Tears welled up but still she offered no explanation, not so much as a smartass comment which was like breathing for this girl.

If I'm honest I was expecting fireworks not waterworks. I concurred with the lieutenant's thoughts and observations, obviously not the phone part or not telling lover boy about Susie as this was all news to me. I was with Dalton on that one. It was pretty strange behaviour all round.

Dalton stopped and took a breath.

My take on this was to give Jess a moment of contemplation.

Her eyes barely left the young girl apart from the occasional glance in my direction.

On seeing her phone light up Dalton broke the silence that had dominated the room by making a grab for it. Although it didn't ring, the vibrating on the hard table startled us all.

Jess shifted her position, displaying an air of confidence all of a sudden, as if she had the upper hand and held all the cards.

Dalton flipped up her phone as she rose from her seat.

"Excuse me, ladies, I need to take this," dashing out of the room as she spoke into the phone.

Detective Simpkins set our drinks in front of us then darted after Dalton. Outwardly displaying an uneasy posture, he swiftly joined the other cops that were gathering in the squad room.

We were left in the company of the friendly cop who'd pointed out to Jess her pizza would be here forthwith. He smiled, and leaving Dalton's chair free he perched himself facing me.

Jess sipped her soda, opting to keep it zipped. Catching her eye, I could tell the cogs were whirring.

She'd mentioned cops meandering round her home. I knew she'd spoken to Andy, Baldwin, Simpkins and now Dalton and she'd said absolutely nada. The girl sure was a weird one.

I stood and took a few steps towards the window adjusting the blinds slightly in order to peek through to the main office area. I wanted to know what all the commotion was about.

My nosiness had got the better of me. Nosiness, boredom and deep frustration. I struggled to relax and I wanted to be doing something to facilitate the release of Susie and my friends.

Through the window overlooking the large open-plan squad room things were happening. There was hustle and bustle on a grand scale. I could hear loud talking and movement. Like worker bees, the police officers were buzzing round the office in a cacophony of noise.

I caught sight of the lieutenant who had finished her call. She was addressing the officers in the squad room with Simpkins positioned nearby hanging on her every word. They were clearly in the midst of something, something very important.

Akin to preparing for battle, they were pulling on bulletproof vests over their normal attire, then outdoor jackets which had the word "POLICE" in large white lettering on them.

I turned to face the friendly cop who I'd learned was called Jimmy. "What's going on, Jimmy?" I muttered.

Just then came a knock on the door and in walked an officer, pizza in hand.

Jess looked up smiling as she saw the pizza box.

"I'm sure the lieutenant will be back to update us if there is anything relevant, Vicky, don't worry," Jimmy remarked. Jess remained quiet and was getting stuck into the food.

I was a little flabbergasted as her relaxed demeanour was something to behold. All this going on around us and she's working her way through a pepperoni pizza. Amazing.

Jimmy joined me at my window station. Although nothing was said, we were probably on the same page regarding the teenager's antics.

Chapter Thirty-Five

How it all Went Down

Baldwin had left the main freeway and was travelling along one of the main highways when the call came in. The crucial call.

A few miles outside of Vegas he caught sight of the massive concrete structures up ahead. A different sight to the evening when every building and attraction exudes bright light and colour.

The strip was teeming with individuals soaking up the atmosphere, enjoying all that Vegas has to offer.

From extravagant shows to magnificent fountains which sway in time to popular music, the vibrance of this adult playground attracted millions of tourists every year like no city on earth.

Then there was the other side to this city.

This the side all too familiar to Baldwin and his colleagues.

In the shadows was a complete contrast. A whole different story. A whole different world.

Poverty, crime, drugs, prostitution and unimaginable violence.

His mind had drifted temporarily, quickly snapping back. Back to where it should be, business. Urgent police business.

Dalton had made the briefest of calls to Baldwin and he was now heading in a new direction.

The call couldn't have caught him more unaware.

He'd spoken to both Dalton and Simpkins within the hour and had the lowdown on the Jack Jones dude, the identification or lack of and was even clued into Jess's antics and food demands.

The fleeting call from the lieutenant got right down to brass tacks as there was new information that could very well turn out to be the clincher. The missing piece of the jigsaw. The deciding factor with regard to bringing these girls home to their families.

"I'm texting you a location. I've had Pratt and Carp tail the suspect vehicle to a warehouse unit downtown. A second vehicle has just shown up and backed into the unit. I told them to sit on it and let me know if there's any sign of movement. I'm not wasting any more time on this. We're going in. By we I mean you and tactical. I've briefed the tactical unit and we're heading out as we speak. I'll meet you there. It is imperative we conclude this today before those bastards take flight. And I know I don't need to say it but suit up. We know they're armed so I'm taking no chances. I'll meet you there in a few." With that she hung up.

Baldwin took in the locality as he read the text. An old abandoned industrial unit on the north side of the city. He attempted to visualise the setting and pull up an image of the place from memory.

The sense of urgency prompted him to go the rest of the way lit up. Sirens blasting, his intention was to switch them off as he got nearer and onto clearer roads as at this time of day the roads were busy with workers, shoppers and sightseeing double deckers equipped with their own version of Elvis. He'd passed them all in the last few minutes.

"Jesus," he muttered, frustrated at the length of time it seemed to be taking to get through the traffic on the strip. It was as if everyone was conspiring against him, even Elvis.

At last Fremont Street and the little wedding chapels were behind him. Staying lit up, he sensibly extinguished the siren.

He decided to risk it and take the back roads. All he could do now was pray, pray they would not be too late.

As Baldwin approached the designated spot where the unmarked police vans had taken root he surveyed the area.

Exit routes were of the upmost importance and top of the list in his head. How many vans had entered the warehouse structure and how many bad guys had the surveillance team spotted? he wondered anxiously.

Considering Pratt and Carp had been assigned to this little number he had a few reservations.

Although not party to the actual conversation, he had it on good authority both Pratt and Carp had been "spoken to" by the lieutenant. The source proclaimed the words, "You are being watched. Get out there and do your job. No cutting corners unless you want to find yourself back on patrol or retiring early."

Both detectives now under scrutiny were unlikely to fuck this one up. At least one would hope not, thought Baldwin, as he exited his police vehicle and joined the rest of the team in the back of the surveillance van.

Dalton nodded in Baldwin's direction before bringing him up to speed.

"There's been no movement since we've rolled up. We're ready to go in and turn the place over. Let's get it over with," said Dalton, in her usual "I mean business tone".

"Do we know for sure if the girls have been transported here?" asked Baldwin hurriedly.

Dalton hesitated and looked across at Detective Pratt who thought he'd better step up and offer up what he'd actually witnessed and what he hadn't.

After listening to a brief summary from Pratt, with Dalton interjecting sporadically, it was determined that the vans had been identified as belonging to the perps.

One of them, the older, tatty one of the two, had been made known to them by way of the CCTV cameras in Henderson.

The other according to DMV records is white or at least should be. Pratt and Carp had seen them both at one property and proceeded to follow them to this location.

They couldn't get eyes on them at location number one, but they and the tag team had followed both vans to this site. He took pains to bring to Dalton and Baldwin's attention that they hadn't been spotted.

"Let's hope you're right," snapped Baldwin still a little annoyed. Baldwin made a decision, enquiring if the tech guy had a mic.

Flynn the tech responded with, "Where do you want it?"

Dalton shook her head disapprovingly.

"You're not doing what I think you're gonna do are you?"

Dalton knew where Baldwin was going with this. She'd been down this road before. Many times in fact, knowing only too well what her best detective had in mind.

Of course, Baldwin didn't answer her. No need, he thought. It's her job to disapprove and to point out the danger and pitfalls of the job. And as usual Baldwin will do what he's going to do. What he feels he has to do.

"Have you got the stuff with you?" asked Dalton.

She was still disapproving but was remembering how many times Baldwin had played the part of the drunk vagrant and how it had worked and produced results. Also recollecting how worryingly authentic he is.

What had they got to lose? Apart from her best detective and a long-time friend, she thought. Oh, and her job if it all went pear-shaped.

Baldwin leapt out of the van closely followed by Flynn and one of the tactical guys. Opening the truck, he grabbed a black trash bag. Pulling out a scruffy plaid shirt and tatty jacket, Baldwin proceeded to tog up.

Flynn was ready to attach the mic under the lapel of the shirt. Baldwin checked the gun he had strapped to his ankle. His other weapon was hidden under the tatty jacket. Just for good measure, he reached into the trunk for a bottle of cheap bourbon.

"Props," he said proudly while shaking the bourbon. "Gotta look the part."

It was his way of attempting to ease the tension.

Flynn cracked a joke about the three-day stubble and bags under Baldwin's eyes making it work for him.

"We're right behind you," said Welsh, the tactical guy, patting him on the shoulder. "As soon as you see signs of the girls we're in."

"Remember, we want these guys alive," Baldwin stated pointedly.

"I know it don't need saying but we want the head of the snake. His minions could be our only lead. There could still be other locations out there where girls are being held."

"Copy that," said Welsh nodding in agreement.

Flynn gave him the thumbs up from the back of the van. He'd checked for sound while listening to Baldwin's declaration to Welsh.

At that the lieutenant poked her head out of the van to wish him luck, but mainly to reiterate he ought to hang fire and was he sure this was the best idea.

"Nope, but I'm gonna do it anyway," came the answer in a determined voice.

"We need eyes on them girls. We could be hanging around here wasting precious time."

At that he turned and edged his way through a hole in the seven-foot fence, the fence surrounding the ramshackle building that was once part of a thriving business park.

"Here goes," he whispered to himself.

A couple of minutes later he found himself at the side of the building, a huge place which, with a bit of luck, he'll hopefully find the kidnapped girls.

Staying close to the building he edged his way to what he took to be a loading area only feet away from the blue vans, one of which had been backed into the loading bay.

He could hear voices and crying, girls crying and whimpering. One male was telling one of them to "shut the fuck up, or I'll take you into another room and you won't be crying you'll be screaming."

Charming, thought Baldwin. I'd like to make you scream.

A second male voice was heard speaking on a mobile. That's two. There should be a third as he'd been told there were two guys in the front of one of the vans.

Thinking on his feet, Baldwin had an idea. A distraction and a delay tactic should any of them decide to scarper once the raid went down.

He opened the passenger side door of the van backed nearest to the loading area. His hand reached for the door handle and he smiled as he realised it wasn't locked. Crawling across the seat he grabbed the keys out of the ignition.

Making a beeline for the other vehicle, again the doors were unlocked, although no keys had been left in the ignition in this one. "Shit," he whispered.

Now to plan B, he thought. Wasting no time, he retrieved a knife he'd brought along for this very purpose, slashing each tyre several times in the hope it may slow the bastards down.

Here we go, now for the hard part.

Although he'd not had eyes on the girls he felt certain they were being held in the warehouse.

Ideally he would have liked visual confirmation. Another quandary, he questioned, was were they all in one place? That would make sense from the perps' perspective, it would be easier to keep eyes on them.

His biggest worry from a logistical point of view was the girls. At the point when the task force guys storm the building there's a chance the girls could be harmed, caught in the crossfire, or used as human shields.

These guys, whoever they are, know the score and are staring down the barrel of life inside. Hopefully, life without parole. Caught here with the victims, they'll have nothing to lose.

The favourite phrase of the DA flashed into his head : "Bring me a smoking gun."

Sure will, grinned Baldwin, determined to bring this to a conclusion without bloodshed, including that of the perpetrators if at all possible.

Contemplating rocking in there like a legless deadbeat with bottle in hand, his original plan was relegated to the back burner. For now at least. He had another idea.

It was hopefully a better and safer move considering what's at stake. The next step requires keying the lieutenant before embarking on his one-man Sundance Kid impersonation.

Plan B was to entice the geniuses out here to see what he's dealing with.

Yeah, they'll likely as not leave one on guard. One's better than three to contend with, he thought to himself.

He quickly got back to the side of the building to whisper directly into the mic, hoping to God it still worked.

Without a moment to lose he put his plan into action.

He grabbed what looked like a T-shirt from one of the vans, soaked it in the booze and spread it across the windshield. He wedged it in the wipers and lit it up.

As quick and simple as that.

The glass cracked and banged noisily. Two of them came bounding out like scuttling rats leaving the ship, shouting and swearing.

Baldwin fled quickly taking cover at the side of the other van near the entrance to the warehouse. His gun was out and he was ready to do whatever necessary.

A split second later all hell broke loose.

He charged into the warehouse arm outstretched shouting, "Police, don't move!"

His gun was aimed at the one perp standing there with a bewildered look on his face.

Baldwin could see girls huddled together behind him. They were blindfolded and terrified.

Worried he may desperately make a grab for one of them, Baldwin advanced purposefully forward keeping the gun trained on the perp. He was ready to make a hole in him if he even looked at the girls, fiercely shouting for him to get down on the floor and repeating it over and over in the same tone.

"Just give me one fucking excuse, asshole. Go on, go for a gun. I've seen the graves. I bet your fingerprints are all over that shovel."

Obviously knowing the game was up, any noise on the inside was eclipsed by the noise outside, the din of the van's crackling windscreen exploding, police sirens, a helicopter hovering above, cops shouting making their presence known, fire trucks and ambulances in the periphery.

The guard, Pete, stood there with his hands above his head. He was in shock, defeated.

"Get down on the floor," hollered the weirdly dressed detective.

Pete complied knowing it was futile to try anything while eyeing the dodgy-looking cop who obviously wanted an excuse to shoot him. Anger and disdain was etched in his face and radiating with every word spoken.

The lieutenant, Simpkins and a bunch of the task force guys sprung into action.

As they strode quickly towards Baldwin the lieutenant announced to the girls that ambulances will be with them any minute. Averting her gaze from Baldwin she was catching sight of the horrific scene. Young women blindfolded, wrists bound, pitifully nestled together waiting for the next instalment of what had become a living nightmare.

Her first question was an automatic reflex question.

"Is anyone hurt?" she asked.

She acknowledged it was a stupid question. Shaking her head at the sight before her the words flowed out from her lips. "They're all hurt."

The terrified girls sat motionless, hardly daring to believe their nightmare could be coming to an end.

Their ears were hearing the words spoken but were too scared to believe them. Feeling the comfort and warmth from each other they stayed put, huddled tightly together.

Suddenly there was more commotion, a flurry of people entering into the mix. Loud footsteps, men's boots.

Welsh marched in with members of his team. He roughly patted down the defeated man who moments prior had been positioned face down on the hard, cold floor. He was motionless and silent with his hands above his head wanting the ground to swallow him whole.

Welsh proceeded to cuff and almost drag him to a waiting police van, reading him his rights as they passed the boss and Baldwin. Pete was now in the hands of law enforcement along with his two criminal buddies.

As he was being forcefully removed one of the young women shifted her body and unsteadily got to her feet. Clearly her intention was to draw attention to herself. She began exuding illegible sounds through the gag, panicking and freaking out the only way to describe her actions.

It was difficult to understand the message she was battling to convey as she struggled to get to her feet, hands zip tied behind her back and tape covering her eyes. The sight was so sorrowful it moved Dalton to tears. Without hesitation, she and Baldwin darted to her aid.

They got that after everything she'd been through she wanted to be free from the binds, but the cops sensed something more, something urgent. Maybe they were missing something.

Baldwin carefully snipped the plastic ties from her sore wrists while Dalton removed the tethering that was clinging to her eyes and lastly her mouth.

Words exploded from her mouth startling the cops.

"Where the fuck were you? Why'd it take you so long?"

Anger. Justifiable anger followed by concern.

"They've taken Susie and another youngster they snatched yesterday," said the frightened young woman.

Turning towards her fellow victims she began carefully removing the blindfolds and mouth tape, all the time offering words of comfort. Gesturing towards Baldwin she asked for help. Armed with the knife he'd used to free her, he got right onto it untying the terrified but clearly relieved girls.

"I'm Detective Baldwin and this is Lieutenant Dalton. We're here to take you home. You'll be admitted to the hospital primarily to be checked out." Pausing for a brief moment he was eyeing the courageous young lady.

"I'm Claire. Claire Hooper. Vicky's friend. Is she OK?" came the emotional words from the young woman.

"She's fine. I'm sure you two have a lot to talk about," said Baldwin in the softest of tones.

The huge warehouse had become quiet and calm after the police action minutes earlier. Serene almost.

The fire in the van was quickly extinguished and police officers were methodically going about their business. They were following protocol, guns at the ready conducting a cursory search.

"Lieutenant."

The shout came from the back of the warehouse close to where the girls had been found. One of the task force stood in the doorway and shouted again, loudly this time. Before Dalton and Baldwin got near the room the officer disappeared into what could be described as an office of sorts.

A scream pierced the air followed by muffled crying.

At the precise moment Dalton and Baldwin arrived at the room, Mike, a task force member, appeared carrying a young girl in his arms. She was younger and smaller than the others and both cops recognised her instantly.

Susie Simmons.

"There's another girl. You need to get in there," said Mike addressing both Baldwin and the lieutenant.

Without hesitation Baldwin rushed into the little office and found another girl roughly Susie's age. Clearly in shock, he found her cowering in a corner. As with the others she was blindfolded with hands tied behind her back and a gag tightly round her mouth. The gag was pulled so tight it was cutting into the corners of her mouth. He caught sight of blood on her face. The tiny girl could be heard whimpering from beneath the gag. Baldwin was now the one on the cusp of tearing up. He wanted to let rip, swear and cuss the evildoers out, but he knew now was not the time.

"Come on, sweetie, you're safe now. We're the police, we've come to take you home. Nobody is going to hurt you."

Steadily removing the binds he took the shocked young girl in his arms while offering words of reassurance and comfort, speaking of family, friends and home. He knew there was nothing he could say to make this right.

The important thing is she's safe and any minute will be on the way to Mercy along with the other girls. Identification and anything else can wait.

Chapter Thirty-Six

Andy Brings News (Vicky)

Out of the corner of my eye I caught sight of a familiar face. A less tired face. A welcome face nonetheless.

I tapped the window gently with my knuckles in the hope of catching Andy's attention.

If nothing else, I wanted to thank him for the coffee and croissant. More importantly, I was itching to know if there had been any developments in the case. My instinct told me all the hoo-ha in the main office had to be connected in some way.

In terms of knowing exactly what was going on we were clueless. I was racking up my own theories and making my own assumptions, fanning the flames of my imagination.

I'd caught his attention as I edged my way to the door. As I turned we nearly bumped heads. Embarrassed, it was my turn with the apologies.

We locked eyes and his smile came with a questioning gaze. "You OK?"

"Yeah, it's just nice to see a friendly face. It's a bit overwhelming and intense here if I'm honest. I've been waiting to view the photos of the missing girls. Hopefully, I'll be able to identify them. I'll give it a go but I think they might have forgotten me. I guess you've been kept up to speed and know about the girls' bodies, eh?" I said trying to fight back the tears.

I think focusing on Jess and trying to keep her in check went a little way in masking what was going on in my head.

"You're not OK, I can see that," said Andy as he stroked my cheek with the back of his hand. Pulling me close he gave me a firm but gentle hug, ignoring the other cop, Jimmy, who at this point was perusing the sports page of the *Nevada Star*.

Jess, still munching on her pizza was attempting to be dainty but not quite pulling it off.

"Pizza?" Andy quietly called out as he took in the sight.

"Don't even ask," I said getting in first, Jess on the cusp of speaking between mouthfuls.

"Yeah, you can have a slice if you fancy," she enthused, happily chomping on the food as if sat in some fast-food joint. Her face lit up at seeing Andy and she was back with the enthusiasm she'd shown earlier.

"No, I'm good thanks. I got a little something from the deli on the corner," he said, lifting up a brown paper bag as way of explanation.

He proceeded to pass the brown bag my way. I took a peek inside. Food, good nutritious grub. My kinda food.

Compared with what had passed for food in my world lately it was a feast to be sure. I spied a thin breaded deli sandwich and a plastic container filled with colourful fruit slices, a protein bar and a banana.

To top it off was a plastic beaker filled to the brim with orange juice, fresh orange evidenced by the pulp at the bottom and little orange bits.

"What's this?" came out of my mouth rather stupidly, my tone feigning surprise although a genuine feeling of gratitude seized me.

"It's what it looks like, freshly squeezed orange juice," knowing exactly where I was coming from but choosing to be cute with his answer.

"No getting away from it, you've read my mind," pointing to the coffee that was now stone cold. I felt bad and ungrateful for having left it.

"This wasn't necessary, you know. But really, thank you. You've done enough already. You don't have to keep doing this," I said meaningfully.

"Not a problem. The coffee in here sucks anyway. Depending on what shift I'm on I swing by the deli on my way here. I took a gamble you'd still be here so I thought you'd like to try one of Franco's legendry deli sandwiches. Drink the juice while it's cold and I'll go see what we can do about the identification images."

He got up and said he would check what was causing the hold up and would be back as soon as he could.

269

After the botched identification I didn't want coming here to be a complete waste of time.

The pizza muncher was still going strong having devoured a few slices. Surprisingly, she'd shared her free lunch with Jimmy who now sat beside her. They were dipping the crusts in the sauce and making small talk. Thankfully, it gave me a few minutes peace.

It was astonishing how much the petite girl could put away. It was even more baffling how she was able to eat at all. One minute she was tense, miserable and dripping with anxiety, the next minute she was acting normal though I'd yet to be party to Jess's normal.

Claustrophobia was rearing its ugly head. I hated this confinement and I longed for Andy to get back. I badly wanted to ask him if he'd any idea what all the palaver was in aid of earlier in the main office.

I am also curious as to where Lieutenant Dalton had disappeared to.

Gazing out into the office my thoughts were pertaining to everything that had come to light.

Out of the corner of my eye I caught sight of Andy making his way through the main thoroughfare in the office, seemingly heading back here.

No sooner had I spotted him there was a sharp rap on the door and in he walked.

"Right then, Vicky, are you ready for the missing persons viewing?" He then turned to Jess. "I'm taking Vicky to a different office as the material required is on a computer. We won't be long."

With that and before she'd opened her mouth in protest we were out the door taking the same path he'd walked seconds before.

My eyes were scouring the office for signs of life. At this juncture it was empty but for a handful of detectives glued to computer screens. There was no Dalton, no Simpkins, no Baldwin.

"Phew, that's better. I'm glad to be out of there," I said, expressing my relief.

"I hear you. She's an acquired taste our Jess. Talk about droning on. And anything apart from what she ought to be opening up with according to Simpkins. Something is seriously going on with that girl. Oh, and nobody's forgotten about the identification photos so don't fret on that score. There's been a development, a break in the case. As I said I've spoken to Simpkins who's on the scene together with Baldwin and Lieutenant Dalton."

My mind was going ten to the dozen wondering what scene. Did he mean the house?

Andy had quit talking as he beckoned me into a light, airy room.

It was a lounge of sorts with comfier chairs, a coffee table, a laminate workbench and kitchen items. Having drunk my orange juice it hit me I'd held onto the bag of food Andy had brought me. Maybe at the back of my mind I had the notion it would go the way the pizza had gone.

My eyes and brain weighed up the room but Andy's disclosure hadn't bypassed me. I was worried. Extremely worried. I had two questions to ask.

"A break in the case? Still on the scene?"

Foreboding gloom engulfed me and there was that all too familiar feeling in the pit of my stomach. A "scene" to me conjured up all manner of things. Bad things. Did I really want to know?

"Sit down, Vicky, I have something extremely important to tell you. It pertains to your friend Claire and the other young women."

I was too scared to listen but knew I had to.

Andy pulled up a chair and adopted a serious look.

The words were taking too long, as if he didn't want to divulge what he knew and be the bearer of bad news.

"It's over, Vicky. It's all over."

Chapter Thirty-Seven

It all Went Down so Fast

Andy took both my hands and held onto me tightly.

"Claire and the others are in ambulances en route to the hospital. I don't know what condition they are in but I can tell you they're alive. I'll take you to see them as soon as we're done here."

I sat staring at him in disbelief. I swallowed hard not quite believing what he had just said.

"I'm not sure if the lieutenant keyed you in on the fact we had eyes on the van. At that point there was no sign of the girls or the perpetrators. The detectives had a surveillance team shadowing the van. Panic set in when a different vehicle, a much larger vehicle, backed up to the building where the subject vehicle had been parked. It was an abandoned warehouse from what I can make out."

Andy hesitated then took a breath.

"To cut a long story short the detectives followed them, radioed in and obtained a warrant. Dalton made the decision to employ the tactical team, the premise that the girls could quite possibly be shifted to another location or over the border to Mexico. The El Torres have strong ties to Mexico. Baldwin and the lieutenant were leading the team who stormed the abandoned building. I'm sure you'll be glad to know it all went according to plan and without casualties which of course is a massive relief all round."

He ceased speaking for a few seconds granting me a moment to absorb the news.

He continued in the same measured tone.

"While this was in motion arrests were made at a second location, a dwelling officers had been able to track to one of the vans cumulating in six arrests in total. The two in the van we are guessing were part of the El Torres gang. Their English is

272

sketchy or that's what they'd like us to believe. They'll talk, they always do. There's always one who wants to make a deal."

He offered a smile and a gentle squeeze of my hands.

I remained rooted to that chair. Stunned. This was the polar opposite to what I was expecting to be told. Not for the first time today I struggled to put two words together.

"And Susie? She's OK?" I enquired, a little perturbed he'd not mentioned her.

"She was held back at the warehouse in a different room to the others along with another young girl that was taken yesterday. Both the younger girls were destined to be shipped out separately according to the intelligence gathered. Evidently, as soon as the girls were rescued Claire went ballistic shouting that they'd taken Susie, but unbeknown to her she was in the same building just a different part of the warehouse. Susie and the other youngster that is. Apparently, Claire took the young girl under her wing after you escaped."

"A good one that Claire. A big gob on her but a heart of gold underneath all that attitude," I said, attempting to hold back the tears which were pricking my eyes. I was struggling to take it all in that it was over at last.

Andy got up and poured me a glass of water. I remained firmly planted in the chair with questions bombarding my brain. Where did Jess and lover boy fit into all this? What part had he played? Is Jake one of the guys in custody?

Taking sips of water, I looked at Andy. "Has someone told Jess about Susie?"

"The lieutenant and Baldwin both said to leave it until they get back. The long and short of it is things don't stack up with that one and of course with Mr Jones. Make no mistake, the lieutenant is dogged in her pursuit for the truth and determined to find out what they're hiding.

"I don't know how much the lieutenant apprised you when she spoke to you both. I guess I'm not divulging state secrets or you're going to hinder the investigation by blabbing to Miss Chatterbox in the other office, but from what I gather they didn't need the tech guys for his phone. He handed it over willingly without any fuss. Password 'an all. There were several pictures of Susie taken over these last few months. How much

Jess knows is anybody's guess. Her sister is snatched just like that. You have to admit it's a bit of a coincidence. Communication between the pair of 'em is scant so there is no evidence pointing to him having knowledge of Susie's disappearance. There are other inconsistencies from what I've heard. It's strange how as soon as she learns about you she heads straight for Mercy, without telling anyone I might add. You've gotta admit, it's mighty suspicious."

"Maybe he's eying up a replacement, someone younger and quieter?" I said.

"Anything is possible. Her folks are on their way down here from what I understand. That's when the fireworks will start, I'm betting," said Andy raising his eyebrows.

I concurred and got the point. But still, rash and misguided as I thought Jess to be, my gut told me she wouldn't put her sister in harm's way. Not knowingly anyway. The smarmy-looking Jack who had been schmoozing a sixteen year old, now there's a different story.

"My focus would be firmly directed his way if I were a cop. Oh yeah, I'd be in there slapping him about a bit," I said, unashamedly expressing what I was thinking.

"You can't be doing that. There are rules you know. Police procedure has to be adhered to. It's not like in films or TV shows." Andy shook his head playfully while trying to keep a straight face.

Breaking the fleeting calm Andy's phone buzzed.

He got to his feet while taking the call and was periodically glancing at me offering the occasional knowing smile.

Picking up on the nuances from his conversation, I was pretty sure he was speaking to Lieutenant Dalton. In fact I was certain.

Eventually closing his phone, Andy turned to me.

"That was the lieutenant. She's on her way back to finish up with Jess, hopefully before her parents show up. Apparently, and I don't want you to get stressed when I tell you this..."

I felt my face drain of colour. Andy's serious face had returned.

"What is it? My friends? Susie?"

"No, no, nothing like that. It's this Jack character. He's lawyered up and we're having to let him go. He has an alibi for the day of Susie's kidnapping. We've checked with the airlines who confirmed he'd taken a flight to London. It doesn't rule him out as he could have an accomplice. He willingly agreed to a DNA swab, no qualms whatsoever, stating, 'go ahead, I've nothing to hide,' against the advice of his expensive lawyer of course. We've no concrete evidence on the jerk with regard to the kidnapping and no criminal history. Not so much as a parking violation, so as a result he's being bailed. Charges pertaining to stalking and sex with a minor are gonna be levied on him. He won't get off scot free, even if the kidnapping is not on him."

I guess he was expecting a strong reaction considering how I'd just let him in on my version of how I'd dish it out to the toerags in custody. Handcuffed to a table, blindfolded, then given a good slapping if I had my way.

"So he's just your everyday common pervert then?" vaulted out my mouth.

Before Andy could respond my mind flashed back to Jess.

"I know I'm not a cop or anything, but maybe we ought to get back to the other office and see Jess? If for no other reason lover boy will probably waltz pass that office we were in on his way outta the building."

I was recollecting how I'd opened the blinds in that room in the hope of catching Andy, also noting at the time her posture was facing the window.

"I can't fathom if Jack getting released is a good thing from her point of view or not. Either way, surely it wouldn't do for her to confront him. If he is going to be charged then she's a witness," I urged.

"Copy that," said Andy.

As I stood up Andy simply couldn't resist making it known how he viewed my recent behaviours. A glint in his eye accompanied that same small smile.

"You might not be a cop, Vicky, but you sure are beginning to sound like one."

With that thought I smiled. Fittingly, me being me had to have the final word.

"Well, I guess I'm bound to considering all the cops I've mingled with the last couple days. Not to mention I feel like I've been in this place forever. I'm betting Jess concurs which is another reason to get back to the other office."

"Oh, I wouldn't worry about Jess, she's probably sent one of the officers out for dessert. She's probably tucking into a Ben & Jerry's as we speak," joked Andy as we made our way back.

He seems to have got her number alright, I mused, attempting to suppress a smile.

Chapter Thirty-Eight

Just When You Thought You'd Heard It All

Just as we'd predicted Jess was tucking into something sweet.

Apparently, after she'd made short work of the pizza a request had been put in for a dessert. A candy bar from a vending machine found its way to her courtesy of Jimmy.

I figured anything to keep her on board in this interrogation box until Dalton puts in an appearance. After all, Jess had been quick to point out she had done her duty.

The girl had adhered to the identification process as requested. Although not exactly under arrest, she can come and go as she pleases and request a lawyer.

My theory, and I suspect Andy's with me on this, is she's waiting for us so we can all trot back to the safe house together. Curiously, she hadn't asked about Susie, her parents or any other matters of which there was a growing list.

Neither had she discussed any of the anomalies put to her by Dalton before her sudden departure. Yep, Andy's on the money, the teenager is definitely hiding something, not that this is in any way news to me.

Jess's eating habits got me thinking. Though food was the last thing on my list of priorities, knowing my next port of call would be the hospital to see my friends it'd be sensible to get something down me.

I opened the brown bag I'd clung onto. The deli sandwich called out to me. I gave my Franco deli sandwich five stars. I felt full, too full for the protein bar, so I thought I would save it as a treat for Claire.

I stayed seated as I finished my yummy sandwich and sipped water from a bottle Jimmy had kindly brought me.

Andy was seated next to me facing Jimmy, and in full sports mode they chatted away.

Absorbing the enormity of what I'm privy to I'm lost in my thoughts. Jess rose from her chair and advanced in the direction of the window, the window incorporating a full view of the squad room.

Suddenly her posture shifted.

As if a firecracker had been lit under her she skyrocketed outta that room. Boy did she move. If the fire alarm had been deployed I doubt she'd have moved with such verve.

A few strides to the door and she was off. Gone in a puff of smoke.

"I hadn't realised she had it in her to move so fast," Andy commented later when we were alone.

Something had spooked her. Something or someone had caught her eye.

Me, Jimmy and Andy jumped to our feet in unison, all as perplexed as each other by the sudden rush of unexpected agility. I figured we all had the same goal, grab her to avert conflict.

Shit, too late.

We just weren't that quick, that energetic, nor that good at babysitting.

The scene erupting before our very eyes was tantamount to an episode from *The Jerry Springer Show*, albeit an upmarket version.

In a matter of seconds the shit had well and truly hit the fan.

The snazzy dressed narcissist I'd had the pleasure of glimpsing earlier stood feet away, the lawyer who'd been lucky enough to bag him for a client close by his side.

New to the scene a designer clad blonde woman was striding gracefully through the squad room, her gaze fixed on Jack who'd ceased moving and the lawyer by his side.

A very striking woman, her glassy, bloodshot eyes did nothing to distract from her beauty. The eyes which remained firmly on the two men in her sights.

An equally smart-looking man accompanied her. His expression exuded venom. Daggers fired from his eyes at one of the men approaching them, and it wasn't the lawyer.

Gunfight at the O.K. Corral zoomed into my mind.

It could've been scripted as they all arrived outside our room within seconds of each other. A face-off.

Evidently Jess had bounded out of the paddock with the intention of snaring her prey. Her man. The newcomers were invisible to her as she only had eyes for one person only.

Knowing what had come out of her mouth after the identification, I'd have put money on her having designs on picking up where they'd left off.

For the very first time I heard the elusive Jack speak. Not to Jess, not the lawyer, or the cops, his words fired at the pretty blonde lady who now stood next to the gobsmacked Jess.

Powerful yet pleading words flowed.

"I'm sorry, Chrissy. I really am. It was unintentional, I bumped into her by accident. You shouldn't have done this to me. You should have let me be part of her life, your life. I wanted to get to know my daughter. She's my girl, you know she's mine. I could have taken care of her and she would have wanted for nothing. She'd be here right now instead of God knows where. Are you listening to me, Chrissy, our girl would be safe."

We are all rooted to the spot mesmerised by the spiel and twisted logic, the smarmy one glaring coldly at the couple.

"This is seriously fucked up," burst out of the mouth of the shocked teenager who was standing just feet away from the guy who yesterday was her whole life.

She was grappling with the news she'd been sleeping with Susie's dad, or was he her dad?

Jess didn't register on his radar. He looked straight through her. Along with the rest of us she was completely invisible.

She's a bit player in the life of that egotistical man, the get what you want when you want it man. The screw everybody man.

Jack Jones's eyes were trained on one person: Chrissy Simmons.

Even the lawyer said nothing and was looking shocked. Another one in the dark by the look of it, I thought.

In utter shock and squinting in disbelief, Jess turned to face her mum.

"Mum? What's he saying? Am I being stupid here? He doesn't mean Susie, surely? How does Jack know you? Dad, please, will someone talk to me and tell me what's going on?" Tears were rolling down her pretty face.

We were all stunned by his revelation, Jess more than anyone, and she was clearly unable to comprehend what was now becoming glaringly obvious.

None of us were quite able to grasp what he'd said, and more to the point what the smartly dressed blonde lady hadn't said or hadn't denied.

It was blatantly obvious these were Jess and Susie's parents.

Make no mistake, Jack Jones knew Dr and Mrs Simmons, Mrs Simmons intimately by the way things were sounding.

The look on her parents' faces as the realisation hit home their oldest daughter and Jack were involved. Involved how and for how long will be the shocker. Oh, and then there's her introducing him to Susie.

"You bastard. You'll stop at nothing to make me pay. You're seriously warped, do you know that?" Chrissy's voice cracked with emotion and hatred.

"Don't flatter yourself. Besides, I've got the next best thing on tap. Willing and pliable. Oh, and so accommodating. I click my finger and she comes running. Who do you think is chasing who here?" His voice was laced with malevolence and spite.

The lawyer butted in taking hold of Jack's arm. "Stop talking."

"Jack, you don't mean that. We're a team. You've always said it's me and you forever. You love me. Please say something."

"Grow up and open your eyes. I'm in this place because you couldn't keep it shut. Where the fuck do you get off bringing my name into it?"

I couldn't gauge what her next move was likely to be. The young girl's confusion was overshadowed by annoyance and anger, incredulous at the fact this could be happening to her.

Andy who was stood directly behind me put his hand on my shoulder. Then he took over.

Jimmy, who'd been party to the whole scene, was rooted to the spot. He was more than likely wondering what to do or if he should intervene at all.

Taking hold of Jess's arm, Andy directed his command to the lawyer.

"Please take Mr Jones out of here now."

When he said the word "now" his tone changed adding emphasis.

The lawyer physically beckoned him out in the direction of the lift.

Barely audible, "We need to talk," skuttled out of Jack's mouth as he sauntered past Dr and Mrs Simmons.

Up to now Dr Simmons had shown decorum and held his tongue. Enough was enough. In no way did he intend to allow this home wrecker to have the last word.

In a past life he had tried to come between them, him and Chrissy. And failed. Through sheer arrogance and spite he'd set his sights on his oldest daughter. An easy target, a young impressionable teenager, and he had taken Susie possibly to make a point.

He'd lived with the knowledge they'd more than likely not heard the last of him, but this? This was inconceivable and beyond the pale. Targeting and using a teenager to get back at her mother and him. He was shameless and devoid of conscience, this disgusting poor excuse for a man.

Dr Simmons' icy stare bore a hole in Jack. Coldly, his voice laced with enmity, he began to demolish him verbally. Clearly his intention was to take that overblown ego down a peg or two.

I for one was eager to hear his take on the unfolding drama.

"You've made a big mistake this time you worthless piece of shit. It took a real effort manipulating and cajoling a teenager to dance to your tune, you pervert. Proud of yourself, eh? Give it your best shot did you? Attempting to ruin my family. You got that, bozo, *my* family. You're not even close. Me and Chrissy swept you out with the trash years ago. As for Jess, she'll have a bright, rewarding future ahead of her, which is more than can be said for you. I'll make damn sure 'sex offender' follows you around for the rest of your natural. Keep the hell away from my family, all of them."

With that he pulled Jess close and gave her a hug.

He then offered his parting words.

"Oh, and I'll see you in court. You won't miss me, I'll have a front row seat."

As Jack and the lawyer took all this in, Jack stayed silent. This time the lawyer added his two cents worth.

"Is that a threat, Mr Simmons?"

"No, it's a promise. And it's Dr Simmons to you and your slimeball client."

With that the two suits walked swiftly to the lift and didn't turn back.

Chapter Thirty-Nine

Picking up the Pieces

Jess was sobbing into her dad's shoulders whispering "I'm sorry" over and over again.

As I would expect Andy took control, ushering Jess and her parents into the interrogation room we'd just left. Jimmy accompanied them.

By now the nasty mouth in the suit and his lawyer were out of earshot.

Not wishing to intrude, I motioned to Andy if it was OK for me to go back to the room the other side of the squad room. He agreed and I gladly left them to it.

The unfolding drama was embarrassing, like airing your dirty laundry in public. I felt for Chrissy. I felt for all of them, especially Susie. One thing's for sure, there's no question they have a loving dad and a stable loving home.

My dad came to mind. Tears pricked my eyes as I wished he were here. Here to hold me and say it'll be alright.

There had been too much drama to get my head round. Too much drama and way too many unanswered questions.

I sat in the same chair I'd occupied earlier and attempted to download the pieces into something which made sense. I struggled.

I kept coming back to why Jess came forward to me about Jack. What brought her to the conclusion he had it in him to take Susie? I guess I won't be the only one to throw that one out there. A more perplexing mystery to me was what the hell do women see in that vile man?

Another humongous question in all this was did he know Jess to be Susie's sister when they started seeing one another?

From the vicious words expelled out of that foul mouth, I take it he thinks she is his daughter. Who knows, Chrissy gave nothing away on that score.

My thoughts were with Susie in all this. As if she hadn't been through enough.

I sat in the bright airy room unable to get to grips with the recent happenings and how quickly things had unfolded.

I needed to see Claire to explain why I'd bolted. How I'd no choice.

I had to let them know that from the second my foot hit that gravel I wasn't resting until they were released. I hadn't abandoned them and did everything in my power to bring them home.

I was shaken out of my ponderances by a rap at the door. In walked my saviour, the man who had taken his job seriously. Who had taken me seriously.

"How do you feel? Are you ready to see your friends?"

With that I got to my feet in readiness for what I'd desperately yearned for, knowing I'd played a small part in the outcome of what had been a harrowing and disturbing time for us all. This knowledge afforded me a modicum of comfort.

Now the hard work must begin for all of us, police and victims alike.

To be continued…

Printed in Great Britain
by Amazon